The Editor

DONALD J. GRAY is Professor Emeritus and Culbertson Chair Emeritus of English at Indiana University. He is the editor of the Norton Critical Edition of *Pride and Prejudice* and of the anthology *Victorian Poetry*, and has written extensively on Victorian poetry and fiction, popular journalism, and the history of literary publishing.

D0144875

W. W. NORTON & COMPANY, INC.
Also Publishes

ENGLISH RENAISSANCE DRAMA: A NORTON ANTHOLOGY
edited by David Bevington et al.

THE NORTON ANTHOLOGY OF AFRICAN AMERICAN LITERATURE
edited by Henry Louis Gates Jr. and Nellie Y. McKay et al.

THE NORTON ANTHOLOGY OF AMERICAN LITERATURE
edited by Nina Baym and Robert Levine et al.

THE NORTON ANTHOLOGY OF CHILDREN'S LITERATURE
edited by Jack Zipes et al.

THE NORTON ANTHOLOGY OF DRAMA
edited by J. Ellen Gainor, Stanton B. Garner Jr., and Martin Puchner

THE NORTON ANTHOLOGY OF ENGLISH LITERATURE
edited by Stephen Greenblatt et al.

THE NORTON ANTHOLOGY OF LATINO LITERATURE
edited by Ilan Stavans et al.

THE NORTON ANTHOLOGY OF LITERATURE BY WOMEN
edited by Sandra M. Gilbert and Susan Gubar

THE NORTON ANTHOLOGY OF MODERN AND CONTEMPORARY POETRY
edited by Jahan Ramazani, Richard Ellmann, and Robert O'Clair

THE NORTON ANTHOLOGY OF POETRY
edited by Margaret Ferguson, Mary Jo Salter, and Jon Stallworthy

THE NORTON ANTHOLOGY OF SHORT FICTION
edited by R. V. Cassill and Richard Bausch

THE NORTON ANTHOLOGY OF THEORY AND CRITICISM
edited by Vincent B. Leitch et al.

THE NORTON ANTHOLOGY OF WORLD LITERATURE
edited by Martin Puchner et al.

THE NORTON FACSIMILE OF THE FIRST FOLIO OF SHAKESPEARE
prepared by Charlton Hinman

THE NORTON INTRODUCTION TO LITERATURE
edited by Kelly J. Mays

THE NORTON READER
edited by Linda H. Peterson and John C. Brereton et al.

THE NORTON SAMPLER
edited by Thomas Cooley

THE NORTON SHAKESPEARE, BASED ON THE OXFORD EDITION
edited by Stephen Greenblatt et al.

For a complete list of Norton Critical Editions, visit
wwnorton.com/college/English/nce

A NORTON CRITICAL EDITION

Lewis Carroll
ALICE IN WONDERLAND

Third Edition

AUTHORITATIVE TEXTS OF
Alice's Adventures in Wonderland
Through the Looking-Glass
The Hunting of the Snark
BACKGROUNDS
CRITICISM

Edited by

DONALD J. GRAY
INDIANA UNIVERSITY

W · W · NORTON & COMPANY · *New York* · *London*

W. W. Norton & Company has been independent since its founding in 1923, when William Warder Norton and Mary D. Herter Norton first published lectures delivered at the People's Institute, the adult education division of New York City's Cooper Union. The firm soon expanded its program beyond the Institute, publishing books by celebrated academics from America and abroad. By mid-century, the two major pillars of Norton's publishing program—trade books and college texts—were firmly established. In the 1950s, the Norton family transferred control of the company to its employees, and today—with a staff of four hundred and a comparable number of trade, college, and professional titles published each year—W. W. Norton & Company stands as the largest and oldest publishing house owned wholly by its employees.

Copyright © 2013, 1992, 1971 by W. W. Norton & Company, Inc.

All rights reserved.
Printed in the United States of America.
Third Edition.

The text of this book is composed in Fairfield Medium
with the display set in Bernhard Modern.
Book design by Antonina Krass.
Composition by Westchester.
Manufacturing by Maple Press.
Production Manager: Sean Mintus.

Library of Congress Cataloging-in-Publication Data
Carroll, Lewis, 1832–1898.
    [Selections. 2013]
    Alice in Wonderland / Lewis Carroll ; authoritative texts of Alice's
Adventures in Wonderland, Through the Looking-Glass, The Hunting
of the Snark, backgrounds, criticism ; edited by Donald J. Gray, Indiana
University. —Third edition.
        pages cm. — (A Norton Critical Edition)
    Includes bibliographical references.
    ISBN 978-0-393-93234-8 (pbk.)
    1. Carroll, Lewis, 1832–1898—Criticism and interpretation.
2. Children's literature, English—History and criticism.   3. Fantasy
literature, English—History and criticism.   4. Alice (Fictitious character :
Carroll)—Fiction.   5. Children—Books and reading—Great Britain—
History—19th century.   6. Alice (Fictitious character : Carroll)
7. Fantasy literature, English.   I. Gray, Donald J.   II. Title.
    PR4611.A4G7   2013
    823'.8—dc23
                                                                    2013001558

W. W. Norton & Company, Inc., 500 Fifth Avenue,
New York, NY 10110-0017
wwnorton.com

W. W. Norton & Company Ltd.
15 Carlisle Street, London W1D 3BS

6 7 8 9 0

Contents

Criticism

Preface to the Third Edition

As I read through the writing published in the past two decades about the Alice books and their author, I found myself thinking almost as much about the life and character of Charles Lutwidge Dodgson as about the writings published under his pseudonym, Lewis Carroll. The biographies by Morton Cohen, David Thomas, and others, the nine volumes containing all of Dodgson's extant diaries, and the several collections of and commentaries on his photographs, taken together present a man who pursued a variety of interests and who maintained a wide network of relationships with friends, acquaintances, members of his family, and colleagues in his several professions. Dodgson was an accomplished entertainer of children, especially young girls, many of whom were warmed and dignified by his attentions, and some of whom remained friends and correspondents when they became young women. But as a young man at Oxford, he was also a familiar of promising contemporaries who moved on to worthy careers, and all through his life he sought and was at home in the company of well-known writers, artists, and actors. An exceptionally gifted photographer of children, he also tirelessly solicited men (usually) of some distinction to sit for photographs in what became a remarkable photographic gallery of eminent Victorians. Dodgson wrote books and pamphlets on mathematics, logic, and the teaching of these subjects, and he was quick to go into print to make public his opinions on other topics—university politics, the economics of the book trade, vivisection, how to assure an equitable result in an election, and how to win at the racetrack. As a member of the clergy he stopped short of ordination as a priest, perhaps in part because of the impediment of his stammer. But in the last years of his life he preached to congregations in Oxford and elsewhere, and when asked he was ready to give advice about matters of religious belief. In the biographical selections of this edition of the Alice books, I have tried to suggest the range and energy of Dodgson's engagement with the many persons, adults and children, and some of the issues, of great and lesser moment, that he knew and cared about in the public as well as the private spaces of his life and times.

Of course, had Dodgson not also been Lewis Carroll, he would be remembered only as a privileged member of a mid-Victorian professional caste who in his abundant leisure created portfolios of very fine photographs. He was fussy about keeping his two identities separate (he was fussy about many things). He knew and emulated the practices of writers and illustrators who made their livings by providing entertainment for magazines and the stage. But his fantasies differ from the work of these writers, and from that of most other nineteenth-century writers for children, because Lewis Carroll also knew what Dodgson knew as a mathematician, logician, and student of language. Carroll was also ready to play with ideas about existence, extinction, authority, and the stability of meaning that people like Dodgson, committed as he was to the axioms of Euclidean geometry and to the governance of a providential deity, took very seriously. His play with these topics continues to exercise the sensibilities and intelligences of literary historians and critics, linguists and psycholinguists, writers who are interested in the role of gender, and writers who are interested in the motives and effects of Carroll's imaginative constructions in print and of Dodgson's subjects and compositions in photographs. The selections I have chosen for the last section of this edition offer at best a sketch of the richness of this commentary. I am grateful to its authors for permission to reprint their writing, and sometimes to lift it out of large arguments whose complexity may not be apparent in the extracts I have chosen. And as anyone must be who reads and writes about the books of Lewis Carroll, I am especially indebted to the annotations and commentary of Martin Gardner and James Kincaid.

The texts of the two Alice books are those of an edition Carroll prepared for publication in 1897. The text of *The Hunting of the Snark* is that of the first edition of 1876. The sources of the texts of the other writing by Dodgson or Carroll are indicated in the notes to each selection.

DONALD GRAY

The Text of
ALICE'S ADVENTURES
IN WONDERLAND

Alice's Adventures in Wonderland

All in the golden afternoon
　　Full leisurely we glide;
For both our oars, with little skill,
　　By little arms are plied,
While little hands make vain pretence
　　Our wanderings to guide.

Ah, cruel Three![1] In such an hour,
　　Beneath such dreamy weather,
To beg a tale of breath too weak
　　To stir the tiniest feather!
Yet what can one poor voice avail
　　Against three tongues together?

Imperious Prima flashes forth
　　Her edict "to begin it":
In gentler tones Secunda hopes
　　"There will be nonsense in it!"
While Tertia interrupts the tale
　　Not *more* than once a minute.

Anon, to sudden silence won,
　　In fancy they pursue
The dream-child moving through a land
　　Of wonders wild and new,
In friendly chat with bird or beast—
　　And half believe it true.

And ever, as the story drained
　　The wells of fancy dry,
And faintly strove that weary one
　　To put the subject by,
"The rest next time—" "It *is* next time!"
　　The happy voices cry.

Thus grew the tale of Wonderland:
　　Thus slowly, one by one,
Its quaint events were hammered out—

1. The three Liddell children, Lorina ("Prima"), Alice ("Secunda"), and Edith ("Tertia").
Alice was ten when the expedition to Godstow during which the story was begun took
place in 1862. She is seven in *Alice's Adventures in Wonderland*, which is set in May;
and seven and a half in *Through the Looking-Glass*, which is set in November. Martin
Gardner in *The Annotated Alice* (p. 9) and James R. Kincaid in the Pennyroyal edition
of *Alice's Adventures in Wonderland* (p. 33) summarize the evidence that the day was
"cool and rather wet," as meteorological records report, or sunny and warm, as Dodgson
and Alice Hargreaves remember (see Selected Bibliography).

And now the tale is done,
And home we steer, a merry crew,
    Beneath the setting sun.

Alice! A childish story take,
    And, with a gentle hand,
Lay it where Childhood's dreams are twined
    In Memory's mystic band.
Like pilgrim's wither'd wreath of flowers
    Pluck'd in a far-off land.

Christmas-Greetings

[FROM A FAIRY TO A CHILD]²

Lady dear, if Fairies may
    For a moment lay aside
Cunning tricks and elfish play,
    'Tis at happy Christmas-tide.

We have heard the children say—
    Gentle children, whom we love—
Long ago, on Christmas Day,
    Came a message from above.

Still, as Christmas-tide comes round,
    They remember it again—
Echo still the joyful sound
    "Peace on earth, good-will to men!"

Yet the hearts must childlike be
    Where such heavenly guests abide;
Unto children, in their glee,
    All the year is Christmas-tide!

Thus, forgetting tricks and play
    For a moment, Lady dear,
We would wish you, if we may,
    Merry Christmas, glad New Year!

               Christmas, 1867

2. This poem was first printed in *Phantasmagoria* (1869). It was attached to the first Alice book when it was reprinted in the facsimile edition of *Alice's Adventures Under Ground* (1886), the manuscript book that Dodgson gave to Alice Liddell as a Christmas gift in 1864. (See Selected Bibliography.)

Chapter I

DOWN THE RABBIT-HOLE

Alice was beginning to get very tired of sitting by her sister on the bank and of having nothing to do: once or twice she had peeped into the book her sister was reading, but it had no pictures or conversations in it, "and what is the use of a book," thought Alice, "without pictures or conversations?"

So she was considering, in her own mind (as well as she could, for the hot day made her feel very sleepy and stupid), whether the pleasure of making a daisy-chain would be worth the trouble of getting up and picking the daisies, when suddenly a White Rabbit with pink eyes ran close by her.[3]

There was nothing so *very* remarkable in that; nor did Alice think it so *very* much out of the way to hear the Rabbit say to itself "Oh dear! Oh dear! I shall be too late!" (when she thought it over afterwards it occurred to her that she ought to have wondered at this, but at the time it all seemed quite natural); but, when the Rabbit actually *took a watch out of its waistcoat-pocket*, and looked at it, and

3. Robinson Duckworth, an Oxford colleague, was a member of the party on the river. In a letter quoted in *The Lewis Carroll Picture Book* (see Selected Bibliography) he remembers asking, "'Dodgson, is this an extempore romance of yours?' And he replied, 'Yes, I am inventing as I go along'" (pp. 358–60).

then hurried on, Alice started to her feet, for it flashed across her mind that she had never before seen a rabbit with either a waistcoat-pocket, or a watch to take out of it, and burning with curiosity, she ran across the field after it, and was just in time to see it pop down a large rabbit-hole under the hedge.

In another moment down went Alice after it, never once considering how in the world she was to get out again.

The rabbit-hole went straight on like a tunnel for some way, and then dipped suddenly down, so suddenly that Alice had not a moment to think about stopping herself before she found herself falling down what seemed to be a very deep well.

relatively Either the well was very deep, or she fell very slowly, for she had plenty of time as she went down to look about her, and to wonder what was going to happen next. First, she tried to look down and make out what she was coming to, but it was too dark to see anything: then she looked at the sides of the well, and noticed that they were filled with cupboards and book-shelves: here and there she saw maps and pictures hung upon pegs. She took down a jar from one of the shelves as she passed: it was labeled "ORANGE MARMALADE," but to her great disappointment it was empty: she did not like to drop the jar, for fear of killing somebody underneath, so managed to put it into one of the cupboards as she fell past it.

"Well!" thought Alice to herself. "After such a fall as this, I shall think nothing of tumbling down-stairs! How brave they'll all think me at home! Why, I wouldn't say anything about it, even if I fell off the top of the house!" (Which was very likely true.) *irony*

narrator Down, down, down. Would the fall *never* come to an end? "I wonder how many miles I've fallen by this time?" she said aloud. "I must be getting somewhere near the centre of the earth. Let me see: that would be four thousand miles down, I think—" (for, you see, Alice had learnt several things of this sort in her lessons in the school-room, and though this was not a *very* good opportunity for showing off her knowledge, as there was no one to listen to her, still it was good practice to say it over) "—yes, that's about the right distance—but then I wonder what Latitude or Longitude I've got to?" (Alice had not the slightest idea what Latitude was, or Longitude either, *narrator* but she thought they were nice grand words to say.)

Presently she began again. "I wonder if I shall fall right *through* the earth! How funny it'll seem to come out among the people that walk with their heads downwards! The antipathies, I think—" (she was rather glad there *was* no one listening, this time, as it didn't sound at all the right word) "—but I shall have to ask them what the name of the country is, you know. Please, Ma'am, is this New Zealand? Or Australia?" (and she tried to curtsey as she spoken—fancy, *curtseying* as you're falling through the air! Do you think you could

narrator addressing reader - narrator as character

manage it?) "And what an ignorant little girl she'll think me for asking! No, it'll never do to ask: perhaps I shall see it written up somewhere."

Down, down, down. There was nothing else to do, so Alice soon began talking again. "Dinah'll miss me very much to-night, I should think!" (Dinah was the cat.[4]) "I hope they'll remember her saucer of milk at tea-time. Dinah, my dear! I wish you were down here with me! There are no mice in the air, I'm afraid, but you might catch a bat, and that's very like a mouse, you know. But do cats eat bats, I wonder?" And here Alice began to get rather sleepy, and went on saying to herself, in a dreamy sort of way, "Do cats eat bats? Do cats eat bats?" and sometimes "Do bats eat cats?" for, you see, as she couldn't answer either question, it didn't much matter which way she put it. She felt that she was dozing off, and had just begun to dream that she was walking hand in hand with Dinah, and was saying to her, very earnestly, "Now, Dinah, tell me the truth: did you ever eat a bat?" when suddenly, thump! thump! down she came upon a heap of sticks and dry leaves, and the fall was over.

Alice was not a bit hurt, and she jumped up on to her feet in a moment: she looked up, but it was all dark overhead: before her was another long passage, and the White Rabbit was still in sight, hurrying down it. There was not a moment to be lost: away went Alice like the wind, and was just in time to hear it say, as it turned a corner, "Oh my ears and whiskers, how late it's getting!" She was close behind it when she turned the corner, but the Rabbit was no longer to be seen: she found herself in a long, low hall, which was lit up by a row of lamps hanging from the roof.

There were doors all round the hall, but they were all locked; and when Alice had been all the way down one side and up the other, trying every door, she walked sadly down the middle, wondering how she was ever to get out again.

Suddenly she came upon a little three-legged table, all made of solid glass: there was nothing on it but a tiny golden key, and Alice's first idea was that this might belong to one of the doors of the hall; but, alas! either the locks were too large, or the key was too small, *relativity* but at any rate it would not open any of them. However, on the second time round, she came upon a low curtain she had not noticed before, and behind it was a little door about fifteen inches high: she tried the little golden key in the lock, and to her great delight it fitted!

Alice opened the door and found that it led into a small passage, not much larger than a rat-hole: she knelt down and looked along

4. Dinah was also the name of the Liddells' cat, named, with her companion Villikens, after the characters in a popular midcentury dialect ballad.

the passage into the loveliest garden you ever saw. How she longed
to get out of that dark hall, and wander about among those beds of
bright flowers and those cool fountains, but she could not even get
her head through the doorway; "and even if my head *would* go
through," thought poor Alice, "it would be of very little use without
my shoulders. Oh, how I wish I could shut up like a telescope! I think
I could, if I only knew how to begin." For, you see, so many out-of-the-
way things had happened lately, that Alice had begun to think that
very few things indeed were really impossible.

There seemed to be no use in waiting by the little door, so she went
back to the table, half hoping she might find another key on it, or at
any rate a book of rules for shutting people up like telescopes: this
time she found a little bottle on it ("which certainly was not here
before," said Alice), and tied around the neck of the bottle was a paper
label, with the words "DRINK ME" beautifully printed on it in large
letters.

It was all very well to say "Drink me," but the wise little Alice was
not going to do *that* in a hurry. "No, I'll look first," she said, "and see
whether it's marked *'poison'* or not"; for she had read several nice
little stories about children who had got burnt, and eaten up by wild
beasts, and other unpleasant things, all because they *would* not
remember the simple rules their friends had taught them:[5] such as,
that a red-hot poker will burn you if you hold it too long; and that, if

---

5. In a traditional kind of children's story popular in the eighteenth and early nineteenth
centuries, lessons of prudence and obedience were taught by visiting terrible calami-
ties on children who transgressed. See the commentary by Charles Dickens and Gillian Avery on pp. 309–10 and pp. 313–15 of this Norton Critical Edition.

you cut your finger *very* deeply with a knife, it usually bleeds; and she had never forgotten that, if you drink much from a bottle marked "poison," it is almost certain to disagree with you, sooner or later.

However, this bottle was *not* marked "poison," so Alice ventured to taste it, and, finding it very nice (it had, in fact, a sort of mixed flavour of cherry-tart, custard, pine-apple, roast turkey, toffy, and hot buttered toast), she very soon finished it off.

✻   ✻   ✻   ✻

✻   ✻   ✻

✻   ✻   ✻   ✻

"What a curious feeling!" said Alice. "I must be shutting up like a telescope!"

And so it was indeed: she was now only ten inches high, and her face brightened up at the thought that she was now the right size for going through the little door into that lovely garden. First, however, she waited for a few minutes to see if she was going to shrink any further: she felt a little nervous about this; "for it might end, you know," said Alice to herself, "in my going out altogether, like a candle. I wonder what I should be like then?" And she tried to fancy what the flame of a candle looks like after the candle is blown out, for she could not remember ever having seen such a thing.

---

*   Dodgson used asterisks to mark passages in which Alice changes size.

After a while, finding that nothing more happened, she decided on going into the garden at once; but, alas for poor Alice! when she got to the door, she found she had forgotten the little golden key, and when she went back to the table for it, she found she could not possibly reach it: she could see it quite plainly through the glass, and she tried her best to climb up one of the legs of the table, but it was too slippery; and when she had tired herself out with trying, the poor little thing sat down and cried.

"Come, there's no use in crying like that!" said Alice to herself rather sharply. "I advise you to leave off this minute!" She generally gave herself very good advice (though she very seldom followed it), and sometimes she scolded herself so severely as to bring tears into her eyes; and once she remembered trying to box her own ears for having cheated herself in a game of croquet she was playing against herself, for this curious child was very fond of pretending to be two people. "But it's no use now," thought poor Alice, "to pretend to be two people! Why, there's hardly enough of me left to make *one* respectable person!"

Soon her eye fell on a little glass box that was lying under the table: she opened it, and found in it a very small cake, on which the words "EAT ME" were beautifully marked in currants. "Well, I'll eat it," said Alice, "and if it makes me grow larger, I can reach the key; and if it makes me grow smaller, I can creep under the door: so either way I'll get into the garden, and I don't care which happens!"

She ate a little bit, and said anxiously to herself "Which way? Which way?", holding her hand on the top of her head to feel which way it was growing; and she was quite surprised to find that she remained the same size. To be sure, this is what generally happens when one eats cake; but Alice had got so much into the way of expecting nothing but out-of-the-way things to happen, that it seemed quite dull and stupid for life to go on in the common way.

So she set to work, and very soon finished off the cake.

✻   ✻   ✻   ✻

✻   ✻   ✻

✻   ✻   ✻   ✻

Chapter II

THE POOL OF TEARS

"Curiouser and curiouser!" cried Alice (she was so much surprised, that for the moment she quite forgot how to speak good English). "Now I'm opening out like the largest telescope that ever was! Good-bye, feet!" (for when she looked down at her feet, they seemed to be almost out of sight, they were getting so far off). "Oh, my poor little feet, I wonder who will put on your shoes and stockings for you now, dears? I'm sure *I* sha'n't be able! I shall be a great deal too far off to trouble myself about you: you must manage the best way you can—but I must be kind to them," thought Alice, "or perhaps they wo'n't walk the way I want to go! Let me see. I'll give them a new pair of boots every Christmas."

And she went on planning to herself how she would manage it. "They must go by the carrier," she thought; "and how funny it'll seem, sending presents to one's own feet! And how odd the directions will look!

> *Alice's Right Foot, Esq.*
> *Hearthrug,*
> *near the Fender,*[6]
> *(with Alice's love).*

Oh dear, what nonsense I'm talking!"

Just at this moment her head struck against the roof of the hall: in fact she was now rather more than nine feet high, and she at once took up the little golden key and hurried off to the garden door.

Poor Alice! It was as much as she could do, lying down on one side, to look through into the garden with one eye; but to get through was more hopeless than ever: she sat down and began to cry again.

"You ought to be ashamed of yourself," said Alice, "a great girl like you," (she might well say this), "to go on crying in this way! Stop this moment, I tell you!" But she went on all the same, shedding gallons of tears, until there was a large pool around her, about four inches deep, and reaching half down the hall.

After a time she heard a little pattering of feet in the distance, and she hastily dried her eyes to see what was coming. It was the White Rabbit returning, splendidly dressed, with a pair of white kid-gloves in one hand and a large fan in the other: he came trotting along in a great hurry, muttering to himself, as he came, "Oh! The Duchess, the Duchess! Oh! *Wo'n't* she be savage if I've kept her waiting!" Alice felt so desperate that she was ready to ask help of any one: so, when the Rabbit came near her, she began, in a low, timid voice, "If you please, Sir—" The Rabbit started violently, dropped the white kid-gloves and the fan, and scurried away into the darkness as hard as he could go.

Alice took up the fan and gloves, and, as the hall was very hot, she kept fanning herself all the time she went on talking. "Dear, dear! How queer everything is to-day! And yesterday things went on just as usual. I wonder if I've changed in the night? Let me think: *was* I the same when I got up this morning? I almost think I can remem-

---

6. A fender is a low metal fence or screen whose purpose is to prevent ashes and coals from falling out of a fireplace.

ber feeling a little different. But if I'm not the same, the next question is 'Who in the world am I?' Ah, *that's* the great puzzle!" And
she began thinking over all the children she knew that were of the
same age as herself, to see if she could have been changed for any
of them.

"I'm sure I'm not Ada," she said, "for her hair goes in such long
ringlets, and mine doesn't go in ringlets at all; and I'm sure I ca'n't
be Mabel, for I know all sorts of things, and she, oh, she knows
such a very little! Besides, *she's* she, and *I'm* I, and—oh dear, how
puzzling it all is! I'll try if I know all the things I used to know. Let
me see: four times five is twelve, and four times six is thirteen, and
four times seven is—oh dear! I shall never get to twenty at that
rate![7] However, the Multiplication-Table doesn't signify: let's try
Geography. London is the capital of Paris, and Paris is the capital

7. Martin Gardner in *The Annotated Alice* (p. 23) suggests that Alice will never reach
   twenty because multiplication tables traditionally stop at twelve, and in the system
   Alice is using four times twelve is nineteen.

of Rome, and Rome—no, *that's* all wrong, I'm certain! I must have been changed for Mabel! I'll try and say *'How doth the little—','*" and she crossed her hands on her lap as if she were saying lessons, and began to repeat it, but her voice sounded hoarse and strange, and the words did not come the same as they used to do:—

allusion
is it necessary to know?
audience?

"How doth the little crocodile
    Improve his shining tail,
And pour the waters of the Nile
    On every golden scale!

"How cheerfully he seems to grin,
    How neatly spreads his claws,
And welcomes little fishes in,
    With gently smiling jaws![8]

"I'm sure those are not the right words," said poor Alice, and her eyes filled with tears again as she went on, "I must be Mabel after all, and I shall have to go and live in that poky little house, and have next to no toys to play with, and oh, ever so many lessons to learn! No, I've made up my mind about it: if I'm Mabel, I'll stay down here. It'll be no use their putting their heads down and saying 'Come up again, dear!' I shall only look up and say 'Who am I, then? Tell me that first, and then, if I like being that person, I'll come up: if not, I'll stay down here till I'm somebody else'—but, oh dear!" cried Alice, with a sudden burst of tears, "I do wish they *would* put their heads down! I am so *very* tired of being all alone here!"

8. Alice's recitation is parody of "Against Idleness and Mischief," by Isaac Watts (1674–1748), included in his *Divine Songs for Children* (1715):

How doth the little busy bee
    Improve each shining hour,
And gather honey all the day
    From every opening flower!

How skillfully she builds her cell!
    How neat she spreads the wax!
And labours hard to store it well
    With the sweet food she makes.

In works of labour or of skill,
    I would be busy too;
For Satan finds some mischief still
    For idle hands to do.

In books, or work, or healthful play,
    Let my first years be past,
That I may give for every day
    Some good account at last.

Watts was a very popular writer whose hymns and poems retained their popularity and authority through the nineteenth century. The best catalogue of Dodgson's parodies, in the Alice books and in his other writing, is the appendix (pp. 307–17) of Sidney Herbert Williams and Falconer Madan's *The Lewis Carroll Handbook*, rev. Roger Lancelyn Green and further revised by Denis Crutch (see Selected Bibliography).

As she said this she looked down at her hands, and was surprised to see that she had put on one of the Rabbit's little white kid-gloves while she was talking. "How *can* I have done that?" she thought. "I must be growing small again." She got up and went to the table to measure herself by it, and found that, as nearly as she could guess, she was now about two feet high, and was going on shrinking rapidly: she soon found out that the cause of this was the fan she was holding, and she dropped it hastily, just in time to save herself from shrinking away altogether.

"That *was* a narrow escape!" said Alice, a good deal frightened at the sudden change, but very glad to find herself still in existence. "And now for the garden!" And she ran with all speed back to the little door; but, alas! the little door was shut again, and the little golden key was lying on the glass table as before, "and things are worse than ever," thought the poor child, "for I never was so small as this before, never! And I declare it's too bad, that it is!"

As she said these words her foot slipped, and in another moment, splash! she was up to her chin in salt-water. Her first idea was that she had somehow fallen into the sea, "and in that case I can go back by railway," she said to herself. (Alice had been to the seaside once in her life, and had come to the general conclusion that wherever you go to on the English coast, you find a number of bathing-machines[9] in the sea, some children digging in the sand with wooden spades, then a row of lodging-houses, and behind them a railway station.) However, she soon made out that she was in the pool of tears which she had wept when she was nine feet high.

"I wish I hadn't cried so much!" said Alice, as she swam about, trying to find her way out. "I shall be punished for it now, I suppose,

9. A bathing machine was a portable shelter that was wheeled into the water before its occupants stepped out into the sea.

by being drowned in my own tears! That *will* be a queer thing, to be sure! However, everything is queer to-day."

Just then she heard something splashing about in the pool a little way off, and she swam nearer to make out what it was: at first she thought it must be a walrus or hippopotamus, but then she remembered how small she was now, and she soon made out that it was only a mouse, that had slipped in like herself.

"Would it be of any use, now," thought Alice, "to speak to this mouse? Everything is so out-of-the-way down here, that I should think very likely it can talk: at any rate, there's no harm in trying." So she began: "O Mouse, do you know the way out of this pool? I am very tired of swimming about here, O Mouse!" (Alice thought this must be the right way of speaking to a mouse: she had never done such a thing before, but she remembered having seen, in her brother's Latin Grammar, "A mouse—of a mouse—to a mouse—a mouse—O mouse!")[1] The mouse looked at her rather inquisitively, and seemed to her to wink with one of its little eyes, but it said nothing.

"Perhaps it doesn't understand English," thought Alice. "I daresay it's a French mouse, come over with William the Conqueror." (For, with all her knowledge of history, Alice had no very clear notion how long ago anything had happened.) So she began again: "Où est ma chatte?" which was the first sentence in her French lesson-book. The Mouse gave a sudden leap out of the water, and seemed to quiver all over with fright. "Oh, I beg your pardon!" cried Alice hastily, afraid that she had hurt the poor animal's feelings. "I quite forgot you didn't like cats."

"Not like cats!" cried the Mouse in a shrill passionate voice. "Would *you* like cats, if you were me?"

"Well, perhaps not," said Alice in a soothing tone: "don't be angry about it. And yet I wish I could show you our cat Dinah. I think you'd take a fancy to cats, if you could only see her. She is such a dear quiet thing," Alice went on, half to herself, as she swam lazily about in the pool, "and she sits purring so nicely by the fire, licking her paws and washing her face—and she is such a nice soft thing to nurse—and she's such a capital one for catching mice—oh, I beg your pardon!" cried Alice again, for this time the Mouse was bristling all over, and she felt certain it must be really offended. "We wo'n't talk about her any more, if you'd rather not."

"We, indeed!" cried the Mouse, who was trembling down to the end of its tail. "As if *I* would talk on such a subject! Our family

---

1. Perhaps another indication of Dodgson's familiarity with midcentury comic entertainments: it has been suggested that this passage is modeled on a mock declension of the Latin word for "muse" (*musa*) in *The Comic Latin Grammar* (1840), written by Percival Leigh, a writer for the comic weekly *Punch*. See Martin Gardner (p. 26) and James R. Kincaid (p. 50).

always *hated* cats: nasty, low, vulgar things! Don't let me hear the name again!"

"I wo'n't indeed!" said Alice, in a great hurry to change the subject of conversation. "Are you—are you fond—of—of dogs?" The Mouse did not answer, so Alice went on eagerly: "There is such a nice little dog, near our house, I should like to show you! A little bright-eyed terrier, you know, with oh, such long curly brown hair! And it'll fetch things when you throw them, and it'll sit up and beg for its dinner, and all sorts of things—I ca'n't remember half of them—and it belongs to a farmer, you know, and he says it's so useful, it's worth a hundred pounds! He says it kills all the rats and—oh dear!" cried Alice in a sorrowful tone. "I'm afraid I've offended it again!" For the Mouse was swimming away from her as hard as it could go, and making quite a commotion in the pool as it went.

So she called softly after it, "Mouse dear! Do come back again, and we wo'n't talk about cats, or dogs either, if you don't like them!" When the Mouse heard this, it turned round and swam slowly back to her: its face was quite pale (with passion, Alice thought), and it said, in a low trembling voice, "Let us get to the shore, and then I'll tell you my history, and you'll understand why it is I hate cats and dogs."

It was high time to go, for the pool was getting quite crowded with the birds and animals that had fallen into it: there was a Duck and a Dodo, a Lory and an Eaglet,[2] and several other curious creatures. Alice led the way, and the whole party swam to the shore.

2. This passage is a relic from the original *Alice's Adventures Under Ground*, the manuscript book that Dodgson prepared for Alice Liddell and that was published in facsimile in 1886. In this passage, Duckworth is the Duck, Dodgson the Dodo, and the Lory and Eaglet are Alice's sisters Lorina and Edith.

Lory - a small Australasian parrot
Dodo - extinct, flightless bird

Chapter III

A CAUCUS-RACE AND A LONG TALE

They were indeed a queer-looking party that assembled on the bank—the birds with draggled feathers, the animals with their fur clinging close to them, and all dripping wet, cross, and uncomfortable.

The first question of course was, how to get dry again: they had a consultation about this, and after a few minutes it seemed quite natural to Alice to find herself talking familiarly with them, as if she had known them all her life. Indeed, she had quite a long argument with the Lory, who at last turned sulky, and would only say, "I'm older than you, and must know better." And this Alice would not allow, without knowing how old it was, and as the Lory positively refused to tell its age, there was no more to be said.

At last the Mouse, who seemed to be a person of some authority among them, called out "Sit down, all of you, and listen to me! *I'll* soon make you dry enough!" They all sat down at once, in a large ring, with the Mouse in the middle. Alice kept her eyes anxiously fixed on it, for she felt sure she would catch a bad cold if she did not get dry very soon.

"Ahem!" said the Mouse with an important air. "Are you all ready? This is the driest thing I know. Silence all round, if you please! 'William the Conqueror, whose cause was favoured by the pope, was soon submitted to by the English, who wanted leaders, and had been of late much accustomed to usurpation and conquest. Edwin and Morcar, the earls of Mercia and Northumbria——'"[3]

"Ugh!" said the Lory, with a shiver.

"I beg your pardon!" said the Mouse, frowning, but very politely. "Did you speak?"

"Not I!" said the Lory, hastily.

"I thought you did," said the Mouse. "I proceed. 'Edwin and Morcar, the earls of Mercia and Northumbria, declared for him; and even Stigand, the patriotic archbishop of Canterbury, found it advisable——'"

"Found *what*?" said the Duck.

"Found *it*," the Mouse replied rather crossly: "of course you know what 'it' means."

"I know what 'it' means well enough, when I find a thing," said the Duck: "it's generally a frog, or a worm. The question is, what did the archbishop find?"

The Mouse did not notice this question, but hurriedly went on, "'—found it advisable to go with Edgar Atheling to meet William and offer him the crown. William's conduct at first was moderate. But the insolence of his Normans——' How are you getting on now, my dear?" it continued, turning to Alice as it spoke.

"As wet as ever," said Alice in a melancholy tone: "it doesn't seem to dry me at all."

"In that case," said the Dodo solemnly, rising to its feet, "I move that the meeting adjourn, for the immediate adoption of more energetic remedies——"

"Speak English!" said the Eaglet. "I don't know the meaning of half those long words, and, what's more, I don't believe you do either!" And the Eaglet bent down its head to hide a smile: some of the other birds tittered audibly.

"What I was going to say," said the Dodo in an offended tone, "was that the best thing to get us dry would be a Caucus-race."[4]

"What *is* a Caucus-race?" said Alice; not that she much wanted to know, but the Dodo had paused as if it thought that *somebody* ought to speak, and no one else seemed inclined to say anything.

---

3. In his now superseded edition of *The Diaries of Lewis Carroll* (see Selected Bibliography), Roger Lancelyn Green identifies this passage as a quotation from Haviland Chepmell's *Short Course of History* (1862) (I, 2).

4. The American word *caucus* was still a strange word in mid-nineteenth-century England. A political term referring to a private meeting of the members of a party or faction, it picked up opprobrious connotations in England. Dodgson often involved himself in the frantic tedium of university politics, and he seems to use the word here both for its strangeness and to suggest the fatuity of politics.

"Why," said the Dodo, "the best way to explain it is to do it." (And, as you might like to try the thing yourself some winter-day, I will tell you how the Dodo managed it.)

First it marked out a race-course, in a sort of circle, ("the exact shape doesn't matter," it said,) and then all the party were placed along the course, here and there. There was no "One, two, three, and away!", but they began running when they liked, and left off when they liked, so that it was not easy to know when the race was over. However, when they had been running half an hour or so, and were quite dry again, the Dodo suddenly called out "The race is over!" and they all crowded round it, panting, and asking "But who has won?"

This question the Dodo could not answer without a great deal of thought, and it stood for a long time with one finger pressed upon its forehead (the position in which you usually see Shakespeare, in the pictures of him), while the rest waited in silence. At last the Dodo said "*Everybody* has won, and *all* must have prizes."

"But who is to give the prizes?" quite a chorus of voices asked.

"Why, *she*, of course," said the Dodo, pointing to Alice with one finger; and the whole party at once crowded round her, calling out, in a confused way, "Prizes! Prizes!"

Alice had no idea what to do, and in despair she put her hand in her pocket, and pulled out a box of comfits[5] (luckily the salt-water had not got into it), and handed them round as prizes. There was exactly one a-piece, all round.

"But she must have a prize herself, you know," said the Mouse.

"Of course," the Dodo replied very gravely. "What else have you got in your pocket?" it went on, turning to Alice.

"Only a thimble," said Alice sadly.

"Hand it over here," said the Dodo.

Then they all crowded round her once more, while the Dodo solemnly presented the thimble, saying "We beg your acceptance of this elegant thimble"; and, when it had finished this short speech, they all cheered.

Alice thought the whole thing very absurd, but they all looked so grave that she did not dare to laugh; and, as she could not think of anything to say, she simply bowed, and took the thimble, looking as solemn as she could.

The next thing was to eat the comfits: this caused some noise and confusion, as the large birds complained that they could not taste theirs, and the small ones choked and had to be patted on the back. However, it was over at last, and they sat down again in a ring, and begged the Mouse to tell them something more.

---

5. Comfits are a confection made of preserved fruit, roots, or seeds coated in sugar.

"You promised to tell me your history, you know," said Alice, "and why it is you hate—C and D," she added in a whisper, half afraid that it would be offended again.

"Mine is a long and sad tale!" said the Mouse, turning to Alice, and sighing.

"It *is* a long tail, certainly," said Alice, looking down with wonder at the Mouse's tail; "but why do you call it sad?" And she kept on puzzling about it while the mouse was speaking, so that her idea of the tale was something like this:—[6]

"You are not attending!" said the Mouse to Alice, severely. "What are you thinking of?"

6. In an essay written by two high-school students, Gary Graham and Jeffrey Maiden, and their teacher, Nancy Fox, the stanzas of "The Mouse's Tale" are printed in conventional form, revealing that each stanza has the shape of a mouse, with the last line as its tail.

> Fury said to the mouse,
> That he met in the house,
> "Let us both go to law: *I* will prosecute *you*."

The authors note that the form of the stanza is that of a "tail-rhyme," a couplet followed by a single line of a different length. See "Tale in Tail(s): A Study Worthy of Alice's Friends," *New York Times*, May 1, 1991, B1.

"Fury said to
a mouse, That
he met in the
house, 'Let
us both go
to law: *I*
will prose-
cute *you*.—
Come, I'll
take no de-
nial: We
must have
the trial;
For really
this morn-
ing I've
nothing
to do.'
Said the
mouse to
the cur,
'Such a
trial, dear
sir, With
no jury
or judge,
would
be wast-
ing our
breath.'
'I'll be
judge,
I'll be
jury,'
said
cun-
ning
old
Fury:
'I'll
try
the
whole
cause,
and
con-
demn
you to
death.'

24

"I beg your pardon," said Alice very humbly: "you had got to the fifth bend, I think?"

"I had *not*!" cried the Mouse, sharply and very angrily.

"A knot!" said Alice, always ready to make herself useful, and looking anxiously about her. "Oh, do let me help to undo it!"

"I shall do nothing of the sort," said the Mouse, getting up and walking away. "You insult me by talking such nonsense!"

"I didn't mean it!" pleaded poor Alice. "But you're so easily offended, you know!"

The Mouse only growled in reply.

"Please come back, and finish your story!" Alice called after it. And the others all joined in chorus "Yes, please do!" But the Mouse only shook its head impatiently, and walked a little quicker.

"What a pity it wouldn't stay!" sighed the Lory, as soon as it was quite out of sight. And an old Crab took the opportunity of saying to her daughter "Ah, my dear! Let this be a lesson to you never to lose *your* temper!" "Hold your tongue, Ma!" said the young Crab, a little snappishly. "You're enough to try the patience of an oyster!"

"I wish I had our Dinah here, I know I do!" said Alice aloud, addressing nobody in particular. *"She'd soon fetch it back!"*

"And who is Dinah, if I might venture to ask the question?" said the Lory.

Alice replied eagerly, for she was always ready to talk about her pet: "Dinah's our cat. And she's such a capital one for catching mice, you ca'n't think! And oh, I wish you could see her after the birds! Why, she'll eat a little bird as soon as look at it!"

This speech caused a remarkable sensation among the party. Some of the birds hurried off at once: one old Magpie began wrapping itself up very carefully, remarking "I really must be getting home: the night-air doesn't suit my throat!" And a Canary called out in a trembling voice, to its children, "Come away, my dears! It's high time you were all in bed!" On various pretexts they all moved off, and Alice was soon left alone.

"I wish I hadn't mentioned Dinah!" she said to herself in a melancholy tone. "Nobody seems to like her, down here, and I'm sure she's the best cat in the world! Oh, my dear Dinah! I wonder if I shall ever see you any more!" And here poor Alice began to cry again, for she felt very lonely and low-spirited. In a little while, however, she again heard a little pattering of footsteps in the distance, and she looked up eagerly, half hoping that the Mouse had changed his mind, and was coming back to finish his story.

Chapter IV

THE RABBIT SENDS IN A LITTLE BILL

It was the White Rabbit, trotting slowly back again, and looking anxiously about as it went, as if it had lost something; and she heard it muttering to itself, "The Duchess! The Duchess! Oh my dear paws! Oh my fur and whiskers! She'll get me executed, as sure as ferrets are ferrets![7] Where *can* I have dropped them, I wonder?" Alice guessed in a moment that it was looking for the fan and the pair of white kid-gloves, and she very good-naturedly began hunting about for them, but they were nowhere to be seen—everything seemed to have changed since her swim in the pool; and the great hall, with the glass table and the little door, had vanished completely.

Very soon the Rabbit noticed Alice, as she went hunting about, and called out to her, in an angry tone, "Why, Mary Ann, what *are* you doing out here? Run home this moment, and fetch me a pair of gloves and a fan! Quick, now!" And Alice was so much frightened that she ran off at once in the direction it pointed to, without trying to explain the mistake that it had made.

"He took me for his housemaid," she said to herself as she ran. "How surprised he'll be when he finds out who I am! But I'd better take him his fan and gloves—that is, if I can find them." As she said this, she came upon a neat little house, on the door of which was a bright brass plate with the name "W. RABBIT" engraved upon it. She went in without knocking, and hurried upstairs, in great fear lest she should meet the real Mary Ann, and be turned out of the house before she had found the fan and gloves.

"How queer it seems," Alice said to herself, "to be going messages for a rabbit! I suppose Dinah'll be sending me on messages next!" And she began fancying the sort of thing that would happen: "'Miss Alice! Come here directly, and get ready for your walk!' 'Coming in a minute, nurse! But I've got to watch this mouse-hole till Dinah comes back, and see that the mouse doesn't get out.' Only I don't think," Alice went on, "that they'd let Dinah stop in the house if it began ordering people about like that!"

By this time she had found her way into a tidy little room with a table in the window, and on it (as she had hoped) a fan and two or three pairs of tiny white kid-gloves: she took up the fan and a pair of the gloves, and was just going to leave the room, when her eye fell upon a little bottle that stood near the looking-glass. There was no label this time with the words "DRINK ME," but nevertheless she

---

7. Martin Gardner in *The Annotated Alice* points out that ferrets are the natural enemies of rabbits (p. 38).

uncorked it and put it to her lips. "I know *something* interesting is sure to happen," she said to herself, "whenever I eat or drink anything: so I'll just see what this bottle does. I do hope it'll make me grow large again, for really I'm quite tired of being such a tiny little thing!"

It did so indeed, and much sooner than she had expected: before she had drunk half the bottle, she found her head pressing against the ceiling, and had to stoop to save her neck from being broken. She hastily put down the bottle, saying to herself "That's quite enough—I hope I sha'n't grow any more—As it is, I ca'n't get out at the door—I do wish I hadn't drunk quite so much!"

Alas! It was too late to wish that! She went on growing, and growing, and very soon had to kneel down on the floor: in another minute there was not even room for this, and she tried the effect of lying down with one elbow against the door, and the other arm curled round her head. Still she went on growing, and, as a last resource, she put one arm out of the window, and one foot up the chimney, and said to herself "Now I can do no more, whatever happens. What *will* become of me?"

Luckily for Alice, the little magic bottle had now had its full effect, and she grew no larger: still it was very uncomfortable, and as there seemed to be no sort of chance of her ever getting out of the room again, no wonder she felt unhappy.

"It was much pleasanter at home," thought poor Alice, "where one wasn't always growing larger and smaller, and being ordered about by mice and rabbits. I almost wish I hadn't gone down that rabbit-hole—and yet—and yet—it's rather curious, you know, this

sort of life! I do wonder what *can* have happened to me! When I used to read fairy tales, I fancied that kind of thing never happened, and now here I am in the middle of one! There ought to be a book written about me, that there ought! And when I grow up, I'll write one—but I'm grown up now," she added in a sorrowful tone; "at least there's no room to grow up any more *here*."

"But then," thought Alice, "shall I *never* get any older than I am now? That'll be a comfort, one way—never to be an old woman— but then—always to have lessons to learn! Oh, I shouldn't like *that*!"

"Oh, you foolish Alice!" she answered herself. "How can you learn lessons in here? Why, there's hardly room for *you*, and no room at all for any lesson-books!"

And so she went on, taking first one side and then the other, and making quite a conversation of it altogether; but after a few minutes she heard a voice outside, and stopped to listen.

"Mary Ann! Mary Ann!" said the voice. "Fetch me my gloves this moment!" Then came a little pattering of feet on the stairs. Alice knew it was the Rabbit coming to look for her, and she trembled till she shook the house, quite forgetting that she was now about a thousand times as large as the Rabbit, and had no reason to be afraid of it.

Presently the Rabbit came up to the door, and tried to open it; but, as the door opened inwards, and Alice's elbow was pressed hard against it, that attempt proved a failure. Alice heard it say to itself "Then I'll go round and get in at the window."

"*That* you wo'n't!" thought Alice, and after waiting till she fancied she heard the Rabbit just under the window, she suddenly spread out her hand, and made a snatch in the air. She did not get hold of anything, but she heard a little shriek and a fall, and a crash of broken glass, from which she concluded that it was just possible it had fallen into a cucumber-frame,[8] or something of the sort.

Next came an angry voice—the Rabbit's—"Pat! Pat! Where are you?" And then a voice she had never heard before, "Sure then I'm here! Digging for apples, yer honour!"[9]

"Digging for apples, indeed!" said the Rabbit angrily. "Here! Come help me out of *this*!" (Sounds of more broken glass.)

"Now tell me, Pat, what's that in the window?"

"Sure, it's an arm, yer honour!" (He pronounced it "arrum.")

---

8. Cucumber-frame: a low construction of wood and glass, like a small greenhouse.
9. Dodgson does not often use dialect. The Irish dialect spoken by Pat, like the lower-class idiom used by the Gryphon later in this book and by the Frog-Footman in *Through the Looking-Glass* ("wexes" for "vexes"), was a common device of nineteenth-century English humorists. The French word for potato, associated with the Irish in the nineteenth century (and after), is *pomme de terre*, apple of the earth.

"An arm, you goose! Who ever saw one that size? Why, it fills the whole window!"

"Sure, it does, yer honour: but it's an arm for all that."

"Well, it's got no business there, at any rate: go and take it away!"

There was a long silence after this, and Alice could only hear whispers now and then; such as "Sure, I don't like it, yer honour, at all, at all!" "Do as I tell you, you coward!", and at last she spread out her hand again, and made another snatch in the air. This time there were *two* little shrieks, and more sounds of broken glass. "What a number of cucumber-frames there must be!" thought

Alice. "I wonder what they'll do next! As for pulling me out of the window, I only wish they *could*! I'm sure I don't want to stay in here any longer!"

She waited for some time without hearing anything more: at last came a rumbling of little cart-wheels, and the sound of a good many voices all talking together: she made out the words: "Where's the other ladder?—Why, I hadn't to bring but one. Bill's got the other—Bill! Fetch it here, lad!—Here, put 'em up at this corner—No, tie 'em together first—they don't reach half high enough yet—Oh, they'll do well enough. Don't be particular—Here, Bill! Catch hold of this rope—Will the roof bear?—Mind that loose slate—Oh, it's coming down! Heads below!" (a loud crash)—"Now, who did that?—It was Bill, I fancy—Who's to go down the chimney?—Nay, *I* sha'n't! *You* do it!—*That* I wo'n't, then!—Bill's got to go down—Here, Bill! The master says you've got to go down the chimney!"

"Oh! So Bill's got to come down the chimney, has he?" said Alice to herself. "Why, they seem to put everything upon Bill! I wouldn't be in Bill's place for a good deal: this fireplace is narrow, to be sure; but I *think* I can kick a little!"

She drew her foot as far down the chimney as she could, and waited till she heard a little animal (she couldn't guess of what sort it was) scratching and scrambling about in the chimney close above her: then, saying to herself "This is Bill", she gave one sharp kick, and waited to see what would happen next.

The first thing she heard was a general chorus of "There goes Bill!" then the Rabbit's voice alone—"Catch him, you by the hedge!" then silence, and then another confusion of voices— "Hold up his head—Brandy now—Don't choke him—How was it, old fellow? What happened to you? Tell us all about it!"

Last came a little feeble, squeaking voice ("That's Bill," thought Alice), "Well, I hardly know—No more, thank ye; I'm better now—but I'm a deal too flustered to tell you—all I know is, something comes at me like a Jack-in-the-box, and up I goes like a sky-rocket!"

"So you did, old fellow!" said the others.

"We must burn the house down!" said the Rabbit's voice. And Alice called out, as loud as she could, "If you do, I'll set Dinah at you!"

There was a dead silence instantly, and Alice thought to herself "I wonder what they *will* do next! If they had any sense, they'd take the roof off." After a minute or two they began moving about again, and Alice heard the Rabbit say "A barrowful will do, to begin with."

"A barrowful of *what*?" thought Alice. But she had not long to doubt, for the next moment a shower of little pebbles came rattling in at the window, and some of them hit her in the face. "I'll put a stop to this," she said to herself, and shouted out "You'd better not do that again!", which produced another dead silence.

Alice noticed, with some surprise, that the pebbles were all turning into little cakes as they lay on the floor, and a bright idea came
into her head. "If I eat one of these cakes," she thought, "it's sure to
make *some* change in my size; and, as it ca'n't possibly make me
larger, it must make me smaller, I suppose."

So she swallowed one of the cakes, and was delighted to find that
she began shrinking directly. As soon as she was small enough to get
through the door, she ran out of the house, and found quite a crowd
of little animals and birds waiting outside. The poor little Lizard,
Bill, was in the middle, being held up by two guinea-pigs, who were
giving it something out of a bottle. They all made a rush at Alice
the moment she appeared; but she ran off as hard as she could, and
soon found herself safe in a thick wood.

"The first thing I've got to do," said Alice to herself, as she wandered about in the wood, "is to grow to my right size again; and the
second thing is to find my way into that lovely garden. I think that
will be the best plan."

It sounded an excellent plan, no doubt, and very neatly and simply
arranged: the only difficulty was, that she had not the smallest idea
how to set about it; and, while she was peering about anxiously
among the trees, a little sharp bark just over her head made her look
up in a great hurry.

An enormous puppy was looking down at her with large round
eyes, and feebly stretching out one paw, trying to touch her. "Poor
little thing!" said Alice, in a coaxing tone, and she tried hard to
whistle to it; but she was terribly frightened all the time at the
thought that it might be hungry, in which case it would be very likely
to eat her up in spite of all her coaxing.

Hardly knowing what she did, she picked up a little bit of stick,
and held it out to the puppy: whereupon the puppy jumped into the
air off all its feet at once, with a yelp of delight, and rushed at the
stick, and made believe to worry it: then Alice dodged behind a
great thistle, to keep herself from being run over; and, the moment
she appeared on the other side, the puppy made another rush at the
stick, and tumbled head over heels in its hurry to get hold of it: then
Alice, thinking it was very like having a game of play with a cart-
horse, and expecting every moment to be trampled under its feet,
ran round the thistle again: then the puppy began a series of short
charges at the stick, running a very little way forwards each time
and a long way back, and barking hoarsely all the while, till at last
it sat down a good way off, panting, with its tongue hanging out of
its mouth, and its great eyes half shut.

This seemed to Alice a good opportunity for making her escape: so
she set off at once, and ran till she was quite tired and out of breath,
and till the puppy's bark sounded quite faint in the distance.

"And yet what a dear little puppy it was!" said Alice, as she leant against a buttercup to rest herself, and fanned herself with one of the leaves. "I should have liked teaching it tricks very much, if—if I'd only been the right size to do it! Oh dear! I'd nearly forgotten that I've got to grow up again! Let me see—how *is* it to be managed? I suppose I ought to eat or drink something or other; but the great question is 'What?'"

The great question certainly was "What?" Alice looked all round her at the flowers and the blades of grass, but she could not see anything that looked like the right thing to eat or drink under the circumstances. There was a large mushroom growing near her, about the same height as herself; and, when she had looked under it, and on both sides of it, and behind it, it occurred to her that she might as well look and see what was on top of it.

She stretched herself up on tiptoe, and peeped over the edge of the mushroom, and her eyes immediately met those of a large blue caterpillar, that was sitting on the top, with its arms folded, quietly smoking a long hookah, and taking not the smallest notice of her or of anything else.

Chapter V

ADVICE FROM A CATERPILLAR

The Caterpillar and Alice looked at each other for some time in silence: at last the Caterpillar took the hookah out of its mouth, and addressed her in a languid, sleepy voice.

"Who are *you*?" said the Caterpillar.

This was not an encouraging opening for a conversation. Alice replied, rather shyly, "I—I hardly know, Sir, just at present—at least I know who I *was* when I got up this morning, but I think I must have been changed several times since then."

"What do you mean by that?" said the Caterpillar, sternly. "Explain yourself!"

"I ca'n't explain *myself*, I'm afraid, Sir," said Alice, "because I'm not myself, you see."

"I don't see," said the Caterpillar.

"I'm afraid I ca'n't put it more clearly," Alice replied, very politely, "for I ca'n't understand it myself, to begin with; and being so many different sizes in a day is very confusing."

"It isn't," said the Caterpillar.

"Well, perhaps you haven't found it so yet," said Alice; "but when you have to turn into a chrysalis—you will some day, you know—

34

and then after that into a butterfly, I should think you'll feel it a little queer, wo'n't you?"

"Not a bit," said the Caterpillar.

"Well, perhaps *your* feelings may be different," said Alice: "all I know is, it would feel very queer to *me*."

"You!" said the Caterpillar contemptuously. "Who are *you?*"

Which brought them back again to the beginning of the conversation. Alice felt a little irritated at the Caterpillar's making such *very* short remarks, and she drew herself up and said, very gravely, "I think you ought to tell me who *you* are, first."

"Why?" said the Caterpillar.

Here was another puzzling question; and, as Alice could not think of any good reason, and the Caterpillar seemed to be in a *very* unpleasant state of mind, she turned away.

"Come back!" the Caterpillar called after her. "I've something important to say!"

This sounded promising, certainly. Alice turned and came back again.

"Keep your temper," said the Caterpillar.

"Is that all?" said Alice, swallowing down her anger as well as she could.

"No," said the Caterpillar.

Alice thought she might as well wait, as she had nothing else to do, and perhaps after all it might tell her something worth hearing. For some minutes it puffed away without speaking; but at last it unfolded its arms, took the hookah out of its mouth again, and said "So you think you're changed, do you?"

"I'm afraid I am, Sir," said Alice. "I ca'n't remember things as I used—and I don't keep the same size for ten minutes together!"

"Ca'n't remember *what* things?" said the Caterpillar.

"Well, I've tried to say '*How doth the little busy bee,*' but it all came different!" Alice replied in a very melancholy voice.

"Repeat '*You are old, Father William,*'"[1] said the Caterpillar.

Alice folded her hands, and began:—

---

1. "You Are Old, Father William" is a parody of Robert Southey's "The Old Man's Comforts, and How He Gained Them," written in 1799. The last two stanzas of Southey's poem suggest the meter and form Dodgson is playing with in his parody, and the pious sentiment he is playing against:

> "You are old, Father William," the young man cried,
> "And life must be hastening away;
> You are cheerful, and love to converse upon death:
> Now tell me the reason, I pray."

> "I am cheerful, young man," Father William replied;
> "Let the cause thy attention engage:
> In the days of my youth, I remembered my God:
> And he hath not forgotten my age."

"You are old, Father William," the young man said,
    "And your hair has become very white;
And yet you incessantly stand on your head—
    Do you think, at your age, it is right?"

"In my youth," Father William replied to his son,
    "I feared it might injure the brain;
But, now that I'm perfectly sure I have none,
    Why, I do it again and again."

"You are old," said the youth, "as I mentioned before,
    And have grown most uncommonly fat;
Yet you turned a back-somersault in at the door—
    Pray, what is the reason of that?"

"In my youth," said the sage, as he shook his grey locks,
    "I kept all my limbs very supple
By the use of this ointment—one shilling the box—
    Allow me to sell you a couple?"

"You are old," said the youth, "and your jaws are too weak
  For anything tougher than suet;
Yet you finished the goose, with the bones and the beak—
  Pray, how did you manage to do it?"

"In my youth," said his father, "I took to the law,
  And argued each case with my wife;
And the muscular strength, which it gave to my jaw
  Has lasted the rest of my life."

"You are old," said the youth, "one would hardly suppose
   That your eye was as steady as ever;
Yet you balanced an eel on the end of your nose—
   What made you so awfully clever?"

"I have answered three questions, and that is enough,"
   Said his father. "Don't give yourself airs!
Do you think I can listen all day to such stuff?
   Be off, or I'll kick you down-stairs!"

"That is not said right," said the Caterpillar.

"Not *quite* right, I'm afraid," said Alice, timidly: "some of the words have got altered."

"It is wrong from beginning to end," said the Caterpillar, decidedly; and there was silence for some minutes.

The Caterpillar was the first to speak.

"What size do you want to be?" it asked.

"Oh, I'm not particular as to size," Alice hastily replied; "only one doesn't like changing so often, you know."

"I *don't* know," said the Caterpillar.

Alice said nothing: she had never been so much contradicted in all her life before, and she felt that she was losing her temper.

"Are you content now?" said the Caterpillar.

"Well, I should like to be a *little* larger, Sir, if you wouldn't mind," said Alice: "three inches is such a wretched height to be."

"It is a very good height indeed!" said the Caterpillar angrily, rearing itself upright as it spoke (it was exactly three inches high).

"But I'm not used to it!" pleaded poor Alice in a piteous tone. And she thought to herself "I wish the creatures wouldn't be so easily offended!"

"You'll get used to it in time," said the Caterpillar; and it put the hookah into its mouth, and began smoking again.

This time Alice waited patiently until it chose to speak again. In a minute or two the Caterpillar took the hookah out of its mouth, and yawned once or twice, and shook itself. Then it got down off the mushroom, and crawled away into the grass, merely remarking, as it went, "One side will make you grow taller, and the other side will make you grow shorter."

"One side of *what*? The other side of *what*?" thought Alice to herself.

"Of the mushroom," said the Caterpillar, just as if she had asked it aloud; and in another moment it was out of sight.

Alice remained looking thoughtfully at the mushroom for a minute, trying to make out which were the two sides of it; and, as it was perfectly round, she found this a very difficult question. However, at last she stretched her arms round it as far as they would go, and broke off a bit of the edge with each hand.

"And now which is which?" she said to herself, and nibbled a little of the right-hand bit to try the effect. The next moment she felt a violent blow underneath her chin: it had struck her foot!

She was a good deal frightened by this very sudden change, but she felt that there was no time to be lost, as she was shrinking rapidly: so she set to work at once to eat some of the other bit. Her chin was pressed so closely against her foot, that there was hardly room to open her mouth; but she did it at last, and managed to swallow a morsel of the left-hand bit.

☆   ☆   ☆   ☆   ☆
  ☆   ☆   ☆   ☆
☆   ☆   ☆   ☆   ☆

"Come, my head's free at last!" said Alice in a tone of delight, which changed into alarm in another moment, when she found that her shoulders were nowhere to be found: all she could see, when she looked down, was an immense length of neck, which seemed to rise like a stalk out of a sea of green leaves that lay far below her.

"What *can* all that green stuff be?" said Alice. "And where *have* my shoulders got to? And oh, my poor hands, how is it I ca'n't see you?" She was moving them about, as she spoke, but no result seemed to follow, except a little shaking among the distant green leaves.

As there seemed to be no chance of getting her hands up to her head, she tried to get her head down to *them*, and was delighted to find that her neck would bend about easily in any direction, like a serpent. She had just succeeded in curving it down into a graceful zigzag, and was going to dive in among the leaves, which she found to be nothing but the tops of the trees under which she had been wandering, when a sharp hiss made her draw back in a hurry: a large pigeon had flown into her face, and was beating her violently with its wings.

"Serpent!" screamed the Pigeon.

"I'm *not* a serpent!" said Alice indignantly. "Let me alone!"

"Serpent, I say again!" repeated the Pigeon, but in a more subdued tone, and added, with a kind of sob, "I've tried every way, but nothing seems to suit them!"

"I haven't the least idea what you're talking about," said Alice.

"I've tried the roots of trees, and I've tried banks, and I've tried hedges," the Pigeon went on, without attending to her; "but those serpents! There's no pleasing them!"

Alice was more and more puzzled, but she thought there was no use in saying anything more till the Pigeon had finished.

"As if it wasn't trouble enough hatching the eggs," said the Pigeon; "but I must be on the look-out for serpents, night and day! Why, I haven't had a wink of sleep these three weeks!"

"I'm very sorry you've been annoyed," said Alice, who was beginning to see its meaning.

"And just as I'd taken the highest tree in the wood," continued the Pigeon, raising its voice to a shriek, "and just as I was thinking

I should be free of them at last, they must needs come wriggling down from the sky! Ugh, Serpent!"

"But I'm *not* a serpent, I tell you!" said Alice. "I'm a—I'm a——"

"Well! *What* are you?" said the Pigeon. "I can see you're trying to invent something!"

"I—I'm a little girl," said Alice, rather doubtfully, as she remembered the number of changes she had gone through, that day.

"A likely story indeed!" said the Pigeon, in a tone of the deepest contempt. "I've seen a good many little girls in my time, but never *one* with such a neck as that! No, no! You're a serpent; and there's no use denying it. I suppose you'll be telling me next that you never tasted an egg!"

"I *have* tasted eggs, certainly," said Alice, who was a very truthful child; "but little girls eat eggs quite as much as serpents do, you know."

"I don't believe it," said the Pigeon; "but if they do, why, then they're a kind of serpent: that's all I can say."

This was such a new idea to Alice, that she was quite silent for a minute or two, which gave the Pigeon the opportunity of adding "You're looking for eggs, I know *that* well enough; and what does it matter to me whether you're a little girl or a serpent?"

"It matters a good deal to *me*," said Alice hastily; "but I'm not looking for eggs, as it happens; and, if I was, I shouldn't want *yours*: I don't like them raw."

"Well, be off, then!" said the Pigeon in a sulky tone, as it settled down again into its nest. Alice crouched down among the trees as well as she could, for her neck kept getting entangled among the branches, and every now and then she had to stop and untwist it. After a while she remembered that she still held the pieces of mushroom in her hands, and she set to work very carefully, nibbling first at one and then at the other, and growing sometimes taller, and sometimes shorter, until she had succeeded in bringing herself down to her usual height.

It was so long since she had been anything near the right size, that it felt quite strange at first; but she got used to it in a few minutes, and began talking to herself, as usual, "Come, there's half my plan done now! How puzzling all these changes are! I'm never sure what I'm going to be, from one minute to another! However, I've got back to my right size: the next thing is, to get into that beautiful garden—how *is* that to be done, I wonder?" As she said this, she came suddenly upon an open place, with a little house in it about four feet high. "Whoever lives there," thought Alice, "it'll never do to come upon them *this* size: why, I should frighten them out of their wits!" So she began nibbling at the right-hand bit again, and did not venture to go near the house till she had brought herself down to nine inches high.

Chapter VI

PIG AND PEPPER

For a minute or two she stood looking at the house, and wondering what to do next, when suddenly a footman in livery came running out of the wood—(she considered him to be a footman because he was in livery: otherwise, judging by his face only, she would have called him a fish)—and rapped loudly at the door with his knuckles. It was opened by another footman in livery, with a round face, and large eyes like a frog; and both footmen, Alice noticed, had powdered hair that curled all over their heads. She felt very curious to know what it was all about, and crept a little way out of the wood to listen.

The Fish-Footman began by producing from under his arm a great letter, nearly as large as himself, and this he handed over to the other, saying, in a solemn tone, "For the Duchess. An invitation from the Queen to play croquet." The Frog-Footman repeated, in the same solemn tone, only changing the order of the words a little, "From the Queen. An invitation for the Duchess to play croquet."

Then they both bowed, and their curls got entangled together.

Alice laughed so much at this, that she had to run back into the wood for fear of their hearing her; and, when she next peeped out, the Fish-Footman was gone, and the other was sitting on the ground near the door, staring stupidly up into the sky.

Alice went timidly up to the door, and knocked.

"There's no sort of use in knocking," said the Footman, "and that for two reasons. First, because I'm on the same side of the door as you are: secondly, because they're making such a noise inside, no one could possibly hear you." And certainly there *was* a most extraordinary noise going on within—a constant howling and sneezing, and every now and then a great crash, as if a dish or kettle had been broken to pieces.

"Please, then," said Alice, "how am I to get in?"

"There might be some sense in your knocking," the Footman went on, without attending to her, "if we had the door between us. For instance, if you were *inside*, you might knock, and I could let you out, you know." He was looking up into the sky all the time he was speaking, and this Alice thought decidedly uncivil. "But perhaps he ca'n't help it," she said to herself; "his eyes are so *very* nearly at the top of his head. But at any rate he might answer questions.—How am I to get in?" she repeated, aloud.

"I shall sit here," the Footman remarked, "till to-morrow——"

At this moment the door of the house opened, and a large plate came skimming out, straight at the Footman's head: it just grazed his nose, and broke to pieces against one of the trees behind him.

"——or next day, maybe," the Footman continued in the same tone, exactly as if nothing had happened.

"How am I to get in?" asked Alice again, in a louder tone.

"*Are* you to get in at all?" said the Footman. "That's the first question, you know."

It was, no doubt: only Alice did not like to be told so. "It's really dreadful," she muttered to herself, "the way all the creatures argue. It's enough to drive one crazy!"

The Footman seemed to think this a good opportunity for repeating his remark, with variations. "I shall sit here," he said, "on and off, for days and days."

"But what am *I* to do?" said Alice.

"Anything you like," said the Footman, and began whistling.

"Oh, there's no use in talking to him," said Alice desperately: "he's perfectly idiotic!" And she opened the door and went in.

The door led right into a large kitchen, which was full of smoke from one end to the other: the Duchess[2] was sitting on a three-legged stool in the middle, nursing a baby: the cook was leaning over the fire, stirring a large cauldron which seemed to be full of soup.

"There's certainly too much pepper in that soup!" Alice said to herself, as well as she could for sneezing.

There was certainly too much of it in the *air*. Even the Duchess sneezed occasionally; and as for the baby, it was sneezing and howling alternately without a moment's pause. The only two creatures in the kitchen, that did *not* sneeze, were the cook, and a large cat, which was lying on the hearth and grinning from ear to ear.

"Please would you tell me," said Alice, a little timidly, for she was not quite sure whether it was good manners for her to speak first, "why your cat grins like that?"

"It's a Cheshire-Cat,"[3] said the Duchess, "and that's why. Pig!"

2. Michael Hancher, in his excellent study of *The Tenniel Illustrations to the "Alice" Books* (see Selected Bibliography), identifies a painting attributed to the Flemish painter Quinten Massys (1465/66–1530) as the most likely source of Tenniel's drawing of the Duchess (pp. 41–48).
3. The phrase "grin like a Cheshire-Cat" is proverbial. Its origins are uncertain, but Dodgson may have read some contributions to *Notes and Queries* in 1852 that attributed the phrase to the custom of making Cheshire cheeses in the shape of grinning cats, or to the practice of a Cheshire signpainter who painted pictures of grinning cats.

She said the last word with such sudden violence that Alice quite jumped; but she saw in another moment that it was addressed to the baby, and not to her, so she took courage, and went on again:—

"I didn't know that Cheshire-Cats always grinned; in fact, I didn't know that cats *could* grin."

"They all can," said the Duchess; "and most of 'em do."

"I don't know of any that do," Alice said very politely, feeling quite pleased to have got into a conversation.

"You don't know much," said the Duchess; "and that's a fact."

Alice did not at all like the tone of this remark, and thought it would be as well to introduce some other subject of conversation. While she was trying to fix on one, the cook took the cauldron of soup off the fire, and at once set to work throwing everything within her reach at the Duchess and the baby—the fire-irons came first; then followed a shower of saucepans, plates, and dishes. The Duchess took no notice of them even when they hit her; and the baby was howling so much already, that it was quite impossible to say whether the blows hurt it or not.

"Oh, *please* mind what you're doing!" cried Alice, jumping up and down in an agony of terror. "Oh, there goes his *precious* nose!", as an unusually large saucepan flew close by it, and very nearly carried it off.

"If everybody minded their own business," the Duchess said, in a hoarse growl, "the world would go round a deal faster than it does."

"Which would *not* be an advantage," said Alice, who felt very glad to get an opportunity of showing off a little of her knowledge. "Just think what work it would make with the day and night! You see the earth takes twenty-four hours to turn round on its axis——"

"Talking of axes," said the Duchess, "chop off her head!"

Alice glanced rather anxiously at the cook, to see if she meant to take the hint; but the cook was busily stirring the soup, and seemed not to be listening, so she went on again: "Twenty-four hours, I *think*; or is it twelve? I——"

"Oh, don't bother *me*!" said the Duchess. "I never could abide figures!" And with that she began nursing her child again, singing a sort of lullaby to it as she did so, and giving it a violent shake at the end of every line:—

> "Speak roughly to your little boy,
>   And beat him when he sneezes:
> He only does it to annoy,
>   Because he knows it teases."

> CHORUS
> (in which the cook and the baby joined):—
>   "Wow! wow! wow!"

While the Duchess sang the second verse of the song, she kept
tossing the baby violently up and down, and the poor little thing
howled so, that Alice could hardly hear the words:—

> "I speak severely to my boy,
>   I beat him when he sneezes;
> For he can thoroughly enjoy
>   The pepper when he pleases!"

CHORUS

> "Wow! wow! wow!"[4]

"Here! You may nurse it a bit, if you like!" the Duchess said to
Alice, flinging the baby at her as she spoke. "I must go and get ready
to play croquet with the Queen," and she hurried out of the room.
The cook threw a frying-pan after her as she went, but it just
missed her.

Alice caught the baby with some difficulty, as it was a queer-
shaped little creature, and held out its arms and legs in all directions, "just like a star-fish," thought Alice. The poor little thing
was snorting like a steam-engine when she caught it, and kept
doubling itself up and straightening itself out again, so that altogether, for the first minute or two, it was as much as she could do
to hold it.

As soon as she had made out the proper way of nursing it (which
was to twist it up into a sort of knot, and then keep tight hold of its
right ear and left foot, so as to prevent its undoing itself), she carried it out into the open air. "If I don't take this child away with
me," thought Alice, "they're sure to kill it in a day or two. Wouldn't
it be murder to leave it behind?" She said the last words out loud,
and the little thing grunted in reply (it had left off sneezing by this
time). "Don't grunt," said Alice; "that's not at all a proper way of
expressing yourself."

The baby grunted again, and Alice looked very anxiously into its
face to see what was the matter with it. There could be no doubt
that it had a *very* turn-up nose, much more like a snout than a real
nose: also its eyes were getting extremely small for a baby: alto-

---

4. "Speak roughly" is a parody of one stanza of a popular children's poem by David Bates,
first published in 1848:

> Speak gently to the little child!
>   Its love be sure to gain;
> Teach it in accents soft and mild—
>   It may not long remain.

The poem is sometimes attributed to G. W. Langford; for the attribution to Bates, see
the appendix (p. 310) to *The Lewis Carroll Handbook* (see Selected Bibliography).

gether Alice did not like the look of the thing at all. "But perhaps it was only sobbing," she thought, and looked into its eyes again, to see if there were any tears.

No, there were no tears. "If you're going to turn into a pig, my dear," said Alice, seriously, "I'll have nothing more to do with you. Mind now!" The poor little thing sobbed again (or grunted, it was impossible to say which), and they went on for some while in silence.

Alice was just beginning to think to herself, "Now, what am I to do with this creature, when I get it home?" when it grunted again, so violently, that she looked down into its face in some alarm. This time there could be *no* mistake about it: it was neither more nor less than a pig, and she felt that it would be quite absurd for her to carry it any further.

So she set the little creature down, and felt quite relieved to see it trot away quietly into the wood. "If it had grown up," she said to herself, "it would have made a dreadfully ugly child: but it makes rather a handsome pig, I think." And she began thinking over other children she knew, who might do very well as pigs, and was just saying to herself "if one only knew the right way to change them——" when she was a little startled by seeing the Cheshire-Cat sitting on a bough of a tree a few yards off.

The Cat only grinned when it saw Alice. It looked good-natured, she thought: still it had *very* long claws and a great many teeth, so she felt that it ought to be treated with respect.

"Cheshire-Puss," she began, rather timidly, as she did not at all know whether it would like the name: however, it only grinned a little wider. "Come, it's pleased so far," thought Alice, and she went on. "Would you tell me, please, which way I ought to go from here?"

"That depends a good deal on where you want to get to," said the Cat.

"I don't much care where——" said Alice.

"Then it doesn't matter which way you go," said the Cat.

"—— so long as I get *somewhere*," Alice added as an explanation.

"Oh, you're sure to do that," said the Cat, "if you only walk long enough."

Alice felt that this could not be denied, so she tried another question. "What sort of people live about here?"

"In *that* direction," the Cat said, waving its right paw round, "lives a Hatter: and in *that* direction," waving the other paw, "lives a March Hare. Visit either you like: they're both mad."[5]

"But I don't want to go among mad people," Alice remarked.

"Oh, you ca'n't help that," said the Cat: "we're all mad here. I'm mad. You're mad."

"How do you know I'm mad?" said Alice.

"You must be," said the Cat, "or you wouldn't have come here."

Alice didn't think that proved it at all: however, she went on: "And how do you know that you're mad?"

"To begin with," said the Cat, "a dog's not mad. You grant that?"

"I suppose so," said Alice.

"Well, then," the Cat went on, "you see a dog growls when it's angry, and wags its tail when it's pleased. Now *I* growl when I'm pleased, and wag my tail when I'm angry. Therefore I'm mad."

"*I* call it purring, not growling," said Alice.

"Call it what you like," said the Cat. "Do you play croquet with the Queen to-day?"

"I should like it very much," said Alice, "but I haven't been invited yet."

"You'll see me there," said the Cat, and vanished.

---

5. "Mad as a hatter" and "mad as a March hare" are both proverbial expressions. The latter may be founded on the mistaken belief that hares mate only in March, and behave erratically in that season. The former may be founded in the fact that the use of mercury in preparing the felt that was made into hats could produce spasmodic convulsions that were taken as symptoms of madness. Tenniel drew the March Hare with straw in his hair, in Dodgson's time a conventional sign of insanity in illustrations and onstage.

The Mad Hatter also bears characteristics of one Theophilus Carter, an eccentric Oxford furniture dealer who customarily stood in the front of his shop wearing a top hat on the back of his head. He was also the inventor of an alarm-clock bed, which at the time for which it was set tipped its occupant onto the floor. See R. L. Green's edition (I, 172–73) of *The Diaries of Lewis Carroll* (see Selected Bibliography).

Alice was not much surprised at this, she was getting so well used to queer things happening. While she was still looking at the place where it had been, it suddenly appeared again.

"By-the-bye, what became of the baby?" said the Cat. "I'd nearly forgotten to ask."

"It turned into a pig," Alice answered very quietly, just as if the Cat had come back in a natural way.

"I thought it would," said the Cat, and vanished again.

Alice waited a little, half expecting to see it again, but it did not appear, and after a minute or two she walked on in the direction in which the March Hare was said to live. "I've seen hatters before," she said to herself: "the March Hare will be much the most interesting, and perhaps, as this is May, it wo'n't be raving mad—at least not so mad as it was in March." As she said this, she looked up, and there was the Cat again, sitting on a branch of a tree.

"Did you say 'pig', or 'fig'?" said the Cat.

"I said 'pig'," replied Alice; "and I wish you wouldn't keep appearing and vanishing so suddenly; you make one quite giddy!"

"All right," said the Cat; and this time it vanished quite slowly, beginning with the end of the tail, and ending with the grin, which remained some time after the rest of it had gone.

"Well! I've often seen a cat without a grin," thought Alice; "but a grin without a cat! It's the most curious thing I ever saw in all my life!"

She had not gone much farther before she came in sight of the house of the March Hare: she thought it must be the right house, because the chimneys were shaped like ears and the roof was thatched with fur. It was so large a house, that she did not like to go nearer till she had nibbled some more of the left-hand bit of mushroom, and raised herself to about two feet high: even then she walked up towards it rather timidly, saying to herself "Suppose it should be raving mad after all! I almost wish I'd gone to see the Hatter instead!"

Chapter VII

A MAD TEA-PARTY

There was a table set out under a tree in front of the house, and the March Hare and the Hatter were having tea at it: a Dormouse was sitting between them, fast asleep,[6] and the other two were using it as a cushion, resting their elbows on it, and talking over its head. "Very uncomfortable for the Dormouse," thought Alice; "only as it's asleep, I suppose it doesn't mind."

The table was a large one, but the three were all crowded together at one corner of it. "No room! No room!" they cried out when they saw Alice coming. "There's *plenty* of room!" said Alice indignantly, and she sat down in a large arm-chair at one end of the table.

"Have some wine," the March Hare said in an encouraging tone.

Alice looked all round the table, but there was nothing on it but tea. "I don't see any wine," she remarked.

"There isn't any," said the March Hare.

"Then it wasn't very civil of you to offer it," said Alice angrily.

"It wasn't very civil of you to sit down without being invited," said the March Hare.

---

6. A dormouse is a rodent that hibernates in the winter and sleeps during the day all year round.

"I didn't know it was *your* table," said Alice: "it's laid for a great many more than three."

"Your hair wants cutting," said the Hatter. He had been looking at Alice for some time with great curiosity, and this was his first speech.

"You should learn not to make personal remarks," Alice said with some severity: "it's very rude."

The Hatter opened his eyes very wide on hearing this; but all he *said* was "Why is a raven like a writing-desk?"[7]

"Come, we shall have some fun now!" thought Alice. "I'm glad they've begun asking riddles—I believe I can guess that," she added aloud.

"Do you mean that you think you can find out the answer to it?" said the March Hare.

"Exactly so," said Alice.

"Then you should say what you mean," the March Hare went on.

"I do," Alice hastily replied; "at least—at least I mean what I say—that's the same thing, you know."

"Not the same thing a bit!" said the Hatter. "Why, you might just as well say that 'I see what I eat' is the same thing as 'I eat what I see'!"

"You might just as well say," added the March Hare, "that 'I like what I get' is the same thing as 'I get what I like'!"

"You might just as well say," added the Dormouse, which seemed to be talking in its sleep, "that 'I breathe when I sleep' is the same thing as 'I sleep when I breathe'!"

"It *is* the same thing with you," said the Hatter, and here the conversation dropped, and the party sat silent for a minute, while Alice thought over all she could remember about ravens and writing-desks, which wasn't much.

The Hatter was the first to break the silence. "What day of the month is it?" he said, turning to Alice: he had taken his watch out of his pocket, and was looking at it uneasily, shaking it every now and then, and holding it to his ear.

Alice considered a little, and then said "The fourth."[8]

"Two days wrong!" sighed the Hatter. "I told you butter wouldn't suit the works!" he added, looking angrily at the March Hare.

"It was the *best* butter," the March Hare meekly replied.

"Yes, but some crumbs must have got in as well," the Hatter grumbled: "you shouldn't have put it in with the bread-knife."

The March Hare took the watch and looked at it gloomily: then he dipped it into his cup of tea, and looked at it again: but he could think of nothing better to say than his first remark, "It was the *best* butter, you know."

---

7. In the Preface to the 1898 edition of *Alice's Adventures in Wonderland*, Dodgson wrote that originally the riddle had no answer, and then he provided one: because it can produce a few notes, though they are very flat; and it is never put with the wrong end in front.
8. May 4 was Alice Liddell's birthday.

Alice had been looking over his shoulder with some curiosity. "What a funny watch!" she remarked. "It tells the day of the month, and doesn't tell what o'clock it is!"

"Why should it?" muttered the Hatter. "Does *your* watch tell you what year it is?"

"Of course not," Alice replied very readily: "but that's because it stays the same year for such a long time together."

"Which is just the case with *mine*," said the Hatter.

Alice felt dreadfully puzzled. The Hatter's remark seemed to her to have no sort of meaning in it, and yet it was certainly English. "I don't quite understand you," she said, as politely as she could.

"The Dormouse is asleep again," said the Hatter, and he poured a little hot tea upon its nose.

The Dormouse shook its head impatiently, and said, without opening its eyes, "Of course, of course: just what I was going to remark myself."

"Have you guessed the riddle yet?" the Hatter said, turning to Alice again.

"No, I give it up," Alice replied. "What's the answer?"

"I haven't the slightest idea," said the Hatter.

"Nor I," said the March Hare.

Alice sighed wearily. "I think you might do something better with the time," she said, "than wasting it in asking riddles that have no answers."

"If you knew Time as well as I do," said the Hatter, "you wouldn't talk about wasting *it*. It's *him*."

"I don't know what you mean," said Alice.

"Of course you don't!" the Hatter said, tossing his head contemptuously. "I dare say you never even spoke to Time!"

"Perhaps not," Alice cautiously replied; "but I know I have to beat time when I learn music."

"Ah! That accounts for it," said the Hatter. "He wo'n't stand beating. Now, if you only kept on good terms with him, he'd do almost anything you liked with the clock. For instance, suppose it were nine o'clock in the morning, just time to begin lessons: you'd only have to whisper a hint to Time, and round goes the clock in a twinkling! Half-past one, time for dinner!"

("I only wish it was," the March Hare said to itself in a whisper.)

"That would be grand, certainly," said Alice thoughtfully; "but then—I shouldn't be hungry for it, you know."

"Not at first, perhaps," said the Hatter: "but you could keep it to half-past one as long as you liked."

"Is that the way *you* manage?" Alice asked.

The Hatter shook his head mournfully. "Not I!" he replied. "We quarreled last March—just before *he* went mad, you know——"

(pointing his teaspoon at the March Hare,) "——it was at the great
concert given by the Queen of Hearts, and I had to sing

> 'Twinkle, twinkle, little bat!
> How I wonder what you're at!'

You know the song, perhaps?"

"I've heard something like it," said Alice.

"It goes on, you know," the Hatter continued, "in this way:—

> 'Up above the world you fly,
> Like a tea-tray in the sky.
>   Twinkle, twinkle—' "[9]

Here the Dormouse shook itself, and began singing in its sleep
"Twinkle, twinkle, twinkle, twinkle——" and went on so long that
they had to pinch it to make it stop.

"Well, I'd hardly finished the first verse," said the Hatter, "when
the Queen bawled out 'He's murdering the time! Off with his head!' "

"How dreadfully savage!" exclaimed Alice.

---

9. "Twinkle, twinkle little bat" is a parody of "The Star" by Jane Taylor, who published a
popular collection, *Rhymes for the Nursery*, in 1806. The first stanza is still familiar:

> Twinkle, twinkle little star!
> How I wonder what you are.
> Up above the world so high,
> Like a diamond in the sky.

Bartholomew Price, a professor of mathematics at Oxford and once Dodgson's tutor,
was nicknamed "the Bat."

"And ever since that," the Hatter went on in a mournful tone, "he wo'n't do a thing I ask! It's always six o'clock now."

A bright idea came into Alice's head. "Is that the reason so many tea-things are put out here?" she asked.

"Yes, that's it," said the Hatter with a sigh: "it's always tea-time, and we've no time to wash the things between whiles."

"Then you keep moving round, I suppose?" said Alice.

"Exactly so," said the Hatter: "as the things get used up."

"But what happens when you come to the beginning again?" Alice ventured to ask.

"Suppose we change the subject," the March Hare interrupted, yawning. "I'm getting tired of this. I vote the young lady tells us a story."

"I'm afraid I don't know one," said Alice, rather alarmed at the proposal.

"Then the Dormouse shall!" they both cried. "Wake up, Dormouse!" And they pinched it on both sides at once.

The Dormouse slowly opened its eyes. "I wasn't asleep," it said in a hoarse, feeble voice, "I heard every word you fellows were saying."

"Tell us a story!" said the March Hare.

"Yes, please do!" pleaded Alice.

"And be quick about it," added the Hatter, "or you'll be asleep again before it's done."

"Once upon a time there were three little sisters," the Dormouse began in a great hurry; "and their names were Elsie, Lacie, and Tillie; and they lived at the bottom of a well——"[1]

"What did they live on?" said Alice, who always took a great interest in questions of eating and drinking.

"They lived on treacle,"[2] said the Dormouse, after thinking a minute or two.

"They couldn't have done that, you know," Alice gently remarked. "They'd have been ill."

"So they were," said the Dormouse; "*very* ill."

Alice tried a little to fancy to herself what such an extraordinary way of living would be like, but it puzzled her too much: so she went on: "But why did they live at the bottom of a well?"

---

1. Another reference to the three girls to whom Alice's adventures were first told: Lacie is an anagram of Alice; Elsie is L. C. (Lorina Charlotte); and Tillie is Edith, who was sometimes called Mathilda in her family. The Dormouse in this passage, telling his story over interruptions and falling asleep during the telling, may recall Dodgson himself. In the introductory poem to *Alice's Adventures in Wonderland*, he refers to the frequency with which his stories were interrupted by the children, and he sometimes pretended to fall asleep while he was telling them (see "Alice's Recollections of Carrollian Days," reprinted on pp. 265–68 of this edition).
2. Treacle: molasses. Martin Gardner in *The Annotated Alice* (p. 76) notes that in an older meaning, "treacle" refers to compounds of elements in water that have healing properties. In Dodgson's time there was such a well in Oxford.

"Take some more tea," the March Hare said to Alice, very earnestly.

"I've had nothing yet," Alice replied in an offended tone: "so I ca'n't take more."

"You mean you ca'n't take *less*," said the Hatter: "it's very easy to take *more* than nothing."

"Nobody asked *your* opinion," said Alice.

"Who's making personal remarks now?" the Hatter asked triumphantly.

Alice did not quite know what to say to this: so she helped herself to some tea and bread-and-butter, and then turned to the Dormouse, and repeated her question. "Why did they live at the bottom of a well?"

The Dormouse again took a minute or two to think about it, and then said "It was a treacle-well."

"There's no such thing!" Alice was beginning very angrily, but the Hatter and the March Hare went "Sh! Sh!" and the Dormouse sulkily remarked "If you ca'n't be civil, you'd better finish the story for yourself."

"No, please go on!" Alice said very humbly. "I wo'n't interrupt you again. I dare say there may be *one*."

"One, indeed!" said the Dormouse indignantly. However, he consented to go on. "And so these three little sisters—they were learning to draw, you know——"

"What did they draw?" said Alice, quite forgetting her promise.

"Treacle," said the Dormouse, without considering at all, this time.

"I want a clean cup," interrupted the Hatter: "let's all move one place on."

He moved on as he spoke, and the Dormouse followed him: the March Hare moved into the Dormouse's place, and Alice rather unwillingly took the place of the March Hare. The Hatter was the only one who got any advantage from the change; and Alice was a good deal worse off than before, as the March Hare had just upset the milk-jug into his plate.

Alice did not wish to offend the Dormouse again, so she began very cautiously: "But I don't understand. Where did they draw the treacle from?"

"You can draw water out of a water-well," said the Hatter; "so I should think you could draw treacle out of a treacle-well—eh, stupid?"

"But they were *in* the well," Alice said to the Dormouse, not choosing to notice this last remark.

"Of course they were," said the Dormouse: "well in."

This answer so confused poor Alice, that she let the Dormouse go on for some time without interrupting it.

"They were learning to draw," the Dormouse went on, yawning and rubbing its eyes, for it was getting very sleepy; "and they drew all manner of things—everything that begins with an M——"

"Why with an M?" said Alice.

"Why not?" said the March Hare.

Alice was silent.

The Dormouse had closed its eyes by this time, and was going off into a doze; but, on being pinched by the Hatter, it woke up again with a little shriek, and went on: "——that begins with an M, such as mouse-traps, and the moon, and memory, and muchness—you know you say things are 'much of a muchness'—did you ever see such a thing as a drawing of a muchness!"

"Really, now you ask me," said Alice, very much confused, "I don't think——"

"Then you shouldn't talk," said the Hatter.

This piece of rudeness was more than Alice could bear: she got up in great disgust, and walked off: the Dormouse fell asleep instantly, and neither of the others took the least notice of her going, though she looked back once or twice, half hoping that they would call after her: the last time she saw them, they were trying to put the Dormouse into the teapot.

"At any rate I'll never go *there* again!" said Alice, as she picked her way through the wood. "It's the stupidest tea-party I ever was at in all my life!"

Just as she said this, she noticed that one of the trees had a door leading right into it. "That's very curious!" she thought. "But everything's curious to-day. I think I may as well go in at once." And in she went.

Once more she found herself in the long hall, and close to the little glass table. "Now, I'll manage better this time," she said to herself, and began by taking the little golden key, and unlocking the door that led into the garden. Then she set to work nibbling at the mushroom (she had kept a piece of it in her pocket) till she was about a foot high; then she walked down the little passage: and *then*—she found herself at last in the beautiful garden, among the bright flower-beds and the cool fountains.

Is this like a video game?

Chapter VIII

THE QUEEN'S CROQUET-GROUND

A large rose-tree stood near the entrance of the garden: the roses growing on it were white, but there were three gardeners at it, busily painting them red. Alice thought this a very curious thing, and she went nearer to watch them, and, just as she came up to them, she heard one of them say "Look out now, Five! Don't go splashing paint over me like that!"

"I couldn't help it," said Five, in a sulky tone. "Seven jogged my elbow."

On which Seven looked up and said "That's right, Five! Always lay the blame on others!"

"*You'd* better not talk!" said Five. "I heard the Queen say only yesterday you deserved to be beheaded."

"What for?" said the one who had spoken first.

"That's none of *your* business, Two!" said Seven.

"Yes, it *is* his business!" said Five. "And I'll tell him—it was for bringing the cook tulip-roots instead of onions."

Seven flung down his brush, and had just begun "Well, of all the unjust things—" when his eye chanced to fall upon Alice, as she stood watching them, and he checked himself suddenly: the others looked round also, and all of them bowed low.

"Would you tell me, please," said Alice, a little timidly, "why you are painting those roses?"

Five and Seven said nothing, but looked at Two. Two began, in a low voice, "Why, the fact is, you see, Miss, this here ought to have been a *red* rose-tree, and we put a white one in by mistake; and, if the Queen was to find out, we should all have our heads cut off, you know. So you see, Miss, we're doing our best, afore she comes, to—" At this moment, Five, who had been anxiously looking across the garden, called out "The Queen! The Queen!" and the three gardeners instantly threw themselves flat upon their faces. There was a sound of many footsteps, and Alice looked round, eager to see the Queen.

First came ten soldiers carrying clubs: these were all shaped like the three gardeners, oblong and flat, with their hands and feet at the corners: next the ten courtiers: these were ornamented all over with diamonds, and walked two and two, as the soldiers did. After these came the royal children: there were ten of them, and the little dears came jumping merrily along, hand in hand, in couples: they were all ornamented with hearts. Next came the guests, mostly Kings and Queens, and among them Alice recognized the White Rabbit: it was talking in a hurried nervous manner, smiling at everything that was said, and went by without noticing her. Then followed the Knave of Hearts, carrying the King's crown on a crimson velvet cushion; and, last of all this grand procession, came THE KING AND THE QUEEN OF HEARTS.

Alice was rather doubtful whether she ought not to lie down on her face like the three gardeners, but she could not remember ever having heard of such a rule at processions; "and besides, what would be the use of a procession," thought she, "if people had all to lie down on their faces, so that they couldn't see it?" So she stood where she was, and waited.

When the procession came opposite to Alice, they all stopped and looked at her, and the Queen said, severely, "Who is this?" She said it to the Knave of Hearts, who only bowed and smiled in reply.

"Idiot!" said the Queen, tossing her head impatiently; and turning to Alice, she went on: "What's your name, child?"

"My name is Alice, so please your Majesty," said Alice very politely; but she added, to herself, "Why, they're only a pack of cards, after all. I needn't be afraid of them!"

"And who are *these*?" said the Queen, pointing to the three gardeners who were lying round the rose-tree; for, you see, as they were lying on their faces, and the pattern on their backs was the same as

the rest of the pack, she could not tell whether they were gardeners, or soldiers, or courtiers, or three of her own children.

"How should *I* know?" said Alice, surprised at her own courage. "It's no business of *mine*."

The Queen turned crimson with fury, and, after glaring at her for a moment like a wild beast, began screaming "Off with her head! Off with——"

"Nonsense!" said Alice, very loudly and decidedly, and the Queen was silent.

The King laid his hand upon her arm, and timidly said "Consider, my dear: she is only a child!"

The Queen turned angrily away from him, and said to the Knave "Turn them over!"

The Knave did so, very carefully, with one foot.

"Get up!" said the Queen in a shrill, loud voice, and the three gardeners instantly jumped up, and began bowing to the King, the Queen, the royal children, and everybody else.

"Leave off that!" screamed the Queen. "You make me giddy." And then, turning to the rose-tree, she went on "What *have* you been doing here?"

"May it please your Majesty," said Two, in a very humble tone, going down on one knee as he spoke, "we were trying—"

"*I* see!" said the Queen, who had meanwhile been examining the roses. "Off with their heads!" and the procession moved on, three of the soldiers remaining behind to execute the unfortunate gardeners, who ran to Alice for protection.

"You sha'n't be beheaded!" said Alice, and she put them into a large flower-pot that stood near. The three soldiers wandered about for a minute or two, looking for them, and then quietly marched off after the others.

"Are their heads off?" shouted the Queen.

"Their heads are gone, if it please your Majesty!" the soldiers shouted in reply.

"That's right!" shouted the Queen. "Can you play croquet?"

The soldiers were silent, and looked at Alice, as the question was evidently meant for her.

"Yes!" shouted Alice.

"Come on, then!" roared the Queen, and Alice joined the procession, wondering very much what would happen next.

"It's—it's a very fine day!" said a timid voice at her side. She was walking by the White Rabbit, who was peeping anxiously into her face.

"Very," said Alice. "Where's the Duchess?"

"Hush! Hush!" said the Rabbit in a low hurried tone. He looked anxiously over his shoulder as he spoke, and then raised himself upon tiptoe, put his mouth close to her ear, and whispered "She's under sentence of execution."

"What for?" said Alice.

"Did you say 'What a pity!'?" the Rabbit said.

"No, I didn't," said Alice. "I don't think it's at all a pity. I said 'What for?'"

"She boxed the Queen's ears—" the Rabbit began. Alice gave a little scream of laughter. "Oh, hush!" the Rabbit whispered in a frightened tone. "The Queen will hear you! You see she came rather late, and the Queen said—"

"Get to your places!" shouted the Queen in a voice of thunder, and people began running about in all directions, tumbling up against each other: however, they got settled down in a minute or two, and the game began.

Alice thought she had never seen such a curious croquet-ground in her life: it was all ridges and furrows: the croquet balls were live hedgehogs, and the mallets live flamingoes, and the soldiers had to double themselves up and stand on their hands and feet, to make the arches.

manipulating/
treatment of
animal world

The chief difficulty Alice found at first was in managing her flamingo: she succeeded in getting its body tucked away, comfortably enough, under her arm, with its legs hanging down, but generally, just as she had got its neck nicely straightened out, and was going to give the hedgehog a blow with its head, it *would* twist itself round and look up in her face, with such a puzzled expression that she could not help bursting out laughing; and, when she had got its head down, and was going to begin again, it was very provoking to find that the hedgehog had unrolled itself, and was in the act of crawling away: besides all this, there was generally a ridge or a furrow in the way wherever she wanted to send the hedgehog to, and, as the doubled-up soldiers were always getting up and walking off to other parts of the ground, Alice soon came to the conclusion that it was a very difficult game indeed.

cf.
p. 66
The players all played at once, without waiting for turns, quarreling all the while, and fighting for the hedgehogs; and in a very short time the Queen was in a furious passion, and went stamping about,

and shouting "Off with his head!" or "Off with her head!" about once in a minute.

Alice began to feel very uneasy: to be sure, she had not as yet had any dispute with the Queen, but she knew that it might happen any minute, "and then," thought she, "what would become of me? They're dreadfully fond of beheading people here: the great wonder is, that there's any one left alive!"

She was looking about for some way of escape, and wondering whether she could get away without being seen, when she noticed a curious appearance in the air: it puzzled her very much at first, but after watching it a minute or two she made it out to be a grin, and she said to herself "It's the Cheshire-Cat: now I shall have somebody to talk to."

"How are you getting on?" said the Cat, as soon as there was mouth enough for it to speak with.

Alice waited till the eyes appeared, and then nodded. "It's no use speaking to it," she thought, "till its ears have come, or at least one of them." In another minute the whole head appeared, and then Alice put down her flamingo, and began an account of the game, feeling very glad she had some one to listen to her. The Cat seemed to think that there was enough of it now in sight, and no more of it appeared.

"I don't think they play at all fairly," Alice began, in rather a complaining tone, "and they all quarrel so dreadfully one ca'n't hear oneself speak—and they don't seem to have any rules in particular: at least, if there are, nobody attends to them—and you've no idea how confusing it is all the things being alive: for instance, there's the arch I've got to go through next walking about at the other end of the ground—and I should have croqueted the Queen's hedgehog just now, only it ran away when it saw mine coming!"

"How do you like the Queen?" said the Cat in a low voice.

"Not at all," said Alice: "she's so extremely—" Just then she noticed that the Queen was close behind her, listening: so she went on "—likely to win, that it's hardly worth while finishing the game."

The Queen smiled and passed on.

"Who *are* you talking to?" said the King, coming up to Alice, and looking at the Cat's head with great curiosity.

"It's a friend of mine—a Cheshire-Cat," said Alice: "allow me to introduce it."

"I don't like the look of it at all," said the King: "however, it may kiss my hand, if it likes."

"I'd rather not," the Cat remarked.

"Don't be impertinent," said the King, "and don't look at me like that!" He got behind Alice as he spoke.

"A cat may look at a king," said Alice. "I've read that in some book, but I don't remember where."[3]

"Well, it must be removed," said the King very decidedly; and he called to the Queen, who was passing at the moment, "My dear! I wish you would have this cat removed!"

The Queen had only one way of settling all difficulties, great or small. "Off with his head!" she said without even looking around.

"I'll fetch the executioner myself," said the King eagerly, and he hurried off.

Alice thought she might as well go back and see how the game was going on, as she heard the Queen's voice in the distance, screaming with passion. She had already heard her sentence three of the players to be executed for having missed their turns, and she did not like the look of things at all, as the game was in such confusion that she never knew whether it was her turn or not. So she went off in search of her hedgehog.

The hedgehog was engaged in a fight with another hedgehog, which seemed to Alice an excellent opportunity for croqueting one of them with the other: the only difficulty was, that her flamingo was gone across the other side of the garden, where Alice could see it trying in a helpless sort of way to fly up into a tree.

By the time she had caught the flamingo and brought it back, the fight was over, and both the hedgehogs were out of sight: "but it doesn't matter much," thought Alice, "as all the arches are gone from this side of the ground." So she tucked it away under her arm, that it might not escape again, and went back to have a little more conversation with her friend.

When she got back to the Cheshire-Cat, she was surprised to find quite a large crowd collected round it: there was a dispute going on between the executioner, the King, and the Queen, who were all talking at once, while all the rest were quite silent, and looked very uncomfortable.

The moment Alice appeared, she was appealed to by all three to settle the question, and they repeated their arguments to her, though, as they all spoke at once, she found it very hard to make out exactly what they said.

The executioner's argument was, that you couldn't cut off a head unless there was a body to cut it off from: that he had never had to do such a thing before, and he wasn't going to begin at *his* time of life.

The King's argument was that anything that had a head could be beheaded, and that you weren't to talk nonsense.

The Queen's argument was that, if something wasn't done about it in less than no time, she'd have everybody executed, all round. (It

---

3. "A cat may look at a king" is another proverbial expression.

was this last remark that had made the whole party look so grave and anxious.)

Alice could think of nothing else to say but "It belongs to the Duchess: you'd better ask *her* about it."

"She's in prison," the Queen said to the executioner: "fetch her here." And the executioner went off like an arrow.

The Cat's head began fading away the moment he was gone, and, by the time he had come back with the Duchess, it had entirely disappeared: so the King and the executioner ran wildly up and down, looking for it, while the rest of the party went back to the game.

Chapter IX

"You ca'n't think how glad I am to see you again, you dear old thing!" said the Duchess, as she tucked her arm affectionately into Alice's, and they walked off together.

Alice was very glad to find her in such a pleasant temper, and thought to herself that perhaps it was only the pepper that had made her so savage when they met in the kitchen.

"When *I'm* a Duchess," she said to herself (not in a very hopeful tone, though), "I wo'n't have any pepper in my kitchen *at all*. Soup does very well without—Maybe it's always pepper that makes people hot-tempered," she went on, very much pleased at having found out a new kind of rule, "and vinegar that makes them sour— and camomile that makes them bitter—and—and barley-sugar[4] and such things that make children sweet-tempered. I only wish people knew *that*: then they wouldn't be so stingy about it, you know——"

She had quite forgotten the Duchess by this time, and was a little startled when she heard her voice close to her ear. "You're thinking about something, my dear, and that makes you forget to talk. I ca'n't tell you just now what the moral of that is, but I shall remember it in a bit."

"Perhaps it hasn't one," Alice ventured to remark.

"Tut, tut, child!" said the Duchess. "Everything's got a moral, if only you can find it." And she squeezed herself up closer to Alice's side as she spoke.

Alice did not much like her keeping so close to her: first because the Duchess was *very* ugly; and secondly, because she was exactly the right height to rest her chin on Alice's shoulder, and it was an uncomfortably sharp chin. However, she did not like to be rude: so she bore it as well as she could.

"The game's going on rather better now," she said, by way of keeping up the conversation a little.

"'Tis so," said the Duchess: "and the moral of that is—'Oh, 'tis love, 'tis love, that makes the world go round!'"

"Somebody said," Alice whispered, "that it's done by everybody minding their own business!"

"Ah well! It means much the same thing," said the Duchess, digging her sharp little chin into Alice's shoulder as she added "and

---

4. Camomile is a plant from which a bitter medicine, often administered as a tea, was made. Barley sugar is hard candy.

Cf. Wilde's aphorisms

the moral of *that* is—'Take care of the sense, and the sounds will take care of themselves.'"[5]

"How fond she is of finding morals in things!" Alice thought to herself.

"I dare say you're wondering why I don't put my arm round your waist," the Duchess said, after a pause: "the reason is, that I'm doubtful about the temper of your flamingo. Shall I try the experiment?"

"He might bite," Alice cautiously replied, not feeling at all anxious to have the experiment tried.

"Very true," said the Duchess: "flamingoes and mustard both bite. And the moral of that is—'Birds of a feather flock together.'"

"Only mustard isn't a bird," Alice remarked.

"Right, as usual," said the Duchess: "what a clear way you have of putting things!"

"It's a mineral, I *think*," said Alice.

5. The proverb is "Take care of the pence, and the pounds will take care of themselves." The rest of the Duchess's morals are unaltered traditional proverbs, except that she seems to have created the moral "The more there is of mine, the less there is of yours," and to be improvising her last incoherent moral.

UT Motto esse quam videri
to be, rather than to seem
70 ALICE IN WONDERLAND

"Of course it is," said the Duchess, who seemed ready to agree to everything that Alice said: "there's a large mustard-mine near here. And the moral of that is—'The more there is of mine, the less there is of yours.'"

"Oh, I know!" exclaimed Alice, who had not attended to this last remark. "It's a vegetable. It doesn't look like one, but it is."

"I quite agree with you," said the Duchess; "and the moral of that is—'Be what you would seem to be'—or, if you'd like it put more simply—'Never imagine yourself not to be otherwise than what it might appear to others that what you were or might have been was not otherwise than what you had been would have appeared to them to be otherwise.'"

"I think I should understand that better," Alice said very politely, "if I had it written down: but I ca'n't quite follow it as you say it."

"That's nothing to what I could say if I chose," the Duchess replied, in a pleased tone.

"Pray don't trouble yourself to say it any longer than that," said Alice.

"Oh, don't talk about trouble!" said the Duchess. "I make you a present of everything I've said as yet."

"A cheap sort of present!" thought Alice. "I'm glad people don't give birthday-presents like that!" But she did not venture to say it out loud.

"Thinking again?" the Duchess asked, with another dig of her sharp little chin.

"I've a right to think," said Alice sharply, for she was beginning to feel a little worried.

"Just about as much right," said the Duchess, "as pigs have to fly; and the m——"

But here, to Alice's great surprise, the Duchess's voice died away, even in the middle of her favourite word "moral", and the arm that was linked into hers began to tremble. Alice looked up, and there stood the Queen in front of them, with her arms folded, frowning like a thunderstorm.

"A fine day, your Majesty!" the Duchess began in a low, weak voice.

"Now, I give you fair warning," shouted the Queen, stamping on the ground as she spoke; "either you or your head must be off, and that in about half no time! Take your choice!"

The Duchess took her choice, and was gone in a moment.

"Let's go on with the game," the Queen said to Alice; and Alice was too much frightened to say a word, but slowly followed her back to the croquet-ground.

The other guests had taken advantage of the Queen's absence, and were resting in the shade: however, the moment they saw her, they hurried back to the game, the Queen merely remarking that a moment's delay would cost them their lives.

All the time they were playing the Queen never left off quarreling with the other players, and shouting "Off with his head!" or "Off with her head!" Those whom she sentenced were taken into custody by the soldiers, who of course had to leave off being arches to do this, so that, by the end of half an hour or so, there were no arches left, and all the players, except the King, the Queen, and Alice, were in custody and under sentence of execution.

Then the Queen left off, quite out of breath, and said to Alice "Have you seen the Mock Turtle yet?"

"No," said Alice. "I don't even know what a Mock Turtle is."

"It's the thing Mock Turtle Soup[6] is made from," said the Queen.

"I never saw one, or heard of one," said Alice.

"Come on, then," said the Queen, "and he shall tell you his history."

As they walked off together, Alice heard the King say in a low voice, to the company, generally, "You are all pardoned." "Come, *that's* a good thing!" she said to herself, for she had felt quite unhappy at the number of executions the Queen had ordered.

They very soon came upon a Gryphon,[7] lying fast asleep in the sun. (If you don't know what a Gryphon is, look at the picture.) "Up, lazy thing!" said the Queen, "and take this young lady to see the

6. Mock turtle soup is usually made of veal.
7. A gryphon, or griffin, is a fabulous creature, common in medieval iconography and heraldry, with the head and wings of an eagle and the body of a lion.

Mock Turtle, and to hear his history. I must go back and see after some executions I have ordered;" and she walked off, leaving Alice alone with the Gryphon. Alice did not quite like the look of the creature, but on the whole she thought it would be quite as safe to stay with it as to go after that savage Queen: so she waited.

The Gryphon sat up and rubbed its eyes: then it watched the Queen till she was out of sight: then it chuckled. "What fun!" said the Gryphon, half to itself, half to Alice.

"What *is* the fun?" said Alice.

"Why, *she*," said the Gryphon. "It's all her fancy, that: they never executes nobody, you know. Come on!"

"Everybody says 'come on!' here," thought Alice, as she went slowly after it: "I never was so ordered about before, in all my life, never!"

They had not gone far before they saw the Mock Turtle in the distance, sitting sad and lonely on a little ledge of rock, and, as they came nearer, Alice could hear him sighing as if his heart would break. She pitied him deeply. "What is his sorrow?" she asked the Gryphon. And the Gryphon answered, very nearly in the same words as before, "It's all his fancy, that: he hasn't got no sorrow, you know. Come on!"

So they went up to the Mock Turtle, who looked at them with large eyes full of tears, but said nothing.

"This here young lady," said the Gryphon, "she wants for to know your history, she do."

"I'll tell it her," said the Mock Turtle in a deep, hollow tone. "Sit down, both of you, and don't speak a word till I've finished."

So they sat down, and nobody spoke for some minutes. Alice thought to herself "I don't see how he can *ever* finish, if he doesn't begin." But she waited patiently.

"Once," said the Mock Turtle at last, with a deep sigh, "I was a real Turtle."

These words were followed by a very long silence, broken only by an occasional exclamation of "Hjckrrh!" from the Gryphon, and the constant heavy sobbing of the Mock Turtle. Alice was very nearly getting up and saying, "Thank you, Sir, for your interesting story," but she could not help thinking there *must* be more to come, so she sat still and said nothing.

"When we were still little," the Mock Turtle went on at last, more calmly, though still sobbing a little now and then, "we went to school in the sea. The master was an old Turtle—we used to call him Tortoise——"

"Why did you call him Tortoise,[8] if he wasn't one?" Alice asked.

8. Alice has in mind the conventional distinction between tortoises, a name often given to land turtles, and turtles, a name given to marine turtles. This entire passage, with its

"We called him Tortoise because he taught us," said the Mock
Turtle angrily. "Really you are very dull!"

"You ought to be ashamed of yourself for asking such a simple
question," added the Gryphon; and then they both sat silent and
looked at poor Alice, who felt ready to sink into the earth. At last
the Gryphon said to the Mock Turtle "Drive on, old fellow! Don't be
all day about it!" and he went on in these words:—

"Yes, we went to school in the sea, though you mayn't believe
it——"

"I never said I didn't!" interrupted Alice.

"You did," said the Mock Turtle.

---

string of puns on the subjects taught in school, is Dodgson's most extensive use of puns
in *Alice's Adventures in Wonderland*. Puns were common in mid-nineteenth-century
British comic writing, especially in the theatrical pantomimes and burlesques of which
Dodgson was fond.

"Hold your tongue!" added the Gryphon, before Alice could speak again. The Mock Turtle went on.

"We had the best of educations—in fact, we went to school every day——"

"*I've* been to a day-school, too," said Alice. "You needn't be so proud as all that."

"With extras?"⁹ asked the Mock Turtle, a little anxiously.

"Yes," said Alice: "we learned French and music."

"And washing?" said the Mock Turtle.

"Certainly not!" said Alice indignantly.

"Ah! Then yours wasn't a really good school," said the Mock Turtle in a tone of great relief. "Now, at *ours*, they had, at the end of the bill, 'French, music, *and washing*—extra.'"

"You couldn't have wanted it much," said Alice; "living at the bottom of the sea."

"I couldn't afford to learn it," said the Mock Turtle with a sigh. "I only took the regular course."

"What was that?" inquired Alice.

"Reeling and Writhing, of course, to begin with," the Mock Turtle replied; "and then the different branches of Arithmetic—Ambition, Distraction, Uglification, and Derision."

"I never heard of 'Uglification,'" Alice ventured to say. "What is it?"

The Gryphon lifted up both its paws in surprise. "Never heard of uglifying!" it exclaimed. "You know what to beautify is, I suppose?"

"Yes," said Alice doubtfully: "it means—to—make—anything—prettier."

"Well, then," the Gryphon went on, "if you don't know what to uglify is, you *are* a simpleton."

Alice did not feel encouraged to ask any more questions about it: so she turned to the Mock Turtle, and said "What else had you to learn?"

"Well, there was Mystery," the Mock Turtle replied, counting off the subjects on his flappers—"Mystery, ancient and modern, with Seaography: then Drawling—the Drawling-master was an old conger-eel, that used to come once a week: *he* taught us Drawling, Stretching, and Fainting in Coils."

"What was *that* like?" said Alice.

"Well, I ca'n't show it you, myself," the Mock Turtle said: "I'm too stiff. And the Gryphon never learnt it."

9. Alice interprets "extras" as subjects for whose teaching an additional charge is levied; the Mock Turtle also means services for which an extra charge is made. Alice, properly brought-up middle-class girl that she is, is indignant at the suggestion that she has been taught servile tasks, such as doing the wash.

"Hadn't time," said the Gryphon: "I went to the Classical master, though. He was an old crab, *he* was."

"I never went to him," the Mock Turtle said with a sigh. "He taught Laughing and Grief, they used to say."

"So he did, so he did," said the Gryphon, sighing in his turn; and both creatures hid their faces in their paws.

"And how many hours a day did you do lessons?" said Alice, in a hurry to change the subject.

"Ten hours the first day," said the Mock Turtle: "nine the next, and so on."

"What a curious plan!" exclaimed Alice.

lessens

"That's the reason they're called lessons," the Gryphon remarked: "because they lessen from day to day."

This was quite a new idea to Alice, and she thought it over a little before she made her next remark. "Then the eleventh day must have been a holiday?"

"Of course it was," said the Mock Turtle.

"And how did you manage on the twelfth?" Alice went on eagerly.

"That's enough about lessons," the Gryphon interrupted in a very decided tone. "Tell her something about the games now."

Chapter X

THE LOBSTER-QUADRILLE

The Mock Turtle sighed deeply, and drew the back of one flapper across his eyes. He looked at Alice and tried to speak, but, for a minute or two, sobs choked his voice. "Same as if he had a bone in his throat," said the Gryphon; and it set to work shaking him and punching him in the back. At last the Mock Turtle recovered his voice, and, with tears running down his cheeks, he went on again:—

"You may not have lived much under the sea—" ("I haven't," said Alice)—"and perhaps you were never even introduced to a lobster—" (Alice began to say "I once tasted——" but checked herself hastily, and said "No never") "——so you can have no idea what a delightful thing a Lobster-Quadrille is!"

"No, indeed," said Alice. "What sort of a dance is it?"

"Why," said the Gryphon, "you first form into a line along the sea-shore——"

"Two lines!" cried the Mock Turtle. "Seals, turtles, salmon, and so on: then, when you've cleared all the jelly-fish out of the way——"

"*That* generally takes some time," interrupted the Gryphon.

"—you advance twice——"

"Each with a lobster as a partner!" cried the Gryphon.

"Of course," the Mock Turtle said: "advance twice, set to partners——"

"—change lobsters, and retire in same order," continued the Gryphon.

"Then, you know," the Mock Turtle went on, "you throw the——"

"The lobsters!" shouted the Gryphon, with a bound into the air.

"—as far out to sea as you can——"

"Swim after them!" screamed the Gryphon.

"Turn a somersault in the sea!" cried the Mock Turtle, capering wildly about.

"'Change lobsters again!" yelled the Gryphon at the top of its voice.

"Back to land again, and—that's all the first figure," said the Mock Turtle, suddenly dropping his voice; and the two creatures, who had been jumping about like mad things all this time, sat down again very sadly and quietly, and looked at Alice.

"It must be a very pretty dance," said Alice timidly.

"Would you like to see a little of it?" said the Mock Turtle.

"Very much indeed," said Alice.

"Come, let's try the first figure!" said the Mock Turtle to the Gryphon. "We can do it without lobsters, you know. Which shall sing?"

"Oh, *you* sing," said the Gryphon. "I've forgotten the words."

So they began solemnly dancing round and round Alice, every now and then treading on her toes when they passed too close, and waving their fore-paws to mark the time, while the Mock Turtle sang this, very slowly and sadly:—

> "Will you walk a little faster?" said a whiting to a snail,
> "There's a porpoise close behind us, and he's treading
>   on my tail.
> See how eagerly the lobsters and the turtles all advance!
> They are waiting on the shingle[1]—will you come and
>   join the dance?
>   Will you, wo'n't you, will you, wo'n't you, will you
>   join the dance?
>   Will you, wo'n't you, will you, wo'n't you, wo'n't you
>   join the dance?

_____
1. Shingle: a stretch of beach strewn with pebbles or rounded stones.

"You can really have no notion how delightful it will be
When they take us up and throw us, with the lobsters,
     out to sea!"
But the snail replied "Too far, too far!", and gave a
     look askance—
Said he thanked the whiting kindly, but he would not
     join the dance.
    Would not, could not, would not, could not, could not
     join the dance.
    Would not, could not, would not, could not, could not
     join the dance.

"What matters it how far we go?" his scaly friend replied.
"There is another shore, you know, upon the other side.
The further off from England the nearer is to France—
Then turn not pale, beloved snail, but come and
     join the dance.
    Will you, wo'n't you, will you, wo'n't you, will you
     join the dance?
    Will you, wo'n't you, will you, wo'n't you, wo'n't you
     join the dance?"[2]

"Thank you, it's a very interesting dance to watch," said Alice, feeling very glad that it was over at last: "and I do so like that curious song about the whiting!"

"Oh, as to the whiting," said the Mock Turtle, "they—you've seen them, of course?"

"Yes," said Alice, "I've often seen them at dinn——" she checked herself hastily.

---

2. On the day before the river trip to Godstow on which he told parts of Alice's adventures, Dodgson records that he heard the Liddell children sing the American minstrel song "Sally Come Up" (*Diaries* 4: 92–93; see full citation on p. 254). The song was parodied in *Alice's Adventures Under Ground* as "Salmon come up! Salmon go down! / Salmon come twist your tail around! / Of all the fishes of the sea / There's none so good as Salmon!" The final version of the song is a parody of Mary Howitt's "The Spider and the Fly," first published in 1834. The poem begins:

> "Will you walk into my parlor?" said the Spider to the Fly,
> "'Tis the prettiest little parlor that ever you did spy;
> The way into my parlor is up a winding stair,
> And I have many curious things to show when you are there."
> "Oh no, no," said the little Fly, "to ask me is in vain;
> For who goes up your winding stair can ne'er come down again."

But the fly, enticed by the spider's tributes to her green-and-purple robes and diamond-bright eyes, flies into the spider's web, is dragged into his "dismal den," and "she ne'er came out again." Like most of the poems Dodgson parodied in the Alice books, Howitt's poem ends with a strong moral:

> And now, dear little children, who may this story read
> To idle, silly, flattering words, I pray you ne'er give heed;
> Unto an evil counsellor close heart, and ear, and eye,
> And take a lesson from the tale of the Spider and the Fly.

"I don't know where Dinn may be," said the Mock Turtle; "but, if you've seen them so often, of course you know what they're like?"

"I believe so," Alice replied thoughtfully. "They have their tails in their mouths—and they're all over crumbs."[3]

"You're wrong about the crumbs," said the Mock Turtle: "crumbs would all wash off in the sea. But they *have* their tails in their mouths; and the reason is——" here the Mock Turtle yawned and shut his eyes. "Tell her about the reason and all that," he said to the Gryphon.

"The reason is," said the Gryphon, "that they *would* go with the lobsters to the dance. So they got thrown out to sea. So they had to fall a long way. So they got their tails fast in their mouths. So they couldn't get them out again. That's all."

"Thank you," said Alice, "it's very interesting. I never knew so much about a whiting before."

"I can tell you more than that, if you like," said the Gryphon. "Do you know why it's called a whiting?"

"I never thought about it," said Alice. "Why?"

"It does the boots and shoes," the Gryphon replied very solemnly.

Alice was thoroughly puzzled. "Does the boots and shoes!" she repeated in a wondering tone.

"Why, what are *your* shoes done with?" said the Gryphon. "I mean, what makes them so shiny?"

Alice looked down at them, and considered a little before she gave her answer. "They're done with blacking, I believe."

"Boots and shoes under the sea," the Gryphon went on in a deep voice, "are done with whiting. Now you know."

"And what are they made of?" Alice asked in a tone of great curiosity.

"Soles and eels, of course," the Gryphon replied, rather impatiently: "any shrimp could have told you that."

"If I'd been the whiting," said Alice, whose thoughts were still running on the song, "I'd have said to the porpoise 'Keep back, please! We don't want *you* with us!'"

"They were obliged to have him with them," the Mock Turtle said. "No wise fish would go anywhere without a porpoise."

"Wouldn't it, really?" said Alice, in a tone of great surprise.

"Of course not," said the Mock Turtle. "Why, if a fish came to *me*, and told me he was going a journey, I should say 'With what porpoise?'"

"Don't you mean 'purpose'?" said Alice.

"I mean what I say," the Mock Turtle replied, in an offended tone. And the Gryphon added "Come, let's hear some of *your* adventures."

3. Whiting is a common food fish, sold with its tail tucked into its mouth or through its eyehole, and served, in Alice's experience, breaded.

"I could tell you my adventures—beginning from this morning," said Alice a little timidly; "but it's no use going back to yesterday, because I was a different person then."

"Explain all that," said the Mock Turtle.

"No, no! The adventures first," said the Gryphon in an impatient tone: "explanations take such a dreadful time."

So Alice began telling them her adventures from the time when she first saw the White Rabbit. She was a little nervous about it, just at first, the two creatures got so close to her, one on each side, and opened their eyes and mouths so *very* wide; but she gained courage as she went on. Her listeners were perfectly quiet till she got to the part about her repeating *"You are old, Father William,"* to the Caterpillar, and the words all coming different, and then the Mock Turtle drew a long breath, and said "That's very curious!"

"It's all about as curious as it can be," said the Gryphon.

"It all came different!" the Mock Turtle repeated thoughtfully. "I should like to hear her try and repeat something now. Tell her to begin." He looked at the Gryphon as if he thought it had some kind of authority over Alice.

"Stand up and repeat *''Tis the voice of the sluggard,'"* said the Gryphon.

"How the creatures order one about, and make one repeat lessons!" thought Alice. "I might just as well be at school at once." However, she got up, and began to repeat it, but her head was so full of the Lobster-Quadrille, that she hardly knew what she was saying; and the words came very queer indeed:—

> "'Tis the voice of the Lobster: I heard him declare
> 'You have baked me too brown, I must sugar my hair.'
> As a duck with his eyelids, so he with his nose
> Trims his belt and his buttons, and turns out his toes.
> When the sands are all dry, he is gay as a lark,
> And will talk in contemptuous tones of the Shark:
> But, when the tide rises and sharks are around,
> His voice has a timid and tremulous sound."[4]

---

4. In the early editions of *Alice's Adventures in Wonderland* Alice's recitation ended after the first four lines. These four lines are a close parody of "The Sluggard," another poem by Isaac Watts, which, like "Against Idleness and Mischief," was published as one of his *Divine Songs for Children* in 1715:

> 'Tis the voice of the Sluggard; I hear him complain,
> "You have waked me too soon, I must slumber again."
> As a Door on its Hinges, so he on his Bed,
> Turns his Sides and his Shoulders, and his heavy Head.

When he revised the poem for a theatrical version of the Alice books prepared by Henry Savile Clarke in 1886, Dodgson added the second four lines of this part of Alice's recitation. This additional quatrain retains nothing of Watts's poem except its meter and rhyme.

"That's different from what *I* used to say when I was a child," said the Gryphon.

"Well, *I* never heard it before," said the Mock Turtle; "but it sounds uncommon nonsense."

Alice said nothing: she had sat down with her face in her hands, wondering if anything would *ever* happen in a natural way again.

"I should like to have it explained," said the Mock Turtle.

"She ca'n't explain it," said the Gryphon hastily. "Go on with the next verse."

"But about his toes?" the Mock Turtle persisted. "How *could* he turn them out with his nose, you know?"

"It's the first position in dancing," Alice said; but she was dreadfully puzzled by the whole thing, and longed to change the subject.

"Go on with the next verse," the Gryphon repeated: "it begins '*I passed by his garden.*'"

Alice did not dare to disobey, though she felt sure it would all come wrong, and she went on in a trembling voice:—

"I passed by his garden, and marked, with one eye,
How the Owl and the Panther were sharing a pie:
The Panther took pie-crust, and gravy, and meat,
While the Owl had the dish as its share of the treat.
When the pie was all finished, the Owl, as a boon,
Was kindly permitted to pocket the spoon:
While the Panther received knife and fork with a growl,
And concluded the banquet by——"[5]

"What *is* the use of repeating all that stuff?" the Mock Turtle interrupted, "if you don't explain it as you go on? It's by far the most confusing thing that *I* ever heard!"

"Yes, I think you'd better leave off," said the Gryphon, and Alice was only too glad to do so.

"Shall we try another figure of the Lobster-Quadrille?" the Gryphon went on. "Or would you like the Mock Turtle to sing you another song?"

"Oh, a song, please, if the Mock Turtle would be so kind," Alice replied, so eagerly that the Gryphon said, in a rather offended tone, "Hm! No accounting for tastes! Sing her '*Turtle Soup*,' will you, old fellow?"

The Mock Turtle sighed deeply, and began, in a voice choked with sobs, to sing this:—

"Beautiful Soup, so rich and green,
Waiting in a hot tureen!
Who for such dainties would not stoop?
Soup of the evening, beautiful Soup!
Soup of the evening, beautiful Soup!
　　Beau—ootiful Soo—oop!
　　Beau—ootiful Soo—oop!

5. Again, in the early editions of *Alice's Adventures in Wonderland* Alice's recitation ended after the first two lines. In this early version, the owl and an oyster shared the pie. Dodgson added two lines to this part of the poem when *The Songs from Alice's Adventures in Wonderland* were published separately in 1870, with music written by William Boyd. (See note 3 on p. 275) The lines Dodgson added in 1870 pick up some of the details of the Caucus-Race:

While the duck and the Dodo, the lizard and cat
Were swimming in milk round the brim of a hat.

Then in 1886, for Savile Clarke's theatrical version of the Alice books, Dodgson changed the oyster to the Panther, and added the concluding six lines of the poem. In his biography of his uncle (see full citation on p. 299), Stuart Collingwood prints (p. 253) yet another version of the last two lines:

But the panther obtained both the fork and the knife,
So, when *he* lost his temper, the owl lost its life.

The third stanza of Watts's "The Sluggard" does begin, "I pass'd by his garden," but there is no other reminiscence of Watts's poem in the remainder of Dodgson's parody.

Soo—oop of the e—e—evening,
Beautiful, beautiful Soup!

"Beautiful Soup! Who cares for fish,
Game, or any other dish?
Who would not give all else for two p
ennyworth only of beautiful Soup?
Pennyworth only of beautiful soup.
Beau—ootiful Soo—oop!
Beau—ootiful Soo—oop!
Soo—oop of the e—e—evening,
Beautiful, beauti—FUL SOUP!"[6]

"Chorus again!" cried the Gryphon, and the Mock Turtle had just begun to repeat it, when a cry of "The trial's beginning!" was heard in the distance.

"Come on!" cried the Gryphon, and, taking Alice by the hand, it hurried off, without waiting for the end of the song.

"What trial is it?" Alice panted as she ran: but the Gryphon only answered "Come on!" and ran the faster, while more and more faintly came, carried on the breeze that followed them, the melancholy words:—

"Soo—oop of the e—e—evening,
Beautiful, beautiful Soup!"

6. "Beautiful Soup" is a parody of "Beautiful Star," a popular song by J. M. Sayles that Dodgson heard the Liddell children sing in August 1862 after the trip to Godstow during which he began to tell some of the adventures of Alice:

Beautiful star in heav'n so bright
Softly falls thy silv'ry light,
As thou movest from earth so far,
Star of the evening, beautiful star,
Beau—ti-ful star,
Beau—ti-ful star,
Star—of the eve—ning
Beautiful, beautiful star.

Green notes in the Appendix to *The Lewis Carroll Handbook* (see Selected Bibliography) that the song had been parodied in a theatrical pantomime in 1860 (p. 311).

Chapter XI

WHO STOLE THE TARTS?

The King and Queen of Hearts were seated on their throne when they arrived, with a great crowd assembled about them—all sorts of little birds and beasts, as well as the whole pack of cards: the Knave was standing before them, in chains, with a soldier on each side to guard him; and near the King was the White Rabbit, with a trumpet in one hand, and a scroll of parchment in the other. In the very middle of the court was a table, with a large dish of tarts upon it: they looked so good, that it made Alice quite hungry to look at them—"I wish they'd get the trial done," she thought, "and hand round the refreshments!" But there seemed to be no chance of this; so she began looking at everything about her to pass away the time.

Alice had never been in a court of justice before, but she had read about them in books, and she was quite pleased to find that she knew the name of nearly everything there. "That's the judge," she said to herself, "because of his great wig."

The judge, by the way, was the King; and, as he wore his crown over the wig (look at the frontispiece if you want to see how he did it), he did not look at all comfortable, and it was certainly not becoming.

"And that's the jury-box," thought Alice; "and those twelve creatures," (she was obliged to say "creatures," you see, because some of them were animals, and some were birds,) "I suppose they are the jurors." She said this last word two or three times over to herself, being rather proud of it: for she thought, and rightly too, that very few little girls of her age knew the meaning of it at all. However, "jurymen" would have done just as well.

The twelve jurors were all writing very busily on slates. "What are they doing?" Alice whispered to the Gryphon. "They ca'n't have anything to put down yet, before the trial's begun."

"They're putting down their names," the Gryphon whispered in reply, "for fear they should forget them before the end of the trial."

"Stupid things!" Alice began in a loud indignant voice; but she stopped herself hastily, for the White Rabbit cried out "Silence in the court!", and the King put on his spectacles and looked anxiously round, to make out who was talking.

Alice could see, as well as if she were looking over their shoulders, that all the jurors were writing down "Stupid things!" on their slates, and she could even make out that one of them didn't know how to spell "stupid," and that he had to ask his neighbour to tell him. "A nice muddle their slates'll be in, before the trial's over!" thought Alice.

One of the jurors had a pencil that squeaked. This, of course, Alice could *not* stand, and she went round the court and got behind him, and very soon found an opportunity of taking it away. She did it so quickly that the poor little juror (it was Bill, the Lizard) could not make out at all what had become of it; so, after hunting all about for it, he was obliged to write with one finger for the rest of the day; and this was of very little use, as it left no mark on the slate.

"Herald, read the accusation!" said the King.

On this the White Rabbit blew three blasts on the trumpet, and then unrolled the parchment-scroll, and read as follows:—

"The Queen of Hearts, she made some tarts,
All on a summer day:
The Knave of Hearts, he stole those tarts
And took them quite away!"[7]

"Consider your verdict," the King said to the jury.

"Not yet, not yet!" the Rabbit hastily interrupted. "There's a great deal to come before that!"

---

7. Dodgson takes over this nursery rhyme unchanged from one of its traditional versions. The traditional versions were collected in *The Nursery Rhymes of England* by James Orchard Halliwell (later Halliwell-Phillipps), first published in 1842.

"Call the first witness," said the King; and the White Rabbit blew three blasts on the trumpet, and called out "First witness!"

The first witness was the Hatter. He came in with a teacup in one hand and a piece of bread-and-butter in the other. "I beg pardon, your Majesty," he began, "for bringing these in; but I hadn't quite finished my tea when I was sent for."

"You ought to have finished," said the King. "When did you begin?"

The Hatter looked at the March Hare, who had followed him into the court, arm-in-arm with the Dormouse. "Fourteenth of March, I *think* it was," he said.

"Fifteenth," said the March Hare.

"Sixteenth," said the Dormouse.

"Write that down," the King said to the jury; and the jury eagerly wrote down all three dates on their slates, and then added them up, and reduced the answer to shillings and pence.

"Take off your hat," the King said to the Hatter.

"It isn't mine," said the Hatter.

"*Stolen!*" the King exclaimed, turning to the jury, who instantly made a memorandum of the fact.

"I keep them to sell," the Hatter added as an explanation. "I've none of my own. I'm a hatter."

Here the Queen put on her spectacles, and began staring hard at the Hatter, who turned pale and fidgeted.

"Give your evidence," said the King: "and don't be nervous, or I'll have you executed on the spot."

This did not seem to encourage the witness at all: he kept shifting from one foot to the other, looking uneasily at the Queen, and in his confusion he bit a large piece out of his teacup instead of the bread-and-butter.

Just at this moment Alice felt a very curious sensation, which puzzled her a good deal until she made out what it was: she was beginning to grow larger again, and she thought at first she would get up and leave the court; but on second thoughts she decided to remain where she was as long as there was room for her.

"I wish you wouldn't squeeze so," said the Dormouse, who was sitting next to her. "I can hardly breathe."

"I ca'n't help it," said Alice very meekly: "I'm growing."

"You've no right to grow *here*," said the Dormouse.

"Don't talk nonsense," said Alice more boldly: "you know you're growing too."

"Yes, but *I* grow at a reasonable pace," said the Dormouse: "not in that ridiculous fashion." And he got up very sulkily and crossed over to the other side of the court.

All this time the Queen had never left off staring at the Hatter, and, just as the Dormouse crossed the court, she said, to one of the officers of the court, "Bring me the list of the singers in the last concert!" on which the wretched Hatter trembled so, that he shook off both his shoes.

"Give your evidence," the King repeated angrily, "or I'll have you executed, whether you are nervous or not."

"I'm a poor man, your Majesty," the Hatter began, in a trembling voice, "and I hadn't begun my tea—not above a week or so—and what with the bread-and-butter getting so thin—and the twinkling of the tea——"

"The twinkling of *what?*" said the King.

"It *began* with the tea," the Hatter replied.

"Of course twinkling *begins* with a T!" said the King sharply. "Do you take me for a dunce? Go on!"

"I'm a poor man," the Hatter went on, "and most things twinkled after that—only the March Hare said——"

"I didn't!" the March Hare interrupted in a great hurry.

"You did!" said the Hatter.

"I deny it!" said the March Hare.

"He denies it," said the King: "leave out that part."

"Well, at any rate, the Dormouse said——" the Hatter went on, looking anxiously around to see if he would deny it too; but the Dormouse denied nothing, being fast asleep.

"After that," continued the Hatter, "I cut some more bread-and-butter——"

"But what did the Dormouse say?" one of the jury asked.

"That I ca'n't remember," said the Hatter.

"You *must* remember," remarked the King, "or I'll have you executed."

The miserable Hatter dropped his teacup and bread-and-butter, and went down on one knee. "I'm a poor man, your Majesty," he began.

"You're a *very* poor *speaker*," said the King.

Here one of the guinea-pigs cheered, and was immediately suppressed by the officers of the court. (As that is rather a hard word, I will just explain to you how it was done. They had a large canvas bag, which tied up at the mouth with strings: into this they slipped the guinea-pig, head first, and then sat upon it.)

"I'm glad I've seen that done," thought Alice. "I've so often read in the newspapers, at the end of trials, 'There was some attempt at applause, which was immediately suppressed by the officers of the court,' and I never understood what it meant till now."

"If that's all you know about it, you may stand down," continued the King.

"I ca'n't go no lower," said the Hatter: "I'm on the floor, as it is."

"Then you may *sit* down," the King replied.

Here the other guinea-pig cheered, and was suppressed.

"Come, that finishes the guinea-pigs!" thought Alice. "Now we shall get on better."

"I'd rather finish my tea," said the Hatter, with an anxious look at the Queen, who was reading the list of singers.

"You may go," said the King, and the Hatter hurriedly left the court, without even waiting to put his shoes on.

"——and just take his head off outside," the Queen added to one of the officers; but the Hatter was out of sight before the officer could get to the door.

"Call the next witness!" said the King.

The next witness was the Duchess's cook. She carried the pepper-box in her hand, and Alice guessed who it was, even before she got into the court, by the way the people near the door began sneezing all at once.

"Give your evidence," said the King.

"Sha'n't," said the cook.

The King looked anxiously at the White Rabbit, who said, in a low voice, "Your Majesty must cross-examine *this* witness."

"Well, if I must, I must," the King said with a melancholy air, and, after folding his arms and frowning at the cook till his eyes were nearly out of sight, he said, in a deep voice, "What are tarts made of?"

"Pepper, mostly," said the cook.

"Treacle," said a sleepy voice behind her.

"Collar that Dormouse!" the Queen shrieked out. "Behead that Dormouse! Turn that Dormouse out of court! Suppress him! Pinch him! Off with his whiskers!"

For some minutes the whole court was in confusion, getting the Dormouse turned out, and, by the time they had settled down again, the cook had disappeared.

"Never mind!" said the King, with an air of great relief. "Call the next witness." And, he added, in an undertone to the Queen, "Really, my dear, *you* must cross-examine the next witness. It quite makes my forehead ache!"

Alice watched the White Rabbit as he fumbled over the list, feeling very curious to see what the next witness would be like, "—for they haven't got much evidence *yet*," she said to herself. Imagine her surprise, when the White Rabbit read out, at the top of his shrill little voice, the name "Alice!"

Chapter XII

ALICE'S EVIDENCE

"Here!" cried Alice, quite forgetting in the flurry of the moment how large she had grown in the last few minutes, and she jumped up in such a hurry that she tipped over the jury-box with the edge of her skirt, upsetting all the jurymen on to the heads of the crowd below, and there they lay sprawling about, reminding her very much of a globe of gold-fish she had accidentally upset the week before.

"Oh, I *beg* your pardon!" she exclaimed in a tone of great dismay, and began picking them up again as quickly as she could, for the accident of the gold-fish kept running in her head, and she had a vague sort of idea that they must be collected at once and put back into the jury-box, or they would die.

"The trial cannot proceed," said the King, in a very grave voice, "until all the jurymen are back in their proper places—*all*," he repeated with great emphasis, looking hard at Alice as he said so.

Alice looked at the jury-box, and saw that, in her haste, she had put the Lizard in head downwards, and the poor little thing was waving its tail about in a melancholy way, being quite unable to move. She soon got it out again, and put it right; "not that it signifies much," she said to herself; "I should think it would be *quite* as much use in the trial one way up as the other."

As soon as the jury had a little recovered from the shock of being upset, and their slates and pencils had been found and handed back to them, they set to work very diligently to write out a history of the accident, all except the Lizard, who seemed too much overcome to do anything but sit with its mouth open, gazing up into the roof of the court.

"What do you know about this business?" the King said to Alice.

"Nothing," said Alice.

"Nothing *whatever*?" persisted the King.

"Nothing whatever," said Alice.

"That's very important," the King said, turning to the jury. They were just beginning to write this down on their slates, when the White Rabbit interrupted: "*Un*important, your Majesty means, of course," he said, in a very respectful tone, but frowning and making faces at him as he spoke.

"*Un*important, of course, I meant," the King hastily said, and went on to himself in an undertone, "important—unimportant—unimportant—important——" as if he were trying which word sounded best.

Some of the jury wrote it down "important," and some "unimportant." Alice could see this, as she was near enough to look over their slates; "but it doesn't matter a bit," she thought to herself.

At this moment the King, who had been for some time busily writing in his note-book, called out "Silence!", and read out from his book, "Rule Forty-two. *All persons more than a mile high to leave the court.*"

Everybody looked at Alice.

"*I'm* not a mile high," said Alice.

"You are," said the King.

"Nearly two miles high," added the Queen.

"Well, I sha'n't go, at any rate," said Alice; "besides, that's not a regular rule: you invented it just now."

"It's the oldest rule in the book," said the King.

"Then it ought to be Number One," said Alice.

The King turned pale, and shut his note-book hastily. "Consider your verdict," he said to the jury, in a low trembling voice.

"There's more evidence to come yet, please your Majesty," said the White Rabbit, jumping up in a great hurry: "this paper has just been picked up."

"What's in it?" said the Queen.

"I haven't opened it yet," said the White Rabbit; "but it seems to be a letter, written by the prisoner to—to somebody."

"It must have been that," said the King, "unless it was written to nobody, which isn't usual, you know."

"Who is it directed to?" said one of the jurymen.

"It isn't directed at all," said the White Rabbit: "in fact, there's nothing written on the *outside*." He unfolded the paper as he spoke, and added "It isn't a letter, after all: it's a set of verses."

"Are they in the prisoner's handwriting?" asked another of the jurymen.

"No, they're not," said the White Rabbit, "and that's the queerest thing about it." (The jury all looked puzzled.)

"He must have imitated somebody else's hand," said the King. (The jury all brightened up again.)

"Please, your Majesty," said the Knave, "I didn't write it, and they ca'n't prove that I did: there's no name signed at the end."

"If you didn't sign it," said the King, "that only makes the matter worse. You *must* have meant some mischief, or else you'd have signed your name like an honest man."

There was a general clapping of hands at this: it was the first really clever thing the King had said that day.

"That *proves* his guilt, of course," said the Queen, "so, off with——"

"It doesn't prove anything of the sort!" said Alice. "Why, you don't even know what they're about!"

"Read them," said the King.

The White Rabbit put on his spectacles. "Where shall I begin, please your Majesty?" he asked.

"Begin at the beginning," the King said, very gravely, "and go on till you come to the end: then stop."

There was dead silence in the court, whilst the White Rabbit read out these verses:—

> "They told me you had been to her,
>   And mentioned me to him:
> She gave me a good character,
>   But said I could not swim.
>
> He sent them word I had not gone
>   (We know it to be true):

If she should push the matter on,
What would become of you?

I gave her one, they gave him two,
You gave us three or more;
They all returned from him to you,
Though they were mine before.

If I or she should chance to be
Involved in this affair,
He trusts to you to set them free,
Exactly as we were.

My notion was that you had been
(Before she had this fit)
An obstacle that came between
Him, and ourselves, and it.

Don't let him know she liked them best,
For this must ever be
A secret, kept from all the rest,
Between yourself and me."[8]

"That's the most important piece of evidence we've heard yet," said the King, rubbing his hands; "so now let the jury——"

"If any one of them can explain it," said Alice, (she had grown so large in the last few minutes that she wasn't a bit afraid of interrupting him,) "I'll give him sixpence. *I* don't believe there's an atom of meaning in it."

The jury all wrote down, on their slates, "*She* doesn't believe there's an atom of meaning in it," but none of them attempted to explain the paper.

"If there's no meaning in it," said the King, "that saves a world of trouble, you know, as we needn't try to find any. And yet I don't know," he went on, spreading out the verses on his knee, and looking at them with one eye; "I seem to see some meaning in them, after all. '—*said I could not swim*—' you ca'n't swim, can you?" he added, turning to the Knave.

8. Dodgson, as Lewis Carroll, published an early version of this poem in *Comic Times* in 1855. Its first stanza: "She's all my fancy painted him / (I make no idle boast): / If he or you had lost a limb, / Which would have suffered most?" The poem is reprinted in *The Complete Works of Lewis Carroll* (pp. 723–24) and in Florence Milner's edition of Dodgson's domestic magazines (pp. 108–09). (See Selected Bibliography.) In the 1855 version, the poem is a close parody of "Alice Gray," by William Mee, published about 1815.

The Knave shook his head sadly. "Do I look like it?" he said. (Which he certainly did *not*, being made entirely of cardboard.)

"All right, so far," said the King; and he went on muttering over the verses to himself: "'*We know it to be true*'—that's the jury, of course—'*If she should push the matter on*'—that must be the Queen—'*What would become of you?*'—What, indeed!—'*I gave her one, they gave him two*'—why, that must be what he did with the tarts, you know——"

"But it goes on '*they all returned from him to you,*'" said Alice.

"Why, there they are!" said the King triumphantly, pointing to the tarts on the table. "Nothing can be clearer than *that*. Then again—'*before she had this fit*'—you never had *fits*, my dear, I think?" he said to the Queen.

"Never!" said the Queen, furiously, throwing an inkstand at the Lizard as she spoke. (The unfortunate little Bill had left off writing on his slate with one finger, as he found it made no mark; but he now hastily began again, using the ink, that was trickling down his face, as long as it lasted.)

"Then the words don't *fit* you," said the King looking round the court with a smile. There was a dead silence.

"It's a pun!" the King added in an angry tone, and everybody laughed. "Let the jury consider their verdict," the King said, for about the twentieth time that day.

"No, no!" said the Queen. "Sentence first—verdict afterwards."

"Stuff and nonsense!" said Alice loudly. "The idea of having the sentence first!"

"Hold your tongue!" said the Queen, turning purple.

"I wo'n't!" said Alice.

"Off with her head!" the Queen shouted at the top of her voice. Nobody moved.

"Who cares for *you*?" said Alice (she had grown to her full size by this time). "You're nothing but a pack of cards!"

At this the whole pack rose up into the air, and came flying down upon her; she gave a little scream, half of fright and half of anger, and tried to beat them off, and found herself lying on the

bank, with her head in the lap of her sister, who was gently brushing away some dead leaves that had fluttered down from the trees upon her face.

"Wake up, Alice dear!" said her sister. "Why, what a long sleep you've had!"

"Oh, I've had such a curious dream!" said Alice. And she told her sister, as well as she could remember them, all these strange Adventures of hers that you have just been reading about; when she had finished, her sister kissed her, and said "It *was* a curious dream, dear, certainly; but now run in to your tea: it's getting late." So Alice got up and ran off, thinking while she ran, as well she might, what a wonderful dream it had been.

But her sister sat still just as she left her, leaning her head on her hand, watching the setting sun, and thinking of little Alice and all her wonderful Adventures, till she too began dreaming after a fashion, and this was her dream:—

First, she dreamed about little Alice herself: once again the tiny hands were clasped upon her knee, and the bright eager eyes were looking up into hers—she could hear the very tones of her voice, and see that queer little toss of her head to keep back the wandering hair that *would* always get into her eyes—and still as she listened, or seemed to listen, the whole place around her became alive with the strange creatures of her little sister's dream.

The long grass rustled at her feet as the White Rabbit hurried by—the frightened Mouse splashed his way through the neighbouring pool—she could hear the rattle of the teacups as the March Hare and his friends shared their never-ending meal, and the shrill voice of the Queen ordering off her unfortunate guests to execution—once more the pig-baby was sneezing on the Duchess's knee, while plates and dishes crashed around it—once more the shriek of the Gryphon, the squeaking of the Lizard's slate-pencil, and the choking of the suppressed guinea-pigs, filled the air, mixed up with the distant sob of the miserable Mock Turtle.

So she sat on, with closed eyes, and half believed herself in Wonderland, though she knew she had but to open them again, and all would change to dull reality—the grass would be only rustling in the wind, and the pool rippling to the waving of the reeds—the rattling teacups would change to tinkling sheep-bells, and the Queen's shrill cries to the voice of the shepherd-boy—and the sneeze of the baby, the shriek of the Gryphon, and all the other queer noises, would change (she knew) to the confused clamour of the busy farm-yard—while the lowing of the cattle in the distance would take the place of the Mock Turtle's heavy sobs.

Lastly, she pictured to herself how this same little sister of hers would, in the after-time, be herself a grown woman; and how she would keep, through all her riper years, the simple and loving heart of her childhood; and how she would gather about her other little children, and make *their* eyes bright and eager with many a strange tale, perhaps even with the dream of Wonderland of long ago; and how she would feel with all their simple sorrows, and find a pleasure in all their simple joys, remembering her own child-life, and the happy summer days.

What's the moral?

The Text of
THROUGH THE
LOOKING-GLASS
and what Alice found there

Through the Looking-Glass and what Alice found there

Child of the pure unclouded brow
    And dreaming eyes of wonder!
Though time be fleet, and I and thou
    Are half a life asunder,
Thy loving smile will surely hail
The love-gift of a fairy-tale.

I have not seen thy sunny face,
    Nor heard thy silver laughter:
No thought of me shall find a place
    In thy young life's hereafter—
Enough that now thou wilt not fail
To listen to my fairy-tale.

A tale begun in other days,
    When summer suns were glowing—
A simple chime, that served to time
    The rhythm of our rowing—
Whose echoes live in memory yet,
Though envious years would say "forget."

Come, hearken then, ere voice of dread,
    With bitter tidings laden,
Shall summon to unwelcome bed
    A melancholy maiden!
We are but older children, dear,
Who fret to find our bedtime near.

Without, the frost, the blinding snow,
    The storm-wind's moody madness—
Within, the firelight's ruddy glow,
    And childhood's nest of gladness.
The magic words shall hold thee fast:
Thou shalt not heed the raving blast.

And, though the shadow of a sigh
    May tremble through the story,
For "happy summer days" gone by,
    And vanish'd summer glory—
It shall not touch, with breath of bale,
The pleasance of our fairy-tale.[1]

---

1. Alice Liddell's middle name was Pleasance. *Through the Looking-Glass* was published in December 1871; its title page bears the date 1872. Alice Liddell was sixteen and a half years old at the end of 1871. In *Through the Looking-Glass* Alice is seven and a half years old, six months older than she is in the first Alice book. The first book is set in May; *Through the Looking-Glass* ("Without, the frost, the blinding snow") is set in November. The phrase set off in quotation marks, "happy summer days," closes the last chapter of *Alice's Adventures in Wonderland*, and thus marks at the start a difference between that story and the tone and autumnal setting of its successor.

White Pawn (Alice) to play, and win in eleven moves.

Preface to the 1897 Edition

As the chess-problem, given on the previous page, has puzzled some of my readers, it may be well to explain that it is correctly worked out, so far as the *moves* are concerned.[2] The *alternation* of Red and White is perhaps not so strictly observed as it might be, and the "castling" of the three Queens is merely a way of saying that they entered the palace; but the "check" of the White King at move 6, the capture of the Red Knight at move 7, and the final "checkmate" of the Red King, will be found, by any one who will take the trouble to set the pieces and play the moves as directed, to be strictly in accordance with the laws of the game.

The new words, in the poem "Jabberwocky," have given rise to some differences of opinion as to their pronunciation: so it may be well to give instructions on *that* point also. Pronounce "slithy" as if it were the two words "sly, the": make the "g" *hard* in "gyre" and "gimble": and pronounce "rath" to rhyme with "bath."

For this sixty-first thousand, fresh electrotypes have been taken from the wood-blocks (which, never having been used for printing from, are in as good condition as when first cut in 1871), and the whole book has been set up afresh with new type. If the artistic qualities of this re-issue fall short, in any particular, of those possessed by the original issue, it will not be for want of painstaking on the part of author, publisher, or printer.[3]

I take this opportunity of announcing that the Nursery "Alice," hitherto priced at four shillings, net, is now to be had on the same terms as the ordinary shilling picture-books—although I feel sure that it is, in every quality (except the *text* itself, on which I am not qualified to pronounce), greatly superior to them. Four shillings was a perfectly reasonable price to charge, considering the very heavy initial outlay I had incurred: still, as the Public have practically said "We will *not* give more than a shilling for a picture-book, however artistically got-up," I am content to reckon my outlay on the book as so much dead loss, and, rather than let the little ones, for whom it was written, go without it, I am selling it at a price which is, to me, much the same thing as *giving* it away.

Christmas, 1896

---

2. As Martin Gardner notes in *The Annotated Alice* (see Selected Bibliography), several commentators have pointed out that Dodgson describes a chess lesson rather than a game (pp. 133–35). In her reminiscence (see pp. 265–68 of this edition), Alice Hargreaves recalls Dodgson teaching the Liddell children how to play chess.
3. Dodgson, who was himself painstaking about the appearance of his books, had agreed to recall 2,000 copies of the first issue of *Alice's Adventures in Wonderland* because Tenniel was dissatisfied with the appearance of the plates. Dodgson was also, as the last paragraph of this preface suggests, acutely interested in the sales and profits of his books. The authors of the 1979 edition of *The Lewis Carroll Handbook* (p. 235: see Selected Bibliography) estimate that 86,000 copies of the standard edition of *Alice's Adventures in Wonderland* were issued before Dodgson's death in 1898 (in addition to 70,000 copies of the cheaper People's Edition). By 1898, 61,000 copies of *Through the Looking-Glass* (plus 46,000 copies of the People's Edition) had been issued, and 11,000 copies of *The Nursery Alice*, a simplified version of the first *Alice* book. Before Dodgson's death Macmillan had printed 20,000 copies of *The Hunting of the Snark*, and 3,000 copies of the facsimile edition of the manuscript book *Alice's Adventures Underground*.

Chapter I

LOOKING-GLASS HOUSE

One thing was certain, that the *white* kitten had had nothing to do with it—it was the black kitten's fault entirely. For the white kitten had been having its face washed by the old cat for the last quarter of an hour (and bearing it pretty well, considering): so you see that it *couldn't* have had any hand in the mischief.

The way Dinah[4] washed her children's faces was this: first she held the poor thing down by its ear with one paw, and then with the other paw she rubbed its face all over, the wrong way, beginning at the nose: and just now, as I said, she was hard at work on the white kitten, which was lying quite still and trying to purr—no doubt feeling that it was all meant for its good.

But the black kitten had been finished with earlier in the afternoon, and so, while Alice was sitting curled up in a corner of the great armchair, half talking to herself and half asleep, the kitten had been having a grand game of romps with the ball of worsted Alice had been trying to wind up, and had been rolling it up and down till it had all come undone again; and there it was, spread over the hearth-rug, all knots and tangles, with the kitten running after its own tail in the middle.

"Oh, you wicked wicked little thing!" cried Alice, catching up the kitten, and giving it a little kiss to make it understand that it was in disgrace. "Really, Dinah ought to have taught you better manners! You *ought*, Dinah, you know you ought!" she added, looking reproachfully at the old cat, and speaking in as cross a voice as she could manage—and then she scrambled back into the armchair, taking

4. Dinah, the Liddells' cat, is also named in *Alice's Adventures in Wonderland*.

the kitten and the worsted with her, and began winding up the ball again. But she didn't get on very fast, as she was talking all the time, sometimes to the kitten, and sometimes to herself. Kitty sat very demurely on her knee, pretending to watch the progress of the winding, and now and then putting out one paw and gently touching the ball, as if it would be glad to help if it might.

"Do you know what to-morrow is, Kitty?" Alice began. "You'd have guessed if you'd been up in the window with me—only Dinah was making you tidy, so you couldn't. I was watching the boys getting in sticks for the bonfire[5]—and it wants plenty of sticks, Kitty! Only it got so cold, and it snowed so, they had to leave off. Never mind, Kitty, we'll go and see the bonfire to-morrow." Here Alice wound two or three turns of the worsted round the kitten's neck, just to see how it would look: this led to a scramble, in which the ball rolled down upon the floor, and yards and yards of it got unwound again.

"Do you know, I was so angry, Kitty," Alice went on, as soon as they were comfortably settled again, "when I saw all the mischief you had been doing, I was very nearly opening the window, and putting you out into the snow! And you'd have deserved it, you little mischievous darling! What have you got to say for yourself? Now don't interrupt me!" she went on, holding up one finger. "I'm going to tell you all your faults. Number one: you squeaked twice while Dinah was washing your face this morning. Now you ca'n't deny it, Kitty: I heard you! What's that you say?" (pretending that the kitten was speaking). "Her paw went into your eye? Well, that's *your* fault, for keeping your eyes open—if you'd shut them tight up, it wouldn't have happened. Now don't make any more excuses, but listen! Number two: you pulled Snowdrop away by the tail just as I had put down the saucer of milk before her! What, you were thirsty, were you? How do you know she wasn't thirsty too? Now for number three: you unwound every bit of the worsted while I wasn't looking!

"That's three faults, Kitty, and you've not been punished for any of them yet. You know I'm saving up all your punishments for Wednesday week[6]—Suppose they had saved up all *my* punishments?" she went on, talking more to herself than the kitten. "What *would* they do at the end of a year? I should be sent to prison, I suppose, when the day came. Or—let me see—suppose each punishment was to be going without a dinner: then, when the miserable day came, I should have to go without fifty dinners at once! Well, I shouldn't mind *that* much! I'd far rather go without them than eat them!

5. If "tomorrow" is Guy Fawkes Day, on which the frustration of a seventeenth-century attempt to blow up the house of Parliament is commemorated by the building of bonfires, then the date of the story is November 4. Alice Liddell's birthday was May 4; later (p. 151) she tells the White Queen that she is exactly seven and a half years old.
6. A week from Wednesday.

"Do you hear the snow against the window-panes, Kitty? How nice and soft it sounds! Just as if someone was kissing the window all over outside. I wonder if the snow *loves* the trees and fields, that it kisses them so gently? And then it covers them up snug, you know, with a white quilt; and perhaps it says 'Go to sleep, darlings, till the summer comes again.' And when they wake up in the summer, Kitty, they dress themselves all in green, and dance about— whenever the wind blows—oh, that's very pretty!" cried Alice, dropping the ball of worsted to clap her hands. "And I do so *wish* it was true! I'm sure the woods look sleepy in the autumn, when the leaves are getting brown.

"Kitty, can you play chess? Now, don't smile, my dear. I'm asking it seriously. Because, when we were playing just now, you watched just as if you understood it: and when I said 'Check!' you purred! Well, it *was* a nice check, Kitty, and really I might have won, if it hadn't been for that nasty Knight, that came wriggling down among my pieces. Kitty dear, let's pretend——" And here I wish I could tell you half the things Alice used to say, beginning with her favourite phrase "Let's pretend." She had had quite a long argument with her sister only the day before—all because Alice had begun with "Let's pretend we're kings and queens;" and her sister, who liked being very exact, had argued that they couldn't, because there were only two of them, and Alice had been reduced at last to say "Well, *you* can be one of them, then, and *I'll* be all the rest." And once she had really frightened her old nurse by shouting suddenly in her ear, "Nurse! Do let's pretend that I'm a hungry hyæna, and you're a bone!"[7]

But this is taking us away from Alice's speech to the kitten. "Let's pretend that you're the Red Queen, Kitty! Do you know, I think if you sat up and folded your arms, you'd look exactly like her. Now do try, there's a dear!" And Alice got the Red Queen off the table, and set it up before the kitten as a model for it to imitate: however, the thing didn't succeed, principally, Alice said, because the kitten wouldn't fold its arms properly. So, to punish it, she held it up to the Looking-glass, that it might see how sulky it was, "—and if you're not good directly," she added, "I'll put you through into Looking-glass House. How would you like *that*?

"Now, if you'll only attend, Kitty, and not talk so much, I'll tell you all my ideas about Looking-glass House. First, there's the room you can see through the glass—that's just the same as our drawing-room, only the things go the other way. I can see all of it when I get upon a chair—all but the bit just behind the fireplace. Oh! I do so wish I could see *that* bit! I want so much to know whether they've a fire in the winter: you never *can* tell, you know, unless our fire smokes, and then smoke comes up in that room too—but that may be only pretence, just to make it look as if they had a fire. Well then, the books are something like our books, only the words go the wrong way: I know *that*, because I've held up one of our books to the glass, and then they hold up one in the other room.

"How would you like to live in Looking-glass House, Kitty? I wonder if they'd give you milk in there? Perhaps Looking-glass milk isn't good to drink—but oh, Kitty! now we come to the passage. You can just see a little *peep* of the passage in Looking-glass House, if you leave the door of our drawing-room wide open: and it's very like our passage as far as you can see, only you know it may be quite

7. The first of many references in the story (as in its predecessor) to the habits of preda-
tors. James R. Kincaid in the Pennyroyal edition of *Through the Looking-Glass* (see
Selected Bibliography): "Alice orders and understands her world largely in terms of
power, and no power is so certain as that belonging to killing and eating. Such certainty, of course, is upset by the chaotic conclusion of the banquet welcoming Alice as
queen, where the food threatens to eat the eaters" (p. 6).

different on beyond. Oh, Kitty, how nice it would be if we could only get through into Looking-glass House! I'm sure it's got, oh! such beautiful things in it! Let's pretend there's a way of getting through into it, somehow, Kitty. Let's pretend the glass has got all soft like gauze, so that we can get through. Why, it's turning into a sort of mist now, I declare! It'll be easy enough to get through——" She was up on the chimney-piece while she said this, though she hardly knew how she had got there. And certainly the glass *was* beginning to melt away, just like a bright silvery mist.[8]

In another moment Alice was through the glass, and had jumped lightly down into the Looking-glass room. The very first thing she

8. One of Dodgson's child-friends, Alice Raikes (later Wilson-Fox), wrote that one day he placed her in front of a mirror with an orange in her right hand and asked, "'which hand the little girl you see there has got it in.' After some perplexed contemplation, I said, 'The left hand.' 'Exactly,' he said, 'and how do you explain that?'" Alice's answer: "'If I was on the *other* side of the glass, wouldn't the orange still be in my right hand?' I can remember his laugh. 'Well done, little Alice,' he said. That's the best answer I've had yet.'" (*Times*, January 22, 1932; reprinted in R. L. Green's edition of *The Diaries* [see Selected Bibliography], II: 272).

did was to look whether there was a fire in the fireplace, and she was quite pleased to find that there was a real one, blazing away as brightly as the one she had left behind. "So I shall be as warm here as I was in the old room," thought Alice: "warmer, in fact, because there'll be no one here to scold me away from the fire. Oh, what fun it'll be, when they see me through the glass in here, and ca'n't get at me!"

Then she began looking about, and noticed that what could be seen from the old room was quite common and uninteresting, but that all the rest was as different as possible. For instance, the pictures on the wall next the fire seemed to be all alive, and the very clock on the chimney-piece (you know you can only see the back of it in the Looking-glass) had got the face of a little old man, and grinned at her.

"They don't keep this room so tidy as the other," Alice thought to herself, as she noticed several of the chessmen down in the hearth among the cinders; but in another moment, with a little "Oh!" of surprise, she was down on her hands and knees watching them. The chessmen were walking about, two and two!

"Here are the Red King and the Red Queen," Alice said (in a whisper, for fear of frightening them), "and there are the White King and the White Queen sitting on the edge of the shovel—and here are two Castles walking arm in arm—I don't think they can hear me," she went on, as she put her head closer down, "and I'm nearly sure they ca'n't see me. I feel somehow as if I was getting invisible——"

Here something began squeaking on the table behind Alice, and made her turn her head just in time to see one of the White Pawns roll over and begin kicking: she watched it with great curiosity to see what would happen next.

"It is the voice of my child!" the White Queen cried out, as she rushed past the King, so violently that she knocked him over among the cinders. "My precious Lily! My imperial kitten!" and she began scrambling wildly up the side of the fender.[9]

"Imperial fiddlestick!" said the King, rubbing his nose, which had been hurt by the fall. He had a right to be a *little* annoyed with the Queen, for he was covered with ashes from head to foot.

9. Fender: see n. 6 on p. 14.

Alice was very anxious to be of use, and, as the poor little Lily was nearly screaming herself into a fit, she hastily picked up the Queen and set her on the table by the side of her noisy little daughter.

The Queen gasped, and sat down: the rapid journey through the air had quite taken away her breath, and for a minute or two she could do nothing but hug the little Lily in silence. As soon as she had recovered her breath a little, she called out to the White King, who was sitting sulkily among the ashes, "Mind the volcano!"

"What volcano?" said the King, looking up anxiously into the fire, as if he thought that was the most likely place to find one.

"Blew—me—up," panted the Queen, who was still a little out of breath. "Mind you come up—the regular way—don't get blown up!"

Alice watched the White King as he slowly struggled up from bar to bar, till at last she said "Why, you'll be hours and hours getting to the table, at that rate. I'd far better help you, hadn't I?" But the King took no notice of the question: it was quite clear that he could neither hear her nor see her.

So Alice picked him up very gently, and lifted him across more slowly than she had lifted the Queen, that she mightn't take his breath away; but, before she put him on the table, she thought she might as well dust him a little, he was so covered with ashes.

She said afterwards that she had never seen in all her life such a face as the King made, when he found himself held in the air by an invisible hand, and being dusted: he was far too much astonished

to cry out, but his eyes and his mouth went on getting larger and larger, and rounder and rounder, till her hand shook so with laughter that she nearly let him drop upon the floor.

"Oh! *please* don't make such faces, my dear!" she cried out, quite forgetting that the King couldn't hear her. "You make me laugh so that I can hardly hold you! And don't keep your mouth so wide open! All the ashes will get into it—there, now I think you're tidy enough!" she added, as she smoothed his hair, and set him upon the table near the Queen.

The King immediately fell flat on his back, and lay perfectly still; and Alice was a little alarmed at what she had done, and went round the room to see if she could find any water to throw over him. However, she could find nothing but a bottle of ink, and when she got back with it she found he had recovered, and he and the Queen were talking together in a frightened whisper—so low, that Alice could hardly hear what they said.

The King was saying "I assure you, my dear, I turned cold to the very ends of my whiskers!"

To which the Queen replied "You haven't got any whiskers."[1]

"The horror of that moment," the King went on, "I shall never, *never* forget!"

"You will, though," the Queen said, "if you don't make a memorandum of it."

Alice looked on with great interest as the King took an enormous memorandum-book out of his pocket, and began writing. A sudden thought struck her, and she took hold of the end of the pencil, which came some way over his shoulder, and began writing for him.

The poor King looked puzzled and unhappy, and struggled with the pencil for some time without saying anything; but Alice was too strong for him, and at last he panted out "My dear! I really *must* get a thinner pencil. I ca'n't manage this one a bit: it writes all manner of things that I don't intend——"

"What manner of things?" said the Queen, looking over the book (in which Alice had put 'The White Knight is sliding down the poker. He balances very badly'). "That's not a memorandum of *your* feelings!"

There was a book lying near Alice on the table, and while she sat watching the White King (for she was still a little anxious about him, and had the ink all ready to throw over him, in case he fainted again), she turned over the leaves, to find some part that she could read, "—for it's all in some language I don't know," she said to herself.

---

1. Tenniel's White King wears a moustache and what looks like a goatee; by "whiskers" the Queen may mean sideburns (Gardner, p. 147).

It was like this.

ʎʞɔoʍɹǝqqɐſ

ˑǝqɐɹƃʇno sɥʇɐɹ ǝɯoɯ ǝɥʇ pu∀
'sǝʌoƃoɹoq ǝɥʇ ǝɹǝʍ ʎsɯᴉɯ ll∀
:ǝqɐʍ ǝɥʇ uᴉ ǝlqɯᴉƃ puɐ ǝɹʎƃ pᴉꓷ
sǝʌoʇ ʎɥʇᴉls ǝɥʇ puɐ 'ƃᴉllᴉɹq sɐʍ⟓'

She puzzled over this for some time, but at last a bright thought
struck her. "Why, it's a Looking-glass book, of course! And, if I hold
it up to a glass, the words will all go the right way again."

This was the poem that Alice read.

JABBERWOCKY

'Twas brillig, and the slithy toves
 Did gyre and gimble in the wabe:
All mimsy were the borogoves,
 And the mome raths outgrabe.

"Beware the Jabberwock, my son!
 The jaws that bite, the claws that catch!
Beware the Jubjub bird, and shun
 The frumious Bandersnatch!"

He took his vorpal sword in hand:
 Long time the manxome foe he sought—
So rested he by the Tumtum tree,
 And stood awhile in thought.

And, as in uffish thought he stood,
  The Jabberwock, with eyes of flame,
Came whiffling through the tulgey wood,
  And burbled as it came!

One, two! One, two! And through and through
  The vorpal blade went snicker-snack!

He left it dead, and with its head
    He went galumphing back.

"And, hast thou slain the Jabberwock?
    Come to my arms, my beamish boy!
O frabjous day! Callooh! Callay!"
    He chortled in his joy.

'Twas brillig, and the slithy toves
    Did gyre and gimble in the wabe:
All mimsy were the borogoves,
    And the mome raths outgrabe.[2]

"It seems very pretty," she said when she had finished it, "but it's *rather* hard to understand!" (You see she didn't like to confess, even to herself, that she couldn't make it out at all.) "Somehow it seems to fill my head with ideas—only I don't exactly know what they are! However, *somebody* killed *something*: that's clear, at any rate——"

"But oh!" thought Alice, suddenly jumping up, "if I don't make haste, I shall have to go back through the Looking-glass, before I've seen what the rest of the house is like! Let's have a look at the garden first!" She was out of the room in a moment, and ran down stairs—or, at least, it wasn't exactly running, but a new invention for getting down stairs quickly and easily, as Alice said to herself. She just kept the tips of her fingers on the hand-rail, and floated gently down without even touching the stairs with her feet: then she floated on through the hall, and would have gone straight out at the door in the same way, if she hadn't caught hold of the doorpost. She was getting a little giddy with so much floating in the air, and was rather glad to find herself walking again in the natural way.

---

2. Dodgson published the first stanza of "Jabberwocky," then titled "Stanza of Anglo-Saxon Poetry" and tricked out in a fake Old English script, in *Mischmasch*, a home miscellany he put together between 1855 and 1862 (see Selected Bibliography for Florence Milner's edition). He defined some of the words in this first version of the poem. He offered other explications in Humpty Dumpty's dialogue in Chapter VI and in the preface to *The Hunting of the Snark* (see pp. 220–21 of this Norton Critical Edition). See also Elizabeth Sewell's "The Balance of Brillig" (pp. 346–50 of this edition), Eric Partridge's "The Nonsense Words of Lear and Carroll" in *Here, There, and Everywhere* (see Selected Bibliography), and Martin Gardner's *The Annotated Alice* (pp. 213–17) for further glosses of the poem.

Roger Lancelyn Green suggests in the *Times Literary Supplement* (March 1, 1957, 126) that the story of the Jabberwocky is a condensation of the plot of a translation by Menella Bute Smedley, Dodgson's cousin, of the German ballad *The Shepherd of the Giant Mountains*. The comma after "and" in the first line of the penultimate stanza was included in the corrections Dodgson made when he prepared an edition of the Alice books near the end of his life, but this correction was one of two not included in an edition published in 1898. See Stanley Godman, "Lewis Carroll's Final Corrections to 'Alice,'" *Times Literary Supplement*, May 2, 1958, 248.

Chapter II

THE GARDEN OF LIVE FLOWERS

"I should see the garden far better," said Alice to herself, "if I could get to the top of that hill: and here's a path that leads straight to it— at least, no, it doesn't do *that*——" (after going a few yards along the path, and turning several sharp corners), "but I suppose it will at last. But how curiously it twists! It's more like a corkscrew than a path! Well, *this* turn goes to the hill, I suppose—no, it doesn't! This goes straight back to the house! Well then, I'll try it the other way."

And so she did: wandering up and down, and trying turn after turn, but always coming back to the house, do what she would. Indeed, once, when she turned a corner rather more quickly than usual, she ran against it before she could stop herself.

"It's no use talking about it," Alice said, looking up at the house and pretending it was arguing with her. "I'm *not* going in again yet. I know I should have to get through the Looking-glass again—back into the old room—and there'd be an end of all my adventures!"

So, resolutely turning her back upon the house, she set out once more down the path, determined to keep straight on till she got to the hill. For a few minutes all went on well, and she was just saying "I really *shall* do it this time——" when the path gave a sudden twist and shook itself (as she described it afterwards), and the next moment she found herself actually walking in at the door.

"Oh, it's too bad!" she cried. "I never saw such a house for getting in the way! Never!"

However, there was the hill full in sight, so there was nothing to be done but start again. This time she came upon a large flower-bed,[3] with a border of daisies, and a willow-tree growing in the middle.

"O Tiger-lily!" said Alice, addressing herself to one that was waving gracefully about in the wind, "I *wish* you could talk!"

---

3. The flowers, and their announcement of the coming of the Red Queen, are taken from a stanza in Tennyson's *Maud* (1855) in which the lover waits for his lady in a garden:

> There has fallen a splendid tear
> From the passion-flower at the gate.
> She is coming, my dove, my dear;
> She is coming, my life, my fate;
> The red rose cries, "She is near,"
> And the white rose weeps, "She is late;"
> The larkspur listens, "I hear;"
> And the lily whispers, "I wait."

Dodgson changed the passion-flower to a tiger-lily when he learned that because of its markings the passion-flower was associated with the passion of Christ. (The same scrupulousness about associating religion with humor is perhaps the reason that he does not name the bishops among the chess pieces.)

"We *can* talk," said the Tiger-lily, "when there's anybody worth talking to."

Alice was so astonished that she couldn't speak for a minute: it quite seemed to take her breath away. At length, as the Tiger-lily only went on waving about, she spoke again, in a timid voice—almost in a whisper. "And can *all* the flowers talk?"

"As well as *you* can," said the Tiger-lily. "And a great deal louder."

"It isn't manners for us to begin, you know," said the Rose, "and I really was wondering when you'd speak! Said I to myself, 'Her face has got *some* sense in it, though it's not a clever one!' Still, you're the right colour, and that goes a long way."

"I don't care about the colour," the Tiger-lily remarked. "If only her petals curled up a little more, she'd be all right."

Alice didn't like being criticized, so she began asking questions. "Aren't you sometimes frightened at being planted out here, with nobody to take care of you?"

"There's the tree in the middle," said the Rose. "What else is it good for?"

"But what could it do, if any danger came?" Alice asked.

"It could bark," said the Rose.

"It says 'Bough-wough!'" cried a Daisy. "That's why its branches are called boughs!"[4]

"Didn't you know *that?*" cried another Daisy. And here they all began shouting together, till the air seemed quite full of little shrill voices. "Silence, every one of you!" cried the Tiger-lily, waving itself passionately from side to side, and trembling with excitement. "They know I ca'n't get at them!" it panted, bending its quivering head towards Alice, "or they wouldn't dare to do it!"

"Never mind!" Alice said in a soothing tone, and, stooping down to the daisies, who were just beginning again, she whispered "If you don't hold your tongues, I'll pick you!"

There was silence in a moment, and several of the pink daisies turned white.

"That's right!" said the Tiger-lily. "The daisies are worst of all. When one speaks, they all begin together, and it's enough to make one wither to hear the way they go on!"

"How is it you can all talk so nicely?" Alice said, hoping to get it into a better temper by a compliment. "I've been in many gardens before, but none of the flowers could talk."

"Put your hand down, and feel the ground," said the Tiger-lily. "Then you'll know why."

Alice did so. "It's very hard," she said; "but I don't see what that has to do with it."

"In most gardens," the Tiger-lily said, "they make the beds too soft—so that the flowers are always asleep."

This sounded a very good reason, and Alice was quite pleased to know it. "I never thought of that before!" she said.

"It's *my* opinion that you never think *at all*," the Rose said, in a rather severe tone.

"I never saw anybody that looked stupider," a Violet said, so suddenly, that Alice quite jumped; for it hadn't spoken before.[5]

"Hold *your* tongue!" cried the Tiger-lily. "As if *you* ever saw anybody! You keep your head under the leaves, and snore away there,

---

4. This is the first of several passages in the book that play with the question of whether words are entirely arbitrary signs or whether, as the Daisy here suggests, the name of a thing is somehow intrinsically connected with its nature. If Dodgson fulfilled his intention, recorded in his diary (see p. 255 of this edition), of reading Horne Tooke's *The Diversions of Purley* (1786; 1805), he would have found there etymologies as fanciful as that advanced by the Daisy: for example, that because the *bark* of a tree and the *bark* of a dog are used for defense, both words derive from *bar*, meaning to defend against. The phrase "bow-wow theory" was also current in nineteenth-century philological study, referring to the idea that human speech developed from animal sounds.

5. Rose (Rhoda) and Violet were Alice's sisters.

till you know no more what's going on in the world, than if you were a bud!"

"Are there any more people in the garden besides me?" Alice said, not choosing to notice the Rose's last remark.

"There's one other flower in the garden that can move about like you," said the Rose. "I wonder how you do it——" ("You're always wondering," said the Tiger-lily), "but she's more bushy than you are."

"Is she like me?" Alice asked eagerly, for the thought crossed her mind, "There's another little girl in the garden, somewhere!"

"Well, she has the same awkward shape as you," the Rose said: "but she's redder—and her petals are shorter, I think."

"They're done up close, like a dahlia," said the Tiger-lily: "not tumbled about, like yours."

"But that's not *your* fault," the Rose added kindly. "You're beginning to fade, you know—and then one ca'n't help one's petals getting a little untidy."

Alice didn't like this idea at all: so, to change the subject, she asked "Does she ever come out here?"

"I daresay you'll see her soon," said the Rose. "She's one of the kind that has nine spikes, you know."

"Where does she wear them?" Alice asked with some curiosity.

"Why, all round her head, of course," the Rose replied. "I was wondering *you* hadn't got some too. I thought it was the regular rule."

"She's coming!" cried the Larkspur. "I hear her footstep, thump, thump, along the gravel-walk!"

Alice looked round eagerly and found that it was the Red Queen. "She's grown a good deal!" was her first remark. She had indeed: when Alice first found her in the ashes, she had been only three inches high—and here she was, half a head taller than Alice herself!

"It's the fresh air that does it," said the Rose: "wonderfully fine air it is, out here."

"I think I'll go and meet her," said Alice, for, though the flowers were interesting enough, she felt that it would be far grander to have a talk with a real Queen.

"You ca'n't possibly do that," said the Rose: "*I* should advise you to walk the other way."

This sounded nonsense to Alice, so she said nothing, but set off at once towards the Red Queen. To her surprise she lost sight of her in a moment, and found herself walking in at the front-door again.

A little provoked, she drew back, and, after looking everywhere for the Queen (whom she spied out at last, a long way off), she thought she would try the plan, this time, of walking in the opposite direction.

It succeeded beautifully. She had not been walking a minute before she found herself face to face with the Red Queen, and full in sight of the hill she had been so long aiming at.

"Where do you come from?" said the Red Queen. "And where are you going? Look up, speak nicely, and don't twiddle your fingers all the time."

Alice attended to all these directions, and explained, as well as she could, that she had lost her way.

"I don't know what you mean by *your* way," said the Queen: "all the ways about here belong to *me*—but why did you come out here at all?" she added in a kinder tone. "Curtsey while you're thinking what to say. It saves time."

Alice wondered a little at this, but she was too much in awe of the Queen to disbelieve it. "I'll try it when I go home," she thought to herself, "the next time I'm a little late for dinner."

"It's time for you to answer now," the Queen said, looking at her watch: "open your mouth a *little* wider when you speak, and always say 'your Majesty.'"

"I only wanted to see what the garden was like, your Majesty——"

"That's right," said the Queen, patting her on the head, which Alice didn't like at all: "though, when you say 'garden'—*I've* seen gardens, compared with which this would be a wilderness."

Alice didn't dare to argue the point, but went on: "—and I thought I'd try and find my way to the top of that hill——"

"When you say 'hill'," the Queen interrupted, "I could show you hills, in comparison with which you'd call that a valley."

"No, I shouldn't," said Alice, surprised into contradicting her at last: "a hill *ca'n't* be a valley, you know. That would be nonsense——"

The Red Queen shook her head. "You may call it 'nonsense' if you like," she said, "but *I've* heard nonsense, compared with which that would be as sensible as a dictionary!"

Alice curtseyed again, as she was afraid from the Queen's tone that she was a *little* offended: and they walked on in silence till they got to the top of the little hill.

For some minutes Alice stood without speaking, looking out in all directions over the country—and a most curious country it was. There were a number of tiny little brooks running straight across it from side to side, and the ground between was divided up into squares by a number of little green hedges, that reached from brook to brook.

"I declare it's marked out just like a large chess-board!" Alice said at last. "There ought to be some men moving about somewhere— and so there are!" she added in a tone of delight, and her heart began to beat quick with excitement as she went on. "It's a great huge game of chess that's being played—all over the world—if this *is* the world

at all, you know. Oh, what fun it is! How I *wish* I was one of them!
I wouldn't mind being a Pawn, if only I might join—though of
course I should *like* to be a Queen, best."

She glanced rather shyly at the real Queen as she said this, but
her companion only smiled pleasantly, and said "That's easily managed. You can be the White Queen's Pawn, if you like, as Lily's too
young to play, and you're in the Second Square to begin with: when
you get to the Eighth Square you'll be a Queen——" Just at this
moment, somehow or other, they began to run.

Alice never could quite make out, in thinking it over afterwards,
how it was that they began: all she remembers is, that they were
running hand in hand, and the Queen went so fast that it was all
she could do to keep up with her: and still the Queen kept crying
"Faster! Faster!", but Alice felt she *could not* go faster, though she
had no breath left to say so.

The most curious part of the thing was, that the trees and the
other things round them never changed their places at all: however
fast they went, they never seemed to pass anything. "I wonder if all
the things move along with us?" thought poor puzzled Alice. And
the Queen seemed to guess her thoughts, for she cried "Faster!
Don't try to talk!"

Not that Alice had any idea of doing *that*. She felt as if she would
never be able to talk again, she was getting so much out of breath:
and still the Queen cried "Faster! Faster!", and dragged her along.
"Are we nearly there?" Alice managed to pant out at last.

"Nearly there!" the Queen repeated. "Why, we passed it ten minutes ago! Faster!" And they ran on for a time in silence, with the
wind whistling in Alice's ears, and almost blowing her hair off her
head, she fancied.

"Now! Now!" cried the Queen. "Faster! Faster!" And they went so fast that at last they seemed to skim through the air, hardly touching the ground with their feet, till suddenly, just as Alice was getting quite exhausted, they stopped, and she found herself sitting on the ground, breathless and giddy.

The Queen propped her up against a tree, and said kindly, "You may rest a little, now."

Alice looked round her in great surprise. "Why, I do believe we've been under this tree the whole time! Everything's just as it was!"

"Of course it is," said the Queen. "What would you have it?"

"Well, in *our* country," said Alice, still panting a little, "you'd generally get to somewhere else—if you ran very fast for a long time as we've been doing."

"A slow sort of country!" said the Queen. "Now, *here*, you see, it takes all the running *you* can do, to keep in the same place. If you want to get somewhere else, you must run at least twice as fast as that!"

"I'd rather not try, please!" said Alice. "I'm quite content to stay here—only I *am* so hot and thirsty!"

"I know what *you'd* like!" the Queen said good-naturedly, taking a little box out of her pocket. "Have a biscuit?"

Alice thought it would not be civil to say "No," though it wasn't at all what she wanted. So she took it, and ate it as well as she could: and it was *very* dry; and she thought she had never been so nearly choked in all her life.

"While you're refreshing yourself," said the Queen, "I'll just take the measurements." And she took a ribbon out of her pocket, marked in inches, and began measuring the ground, and sticking little pegs in here and there.

"At the end of two yards," she said, putting in a peg to mark the distance, "I shall give you your directions—have another biscuit?"

"No, thank you," said Alice: "one's *quite* enough!"

"Thirst quenched, I hope?" said the Queen.

Alice did not know what to say to this, but luckily the Queen did not wait for an answer, but went on. "At the end of *three* yards I shall repeat them—for fear of your forgetting them. At the end of *four*, I shall say good-bye. And at the end of *five*, I shall go!"

She had got all the pegs put in by this time, and Alice looked on with great interest as she returned to the tree, and then began slowly walking down the row.

At the two-yard peg she faced round, and said "A pawn goes two squares in its first move, you know. So you'll go *very* quickly through the Third Square—by railway, I should think—and you'll find yourself in the Fourth Square in no time. Well, *that* square belongs to Tweedledum and Tweedledee—the Fifth is mostly water—the Sixth belongs to Humpty Dumpty—But you make no remark?"

"I—I didn't know I had to make one—just then," Alice faltered out.

"You *should* have said," the Queen went on in a tone of grave reproof, "'It's extremely kind of you to tell me all this'—however, we'll suppose it said—the Seventh Square is all forest—however, one of the Knights will show you the way—and in the Eighth Square we shall be Queens together, and it's all feasting and fun!" Alice got up and curtseyed, and sat down again.

At the next peg the Queen turned again, and this time she said "Speak in French when you ca'n't think of the English for a thing— turn out your toes as you walk—and remember who you are!" She did not wait for Alice to curtsey, this time, but walked on quickly to the next peg, where she turned for a moment to say "Good-bye," and then hurried on to the last.

How it happened, Alice never knew, but exactly as she came to the last peg, she was gone.[6] Whether she vanished into the air, or whether she ran quickly into the wood ("and she *can* run very fast!" thought Alice), there was no way of guessing, but she was gone, and Alice began to remember that she was a Pawn, and that it would soon be time for her to move.

6. After marking off the stages of Alice's progress to queen, the Red Queen disappears by making a move that Alice, as pawn, cannot make.

Chapter III

Of course the first thing to do was to make a grand survey of the country she was going to travel through. "It's something very like learning geography," thought Alice, as she stood on tiptoe in hopes of being able to see a little further. "Principal rivers—there *are* none. Principal mountains—I'm on the only one, but I don't think it's got any name. Principal towns—why, what *are* those creatures, making honey down there? They ca'n't be bees—nobody ever saw bees a mile off, you know——" and for some time she stood silent, watching one of them that was bustling about among the flowers, poking its proboscis into them, "just as if it was a regular bee," thought Alice.

However, this was anything but a regular bee: in fact, it was an elephant—as Alice soon found out, though the idea quite took her breath away at first. "And what enormous flowers they must be!" was her next idea. "Something like cottages with the roofs taken off, and stalks put to them—and what quantities of honey they must make! I think I'll go down and—no, I wo'n't go *just* yet," she went on, checking herself just as she was beginning to run down the hill, and trying to find some excuse for turning shy so suddenly. "It'll never do to go down among them without a good long branch to brush them away—and what fun it'll be when they ask me how I liked my walk. I shall say 'Oh, I liked it well enough——' (here came the favourite little toss of the head), 'only it *was* so dusty and hot, and the elephants *did* tease so!'"

"I think I'll go down the other way," she said after a pause; "and perhaps I may visit the elephants later on. Besides, I *do* so want to get into the Third Square!"

So, with this excuse, she ran down the hill, and jumped over the first of the six little brooks.

    ✳   ✳   ✳   ✳   ✳

      ✳   ✳   ✳   ✳

    ✳   ✳   ✳   ✳   ✳7

"Tickets, please!" said the Guard, putting his head in at the window. In a moment everybody was holding out a ticket: they were about the same size as the people, and quite seemed to fill the carriage.

---

7. Asterisks mark Alice's progress from one square on the chessboard to another.

"Now then! Show your ticket, child!" the Guard went on, looking angrily at Alice. And a great many voices all said together ("like the chorus of a song," thought Alice) "Don't keep him waiting, child! Why, his time is worth a thousand pounds a minute!"

"I'm afraid I haven't got one," Alice said in a frightened tone: "there wasn't a ticket-office where I came from." And again the chorus of voices went on. "There wasn't room for one where she came from. The land there is worth a thousand pounds an inch!"

"Don't make excuses," said the Guard: "you should have bought one from the engine-driver." And once more the chorus of voices went on with "The man that drives the engine. Why, the smoke alone is worth a thousand pounds a puff!"

Alice thought to herself "Then there's no use in speaking." The voices didn't join in, *this* time, as she hadn't spoken, but, to her great surprise, they all *thought* in chorus (I hope you understand what *thinking in chorus* means—for I must confess that *I* don't), "Better say nothing at all. Language is worth a thousand pounds a word!"

"I shall dream about a thousand pounds to-night, I know I shall!" thought Alice.

All this time the Guard was looking at her, first through a telescope, then through a microscope, and then through an opera-glass. At last he said "You're traveling the wrong way," and shut up the window, and went away.

"So young a child," said the gentleman sitting opposite to her, (he was dressed in white paper,)[8] "ought to know which way she's going, even if she doesn't know her own name!"

A Goat, that was sitting next to the gentleman in white, shut his eyes and said in a loud voice, "She ought to know her way to the ticket-office, even if she doesn't know her alphabet!"

There was a Beetle sitting next the Goat (it was a very queer carriage-full of passengers altogether), and, as the rule seemed to be that they should all speak in turn, *he* went on with "She'll have to go back from here as luggage!"

Alice couldn't see who was sitting beyond the Beetle, but a hoarse voice spoke next. "Change engines——" it said, and there it choked and was obliged to leave off.

"It sounds like a horse," Alice thought to herself. And an extremely small voice, close to her ear, said "You might make a joke on that—something about 'horse' and 'hoarse,' you know."

Then a very gentle voice in the distance said, "She must be labeled 'Lass, with care,'[9] you know——"

And after that other voices went on ("What a number of people there are in the carriage!" thought Alice), saying "She must go by post, as she's got a head[1] on her——" "She must be sent as a message by the telegraph——" "She must draw the train herself the rest of the way——," and so on.

But the gentleman dressed in white paper leaned forwards and whispered in her ear, "Never mind what they all say, my dear, but take a return-ticket every time the train stops."

"Indeed I sha'n't!" Alice said rather impatiently. "I don't belong to this railway journey at all—I was in a wood just now—and I wish I could get back there!'"

"You might make a joke on *that*," said the little voice close to her ear: "something about 'you *would* if you could,' you know."

"Don't tease so," said Alice, looking about in vain to see where the voice came from. "If you're so anxious to have a joke made, why don't you make one yourself?"

The little voice sighed deeply. It was *very* unhappy, evidently, and Alice would have said something pitying to comfort it, "if it would only sigh like other people!" she thought. But this was such a wonderfully small sigh, that she wouldn't have heard it all, if it hadn't come *quite* close to her ear. The consequence of this was that it

---

8. Although Tenniel's drawing unmistakably resembles him, there is nothing in the text to suggest that man dressed in paper is intended to represent Benjamin Disraeli. Disraeli held ministerial posts off and on in the 1850s and 1860s ("take a return ticket"), became prime minister briefly in 1868 and again, for a long period, in 1878.
9. I.e., "Glass, with care."
1. Mid-nineteenth-century postage stamps bore a portrait of the head of Queen Victoria.

tickled her ear very much, and quite took off her thoughts from the unhappiness of the poor little creature.

"I know you are a friend," the little voice went on: "a dear friend, and an old friend. And you wo'n't hurt me, though I am an insect."

"What kind of insect?" Alice inquired, a little anxiously. What she really wanted to know was, whether it could sting or not, but she thought this wouldn't be quite a civil question to ask.

"What, then you don't—" the little voice began, when it was drowned by a shrill scream from the engine, and everybody jumped up in alarm, Alice among the rest.

The Horse, who had put his head out of the window, quietly drew it in and said "It's only a brook we have to jump over." Everybody seemed satisfied with this, though Alice felt a little nervous at the idea of trains jumping at all. "However, it'll take us into the Fourth Square, that's some comfort!" she said to herself. In another moment she felt the carriage rise straight up into the air, and in her fright she caught at the thing nearest to her hand, which happened to be the Goat's beard.

✻   ✻   ✻   ✻   ✻
✻   ✻   ✻   ✻
✻   ✻   ✻   ✻   ✻

But the beard seemed to melt away as she touched it, and she found herself sitting quietly under a tree—while the Gnat (for that was the insect she had been talking to) was balancing itself on a twig just over her head, and fanning her with its wings.

It certainly was a *very* large Gnat: "about the size of a chicken," Alice thought. Still, she couldn't feel nervous with it, after they had been talking together so long.

"—then you don't like *all* insects?" the Gnat went on, as quietly as if nothing had happened.

"I like them when they can talk," Alice said. "None of them ever talk, where I come from."

"What sort of insects do you rejoice in, where *you* come from?" the Gnat inquired.

"I don't *rejoice* in insects at all," Alice explained, "because I'm rather afraid of them—at least the large kinds. But I can tell you the names of some of them."

"Of course they answer to their names?" the Gnat remarked carelessly.

"I never knew them do it."

"What's the use of their having names," the Gnat said, "if they wo'n't answer to them?"

"No use to *them*," said Alice; "but it's useful to the people that name them, I suppose. If not, why do things have names at all?"[2]

"I ca'n't say," the Gnat replied. "Further on, in the wood down there, they've got no names—however, go on with your list of insects: you're wasting time."

"Well, there's the Horse-fly," Alice began, counting off the names on her fingers.

"All right," said the Gnat. "Half way up that bush, you'll see a Rocking-horse-fly, if you look. It's made entirely of wood, and gets about by swinging itself from branch to branch."

"What does it live on?" Alice asked, with great curiosity.

"Sap and sawdust," said the Gnat. "Go on with the list."

2. Alice here plays with another theory of language, later to be developed by Humpty Dumpty: that names are arbitrary designations imposed on things for the convenience of humans.

Alice looked at the Rocking-horse-fly with great interest, and made up her mind that it must have been just repainted, it looked so bright and sticky; and then she went on.

"And there's the Dragon-fly."

"Look on the branch above your head," said the Gnat, "and there you'll find a Snap-dragon-fly. Its body is made of plum-pudding, its wings of holly-leaves, and its head is a raisin burning in brandy."

"And what does it live on?" Alice asked, as before.

"Frumenty[3] and mince-pie," the Gnat replied; "and it makes its nest in a Christmas-box."

"And then there's the Butterfly," Alice went on, after she had taken a good look at the insect with its head on fire, and had thought to herself, "I wonder if that's the reason insects are so fond of flying into candles—because they want to turn into Snap-dragon-flies!"

"Crawling at your feet," said the Gnat (Alice drew her feet back in some alarm), "you may observe a Bread-and-butter-fly. Its wings are thin slices of bread-and-butter, its body is a crust, and its head is a lump of sugar."

"And what does *it* live on?"

"Weak tea with cream in it."

A new difficulty came into Alice's head. "Supposing it couldn't find any?" she suggested.

"Then it would die, of course."

"But that must happen very often," Alice remarked thoughtfully.

"It always happens," said the Gnat.

3. Frumenty is a dessert made of boiled wheat flavored with sugar, spice, or raisins.

After this, Alice was silent for a minute or two, pondering. The Gnat amused itself meanwhile by humming round and round her head: at last it settled again and remarked "I suppose you don't want to lose your name?"

"No, indeed," Alice said, a little anxiously.

"And yet I don't know," the Gnat went on in a careless tone: "only think how convenient it would be if you could manage to go home without it! For instance, if the governess wanted to call you to your lessons, she would call out 'Come here——,' and there she would have to leave off, because there wouldn't be any name for her to call, and of course you wouldn't have to go, you know."

"That would never do, I'm sure," said Alice: "the governess would never think of excusing me lessons for that. If she couldn't remember my name, she'd call me 'Miss,' as the servants do."

"Well, if she said 'Miss,' and didn't say anything more," the Gnat remarked, "of course you'd miss your lessons. That's a joke. I wish *you* had made it."

"Why do you wish *I* had made it?" Alice asked. "It's a very bad one."

But the Gnat only sighed deeply, while two large tears came rolling down its cheeks.

"You shouldn't make jokes," Alice said, "if it makes you so unhappy."

Then came another of those melancholy little sighs, and this time the poor Gnat really seemed to have sighed itself away, for, when Alice looked up, there was nothing whatever to be seen on the twig, and, as she was getting quite chilly with sitting still so long, she got up and walked on.

She very soon came to an open field, with a wood on the other side of it: it looked much darker than the last wood, and Alice felt a *little* timid about going into it. However, on second thoughts, she made up her mind to go on: "for I certainly won't go *back*," she thought to herself, and this was the only way to the Eighth Square.

"This must be the wood," she said thoughtfully to herself, "where things have no names. I wonder what'll become of *my* name when I go in? I shouldn't like to lose it at all—because they'd have to give me another, and it would be almost certain to be an ugly one. But then the fun would be, trying to find the creature that had got my old name! That's just like the advertisements, you know, when people lose dogs——'answers to the name of "Dash": had on a brass collar'—just fancy calling everything you met 'Alice,' till one of them answered! Only they wouldn't answer at all, if they were wise."

She was rambling on in this way when she reached the wood: it looked very cool and shady. "Well, at any rate it's a great comfort," she said as she stepped under the trees, "after being so hot, to get into the—into the—into *what?*" she went on, rather surprised at not being able to think of the word. "I mean to get under the—under the—under *this*, you know!" putting her hand on the trunk of the tree. "What *does* it call itself, I wonder? I do believe it's got no name—why, to be sure it hasn't!"

She stood silent for a minute, thinking: then she suddenly began again. "Then it really *has* happened, after all! And now, who am I? I *will* remember, if I can! I'm determined to do it!" But being determined didn't help her much, and all she could say, after a great deal of puzzling, was "L, I *know* it begins with L!"[4]

Just then a Fawn came wandering by: it looked at Alice with its large gentle eyes, but didn't seem at all frightened. "Here then! Here then!" Alice said, as she held out her hand and tried to stroke it; but it only started back a little, and then stood looking at her again.

"What do you call yourself?" the Fawn said at last. Such a soft sweet voice it had!

"I wish I knew!" thought poor Alice. She answered, rather sadly, "Nothing, just now."

"Think again," it said: "that wo'n't do."

Alice thought, but nothing came of it. "Please, would you tell me what *you* call yourself?" she said timidly. "I think that might help a little."

4. Liddell begins with *L*.

"I'll tell you, if you'll come a little further on," the Fawn said. "I ca'n't remember *here*."

So they walked on together through the wood, Alice with her arms clasped lovingly round the soft neck of the Fawn, till they came out into another open field, and here the Fawn gave a sudden bound into the air, and shook itself free from Alice's arm. "I'm a Fawn!" it cried out in a voice of delight. "And, dear me! you're a human child!" A sudden look of alarm came into its beautiful brown eyes, and in another moment it had darted away at full speed.

Alice stood looking after it, almost ready to cry with vexation at having lost her dear little fellow-traveler so suddenly. "However, I know my name now," she said: "that's *some* comfort. Alice— Alice—I wo'n't forget it again. And now, which of these finger-posts ought I to follow, I wonder?"

It was not a very difficult question to answer, as there was only one road through the wood, and the two finger-posts both pointed along it. "I'll settle it," Alice said to herself, "when the road divides and they point different ways."

But this did not seem likely to happen. She went on and on, a long way, but, wherever the road divided, there were sure to be two finger-posts pointing the same way, one marked "TO TWEEDLEDUM'S HOUSE," and the other "TO THE HOUSE OF TWEEDLEDEE."

"I do believe," said Alice at last, "that they live in the *same* house! I wonder I never thought of that before—But I ca'n't stay there long. I'll just call and say 'How d'ye do?' and ask them the way out of the wood. If I could only get to the Eighth Square before it gets dark!" So she wandered on, talking to herself as she went, till, on turning a sharp corner, she came upon two fat little men, so suddenly that she could not help starting back, but in another moment she recovered herself, feeling sure that they must be

Chapter IV

TWEEDLEDUM AND TWEEDLEDEE

They were standing under a tree, each with an arm round the other's neck, and Alice knew which was which in a moment, because one of them had 'DUM' embroidered on his collar, and the other 'DEE.' "I suppose they've each got 'TWEEDLE' round at the back of the collar," she said to herself.

They stood so still that she quite forgot they were alive, and she was just going round to see if the word 'TWEEDLE' was written at the back of each collar, when she was startled by a voice coming from the one marked 'DUM.'

"If you think we're wax-works," he said, "you ought to pay, you know. Wax-works weren't made to be looked at for nothing. Nohow!"

"Contrariwise," added the one marked 'DEE,' "if you think we're alive, you ought to speak."

"I'm sure I'm very sorry," was all Alice could say; for the words of the old song kept ringing through her head like the ticking of a clock, and she could hardly help saying them out loud:—

> "Tweedledum and Tweedledee
>   Agreed to have a battle;
> For Tweedledum said Tweedledee
>   Had spoiled his nice new rattle.

"Just then flew down a monstrous crow,
  As black as a tar-barrel;
Which frightened both the heroes so,
  They quite forgot their quarrel."[5]

"I know what you're thinking about," said Tweedledum; "but it isn't so, nohow."

"Contrariwise," continued Tweedledee, "if it was so, it might be; and if it were so, it would be; but as it isn't, it ain't. That's logic."

"I was thinking," Alice said politely, "which is the best way out of this wood: it's getting so dark. Would you tell me, please?"

But the fat little men only looked at each other and grinned.

They looked so exactly like a couple of great schoolboys, that Alice couldn't help pointing her finger at Tweedledum, and saying "First Boy!"

"Nohow!" Tweedledum cried out briskly, and shut his mouth up again with a snap.

"Next Boy!" said Alice, passing on to Tweedledee, though she felt quite certain he would only shout out "Contrariwise!" and so he did.

"You've begun wrong!" cried Tweedledum. "The first thing in a visit is to say 'How d'ye do?' and shake hands!" And here the two brothers gave each other a hug, and then they held out the two hands that were free, to shake hands with her.

Alice did not like shaking hands with either of them first, for fear of hurting the other one's feelings; so, as the best way out of the difficulty, she took hold of both hands at once: the next moment they were dancing round in a ring. This seemed quite natural (she remembered afterwards), and she was not even surprised to hear music playing: it seemed to come from the tree under which they were dancing, and it was done (as well as she could make it out) by the branches rubbing one across the other, like fiddles and fiddle-sticks.

"But it certainly *was* funny," (Alice said afterwards, when she was telling her sister the history of all this,) "to find myself singing '*Here we go round the mulberry bush.*' I don't know when I began it, but somehow I felt as if I'd been singing it a long long time!"

The other two dancers were fat, and very soon out of breath. "Four times round is enough for one dance," Tweedledum panted out, and they left off dancing as suddenly as they had begun: the music stopped at the same moment.

Then they let go of Alice's hands, and stood looking at her for a minute: there was a rather awkward pause, as Alice didn't know

5. Dodgson takes over this nursery rhyme unaltered from one of its traditional versions. The rhyme was collected in James Orchard Halliwell's *The Nursery Rhymes of England* (first edition, 1842).

how to begin a conversation with people she had just been dancing with. "It would never do to say 'How d'ye do?' *now*," she said to herself: "we seem to have got beyond that, somehow!"

"I hope you're not much tired?" she said at last.

"Nohow. And thank you *very* much for asking," said Tweedledum.

"So *much* obliged!" added Tweedledee. "You like poetry?"

"Ye-es, pretty well—*some* poetry," Alice said doubtfully. "Would you tell me which road leads out of the wood?"

"What shall I repeat to her?" said Tweedledee, looking round at Tweedledum with great solemn eyes, and not noticing Alice's question.

"'*The Walrus and the Carpenter*' is the longest," Tweedledum replied, giving his brother an affectionate hug.

Tweedledee began instantly:

"The sun was shining——"

Here Alice ventured to interrupt him. "If it's *very* long," she said, as politely as she could, "would you please tell me first which road——"

Tweedledee smiled gently, and began again: ·

"The sun was shining on the sea,
    Shining with all his might:
He did his very best to make
    The billows smooth and bright—
And this was odd, because it was
    The middle of the night.

The moon was shining sulkily,
    Because she thought the sun
Had got no business to be there
    After the day was done—
'It's very rude of him,' she said,
    'To come and spoil the fun!'

The sea was wet as wet could be,
    The sands were dry as dry.
You could not see a cloud, because
    No cloud was in the sky:
No birds were flying overhead—
    There were no birds to fly.

The Walrus and the Carpenter
    Were walking close at hand:
They wept like anything to see
    Such quantities of sand:

'If this were only cleared away,'
　　They said, 'it *would* be grand!'

'If seven maids with seven mops
　　Swept it for half a year,
Do you suppose,' the Walrus said,
　　'That they could get it clear?'
'I doubt it,' said the Carpenter,
　　And shed a bitter tear.

'O Oysters, come and walk with us!'
　　The Walrus did beseech.
'A pleasant walk, a pleasant talk,
　　Along the briny beach:
We cannot do with more than four,
　　To give a hand to each.'

The eldest Oyster looked at him,
　　But never a word he said:
The eldest Oyster winked his eye,
　　And shook his heavy head—
Meaning to say he did not choose
　　To leave the oyster-bed.

But four young Oysters hurried up,
　　All eager for the treat:
Their coats were brushed, their faces washed,
　　Their shoes were clean and neat—
And this was odd, because, you know,
　　They hadn't any feet.

Four other Oysters followed them,
   And yet another four;
And thick and fast they came at last,
   And more, and more, and more—
All hopping through the frothy waves,
   And scrambling to the shore.

The Walrus and the Carpenter
   Walked on a mile or so,
And then they rested on a rock
   Conveniently low:
And all the little Oysters stood
   And waited in a row.

'The time has come,' the Walrus said,
   'To talk of many things:
Of shoes—and ships—and sealing wax—
   Of cabbages—and kings—
And why the sea is boiling hot—
   And whether pigs have wings.'

'But wait a bit,' the Oysters cried,
   'Before we have our chat;
For some of us are out of breath,
   And all of us are fat!'
'No hurry!' said the Carpenter.
   They thanked him much for that.

'A loaf of bread,' the Walrus said,
   'Is what we chiefly need:

Pepper and vinegar besides
   Are very good indeed—
Now, if you're ready, Oysters dear,
   We can begin to feed.'

'But not on us!' the Oysters cried,
   Turning a little blue.
'After such kindness, that would be
   A dismal thing to do!'
'The night is fine,' the Walrus said.
   'Do you admire the view?

'It was so kind of you to come!
   And you are very nice!'
The Carpenter said nothing but
   'Cut us another slice.
I wish you were not quite so deaf—
   I've had to ask you twice!'

'It seems a shame,' the Walrus said,
   'To play them such a trick,
After we've brought them out so far,
   And made them trot so quick!'
The Carpenter said nothing but
   'The butter's spread too thick!'

'I weep for you,' the Walrus said:
   'I deeply sympathize.'
With sobs and tears he sorted out

Those of the largest size,
Holding his pocket-handkerchief
Before his streaming eyes.

'O Oysters,' said the Carpenter,
'You've had a pleasant run!
Shall we be trotting home again?'
But answer came there none—
And this was scarcely odd, because
They'd eaten every one."[6]

"I like the Walrus best," said Alice: "because he was a *little* sorry for the poor oysters."

"He ate more than the Carpenter, though," said Tweedledee. "You see he held his handkerchief in front, so that the Carpenter couldn't count how many he took: contrariwise."

"That was mean!" Alice said indignantly. "Then I like the Carpenter best—if he didn't eat so many as the Walrus."

"But he ate as many as he could get," said Tweedledum.

This was a puzzler. After a pause, Alice began, "Well! They were *both* very unpleasant characters——" Here she checked herself in some alarm, at hearing something that sounded to her like the puffing of a large steam-engine in the wood near them, though she feared it was more likely to be a wild beast. "Are there any lions or tigers about here?" she asked timidly.

"It's only the Red King snoring," said Tweedledee.

"Come and look at him!" the brothers cried, and they each took one of Alice's hands, and led her up to where the King was sleeping.

"Isn't he a *lovely* sight?" said Tweedledum.

Alice couldn't say honestly that he was. He had a tall red night-cap on, with a tassel, and he was lying crumpled up into a sort of untidy heap, and snoring loud—"fit to snore his head off!" as Tweedledum remarked.

---

6. Although "The Walrus and the Carpenter" is written in the meter of Thomas Hood's "The Dream of Eugene Aram," a poem about a schoolteacher who is discovered to be a murderer, Dodgson claimed that he "had no particular poem in mind" (*Letters* 1,177; see full citation on p. 251). For Savile Clarke's theatrical version of the Alice books, Dodgson added a final stanza:

The Carpenter he ceased to sob
The Walrus ceased to weep;
They'd finished all the oysters;
And they laid them down to sleep—
And of their craft and cruelty
The punishment to reap.

This verse was followed by a scene in which the ghosts of three oysters stamp on the chests of the sleeping Walrus and Carpenter. The scene is reprinted in R. L. Green's edition of *The Diaries of Lewis Carroll* (II, 446–47: see Selected Bibliography).

"I'm afraid he'll catch cold with lying on the damp grass," said Alice, who was a very thoughtful little girl.

"He's dreaming now," said Tweedledee: "and what do you think he's dreaming about?"

Alice said "Nobody can guess that."

"Why, about *you!*" Tweedledee exclaimed, clapping his hands triumphantly. "And if he left off dreaming about you, where do you suppose you'd be?"

"Where I am now, of course," said Alice.

"Not you!" Tweedledee retorted contemptuously. "You'd be nowhere. Why, you're only a sort of thing in his dream!"

"'If that there King was to wake," added Tweedledum, "you'd go out—bang!—just like a candle!"

"I shouldn't!" Alice exclaimed indignantly. "Besides, if *I'm* only a sort of thing in his dream, what are *you*, I should like to know?"

"Ditto," said Tweedledum.

"Ditto, ditto!" cried Tweedledee.

He shouted this so loud that Alice couldn't help saying "Hush! You'll be waking him, I'm afraid, if you make so much noise."

"Well, it's no use *your* talking about waking him," said Tweedledum, "when you're only one of the things in his dream. You know very well you're not real."

"I *am* real!" said Alice, and began to cry.

"You wo'n't make yourself a bit realler by crying," Tweedledee remarked: "there's nothing to cry about."

"If I wasn't real," Alice said—half laughing through her tears, it all seemed so ridiculous—"I shouldn't be able to cry."

"I hope you don't suppose those are *real* tears?" Tweedledum interrupted in a tone of great contempt.

"I know they're talking nonsense," Alice thought to herself: "and it's foolish to cry about it." So she brushed away her tears, and went on, as cheerfully as she could, "At any rate I'd better be getting out of the wood, for really it's coming on very dark. Do you think it's going to rain?"

Tweedledum spread a large umbrella over himself and his brother, and looked up into it. "No, I don't think it is," he said: "at least—not under *here*. Nohow."

"But it may rain *outside*?"

"It may—if it chooses," said Tweedledee: "we've no objection. Contrariwise."

"Selfish things!" thought Alice, and she was just going to say "Good-night" and leave them, when Tweedledum sprang out from under the umbrella, and seized her by the wrist.

"Do you see *that*?" he said, in a voice choking with passion, and his eyes grew large and yellow all in a moment, as he pointed with a trembling finger at a small white thing lying under the tree.

"It's only a rattle," Alice said, after a careful examination of the little white thing. "Not a rattle-*snake*, you know," she added hastily, thinking that he was frightened: "only an old rattle—quite old and broken."

"I knew it was!" cried Tweedledum, beginning to stamp about wildly and tear his hair. "It's spoilt, of course!" Here he looked at Tweedledee, who immediately sat down on the ground, and tried to hide himself under the umbrella.

Alice laid her hand upon his arm, and said, in a soothing tone, "You needn't be so angry about an old rattle."

"But it *isn't* old!" Tweedledum cried, in a greater fury than ever. "It's *new*, I tell you——I bought it yesterday—my nice NEW RATTLE!" and his voice rose to a perfect scream.[7]

All this time Tweedledee was trying his best to fold up the umbrella, with himself in it: which was such an extraordinary thing to do, that it quite took off Alice's attention from the angry brother. But he couldn't quite succeed, and it ended in his rolling over, bundled up in the umbrella, with only his head out: and there he lay, opening and shutting his mouth and his large eyes—"looking more like a fish than anything else," Alice thought.

"Of course you agree to have a battle?" Tweedledum said in a calmer tone.

"I suppose so," the other sulkily replied, as he crawled out of the umbrella: "only *she* must help us to dress up, you know."

So the two brothers went off hand-in-hand into the wood, and returned in a minute with their arms full of things—such as bolsters, blankets, hearth-rugs, table-cloths, dish-covers, and coalscuttles. "I hope you're a good hand at pinning and tying strings?" Tweedledum remarked. "Every one of these things has got to go on, somehow or other."

Alice said afterwards she had never seen such a fuss made about anything in all her life—the way those two bustled about—and the quantity of things they put on—and the trouble they gave her in tying strings and fastening buttons—"Really they'll be more like bundles of old clothes than anything else, by the time they're ready!" she said to herself, as she arranged a bolster round the neck of Tweedledee, "to keep his head from being cut off," as he said.

"You know," he added very gravely, "it's one of the most serious things that can possibly happen to one in a battle—to get one's head cut off."

Alice laughed loud: but she managed to turn it into a cough, for fear of hurting his feelings.

"Do I look very pale?" said Tweedledum, coming up to have his helmet tied on. (He *called* it a helmet, though it certainly looked much more like a saucepan.)

"Well—yes—a *little*," Alice replied gently.

"I'm very brave, generally," he went on in a low voice: "only to-day I happen to have a headache."

"And *I've* got a toothache!" said Tweedledee, who had overheard the remark. "I'm far worse than you!"

---

7. The rattle by Tweedledum's foot in Tenniel's drawing is not a baby's rattle, but rather one used by watchmen as an instrument of alarm or warning (Gardner, p. 191).

"Then you'd better not fight to-day," said Alice, thinking it a good opportunity to make peace.

"We *must* have a bit of a fight, but I don't care about going on long," said Tweedledum. "What's the time now?"

Tweedledee looked at his watch, and said "Half-past four."

"Let's fight till six, and then have dinner," said Tweedledum.

"Very well," the other said, rather sadly: "and *she* can watch us— only you'd better not come *very* close," he added: "I generally hit every thing I can see—when I get really excited."

"And *I* hit every thing within reach," cried Tweedledum, "whether I can see it or not!"

Alice laughed. "You must hit the *trees* pretty often, I should think," she said.

Tweedledum looked round him with a satisfied smile. "I don't suppose," he said, "there'll be a tree left standing, for ever so far round, by the time we've finished!"

"And all about a rattle!" said Alice, still hoping to make them a *little* ashamed of fighting for such a trifle.

"I shouldn't have minded it so much," said Tweedledum, "if it hadn't been a new one."

"I wish the monstrous crow would come!" thought Alice.

"There's only one sword, you know," Tweedledum said to his brother: "but *you* can have the umbrella—it's quite as sharp. Only we must begin quick. It's getting as dark as it can."

"And darker," said Tweedledee.

It was getting dark so suddenly that Alice thought there must be a thunderstorm coming on. "What a thick black cloud that is!" she said. "And how fast it comes! Why, I do believe it's got wings!"

"It's the crow!" Tweedledum cried out in a shrill voice of alarm; and the two brothers took to their heels and were out of sight in a moment.

Alice ran a little way into the wood, and stopped under a large tree. "It can never get at me *here*," she thought: "it's far too large to squeeze itself in among the trees. But I wish it wouldn't flap its wings so—it makes quite a hurricane in the wood—here's somebody's shawl being blown away!"

Chapter V

WOOL AND WATER

She caught the shawl as she spoke, and looked about for the owner: in another moment the White Queen came running wildly through the wood, with both arms stretched out wide, as if she were flying, and Alice very civilly went to meet her with the shawl.

"I'm very glad I happened to be in the way," Alice said, as she helped her to put on her shawl again.

The White Queen only looked at her in a helpless frightened sort of way, and kept repeating something in a whisper to herself that sounded like "Bread-and-butter, bread-and-butter," and Alice felt that if there was to be any conversation at all, she must manage it herself. So she began rather timidly: "Am I addressing the White Queen?"

"Well, yes, if you call that a-dressing," the Queen said. "It isn't *my* notion of the thing, at all."

Alice thought it would never do to have an argument at the very beginning of their conversation, so she smiled and said "If your Majesty will only tell me the right way to begin, I'll do it as well as I can."

"But I don't want it done at all!" groaned the poor Queen. "I've been a-dressing myself for the last two hours."

It would have been all the better, as it seemed to Alice, if she had got some one else to dress her, she was so dreadfully untidy. "Every single thing's crooked," Alice thought to herself, "and she's all over pins!—May I put your shawl straight for you?" she added aloud.

"I don't know what's the matter with it!" the Queen said, in a melancholy voice. "It's out of temper, I think. I've pinned it here, and I've pinned it there, but there's no pleasing it!"

"It *ca'n't* go straight, you know, if you pin it all on one side," Alice said as she gently put it right for her; "and dear me, what a state your hair is in!"

"The brush has got entangled in it!" the Queen said with a sigh. "And I lost the comb yesterday."

Alice carefully released the brush, and did her best to get the hair into order. "Come, you look rather better now!" she said, after altering most of the pins. "But really you should have a lady's maid!"

"I'm sure I'll take *you* with pleasure!" the Queen said. "Two pence a week, and jam every other day."

Alice couldn't help laughing, as she said "I don't want you to hire *me*—and I don't care for jam."

"It's very good jam," said the Queen.

"Well, I don't want any to-*day*, at any rate."

"You couldn't have it if you *did* want it," the Queen said. "The rule is, jam to-morrow and jam yesterday—but never jam *to*-day."[8]

"It *must* come sometimes to 'jam to-day,'" Alice objected.

"No, it ca'n't," said the Queen. "It's jam every *other* day: to-day isn't any *other* day, you know."

"I don't understand you," said Alice. "It's dreadfully confusing!"

"That's the effect of living backwards," the Queen said kindly: "it always makes one a little giddy at first—"

"Living backwards!" Alice repeated in great astonishment. "I never heard of such a thing!"

"—but there's one great advantage in it, that one's memory works both ways."

"I'm sure *mine* only works one way," Alice remarked. "I ca'n't remember things before they happen."

"It's a poor sort of memory that only works backwards," the Queen remarked.

"What sort of things do *you* remember best?" Alice ventured to ask.

8. Martin Gardner (p. 196) writes that he has been instructed by several Latin teachers that the Latin word "iam" or "jam" (the letters "i" and "j" may be substituted for one another) means "now" in the past and future tenses, but in the present tense the proper word is "nunc." So one cannot use "iam/jam" in the present, and teachers invoke the Queen's sentence to remind students of this proper usage.

"Oh, things that happened the week after next," the Queen replied in a careless tone. "For instance, now," she went on, sticking a large piece of plaster[9] on her finger as she spoke, "there's the King's Messenger. He's in prison now, being punished: and the trial doesn't even begin till next Wednesday: and of course the crime comes last of all."

"Suppose he never commits the crime?" said Alice.

"That would be all the better, wouldn't it?" the Queen said, as she bound the plaster round her finger with a bit of ribbon.

Alice felt there was no denying *that*. "Of course it would be all the better," she said: "but it wouldn't be all the better his being punished."

"You're wrong *there*, at any rate," said the Queen. "Were *you* ever punished?"

"Only for faults," said Alice.

"And you were all the better for it, I know!" the Queen said triumphantly.

"Yes, but then I *had* done the things I was punished for," said Alice: "that makes all the difference."

"But if you *hadn't* done them," the Queen said, "that would have been better still; better, and better, and better!" Her voice went higher with each "better," till it got quite to a squeak at last.

9. An adhesive bandage.

Alice was just beginning to say "There's a mistake some-where——," when the Queen began screaming, so loud that she had to leave the sentence unfinished. "Oh, oh, oh!" shouted the Queen, shaking her hand about as if she wanted to shake it off. "My finger's bleeding! Oh, oh, oh, oh!"

Her screams were so exactly like the whistle of a steam-engine, that Alice had to hold both her hands over her ears.

"What *is* the matter?" she said, as soon as there was a chance of making herself heard. "Have you pricked your finger?"

"I haven't pricked it *yet*," the Queen said, "but I soon shall—oh, oh, oh!"

"When do you expect to do it?" Alice said, feeling very much inclined to laugh.

"When I fasten my shawl again," the poor Queen groaned out: "the brooch will come undone directly. Oh, oh!" As she said the words the brooch flew open, and the Queen clutched wildly at it, and tried to clasp it again.

"Take care!" cried Alice. "You're holding it all crooked!" And she caught at the brooch; but it was too late: the pin had slipped, and the Queen had pricked her finger.

"That accounts for the bleeding, you see," she said to Alice with a smile. "Now you understand the way things happen here."

"But why don't you scream *now*?" Alice asked, holding her hands ready to put over her ears again.

"Why, I've done all the screaming already," said the Queen. "What would be the good of having it all over again?"

By this time it was getting light. "The crow must have flown away, I think," said Alice: "I'm so glad it's gone. I thought it was the night coming on."

"I wish *I* could manage to be glad!" the Queen said. "Only I never can remember the rule. You must be very happy, living in this wood, and being glad whenever you like!"

"Only it is so *very* lonely here!" Alice said in a melancholy voice; and, at the thought of her loneliness, two large tears came rolling down her cheeks.

"Oh, don't go on like that!" cried the poor Queen, wringing her hands in despair. "Consider what a great girl you are. Consider what a long way you've come to-day. Consider what o'clock it is. Consider anything, only don't cry!"

Alice could not help laughing at this, even in the midst of her tears. "Can *you* keep from crying by considering things?" she asked.[1]

---

1. In the preface to *Pillow-Problems*, the second part of *Curiosa Mathematica*, published in 1893 under Dodgson's own name, he recommends the working-out in one's head of mathematical problems as a way to keep skeptical, blasphemous, and unholy thoughts at bay during wakeful night-time hours.

"That's the way it's done," the Queen said with great decision: "nobody can do two things at once, you know. Let's consider your age to begin with——how old are you?"

"I'm seven and a half, exactly."

"You needn't say 'exactly,'" the Queen remarked. "I can believe it without that. Now I'll give *you* something to believe. I'm just one hundred and one, five months and a day."

"I ca'n't believe *that*!" said Alice.

"Ca'n't you?" the Queen said in a pitying tone. "Try again: draw a long breath, and shut your eyes."

Alice laughed. "There's no use trying," she said: "one *ca'n't* believe impossible things."

"I daresay you haven't had much practice," said the Queen. "When I was your age, I always did it for half-an-hour a day. Why, sometimes I've believed as many as six impossible things before breakfast. There goes the shawl again!"

The brooch had come undone as she spoke, and a sudden gust of wind blew the Queen's shawl across a little brook. The Queen spread out her arms again, and went flying after it, and this time she succeeded in catching it for herself. "I've got it!" she cried in a triumphant tone. "Now you shall see me pin it on again, all by myself!"

"Then I hope your finger is better now?" Alice said very politely, as she crossed the little brook after the Queen.

*   *   *   *   *

   *   *   *   *

*   *   *   *   *

"Oh, much better!" cried the Queen, her voice rising into a squeak as she went on. "Much be-etter! Be-etter! Be-e-e-etter! Be-e-ehh!" The last word ended in a long bleat, so like a sheep that Alice quite started.

She looked at the Queen, who seemed to have suddenly wrapped herself up in wool. Alice rubbed her eyes, and looked again. She couldn't make out what had happened at all. Was she in a shop? And was that really—was it really a *sheep* that was sitting on the other side of the counter? Rub as she would, she could make nothing more of it: she was in a little dark shop, leaning with her elbows on the counter, and opposite to her was an old Sheep, sitting in an arm-chair, knitting, and every now and then leaving off to look at her through a great pair of spectacles.[2]

---

2. One of the central features of the theatrical pantomimes Dodgson frequently attended was a series of transformation scenes in which one setting was ingeniously transformed into another. This transformation, like others in *Through the Looking-Glass*, owes something to pantomime. Tenniel's illustration of the Shop itself is modeled on a shop in Oxford.

"What is it you want to buy?" the Sheep said at last, looking up for a moment from her knitting.

"I don't *quite* know yet," Alice said very gently. "I should like to look all round me first, if I might."

"You may look in front of you, and on both sides, if you like," said the Sheep; "but you ca'n't look *all* round you—unless you've got eyes at the back of your head."

But these, as it happened, Alice had *not* got: so she contented herself with turning round, looking at the shelves as she came to them.

The shop seemed to be full of all manner of curious things—but the oddest part of it all was that, whenever she looked hard at any shelf, to make out exactly what it had on it, that particular shelf was always quite empty, though the others round it were crowded as full as they could hold.

"Things flow about so here!" she said at last in a plaintive tone, after she had spent a minute or so in vainly pursuing a large bright thing that looked sometimes like a doll and sometimes like a work-box, and was always in the shelf next above the one she was looking at. "And this one is the most provoking of all—but I'll tell you what——" she added, as a sudden thought struck her. "I'll follow it up to the very top shelf of all. It'll puzzle it to go through the ceiling, I expect!"

But even this plan failed: the 'thing' went through the ceiling as quietly as possible, as if it were quite used to it.

"Are you a child or a teetotum?"[3] the Sheep said, as she took up another pair of needles. "You'll make me giddy soon, if you go on turning round like that." She was now working with fourteen pairs at once, and Alice couldn't help looking at her in great astonishment.

"How *can* she knit with so many?" the puzzled child thought to herself. "She gets more and more like a porcupine every minute!"

"Can you row?" the Sheep asked, handing her a pair of knitting-needles as she spoke.

"Yes, a little—but not on land—and not with needles——" Alice was beginning to say, when suddenly the needles turned into oars in her hands, and she found they were in a little boat, gliding along between banks: so there was nothing for it but to do her best.

"Feather!" cried the Sheep, as she took up another pair of needles.

This didn't sound like a remark that needed any answer: so Alice said nothing, but pulled away. There was something very queer about the water, she thought, as every now and then the oars got fast in it, and would hardly come out again.

"Feather! Feather!" the Sheep cried again, taking more needles. "You'll be catching a crab directly."[4]

"A dear little crab!" thought Alice. "I should like that."

"Didn't you hear me say 'Feather'?" the Sheep cried angrily, taking up quite a bunch of needles.

"Indeed I did," said Alice: "you've said it very often—and very loud. Please, where *are* the crabs?"

"In the water, of course!" said the Sheep, sticking some of the needles into her hair, as her hands were full. "Feather, I say!"

"*Why* do you say 'Feather' so often?" Alice asked at last, rather vexed. "I'm not a bird!"

"You are," said the Sheep: "you're a little goose."

This offended Alice a little, so there was no more conversation for a minute or two, while the boat glided gently on, sometimes among beds of weeds (which made the oars stick fast in the water,

3. A small top with several flat surfaces bearing numbers. It is used to play games—to direct players the number of spaces they may move on a board, for example.
4. To feather is to turn an oar-blade horizontally on the return stroke. If the blade touches the water on the return stroke, the rower has caught a crab. Because the rower's body is moving forward on the return stroke, to catch a crab may drive the oar handle into her chest or chin and even, as happens to Alice, unseat her.

worse than ever), and sometimes under trees, but always with the same tall river-banks frowning over their heads.

"Oh, please! There are some scented rushes!" Alice cried in a sudden transport of delight. "There really are—and *such* beauties!"

"You needn't say 'please' to *me* about 'em," the Sheep said, without looking up from her knitting: "I didn't put 'em there, and I'm not going to take 'em away."

"No, but I meant—please, may we wait and pick some?" Alice pleaded. "If you don't mind stopping the boat for a minute."

"How am *I* to stop it?" said the Sheep. "If you leave off rowing, it'll stop of itself."

So the boat was left to drift down the stream as it would, till it glided gently in among the waving rushes. And then the little sleeves were carefully rolled up, and the little arms were plunged in elbow-deep, to get hold of the rushes a good long way down before breaking them off—and for a while Alice forgot all about the Sheep and the knitting, as she bent over the side of the boat, with just the ends of her tangled hair dipping into the water—while with bright eager eyes she caught at one bunch after another of the darling scented rushes.

"I only hope the boat wo'n't tipple over!" she said to herself. "Oh, *what* a lovely one! Only I couldn't quite reach it." And it certainly *did* seem a little provoking ("almost as if it happened on purpose," she thought) that, though she managed to pick plenty of beautiful rushes as the boat glided by, there was always a more lovely one that she couldn't reach.

"The prettiest are always further!" she said at last, with a sigh at the obstinacy of the rushes in growing so far off, as, with flushed cheeks and dripping hair and hands, she scrambled back into her place, and began to arrange her new-found treasures.

What mattered it to her just then that the rushes had begun to fade, and to lose all their scent and beauty, from the very moment that she picked them? Even real scented rushes, you know, last only a very little while—and these, being dream-rushes, melted away almost like snow, as they lay in heaps at her feet—but Alice hardly noticed this, there were so many other curious things to think about.

They hadn't gone much farther before the blade of one of the oars got fast in the water and *wouldn't* come out again (so Alice explained it afterwards), and the consequence was that the handle of it caught her under the chin, and, in spite of a series of little shrieks of "Oh, oh, oh!" from poor Alice, it swept her straight off the seat, and down among the heap of rushes.

However, she wasn't a bit hurt, and was soon up again: the Sheep went on with her knitting all the while, just as if nothing had happened. "That was a nice crab you caught!" she remarked, as Alice

got back into her place, very much relieved to find herself still in the boat.

"Was it? I didn't see it," said Alice, peeping cautiously over the side of the boat into the dark water. "I wish it hadn't let go—I should so like a little crab to take home with me!" But the Sheep only laughed scornfully, and went on with her knitting.

"Are there many crabs here?" said Alice.

"Crabs, and all sorts of things," said the Sheep: "plenty of choice, only make up your mind. Now, what *do* you want to buy?"

"To buy!" Alice echoed in a tone that was half astonished and half frightened—for the oars, and the boat, and the river, had vanished all in a moment, and she was back again in the little dark shop.

"I should like to buy an egg, please," she said timidly. "How do you sell them?"

"Fivepence farthing for one—twopence for two," the Sheep replied.

"Then two are cheaper than one?" Alice said in a surprised tone, taking out her purse.

"Only you *must* eat them both, if you buy two," said the Sheep.

"Then I'll have *one*, please," said Alice, as she put the money down on the counter. For she thought to herself, "They mightn't be at all nice, you know."[5]

The Sheep took the money, and put it away in a box: then she said "I never put things into people's hands—that would never do—you must get it for yourself." And so saying, she went off to the other end of the shop, and set the egg upright on a shelf.

"I wonder *why* it wouldn't do?" thought Alice, as she groped her way among the tables and chairs, for the shop was very dark towards the end. "The egg seems to get further away the more I walk towards it. Let me see, is this a chair? Why, it's got branches, I declare! How very odd to find trees growing here! And actually here's a little brook! Well, this is the very queerest shop I ever saw!"

✲   ✲   ✲   ✲   ✲

✲   ✲   ✲   ✲

✲   ✲   ✲   ✲   ✲

So she went on, wondering more and more at every step, as everything turned into a tree the moment she came up to it, and she quite expected the egg to do the same.

---

5. In his edition of Dodgson's diaries (see Selected Bibliography), R. L. Green quotes one of Dodgson's contemporaries at Oxford as saying that "a Christ Church undergraduate knew that if he ordered one boiled egg he was served with two, but one was invariably bad" (I, 176).

Chapter VI

HUMPTY DUMPTY

However, the egg only got larger and larger, and more and more human: when she had come within a few yards of it, she saw that it had eyes and a nose and a mouth; and, when she had come close to it, she saw clearly that it was HUMPTY DUMPTY himself. "It ca'n't be anybody else!" she said to herself. "I'm as certain of it, as if his name were written all over his face!"

It might have been written a hundred times, easily, on that enormous face. Humpty Dumpty was sitting, with his legs crossed like a Turk, on the top of a high wall—such a narrow one that Alice quite wondered how he could keep his balance—and, as his eyes were steadily fixed in the opposite direction, and he didn't take the least notice of her, she thought he must be a stuffed figure after all.

"And how exactly like an egg he is!" she said aloud, standing with her hands ready to catch him, for she was every moment expecting him to fall.

"It's *very* provoking," Humpty Dumpty said after a long silence, looking away from Alice as he spoke, "to be called an egg—*very*!"

"I said you *looked* like an egg, Sir," Alice gently explained. "And some eggs are very pretty, you know," she added, hoping to turn her remark into a sort of compliment.

"Some people," said Humpty Dumpty, looking away from her as usual, "have no more sense than a baby!"

Alice didn't know what to say to this: it wasn't at all like conversation, she thought, as he never said anything to *her*; in fact, his last remark was evidently addressed to a tree—so she stood and softly repeated to herself:—

> "Humpty Dumpty sat on a wall:
> Humpty Dumpty had a great fall.
> All the King's horses and all the King's men
> Couldn't put Humpty Dumpty in his place again."[6]

"That last line is much too long for the poetry," she added, almost out loud, forgetting that Humpty Dumpty would hear her.

---

6. This nursery rhyme, which again Dodgson takes over in one of its traditional forms, is very old and common in several languages. It is, as Iona and Peter Opie point out in *The Oxford Dictionary of Nursery Rhymes* (Oxford, 1951: pp. 213–16), a riddle, which may explain why Humpty Dumpty does not know or will not admit that he is an egg, and begins his conversation with Alice with a riddling contest.

The usual last line is: "Couldn't put Humpty together again." Alice's misremembering of the line not only gives it two additional syllables, as she notices, but also charitably protects Humpty from a graphic description of his fate.

"Don't stand chattering to yourself like that," Humpty Dumpty said, looking at her for the first time, "but tell me your name and your business."

"My *name* is Alice, but——"

"It's a stupid name enough!" Humpty Dumpty interrupted impatiently. "What does it mean?"

"*Must* a name mean something?" Alice asked doubtfully.

"Of course it must," Humpty Dumpty said with a short laugh: "*my* name means the shape I am[7]—and a good handsome shape it is, too. With a name like yours, you might be any shape, almost."

"Why do you sit out here all alone?" said Alice, not wishing to begin an argument.

"Why, because there's nobody with me!" cried Humpty Dumpty. "Did you think I didn't know the answer to *that*? Ask another."

"Don't you think you'd be safer down on the ground?" Alice went on, not with any idea of making another riddle, but simply in her good-natured anxiety for the queer creature. "That wall is so *very* narrow!"

"What tremendously easy riddles you ask!" Humpty Dumpty growled out. "Of course I don't think so! Why, if ever I *did* fall off—which there's no chance of—but *if* I did——" Here he pursed up his lips, and looked so solemn and grand that Alice could hardly help laughing. "*If* I *did* fall," he went on, "*the King has promised me*—ah, you may turn pale, if you like! You didn't think I was going to say that, did you? *The King has promised me—with his very own mouth*—to—to——"

"To send all his horses and all his men," Alice interrupted, rather unwisely.

"Now I declare that's too bad!" Humpty Dumpty cried, breaking into a sudden passion. "You've been listening at doors—and behind trees—and down chimneys—or you couldn't have known it!"

"I haven't indeed!" Alice said very gently. "It's in a book."

"Ah, well! They may write such things in a *book*," Humpty Dumpty said in a calmer tone. "That's what you call a History of England, that is. Now, take a good look at me! I'm one that has spoken to a King, *I* am: mayhap you'll never see such another: and, to show you I'm not proud, you may shake hands with me!" And he grinned almost from ear to ear, as he leant forwards (and as nearly as possible fell off the wall in doing so) and offered Alice his hand. She watched him a little anxiously as she took it. "If he smiled much more the ends of his mouth might meet behind," she thought: "And

---

7. Humpty Dumpty here advances the theory that names have something to do with the nature of the thing they name. Later, in his remarks about "glory," he picks up the other theory Dodgson plays with in this book, that words are wholly arbitrary signs.

then I don't know *what* would happen to his head! I'm afraid it would come off!"

"Yes, all his horses and all his men," Humpty Dumpty went on. "They'd pick me up again in a minute, *they* would! However, this conversation is going on a little too fast: let's go back to the last remark but one."

"I'm afraid I ca'n't quite remember it," Alice said, very politely.

"In that case we start afresh," said Humpty Dumpty, "and it's my turn to choose a subject——" ("He talks about it just as if it was a game!" thought Alice.) "So here's a question for you. How old did you say you were?"

Alice made a short calculation, and said "Seven years and six months."

"Wrong!" Humpty Dumpty exclaimed triumphantly. "You never said a word like it!"

"I thought you meant 'How old *are* you?'" Alice explained.

"If I'd meant that, I'd have said it," said Humpty Dumpty.

Alice didn't want to begin another argument, so she said nothing.

"Seven years and six months!" Humpty Dumpty repeated thoughtfully. "An uncomfortable sort of age. Now if you'd asked *my* advice, I'd have said 'Leave off at seven'——but it's too late now."

"I never ask advice about growing," Alice said indignantly.

"Too proud?" the other enquired.

Alice felt even more indignant at this suggestion. "I mean," she said, "that one ca'n't help growing older."

"*One* ca'n't, perhaps," said Humpty Dumpty; "but *two* can. With proper assistance, you might have left off at seven."

"What a beautiful belt you've got on!" Alice suddenly remarked. (They had had quite enough of the subject of age, she thought: and, if they really were to take turns in choosing subjects, it was *her* turn now.) "At least," she corrected herself on second thoughts, "a beautiful cravat, I should have said—no, a belt, I mean—I beg your pardon!" she added in dismay, for Humpty Dumpty looked thoroughly offended, and she began to wish she hadn't chosen that subject. "If only I knew," she thought to herself, "which was neck and which was waist!"

Evidently Humpty Dumpty was very angry, though he said nothing for a minute or two. When he *did* speak again, it was in a deep growl.

"It is a—*most*—*provoking*—thing," he said at last, "when a person doesn't know a cravat from a belt!"

"I know it's very ignorant of me," Alice said, in so humble a tone that Humpty Dumpty relented.

"It's a cravat, child, and a beautiful one, as you say. It's a present from the White King and Queen. There now!"

"It is really?" said Alice, quite pleased to find that she *had* chosen a good subject, after all.

"They gave it me," Humpty Dumpty continued thoughtfully, as he crossed one knee over the other and clasped his hands round it, "they gave it me—for an un-birthday present."

"I beg your pardon?" Alice said with a puzzled air.

"I'm not offended," said Humpty Dumpty.

"I mean, what *is* an un-birthday present?"

"A present given when it isn't your birthday, of course."

Alice considered a little. "I like birthday presents best," she said at last.

"You don't know what you're talking about!" cried Humpty Dumpty. "How many days are there in a year?"

"Three hundred and sixty-five," said Alice.

"And how many birthdays have you?"

"One."

"And if you take one from three hundred and sixty-five what remains?"

"Three hundred and sixty-four, of course."

Humpty Dumpty looked doubtful. "I'd rather see that done on paper," he said.

Alice couldn't help smiling as she took out her memorandum-book, and worked the sum for him:

$$\frac{\begin{array}{r}365 \\ 1\end{array}}{364}$$

Humpty Dumpty took the book, and looked at it carefully. "That *seems* to be done right——" he began.

"You're holding it upside down!" Alice interrupted.

"To be sure I was!" Humpty Dumpty said gaily, as she turned it round for him. "I thought it looked a little queer. As I was saying, that *seems* to be done right—though I haven't time to look it over thoroughly just now—and that shows that there are three hundred and sixty-four days when you might get un-birthday presents——"

"Certainly," said Alice.

"And only *one* for birthday presents, you know. There's glory for you!"

"I don't know what you mean by 'glory,'" Alice said.

Humpty Dumpty smiled contemptuously. "Of course you don't—till I tell you. I meant 'there's a nice knock-down argument for you!'"

"But 'glory' doesn't mean 'a nice knock-down argument,'" Alice objected.

"When *I* use a word," Humpty Dumpty said, in rather a scornful tone, "it means just what I choose it to mean—neither more nor less."[8]

"The question is," said Alice, "whether you *can* make words mean so many different things."

"The question is," said Humpty Dumpty, "which is to be master——that's all."

Alice was too much puzzled to say anything; so after a minute Humpty Dumpty began again. "They've a temper, some of them—particularly verbs: they're the proudest—adjectives you can do anything with, but not verbs—however, *I* can manage the whole lot of them! Impenetrability! That's what *I* say!"

"Would you tell me, please," said Alice, "what that means?"

"Now you talk like a reasonable child," said Humpty Dumpty, looking very much pleased. "I meant by 'impenetrability' that we've had enough of that subject, and it would be just as well if you'd

8. In *The Annotated Alice* Martin Gardner (p. 214) quotes a passage from Dodgson's *Symbolic Logic: Part I* (1896; see Bartley, Selected Bibliography). Logicians, Dodgson writes, "speak of the Copula of a Proposition 'with bated breath,' almost as if it were a living, conscious Entity, capable of declaring for itself *what* it chooses to mean, and that we, poor human creatures, had nothing to do but to ascertain *what* was its sovereign will and pleasure, and submit to it." As Dodgson prepares for his practice in the book of using words simply as counters in his illustrations of the pleasures of doing logic ("No person is despised who can manage a crocodile"), he maintains "that any writer of a book is fully authorized in attaching any meaning he likes to any word or phrase he intends to use" (p. 165).

mention what you mean to do next, as I suppose you don't mean to stop here all the rest of your life."

"That's a great deal to make one word mean," Alice said in a thoughtful tone.

"When I make a word do a lot of work like that," said Humpty Dumpty, "I always pay it extra."

"Oh!" said Alice. She was too much puzzled to make any other remark.

"Ah, you should see 'em come round me of a Saturday night," Humpty Dumpty went on, wagging his head gravely from side to side, "for to get their wages, you know."

(Alice didn't venture to ask what he paid them with; and so you see I ca'n't tell *you*.)

"You seem very clever at explaining words, Sir," said Alice. "Would you kindly tell me the meaning of the poem called 'Jabberwocky'?"

"Let's hear it," said Humpty Dumpty. "I can explain all the poems that ever were invented—and a good many that haven't been invented just yet."

This sounded very hopeful, so Alice repeated the first verse:—

> " 'Twas brillig, and the slithy toves
>   Did gyre and gimble in the wabe:
> All mimsy were the borogoves,
>   And the mome raths outgrabe."

"That's enough to begin with," Humpty Dumpty interrupted: "there are plenty of hard words there. *'Brillig'* means four o'clock in the afternoon—the time when you begin *broiling* things for dinner."

"That'll do very well," said Alice: "and *'slithy'*?"

"Well, *'slithy'* means 'lithe and slimy.' 'Lithe' is the same as 'active.' You see it's like a portmanteau[9]—there are two meanings packed up into one word."

"I see it now," Alice remarked thoughtfully: "and what are *'toves'*?"

"Well *'toves'* are something like badgers—they're something like lizards—and they're something like corkscrews."

"They must be very curious-looking creatures."

"They are that," said Humpty Dumpty; "also they make their nests under sun-dials—also they live on cheese."

"And what's to *'gyre'*; and to *'gimble'*?"

"To *'gyre'* is to go round and round like a gyroscope. To *'gimble'* is to make holes like a gimblet."

---

9. A portmanteau is a traveling bag that opens, like a book, into two equal compartments. For a further discussion by Dodgson of the portmanteau words of "Jabberwocky," see the preface to *The Hunting of the Snark*, on pp. 220–21 this Norton Critical Edition.

"And '*the wabe*' is the grass-plot round a sun-dial, I suppose?" said Alice, surprised at her own ingenuity.

"Of course it is. It's called '*wabe*', you know, because it goes a long way before it, and a long way behind it——"

"And a long way beyond it on each side," Alice added.

"Exactly so. Well then, '*mimsy*' is 'flimsy and miserable' (there's another portmanteau for you). And a '*borogove*' is a thin shabby-looking bird with its feathers sticking out all round—something like a live mop."

"And then '*mome raths*'?" said Alice. "I'm afraid I'm giving you a great deal of trouble."

"Well, a '*rath*' is a sort of green pig: but '*mome*' I'm not certain about. I think it's short for 'from home'—meaning that they'd lost their way, you know."

"And what does '*outgrabe*' mean?"

"Well, '*outgribing*' is something between bellowing and whistling, with a kind of sneeze in the middle: however, you'll hear it done, maybe—down in the wood yonder—and, when you've once heard it, you'll be *quite* content. Who's been repeating all that hard stuff to you?"

"I read it in a book," said Alice. "But I *had* some poetry repeated to me much easier than that, by—Tweedledee, I think it was."

"As to poetry, you know," said Humpty Dumpty, stretching out one of his great hands, "*I* can repeat poetry as well as other folk, if it comes to that——"

"Oh, it needn't come to that!" Alice hastily said, hoping to keep him from beginning.

"The piece I'm going to repeat," he went on without noticing her remark, "was written entirely for your amusement."

Alice felt that in that case she really *ought* to listen to it; so she sat down, and said "Thank you" rather sadly,

> "In winter, when the fields are white,
> I sing this song for your delight——

only I don't sing it," he added, as an explanation.

"I see you don't," said Alice.

"If you can *see* whether I'm singing or not, you've sharper eyes than most," Humpty Dumpty remarked severely. Alice was silent.

> "In spring, when woods are getting green,
> I'll try and tell you what I mean:"

"Thank you very much," said Alice.

> "In summer, when the days are long,
> Perhaps you'll understand the song:
>
> In autumn, when the leaves are brown,
> Take pen and ink, and write it down."

"I will, if I can remember it so long," said Alice.

"You needn't go on making remarks like that," Humpty Dumpty said: "they're not sensible, and they put me out."

> "I sent a message to the fish:
> I told them 'This is what I wish.'
>
> The little fishes of the sea,
> They sent an answer back to me.

> The little fishes' answer was
> 'We cannot do it, Sir, because———' "

"I'm afraid I don't quite understand," said Alice.
"It gets easier further on," Humpty Dumpty replied.

> "I sent to them again to say
> 'It will be better to obey.'
>
> The fishes answered, with a grin,
> 'Why, what a temper you are in!'
>
> I told them once, I told them twice:
> They would not listen to advice.
>
> I took a kettle large and new,
> Fit for the deed I had to do.
>
> My heart went hop, my heart went thump:
> I filled the kettle at the pump.
>
> Then some one came to me and said
> 'The little fishes are in bed.'

> I said to him, I said it plain,
> 'Then you must wake them up again.'
>
> I said it very loud and clear:
> I went and shouted in his ear."

Humpty Dumpty raised his voice almost to a scream as he repeated this verse, and Alice thought, with a shudder, "I wouldn't have been the messenger for *anything*!"

> "But he was very stiff and proud:
> He said, 'You needn't shout so loud!'
>
> And he was very proud and stiff:
> He said 'I'd go and wake them, if——'
>
> I took a corkscrew from the shelf:
> I went to wake them up myself.
>
> And when I found the door was locked,
> I pulled and pushed and kicked and knocked.
>
> And when I found the door was shut,
> I tried to turn the handle, but——"

There was a long pause.

"Is that all?" Alice timidly asked.

"That's all," said Humpty Dumpty. "Good-bye."

This was rather sudden, Alice thought: but, after such a *very* strong hint that she ought to be going, she felt that it would hardly be civil to stay. So she got up, and held out her hand. "Good-bye, till we meet again!" she said as cheerfully as she could.

"I shouldn't know you again if we *did* meet," Humpty Dumpty replied in a discontented tone, giving her one of his fingers to shake: "you're so exactly like other people."

"The *face* is what one goes by, generally," Alice remarked in a thoughtful tone.

"That's just what I complain of," said Humpty Dumpty. "Your face is the same as everybody has—the two eyes, so——" (marking their places in the air with his thumb) "nose in the middle, mouth under. It's always the same. Now if you had the two eyes on the same side of the nose, for instance—or the mouth at the top—that would be *some* help."

"It wouldn't look nice," Alice objected. But Humpty Dumpty only shut his eyes, and said "Wait till you've tried."

Alice waited a minute to see if he would speak again, but, as he never opened his eyes or took any further notice of her, she said

"Good-bye!" once more, and, getting no answer to this, she quietly walked away: but she couldn't help saying to herself, as she went, "Of all the unsatisfactory——" (she repeated this aloud, as it was a great comfort to have such a long word to say) "of all the unsatisfactory people I *ever* met——" She never finished the sentence, for at this moment a heavy crash shook the forest from end to end.

Chapter VII

THE LION AND THE UNICORN

The next moment soldiers came running through the wood, at first in twos and threes, then ten or twenty together, and at last in such crowds that they seemed to fill the whole forest. Alice got behind a tree, for fear of being run over, and watched them go by.

She thought that in all her life she had never seen soldiers so uncertain on their feet: they were always tripping over something or other, and whenever one went down, several more always fell over him, so that the ground was soon covered with little heaps of men.

Then came the horses. Having four feet, these managed rather better than the foot-soldiers; but even *they* stumbled now and then;

and it seemed to be a regular rule that, whenever a horse stumbled, the rider fell off instantly. The confusion got worse every moment, and Alice was very glad to get out of the wood into an open place, where she found the White King seated on the ground, busily writing in his memorandum-book.

"I've sent them all!" the King cried in a tone of delight, on seeing Alice. "Did you happen to meet any soldiers, my dear, as you came through the wood?"

"Yes, I did," said Alice: "several thousand, I should think."

"Four thousand two hundred and seven, that's the exact number," the King said, referring to his book. "I couldn't send all the horses, you know, because two of them are wanted in the game.[1] And I haven't sent the two Messengers, either. They're both gone to the town. Just look along the road, and tell me if you can see either of them."

"I see nobody on the road," said Alice.

"I only wish *I* had such eyes," the King remarked in a fretful tone. "To be able to see Nobody! And at that distance too! Why, it's as much as *I* can do to see real people, by this light!"

All this was lost on Alice, who was still looking intently along the road, shading her eyes with one hand. "I see somebody now!" she exclaimed at last. "But he's coming very slowly—and what curious attitudes he goes into!" (For the Messenger kept skipping up and down, and wriggling like an eel, as he came along, with his great hands spread out like fans on each side.)

"Not at all," said the King. "He's an Anglo-Saxon Messenger—and those are Anglo-Saxon attitudes.[2] He only does them when he's happy. His name is Haigha." (He pronounced it so as to rhyme with 'mayor.')

"I love my love with an H," Alice couldn't help beginning, "because he is Happy. I hate him with an H, because he is Hideous. I fed him with—with—with Ham-sandwiches and Hay. His name is Haigha, and he lives——"

"He lives on the Hill," the King remarked simply, without the least idea that he was joining in the game, while Alice was still hesitating for the name of a town beginning with H. "The other Mes-

1. The White King holds back two horses (knights) for the chess game.
2. Harry Morgan Ayres, in *Carroll's Alice* (see Selected Bibliography), reproduces (pp. 70–71) some illustrations from a tenth-century Old English manuscript in which figures strike attitudes similar to those described in this passage. The burlesque of the seemingly rude and awkward line and composition of medieval tapestry and woodcuts was a common practice of mid-nineteenth-century comic draftsmen: Richard Doyle, for example, published a popular series in *Punch* in the 1850s in which he parodied the style of the eleventh-century Bayeux tapestry to depict the customs of nineteenth-century England.

senger's called Hatta. I must have *two*, you know—to come and go. One to come, and one to go."[3]

"I beg your pardon?" said Alice.

"It isn't respectable to beg," said the King.

"I only meant that I didn't understand," said Alice. "Why one to come and one to go?"

"Don't I tell you?" the King repeated impatiently. "I must have *two*—to fetch and carry. One to fetch, and one to carry."

At this moment the Messenger arrived: he was far too much out of breath to say a word, and could only wave his hands about, and make the most fearful faces at the poor King.

"This young lady loves you with an H," the King said, introducing Alice in the hope of turning off the Messenger's attention from himself—but it was of no use—the Anglo-Saxon attitudes only got more extraordinary every moment, while the great eyes rolled wildly from side to side.

3. In *Carroll's Alice*, Ayres also suggests (pp. 66–72) that the name of Haigha is derived from that of Daniel Henry Haigh, a nineteenth-century student of Anglo-Saxon language and literature; and that the name of Hatta may derive from a misconception by an early nineteenth-century author of a history of the Anglo-Saxons that the word *hatte* ("is called") in an early manuscript is a surname. *Hatte, Hatta,* and *Hatter*—Hatta turns out to be the Mad Hatter—is a conjunction of words and sounds that Dodgson may very well have exploited in a book so interested in words.

   The White King's interruption in a sense saves Alice. She is playing a parlor game in which each player must complete a set of statements with words beginning with the same letter. If she fails to think of a town whose name begins with an H, she will fall out of the game.

"You alarm me!" said the King. "I feel faint—Give me a ham sandwich!"

On which the Messenger, to Alice's great amusement, opened a bag that hung round his neck, and handed a sandwich to the King, who devoured it greedily.

"Another sandwich!" said the King.

"There's nothing but hay left now," the Messenger said, peeping into the bag.

"Hay, then," the King murmured in a faint whisper.

Alice was glad to see that it revived him a good deal. "There's nothing like eating hay when you're faint," he remarked to her, as he munched away.

"I should think throwing cold water over you would be better," Alice suggested: "—or some sal-volatile."[4]

"I didn't say there was nothing *better*," the King replied. "I said there was nothing *like* it." Which Alice did not venture to deny.

"Who did you pass on the road?" the King went on, holding out his hand to the Messenger for some hay.

"Nobody," said the Messenger.

"Quite right," said the King: "this young lady saw him too. So of course Nobody walks slower than you."

"I do my best," the Messenger said in a sullen tone. "I'm sure nobody walks much faster than I do!"

"He ca'n't do that," said the King, "or else he'd have been here first. However, now you've got your breath, you may tell us what's happened in the town."

"I'll whisper it," said the Messenger, putting his hands to his mouth in the shape of a trumpet and stooping so as to get close to the King's ear. Alice was sorry for this, as she wanted to hear the news too. However, instead of whispering, he simply shouted, at the top of his voice, "They're at it again!"

"Do you call *that* a whisper?" cried the poor King, jumping up and shaking himself. "If you do such a thing again, I'll have you buttered! It went through and through my head like an earthquake!"

"It would have to be a very tiny earthquake!" thought Alice. "Who are at it again?" she ventured to ask.

"Why, the Lion and the Unicorn, of course," said the King.

"Fighting for the crown?"

"Yes, to be sure," said the King: "and the best of the joke is, that it's *my* crown all the while! Let's run and see them." And they trotted off, Alice repeating to herself, as she ran, the words of the old song:—

4. An ammonia solution used as smelling salts.

"The Lion and the Unicorn were fighting for the crown:
The Lion beat the Unicorn all round the town.
Some gave them white bread, some gave them brown:
Some gave them plum-cake and drummed them out of town."[5]

"Does——the one——that wins——get the crown?" she asked,
as well as she could, for the run was putting her quite out of breath.

"Dear me, no!" said the King. "What an idea!"

"Would you——be good enough——" Alice panted out, after
running a little further, "to stop a minute—just to get—one's breath
again?"

"I'm *good* enough," the King said, "only I'm not *strong* enough.
You see, a minute goes by so fearfully quick. You might as well try
to stop a Bandersnatch!"

Alice had no more breath for talking; so they trotted on in silence,
till they came into sight of a great crowd, in the middle of which the
Lion and Unicorn were fighting. They were in such a cloud of dust,
that at first Alice could not make out which was which; but she
soon managed to distinguish the Unicorn by his horn.

They placed themselves close to where Hatta, the other Messenger, was standing watching the fight, with a cup of tea in one hand
and a piece of bread-and-butter in the other.

"He's only just out of prison[6] and he hadn't finished his tea when
he was sent in," Haigha whispered to Alice: "and they only give
them oyster-shells in there—so you see he's very hungry and thirsty.
How are you, dear child?" he went on, putting his arm affectionately round Hatta's neck.

Hatta looked round and nodded, and went on with his
bread-and-butter.

"Were you happy in prison, dear child?" said Haigha.

Hatta looked round once more, and this time a tear or two trickled down his cheek; but not a word would he say.

---

5. Again, Dodgson takes over a traditional version of this nursery rhyme. The contest
   between the lion and the unicorn is traditional too, and in this rhyme, which was current in England in the eighteenth century, the contest may specifically refer to the
   placing of the unicorn from the Scottish coat of arms on the British coat of arms after
   the union of Scotland and England. Tenniel's unicorn looks a good deal like Disraeli
   and his lion somewhat like William Ewart Gladstone, Disraeli's great parliamentary
   rival who succeeded him as prime minister in 1868. At the time he illustrated the Alice
   books, Tenniel was best known for his political cartoons in *Punch*. In his book on Tenniel's illustrations (see Selected Bibliography), Michael Hancher remarks many simi-
   larities between Tenniel's work in *Punch* and his illustrations of the Alice books.
6. Although the White Queen does not name Hatta in an earlier reference (p. 149) to one
   of the King's messengers, Tenniel has already pictured him as the Mad Hatter, who left
   the King of Hearts' court hurriedly at the end of *Alice's Adventures in Wonderland*, just
   before the Queen of Hearts ordered his execution.

"Speak, ca'n't you!" Haigha cried impatiently. But Hatta only munched away, and drank some more tea.

"Speak, wo'n't you!" cried the King. "How are they getting on with the fight?"

Hatta made a desperate effort, and swallowed a large piece of bread-and-butter. "They're getting on very well," he said in a choking voice: "each of them has been down about eighty-seven times."

"Then I suppose they'll soon bring the white bread and the brown?" Alice ventured to remark.

"It's waiting for 'em now," said Hatta; "this is a bit of it as I'm eating."

There was a pause in the fight just then, and the Lion and the Unicorn sat down, panting, while the King called out "Ten minutes allowed for refreshments!" Haigha and Hatta set to work at once, carrying round trays of white and brown bread. Alice took a piece to taste, but it was *very* dry.

"I don't think they'll fight any more to-day," the King said to Hatta: "go and order the drums to begin." And Hatta went bounding away like a grasshopper

For a minute or two Alice stood silent, watching him. Suddenly she brightened up. "Look, look!" she cried, pointing eagerly. "There's the White Queen running across the country! She came flying out of the wood over yonder——How fast those Queens *can* run!"

"There's some enemy after her, no doubt," the King said, without even looking round. "That wood's full of them."

"But aren't you going to run and help her?" Alice asked, very much surprised at his taking it so quietly.

"No use, no use!" said the King. "She runs so fearfully quick. You might as well try to catch a Bandersnatch! But I'll make a memorandum about her, if you like——She's a dear good creature," he repeated softly to himself, as he opened his memorandum-book. "Do you spell 'creature' with a double 'e'?"

At this moment the Unicorn sauntered by them, with his hands in his pockets. "I had the best of it this time?" he said to the King, just glancing at him as he passed.

"A little—a little," the King replied, rather nervously. "You shouldn't have run him through with your horn, you know."

"It didn't hurt him," the Unicorn said carelessly, and he was going on, when his eye happened to fall upon Alice: he turned round instantly, and stood for some time looking at her with an air of the deepest disgust.

"What—is—this?" he said at last.

"This is a child!" Haigha replied eagerly, coming in front of Alice to introduce her, and spreading out both his hands towards her in an Anglo-Saxon attitude. "We only found it to-day. It's as large as life, and twice as natural!"

"I always thought they were fabulous monsters!" said the Unicorn. "Is it alive?"

"It can talk," said Haigha solemnly.

The Unicorn looked dreamily at Alice, and said "Talk, child."

Alice could not help her lips curling up into a smile as she began: "Do you know, I always thought Unicorns were fabulous monsters, too? I never saw one alive before!"

"Well, now that we *have* seen each other," said the Unicorn, "if you'll believe in me, I'll believe in you. Is that a bargain?"

"Yes, if you like," said Alice.

"Come, fetch out the plum-cake, old man!" the Unicorn went on, turning from her to the King. "None of your brown bread for me!"

"Certainly—certainly!" the King muttered, and beckoned to Haigha. "Open the bag!" he whispered. "Quick! Not that one—that's full of hay!"

Haigha took a large cake out of the bag, and gave it to Alice to hold, while he got out a dish and carving-knife. How they all came out of it Alice couldn't guess. It was just like a conjuring-trick, she thought.

The Lion had joined them while this was going on: he looked very tired and sleepy, and his eyes were half shut. "What's this!" he said, blinking lazily at Alice, and speaking in a deep hollow tone that sounded like the tolling of a great bell.

"Ah, what *is* it, now?" the Unicorn cried eagerly. "You'll never guess! *I* couldn't."

The Lion looked at Alice wearily. "Are you animal—or vegetable—or mineral?" he said, yawning at every other word.[7]

"It's a fabulous monster!" the Unicorn cried out, before Alice could reply.

"Then hand round the plum-cake, Monster," the Lion said, lying down and putting his chin on his paws. "And sit down, both of you," (to the King and the Unicorn): "fair play with the cake, you know!"

The King was evidently very uncomfortable at having to sit down between the two great creatures; but there was no other place for him.

"What a fight we might have for the crown, *now*!" the Unicorn said, looking slyly up at the crown, which the poor King was nearly shaking off his head, he trembled so much.

"I should win easy," said the Lion.

"I'm not so sure of that," said the Unicorn.

"Why, I beat you all round the town, you chicken!" the Lion replied angrily, half getting up as he spoke.

Here the King interrupted, to prevent the quarrel going on: he was very nervous, and his voice quite quivered. "All round the

---

7. A question often asked at the beginning of a parlor game, such as "Twenty Questions," in which players try to guess the object or person that another player is thinking of.

town?" he said. "That's a good long way. Did you go by the old bridge, or the market-place? You get the best view by the old bridge."

"I'm sure I don't know," the Lion growled out as he lay down again. "There was too much dust to see anything. What a time the Monster is, cutting up that cake!"

Alice had seated herself on the bank of a little brook, with the great dish on her knees, and was sawing away diligently with the knife. "It's very provoking!" she said, in reply to the Lion (she was getting quite used to being called 'the Monster'). "I've cut several slices already, but they always join on again!"

"You don't know how to manage Looking-glass cakes," the Unicorn remarked. "Hand it round first, and cut it afterwards."

This sounded nonsense, but Alice very obediently got up, and carried the dish round, and the cake divided itself into three pieces as she did so. "*Now* cut it up," said the Lion, as she returned to her place with the empty dish.

"I say, this isn't fair!" cried the Unicorn, as Alice sat with the knife in her hand, very much puzzled how to begin. "The Monster has given the Lion twice as much as me!"

"She's kept none for herself, anyhow," said the Lion. "Do you like plum-cake, Monster?"

But before Alice could answer him, the drums began.

Where the noise came from, she couldn't make out: the air
seemed full of it, and it rang through and through her head till she
felt quite deafened. She started to her feet and sprang across the

           *   *   *   *   *

              *   *   *   *

      *   *   *   *   *

little brook in her terror, and had just time to see the Lion and the
Unicorn rise to their feet, with angry looks at being interrupted in
their feast, before she dropped to her knees, and put her hands over
her ears, vainly trying to shut out the dreadful uproar.

"If *that* doesn't 'drum them out of town,'" she thought to herself,
"nothing ever will!"

Chapter VIII

"IT'S MY OWN INVENTION"

After a while the noise seemed gradually to die away, till all was dead silence, and Alice lifted up her head in some alarm. There was no one to be seen, and her first thought was that she must have been dreaming about the Lion and the Unicorn and those queer Anglo-Saxon Messengers. However, there was the great dish still lying at her feet, on which she had tried to cut the plum-cake, "So I wasn't dreaming, after all," she said to herself, "unless—unless we're all part of the same dream. Only I do hope it's *my* dream, and not the Red King's! I don't like belonging to another person's dream," she went on in a rather complaining tone: "I've a great mind to go and wake him, and see what happens!"

At this moment her thoughts were interrupted by a loud shouting of "Ahoy! Ahoy! Check!" and a Knight, dressed in crimson armour, came galloping down upon her, brandishing a great club. Just as he reached her, the horse stopped suddenly: "You're my prisoner!" the Knight cried, as he tumbled off his horse.

Startled as she was, Alice was more frightened for him than for herself at the moment, and watched him with some anxiety as he mounted again. As soon as he was comfortably in the saddle, he began once more "You're my——" but here another voice broke in "Ahoy! Ahoy! Check!" and Alice looked round in some surprise for the new enemy.

This time it was a White Knight. He drew up at Alice's side, and tumbled off his horse just as the Red Knight had done: then he got on again, and the two Knights sat and looked at each other for some time without speaking. Alice looked from one to the other in some bewilderment.

"She's *my* prisoner, you know!" the Red Knight said at last.

"Yes, but then *I* came and rescued her!" the White Knight replied.

"Well, we must fight for her, then," said the Red Knight, as he took up his helmet (which hung from the saddle, and was something the shape of a horse's head) and put it on.

"You will observe the Rules of Battle, of course?" the White Knight remarked, putting on his helmet too.

"I always do," said the Red Knight, and they began banging away at each other with such fury that Alice got behind a tree to be out of the way of the blows.

"I wonder, now, what the Rules of Battle are," she said to herself, as she watched the fight, timidly peeping out from her hiding-place. "One Rule seems to be, that if one Knight hits the other, he knocks him off his horse; and, if he misses, he tumbles off himself—and

another Rule seems to be that they hold their clubs with their arms,
as if they were Punch and Judy[8]——What a noise they make when
they tumble! Just like a whole set of fire-irons falling into the
fender! And how quiet the horses are! They let them get on and off
them just as if they were tables!"

Another Rule of Battle, that Alice had not noticed, seemed to be
that they always fell on their heads; and the battle ended with their
both falling off in this way, side by side. When they got up again, they
shook hands, and then the Red Knight mounted and galloped off.

"It was a glorious victory, wasn't it?" said the White Knight, as he
came up panting.

"I don't know," Alice said doubtfully. "I don't want to be anybody's prisoner. I want to be a Queen."

"So you will, when you've crossed the next brook," said the White
Knight. "I'll see you safe to the end of the wood—and then I must
go back, you know. That's the end of my move."

---

8. The hand puppets in a Punch and Judy show necessarily hold their clubs (there is a
   good deal of beating in the Punch and Judy story) pressed between their bodies and
   their crossed arms, as in Tenniel's illustration.

"Thank you very much," said Alice. "May I help you off with your helmet?" It was evidently more than he could manage by himself: however, she managed to shake him out of it at last.

"Now one can breathe more easily," said the Knight, putting back his shaggy hair with both hands, and turning his gentle face and large mild eyes to Alice. She thought she had never seen such a strange-looking soldier in all her life.

He was dressed in tin armour, which seemed to fit him very badly, and he had a queer-shaped little deal box[9] fastened across his shoulders, upside-down, and with the lid hanging open. Alice looked at it with great curiosity.

"I see you're admiring my little box," the Knight said in a friendly tone. "It's my own invention[1]—to keep clothes and sandwiches in. You see I carry it upside-down, so that the rain ca'n't get in."

"But the things can get *out*," Alice gently remarked. "Do you know the lid's open?"

"I didn't know it," the Knight said, a shade of vexation passing over his face. "Then all the things must have fallen out! And the box is no use without them." He unfastened it as he spoke, and was just going to throw it into the bushes, when a sudden thought seemed to strike him, and he hung it carefully on a tree. "Can you guess why I did that?" he said to Alice.

Alice shook her head.

"In hopes some bees may make a nest in it—then I should get the honey."

"But you've got a bee-hive—or something like one—fastened to the saddle," said Alice.

"Yes, it's a very good bee-hive," the Knight said in a discontented tone, "one of the best kind. But not a single bee has come near it yet. And the other thing is a mouse-trap. I suppose the mice keep the bees out—or the bees keep the mice out, I don't know which."

"I was wondering what the mouse-trap was for," said Alice. "It isn't very likely there would be any mice on the horse's back."

"Not very likely, perhaps," said the Knight; "but, if they *do* come, I don't choose to have them running all about."

"You see," he went on after a pause, "it's as well to be provided for *everything*. That's the reason the horse has all those anklets round his feet."

9. A deal box is made of pine.
1. Many commentators have found Dodgson in the White Knight. Dodgson too was an inventor of such devices as a map of London cut in sections so that it could be carried as a book in a pocket, and the Nyctograph, an invention designed to assist writing in the dark. The association between Dodgson and the White Knight is both strengthened and made poignant by the ending of this scene, in which the knight continues on his way and Alice leaves him to become a queen.

"But what are they for?" Alice asked in a tone of great curiosity.

"To guard against the bites of sharks," the Knight replied. "It's an invention of my own. And now help me on. I'll go with you to the end of the wood—What's that dish for?"

"It's meant for plum-cake," said Alice.

"We'd better take it with us," the Knight said. "It'll come in handy if we find any plum-cake. Help me to get it into this bag."

This took a long time to manage, though Alice held the bag open very carefully, because the Knight was so *very* awkward in putting in the dish: the first two or three times that he tried he fell in himself instead. "It's rather a tight fit, you see," he said, as they got it in at last; "there are so many candlesticks in the bag." And he hung it to the saddle, which was already loaded with bunches of carrots, and fire-irons, and many other things.

"I hope you've got your hair well fastened on?" he continued, as they set off.

"Only in the usual way," Alice said, smiling.

"That's hardly enough," he said, anxiously. "You see the wind is so *very* strong here. It's as strong as soup."

"Have you invented a plan for keeping the hair from being blown off?" Alice enquired.

"Not yet," said the Knight. "But I've got a plan for keeping it from *falling* off."

"I should like to hear it, very much."

"First you take an upright stick," said the Knight. "Then you make your hair creep up it, like a fruit-tree. Now the reason hair falls off is because it hangs *down*—things never fall *upwards*, you know. It's a plan of my own invention. You may try it if you like."

It didn't sound a comfortable plan, Alice thought, and for a few minutes she walked on in silence, puzzling over the idea, and every now and then stopping to help the poor Knight, who certainly was *not* a good rider.

Whenever the horse stopped (which it did very often), he fell off in front; and, whenever it went on again (which it generally did rather suddenly), he fell off behind. Otherwise he kept on pretty well, except that he had a habit of now and then falling off sideways; and, as he generally did this on the side on which Alice was walking, she soon found that it was the best plan not to walk *quite* close to the horse.

"I'm afraid you've not had much practice in riding," she ventured to say, as she was helping him up from his fifth tumble.

The Knight looked very much surprised, and a little offended at the remark. "What makes you say that?" he asked, as he scrambled

back into the saddle, keeping hold of Alice's hair with one hand, to
save himself from falling over on the other side.

"Because people don't fall off quite so often, when they've had
much practice."

"I've had plenty of practice," the Knight said very gravely: "plenty
of practice!"

Alice could think of nothing better to say than "Indeed?" but she
said it as heartily as she could. They went on a little way in silence
after this, the Knight with his eyes shut, muttering to himself, and
Alice watching anxiously for the next tumble.

"The great art of riding," the Knight suddenly began in a loud
voice, waving his right arm as he spoke, "is to keep——" Here the
sentence ended as suddenly as it had begun, as the Knight fell
heavily on the top of his head exactly in the path where Alice was
walking. She was quite frightened this time, and said in an anxious
tone, as she picked him up, "I hope no bones are broken?"

"None to speak of," the Knight said, as if he didn't mind breaking
two or three of them. "The great art of riding, as I was saying is—to
keep your balance properly. Like this, you know——"

He let go the bridle, and stretched out both his arms to show Alice
what he meant, and this time he fell flat on his back, right under the
horse's feet.

"Plenty of practice!" he went on repeating, all the time that Alice was getting him on his feet again. "Plenty of practice!"

"It's too ridiculous!" cried Alice, losing all her patience this time. "You ought to have a wooden horse on wheels, that you ought!"

"Does that kind go smoothly?" the Knight asked in a tone of great interest, clasping his arms round the horse's neck as he spoke, just in time to save himself from tumbling off again.

"Much more smoothly than a live horse," Alice said, with a little scream of laughter, in spite of all she could do to prevent it.

"I'll get one," the Knight said thoughtfully to himself. "One or two—several."

There was a short silence after this, and then the Knight went on again. "I'm a great hand at inventing things. Now, I daresay you noticed, the last time you picked me up, that I was looking rather thoughtful?"

"You *were* a little grave," said Alice.

"Well, just then I was inventing a new way of getting over a gate—would you like to hear it?"

"Very much indeed," Alice said politely.

"I'll tell you how I came to think of it," said the Knight. "You see, I said to myself 'The only difficulty is with the feet: the *head* is high enough already.' Now, first I put my head on the top of the gate—then the head's high enough—then I stand on my head—then the feet are high enough, you see—then I'm over, you see."

"Yes, I suppose you'd be over when that was done," Alice said thoughtfully: "but don't you think it would be rather hard?"

"I haven't tried it yet," the Knight said, gravely; "so I ca'n't tell for certain—but I'm afraid it *would* be a little hard."

He looked so vexed at the idea, that Alice changed the subject hastily. "What a curious helmet you've got!" she said cheerfully. "Is that your invention too?"

The Knight looked down proudly at his helmet, which hung from the saddle. "Yes," he said; "but I've invented a better one than that—like a sugar-loaf.[2] When I used to wear it, if I fell off the horse, it always touched the ground directly. So I had a *very* little way to fall, you see—But there *was* the danger of falling *into* it, to be sure. That happened to me once—and the worst of it was, before I could get out again, the other White Knight came and put it on. He thought it was his own helmet."

The Knight looked so solemn about it that Alice did not dare to laugh. "I'm afraid you must have hurt him," she said in a trembling voice, "being on the top of his head."

2. A sugar-loaf is usually cone-shaped. Hats called "sugar-loaf hats" were common in the sixteenth and seventeenth centuries.

"I had to kick him, of course," the Knight said, very seriously. "And then he took the helmet off again—but it took hours and hours to get me out. I was as fast as—as lightning, you know."

"But that's a different kind of fastness," Alice objected.

The Knight shook his head. "It was all kinds of fastness with me, I can assure you!" he said. He raised his hands in some excitement as he said this, and instantly rolled out of the saddle, and fell head-long into a deep ditch.

Alice ran to the side of the ditch to look for him. She was rather startled by the fall, as for some time he had kept on very well, and she was afraid that he really *was* hurt this time. However, though she could see nothing but the soles of his feet, she was much relieved to hear that he was talking on in his usual tone. "All kinds of fastness," he repeated: "but it was careless of him to put another man's helmet on—with the man in it, too."

"How *can* you go on talking so quietly, head downwards?" Alice asked, as she dragged him out by the feet, and laid him in a heap on the bank.

The Knight looked surprised at the question. "What does it matter where my body happens to be?" he said. "My mind goes on working all the same. In fact, the more head-downwards I am, the more I keep inventing new things."

"Now the cleverest thing of the sort that I ever did," he went on after a pause, "was inventing a new pudding during the meat-course."

"In time to have it cooked for the next course?" said Alice. "Well, that *was* quick work, certainly!"

"Well, not the *next* course," the Knight said in slow thoughtful tone: "no, certainly not the next *course*."

"Then it would have to be the next day. I suppose you wouldn't have two pudding-courses in one dinner?"

"Well, not the *next* day," the Knight repeated as before: "not the next *day*. In fact," he went on, holding his head down, and his voice getting lower and lower, "I don't believe that pudding ever *was* cooked! In fact, I don't believe that pudding ever *will* be cooked! And yet it was a very clever pudding to invent."

"What did you mean it to be made of?" Alice asked, hoping to cheer him up, for the poor Knight seemed quite low-spirited about it.

"It began with blotting-paper," the Knight answered with a groan.

"That wouldn't be very nice, I'm afraid——"

"Not very nice *alone*," he interrupted, quite eagerly: "but you've no idea what a difference it makes, mixing it with other things—such as gunpowder and sealing-wax. And here I must leave you." They had just come to the end of the wood.

Alice could only look puzzled: she was thinking of the pudding.

"You are sad," the Knight said in an anxious tone: "let me sing you a song to comfort you."

"Is it very long?" Alice asked, for she had heard a good deal of poetry that day.

"It's long," said the Knight, "but it's very, *very* beautiful. Everybody that hears me sing it—either it brings the *tears* into their eyes, or else——"

"Or else what?" said Alice, for the Knight had made a sudden pause.

"Or else it doesn't, you know. The name of the song is called '*Haddocks' Eyes*.'"

"Oh, that's the name of the song, is it?" Alice said, trying to feel interested.

"No, you don't understand," the Knight said, looking a little vexed. "That's what the name *is called*. The name really *is* '*The Aged Aged Man*.'"

"Then I ought to have said 'That's what the *song* is called'?" Alice corrected herself.

"No, you oughtn't: that's quite another thing! The *song* is called '*Ways and Means*': but that's only what it's *called*, you know!"

"Well, what *is* the song, then?" said Alice, who was by this time completely bewildered.

"I was coming to that," the Knight said. "The song really *is* '*A-sitting On A Gate*': and the tune's my own invention."

So saying, he stopped his horse and let the reins fall on its neck: then, slowly beating time with one hand, and with a faint smile lighting up his gentle foolish face, as if he enjoyed the music of his song, he began.

Of all the strange things that Alice saw in her journey Through The Looking-Glass, this was the one that she always remembered most clearly. Years afterwards she could bring the whole scene back again, as if it had been only yesterday—the mild blue eyes and kindly smile of the Knight—the setting sun gleaming through his hair, and shining on his armour in a blaze of light that quite dazzled her—the horse quietly moving about, with the reins hanging loose on his neck, cropping the grass at her feet—and the black shadows of the forest behind—all this she took in like a picture, as, with one hand shading her eyes, she leant against a tree, watching the strange pair, and listening, in a half-dream, to the melancholy music of the song.

"But the tune *isn't* his own invention," she said to herself: "it's '*I give thee all, I can no more.*'"[3] She stood and listened very attentively, but no tears came into her eyes.

> "I'll tell thee everything I can:
>   There's little to relate.
> I saw an aged aged man,
>   A-sitting on a gate.
> 'Who are you, aged man?' I said.
>   'And how is it you live?'
> And his answer trickled through my head,
>   Like water through a sieve.
>
> He said 'I look for butterflies
>   That sleep among the wheat:
> I make them into mutton pies,
>   And sell them in the street.
> I sell them unto men,' he said,
>   'Who sail on stormy seas;
> And that's the way I get my bread—
>   A trifle, if you please.'
>
> But I was thinking of a plan
>   To dye one's whiskers green,
> And always use so large a fan

---

3. "I give thee all—I can no more" is the first line of a song entitled "My Heart and Lute," by Thomas Moore (1779–1852). The White Knight's song retains, until the last lines of the poem, the meter and rhyme scheme of Moore's song. But Dodgson's poem itself is a burlesque of Wordsworth's "Resolution and Independence," in which an inexplicably saddened speaker is heartened by a colloquy with an aged but resolute leech-gatherer. Dodgson contributed an early version of this parody to the comic journal *The Train* (1856). It is included in *The Complete Works of Lewis Carroll* (see Selected Bibliography), pp. 727–30.

That they could not be seen.
So, having no reply to give
    To what the old man said,
I cried 'Come, tell me how you live!'
    And thumped him on the head.

His accents mild took up the tale:
    He said 'I go my ways,
And when I find a mountain-rill,
    I set it in a blaze;
And thence they make a stuff they call
    Rowland's Macassar-Oil—[4]
Yet twopence-halfpenny is all
    They give me for my toil.'

But I was thinking of a way
    To feed oneself on batter,
And so go on from day to day
    Getting a little fatter.
I shook him well from side to side,
    Until his face was blue:
'Come, tell me how you live,' I cried,
    'And what it is you do!'

He said 'I hunt for haddocks' eyes
    Among the heather bright,
And work them into waistcoat-buttons
    In the silent night.
And these I do not sell for gold
    Or coin of silvery shine,
But for a copper halfpenny,
    And that will purchase nine.

'I sometimes dig for buttered rolls,
    Or set limed twigs for crabs:[5]
I sometimes search for grassy knolls
    For wheels of Hansom-cabs.[6]
And that's the way' (he gave a wink)
    'By which I get my wealth—
And very gladly will I drink
    Your Honour's noble health.'

4. Rowland's Macassar-Oil was a widely advertised hairdressing.
5. Limed twigs are branches covered with bird lime, used to catch birds.
6. A hansom-cab is a two-wheeled carriage; it became very common as a hired convey-
   ance, especially in London, in the latter half of the nineteenth century.

I heard him then, for I had just
    Completed my design
To keep the Menai bridge[7] from rust
    By boiling it in wine.
I thanked him much for telling me
    The way he got his wealth,
But chiefly for his wish that he
    Might drink my noble health.

And now, if e'er by chance I put
    My fingers into glue,
Or madly squeeze a right-hand foot
    Into a left-hand shoe,
Or if I drop upon my toe
    A very heavy weight,
I weep, for it reminds me so
Of that old man I used to know—

Whose look was mild, whose speech was slow,
Whose hair was whiter than the snow,
Whose face was very like a crow,
With eyes, like cinders, all aglow,
Who seemed distracted with his woe,
Who rocked his body to and fro,
And muttered mumblingly and low,

7. The Menai Bridge is a suspension bridge in Wales.

As if his mouth were full of dough,
Who snorted like a buffalo——
That summer evening long ago,
    A-sitting on a gate."

As the Knight sang the last words of the ballad, he gathered up
the reins, and turned his horse's head along the road by which they
had come. "You've only a few yards to go," he said, "down the hill
and over that little brook, and then you'll be a Queen——But you'll
stay and see me off first?" he added as Alice turned with an eager
look in the direction to which he pointed. "I sha'n't be long. You'll
wait and wave your handkerchief when I get to that turn in the road?
I think it'll encourage me, you see."

"Of course I'll wait," said Alice: "and thank you very much for
coming so far—and for the song—I liked it very much."

"I hope so," the Knight said doubtfully: "but you didn't cry so
much as I thought you would."

So they shook hands, and then the Knight rode slowly away into
the forest. "It wo'n't take long to see him *off*, I expect," Alice said to
herself, as she stood watching him. "There he goes! Right on his
head as usual! However, he gets on again pretty easily—that comes
of having so many things hung round the horse——" So she went
on talking to herself, as she watched the horse walking leisurely
along the road, and the Knight tumbling off, first on one side and
then on the other. After the fourth or fifth tumble he reached the
turn, and then she waved her handkerchief to him, and waited till he
was out of sight.

"I hope it encouraged him," she said, as she turned to run down
the hill: "and now for the last brook, and to be a Queen! How grand
it sounds!" A very few steps brought her to the edge of the brook.[8]
"The Eighth Square at last!" she cried as she bounded across,

    *   *   *   *   *

     *   *   *   *

   *   *   *   *   *

and threw herself down to rest on a lawn as soft as moss, with little
flowerbeds dotted about it here and there. "Oh, how glad I am to
get here! And what *is* this on my head?" she exclaimed in a tone of
dismay, as she put her hands up to something very heavy, that fitted
tight round her head.

8. Dodgson wrote an episode about Alice and "The Wasp in a Wig" and placed it at this
point in Alice's journey. He deleted the episode after the book had been set in galley
proofs. See pp. 209–13 in this Norton Critical Edition.

"But how *can* it have got there without my knowing it?" she said to herself, as she lifted it off, and set it on her lap to make out what it could possibly be.

It was a golden crown.

Chapter IX

QUEEN ALICE

"Well, this *is* grand!" said Alice. "I never expected I should be a Queen so soon—and I'll tell you what it is, your Majesty," she went on, in a severe tone (she was always rather fond of scolding herself), "it'll never do for you to be lolling about on the grass like that! Queens have to be dignified, you know!"

So she got up and walked about—rather stiffly just at first, as she was afraid that the crown might come off: but she comforted herself with the thought that there was nobody to see her, "and if I really am a Queen," she said as she sat down again, "I shall be able to manage it quite well in time."

Everything was happening so oddly that she didn't feel a bit surprised at finding the Red Queen and the White Queen sitting close to her, one on each side: she would have liked very much to ask them how they came there, but she feared it would not be quite civil. However, there would be no harm, she thought, in asking if the game was over. "Please, would you tell me——" she began, looking timidly at the Red Queen.

"Speak when you're spoken to!" the Queen sharply interrupted her.

"But if everybody obeyed that rule," said Alice, who was always ready for a little argument, "and if you only spoke when you were spoken to, and the other person always waited for *you* to begin, you see nobody would ever say anything, so that——"

"Ridiculous!" cried the Queen. "Why, don't you see, child——" here she broke off with a frown, and, after thinking for a minute, suddenly changed the subject of the conversation. "What do you mean by 'If you really are a Queen'? What right have you to call yourself so? You ca'n't be a Queen, you know, till you've passed the proper examination. And the sooner we begin it, the better."

"I only said 'if'!" poor Alice pleaded in a piteous tone.

The two Queens looked at each other, and the Red Queen remarked, with a little shudder, "She *says* she only said 'if'——"

"But she said a great deal more than that!" the White Queen moaned, wringing her hands. "Oh, ever so much more than that!"

"So you did, you know," the Red Queen said to Alice. "Always speak the truth—think before you speak—and write it down afterwards."

"I'm sure I didn't mean——" Alice was beginning, but the Red Queen interrupted her impatiently.

"That's just what I complain of! You *should* have meant! What do you suppose is the use of a child without any meaning? Even a joke should have some meaning—and a child's more important than a joke, I hope. You couldn't deny that, even if you tried with both hands."

"I don't deny things with my *hands*," Alice objected.

"Nobody said you did," said the Red Queen. "I said you couldn't if you tried."

"She's in that state of mind," said the White Queen, "that she wants to deny *something*—only she doesn't know what to deny!"

"A nasty, vicious temper," the Red Queen remarked; and then there was an uncomfortable silence for a minute or two.

The Red Queen broke the silence by saying, to the White Queen, "I invite you to Alice's dinner-party this afternoon."

The White Queen smiled feebly, and said "And I invite *you*."

"I didn't know I was to have a party at all," said Alice; "but, if there *is* to be one, I think *I* ought to invite the guests."

"We gave you the opportunity of doing it," the Red Queen remarked: "but I daresay you've not had many lessons in manners yet?"

"Manners are not taught in lessons," said Alice. "Lessons teach you to do sums, and things of that sort."

"Can you do Addition?" the White Queen asked. "What's one and one and one and one and one and one and one and one and one and one?"[9]

"I don't know," said Alice. "I lost count."

"She ca'n't do Addition," the Red Queen interrupted. "Can you do Subtraction? Take nine from eight."

9. In the Pennyroyal edition of *Through the Looking-Glass* (see Selected Bibliography), James R. Kincaid cites a suggestion that Dodgson is here parodying a popular and dismally pedagogic nineteenth-century children's book, set up as a catechism, in which useful knowledge is pounded home in a series of questions and answers (p. 101).

"Nine from eight I ca'n't, you know," Alice replied very readily: "but——"

"She ca'n't do Subtraction," said the White Queen. "Can you do Division? Divide a loaf by a knife—what's the answer to *that*?"

"I suppose——" Alice was beginning, but the Red Queen answered for her. "Bread-and-butter, of course. Try another Subtraction sum. Take a bone from a dog: what remains?"

Alice considered. "The bone wouldn't remain, of course, if I took it—and the dog wouldn't remain: it would come to bite me—and I'm sure *I* shouldn't remain!"

"Then you think nothing would remain?" said the Red Queen.

"I think that's the answer."

"Wrong, as usual," said the Red Queen: "the dog's temper would remain."

"But I don't see how——"

"Why, look here!" the Red Queen cried. "The dog would lose its temper, wouldn't it?"

"Perhaps it would," Alice replied cautiously.

"Then if the dog went away, its temper would remain!" the Queen exclaimed triumphantly.

Alice said, as gravely as she could, "They might go different ways." But she couldn't help thinking to herself "What dreadful nonsense we *are* talking!"

"She ca'n't do sums a *bit*!" the Queens said together, with great emphasis.

"Can *you* do sums?" Alice said, turning suddenly on the White Queen, for she didn't like being found fault with so much.

The Queen gasped and shut her eyes. "I can do Addition," she said, "if you give me time—but I ca'n't do Subtraction under *any* circumstances!"

"Of course you know your ABC?" said the Red Queen.

"To be sure I do," said Alice.

"So do I," the White Queen whispered: "we'll often say it over together, dear. And I'll tell you a secret—I can read words of one letter! Isn't *that* grand? However, don't be discouraged. You'll come to it in time."

Here the Red Queen began again. "Can you answer useful questions?" she said. "How is bread made?"

"I know *that*!" Alice cried eagerly. "You take some flour——"

"Where do you pick the flower?" the White Queen asked: "In a garden or in the hedges?"

"Well, it isn't *picked* at all," Alice explained: "it's *ground*——"

"How many acres of ground?" said the White Queen. "You mustn't leave out so many things."

"Fan her head!" the Red Queen anxiously interrupted. "She'll be feverish after so much thinking." So they set to work and fanned her with bunches of leaves, till she had to beg them to leave off, it blew her hair about so.

"She's all right again now," said the Red Queen. "Do you know Languages? What's the French for fiddle-de-dee?"

"Fiddle-de-dee's not English," Alice replied gravely.

"Who ever said it was?" said the Red Queen.

Alice thought she saw a way out of the difficulty, this time. "If you'll tell me what language 'fiddle-de-dee' is, I'll tell you the French for it!" she exclaimed triumphantly.

But the Red Queen drew herself up rather stiffly, and said "Queens never make bargains."

"I wish Queens never asked questions," Alice thought to herself.

"Don't let us quarrel," the White Queen said in an anxious tone. "What is the cause of lightning?"

"The cause of lightning," Alice said very decidedly, for she felt quite certain about this, "is the thunder—no, no!" she hastily corrected herself. "I meant the other way."

"It's too late to correct it," said the Red Queen: "when you've once said a thing, that fixes it, and you must take the consequences."

"Which reminds me——" the White Queen said, looking down and nervously clasping and unclasping her hands, "we had *such* a thunderstorm last Tuesday—I mean one of the last set of Tuesdays, you know."

Alice was puzzled. "In *our* country," she remarked, "there's only one day at a time."

The Red Queen said "That's a poor thin way of doing things. Now *here*, we mostly have days and nights two or three at a time, and sometimes in the winter we take as many as five nights together—for warmth, you know."

"Are five nights warmer than one night, then?" Alice ventured to ask.

"Five times as warm, of course."

"But they should be five times as *cold*, by the same rule——"

"Just so!" cried the Red Queen. "Five times as warm, *and* five times as cold—just as I'm five times as rich as you are, *and* five times as clever!"

Alice sighed and gave it up. "It's exactly like the riddle with no answer!" she thought.[1]

---

1. In the Red Queen's formulation of this set of oppositions, it makes no more sense to think of someone as being both rich and clever than it does to think of something as being both warm and cold. In her exasperation, Alice remembers the riddle about the raven and the writing desk she heard during the mad tea-party in *Alice's Adventures in Wonderland*.

"Humpty Dumpty saw it too," the White Queen went on in a low voice, more as if she were talking to herself. "He came to the door with a corkscrew in his hand——"

"What did he want?" said the Red Queen.

"He said he *would* come in," the White Queen went on, "because he was looking for a hippopotamus. Now, as it happened, there wasn't such a thing in the house, that morning."

"Is there generally?" Alice asked in an astonished tone.

"Well, only on Thursdays," said the Queen.

"I know what he came for," said Alice: "he wanted to punish the fish, because——"[2]

Here the White Queen began again. "It was *such* a thunderstorm, you ca'n't think!" ("She *never* could, you know," said the Red Queen.) "And part of the roof came off, and ever so much thunder got in—and it went rolling round the room in great lumps—and knocking over the tables and things—till I was so frightened, I couldn't remember my own name!"

Alice thought to herself "I never should *try* to remember my name in the middle of an accident! Where would be the use of it?" but she did not say this aloud, for fear of hurting the poor Queen's feelings.

"Your Majesty must excuse her," the Red Queen said to Alice, taking one of the White Queen's hands in her own, and gently stroking it: "she means well, but she ca'n't help saying foolish things, as a general rule."

The White Queen looked timidly at Alice, who felt she *ought* to say something kind, but really couldn't think of anything at the moment.

"She never was really well brought up," the Red Queen went on: "but it's amazing how good-tempered she is! Pat her on the head, and see how pleased she'll be!" But this was more than Alice had courage to do.

"A little kindness—and putting her hair in papers[3]—would do wonders with her—"

The White Queen gave a deep sigh, and laid her head on Alice's shoulder. "I *am* so sleepy!" she moaned.

"She's tired, poor thing!" said the Red Queen. "Smoothe[4] her hair—lend her your nightcap—and sing her a soothing lullaby."

"I haven't got a nightcap with me," said Alice, as she tried to obey the first direction: "and I don't know any soothing lullabies."

---

2. See Humpty Dumpty's song on pp. 164–66 of this Norton Critical Edition.
3. Curlers.
4. "Smoothe" for "Smooth" is the second (and last) of the corrections by Dodgson intended for an 1897 edition of the two Alice books that were not included in the edition. See Stanley Godman. "Lewis Carroll's Final Corrections to Alice,'" *Times Literary Supplement*, May 2 1958, p. 248.

"I must do it myself, then," said the Red Queen, and she began:—

> "Hush-a-by lady, in Alice's lap!
> 'Till the feast's ready, we've time for a nap.
> When the feast's over, we'll go to the ball—
> Red Queen, and White Queen, and Alice, and all![5]

"And now you know the words," she added, as she put her head down on Alice's other shoulder, "just sing it through to *me*. I'm getting sleepy, too." In another moment both Queens were fast asleep, and snoring loud.

"What *am* I to do?" exclaimed Alice, looking about in great perplexity, as first one round head, and then the other, rolled down from her shoulder, and lay like a heavy lump in her lap. "I don't think it *ever* happened before, that any one had to take care of two Queens asleep at once! No, not in all the History of England—it couldn't, you know, because there never was more than one Queen at a time. Do wake up, you heavy things!" she went on in an impatient tone; but there was no answer but a gentle snoring.

The snoring got more distinct every minute, and sounded more like a tune: at last she could even make out words, and she listened so eagerly that, when the two great heads suddenly vanished from her lap, she hardly missed them.

---

5. This song is the only parody of a nursery rhyme in the Alice books. The rhyme, "Hush-a-by baby" or "Rock-a-by baby," was well known by the eighteenth century.

She was standing before an arched doorway, over which were the words "QUEEN ALICE" in large letters, and on each side of the arch there was a bell-handle; one was marked "Visitors' Bell," and the other "Servants' Bell."[6]

"I'll wait till the song's over," thought Alice, "and then I'll ring the—the—*which* bell must I ring?" she went on, very much puzzled by the names. "I'm not a visitor, and I'm not a servant. There *ought* to be one marked 'Queen,' you know——"

Just then the door opened a little way, and a creature with a long beak put its head out for a moment and said "No admittance till the week after next!" and shut the door again with a bang.

Alice knocked and rang in vain for a long time; but at last a very old Frog, who was sitting under a tree, got up and hobbled slowly towards her: he was dressed in bright yellow, and had enormous boots on.

"What is it, now?" the Frog said in a deep hoarse whisper.

6. A. L. Taylor in *The White Knight* (see Selected Bibliography) speculates that Alice has come full circle to a point where several sets of opposites meet: front door ("Visitors' Bell") and back door ("Servants' Bell"), the two ends of the chess board, beginning and end (pp. 106–07). This scene is the last of the transformation scenes in the book, except for the final dissolving scene.

Alice turned round, ready to find fault with anybody. "Where's the servant whose business it is to answer the door?" she began angrily.

"Which door?" said the Frog.

Alice almost stamped with irritation at the slow drawl in which he spoke. "*This* door, of course!"

The Frog looked at the door with his large dull eyes for a minute: then he went nearer and rubbed it with his thumb, as if he were trying whether the paint would come off: then he looked at Alice.

"To answer the door?" he said. "What's it been asking of?" He was so hoarse that Alice could scarcely hear him.

"I don't know what you mean," she said.

"I speaks English, doesn't I?" the Frog went on. "Or are you deaf? What did it ask you?"

"Nothing!" Alice said impatiently. "I've been knocking at it!"

"Shouldn't do that—shouldn't do that——" the Frog muttered. "Wexes it, you know." Then he went up and gave the door a kick with one of his great feet. "You let *it* alone," he panted out, as he hobbled back to his tree, "and it'll let *you* alone, you know."

At this moment the door was flung open, and a shrill voice was heard singing:—

> "To the Looking-Glass world it was Alice that said
> 'I've a sceptre in hand, I've a crown on my head.
> Let the Looking-Glass creatures, whatever they be,
> Come and dine with the Red Queen, the White Queen,
>   and me!'"

And hundreds of voices joined in the chorus:—

> "Then fill up the glasses as quick as you can,
> And sprinkle the table with buttons and bran:
> Put cats in the coffee, and mice in the tea—
> And welcome Queen Alice with thirty-times-three!"

Then followed a confused noise of cheering, and Alice thought to herself "Thirty times three makes ninety. I wonder if any one's counting?" In a minute there was silence again, and the same shrill voice sang another verse:—

> "'O Looking-Glass creatures,' quoth Alice, 'draw near!
> 'Tis an honour to see me, a favour to hear:
> 'Tis a privilege high to have dinner and tea
> Along with the Red Queen, the White Queen, and me!'"

Then came the chorus again:—

> "Then fill up the glasses with treacle and ink,
> Or anything else that is pleasant to drink:

Mix sand with the cider, and wool with the wine—
And welcome Queen Alice with ninety-times-nine!"[7]

"Ninety times nine!" Alice repeated in despair. "Oh, that'll never be done! I'd better go in at once——" and in she went, and there was a dead silence the moment she appeared.

Alice glanced nervously along the table, as she walked up the large hall, and noticed that there were about fifty guests, of all kinds: some were animals, some birds, and there were even a few flowers among them. "I'm glad they've come without waiting to be asked," she thought: "I should never have known who were the right people to invite!"

There were three chairs at the head of the table: the Red and White Queens had already taken two of them, but the middle one was empty. Alice sat down in it, rather uncomfortable at the silence, and longing for some one to speak.

At last the Red Queen began. "You've missed the soup and fish," she said. "Put on the joint!" And the waiters set a leg of mutton before Alice, who looked at it rather anxiously, as she had never had to carve a joint before.

"You look a little shy: let me introduce you to that leg of mutton," said the Red Queen. "Alice——Mutton: Mutton——Alice." The leg of mutton got up in the dish and made a little bow to Alice; and Alice returned the bow, not knowing whether to be frightened or amused.

"May I give you a slice?" she said, taking up the knife and fork, and looking from one Queen to the other.

"Certainly not," the Red Queen said, very decidedly: "it isn't etiquette to cut[8] any one you've been introduced to. Remove the joint!" And the waiters carried it off, and brought a large plum-pudding in its place.

"I wo'n't be introduced to the pudding, please," Alice said rather hastily, "or we shall get no dinner at all. May I give you some?"

But the Red Queen looked sulky, and growled "Pudding—— Alice: Alice——Pudding. Remove the pudding!", and the waiters took it away so quickly that Alice couldn't return its bow.

However, she didn't see why the Red Queen should be the only one to give orders; so, as an, experiment, she called out "Waiter! Bring back the pudding!" and there it was again in a moment, like a conjuring-trick. It was so large that she couldn't help feeling a *little* shy with it, as she had been with the mutton; however, she conquered

---

7. The song that greets Alice is a parody of "Bonny Dundee," by Walter Scott, first published in 1830. Scott's poem begins, "To the Lords of Convention 'twas Claver'se who spoke"; and its chorus begins with the line "Come fill my cup, come fill my can."
8. To "cut" someone is to fail to acknowledge his or her greeting.

her shyness by a great effort, and cut a slice and handed it to the Red Queen.

"What impertinence!" said the Pudding. "I wonder how you'd like it, if I were to cut a slice out of *you*, you creature!"

It spoke in a thick, suety sort of voice, and Alice hadn't a word to say in reply: she could only sit and look at it and gasp.

"Make a remark," said the Red Queen: "it's ridiculous to leave all the conversation to the pudding!"

"Do you know, I've had such a quantity of poetry repeated to me to-day," Alice began, a little frightened at finding that, the moment she opened her lips, there was dead silence, and all eyes were fixed upon her; "and it's a very curious thing, I think—every poem was about fishes in some way. Do you know why they're so fond of fishes, all about here?"

She spoke to the Red Queen, whose answer was a little wide of the mark. "As to fishes," she said, very slowly and solemnly, putting her mouth close to Alice's ear, "her White Majesty knows a lovely riddle—all in poetry—all about fishes. Shall she repeat it?"

"Her Red Majesty's very kind to mention it," the White Queen murmured into Alice's other ear, in a voice like the cooing of a pigeon. "It would be *such* a treat! May I?"

"Please do," Alice said very politely.

The White Queen laughed with delight, and stroked Alice's cheek. Then she began:

> "'First, the fish must be caught.'
> That is easy: a baby, I think, could have caught it.
> 'Next, the fish must be bought.'
> That is easy: a penny, I think, could have bought it.
>
> 'Now cook me the fish!'
> That is easy, and will not take more than a minute.
> 'Let it lie in a dish!'
> That is easy, because it already is in it.
>
> 'Bring it here! Let me sup!'
> It is easy to set such a dish on the table.
> 'Take the dish-cover up!'
> Ah, *that* is so hard that I fear I'm unable!
>
> For it holds it like glue—
> Holds the lid to the dish, while it lies in the middle:
> Which is easiest to do,
> Un-dish-cover the fish, or dishcover the riddle?"[9]

"Take a minute to think about it, and then guess," said the Red Queen. "Meanwhile, we'll drink your health—Queen Alice's health!" she screamed at the top of her voice, and all the guests began drinking it directly, and very queerly they managed it: some of them put their glasses upon their heads like extinguishers, and drank all that trickled down their faces—others upset the decanters, and drank the wine as it ran off the edges of the table—and three of them (who looked like kangaroos) scrambled into the dish of roast mutton, and began eagerly lapping up the gravy, "just like pigs in a trough!" thought Alice.

"You ought to return thanks in a neat speech," the Red Queen said, frowning at Alice as she spoke.

"We must support you, you know," the White Queen whispered, as Alice got up to do it, very obediently, but a little frightened.

"Thank you very much," she whispered in reply, "but I can do quite well without."

"That wouldn't be at all the thing," the Red Queen said very decidedly: so Alice tried to submit to it with good grace.

---

9. Dodgson did not provide an answer to this riddle, as he later did to the Mad Hatter's riddle in *Alice's Adventures in Wonderland*. Martin Gardner in *The Annotated Alice* suggests that the answer is an oyster (p. 264).

("And they *did* push so!" she said afterwards, when she was telling her sister the history of her feast. "You would have thought they wanted to squeeze me flat!")

In fact it was rather difficult for her to keep in her place while she made her speech: the two Queens pushed her so, one on each side, that they nearly lifted her up into the air. "I rise to return thanks——" Alice began: and she really *did* rise as she spoke, several inches; but she got hold of the edge of the table, and managed to pull herself down again.

"Take care of yourself!" screamed the White Queen, seizing Alice's hair with both her hands. "Something's going to happen!"

And then (as Alice afterwards described it) all sorts of things happened in a moment. The candles all grew up to the ceiling, looking something like a bed of rushes with fireworks at the top. As to the bottles, they each took a pair of plates, which they hastily fitted on as wings, and so, with forks for legs, went fluttering about in all directions: "and very like birds they look," Alice thought to herself, as well as she could in the dreadful confusion that was beginning.

At this moment she heard a hoarse laugh at her side, and turned to see what was the matter with the White Queen; but, instead of the Queen, there was the leg of mutton sitting in the chair. "Here I am!" cried a voice from the soup-tureen, and Alice turned again, just in time to see the Queen's broad good-natured face grinning at her for a moment over the edge of the tureen, before she disappeared into the soup.

There was not a moment to be lost. Already several of the guests were lying down in the dishes, and the soup ladle was walking up the table towards Alice's chair, and beckoning to her impatiently to get out of its way.

"I ca'n't stand this any longer!" she cried, as she jumped up and seized the tablecloth with both hands: one good pull, and plates, dishes, guests, and candles came crashing down together in a heap on the floor.

"And as for *you*," she went on, turning fiercely upon the Red Queen, whom she considered as the cause of all the mischief—but the Queen was no longer at her side—she had suddenly dwindled down to the size of a little doll, and was now on the table, merrily running round and round after her own shawl, which was trailing behind her.

At any other time, Alice would have felt surprised at this, but she was far too much excited to be surprised at anything *now*. "As for *you*," she repeated, catching hold of the little creature in the very act of jumping over a bottle which had just lighted upon the table, "I'll shake you into a kitten, that I will!"

Chapter X

SHAKING

She took her off the table as she spoke, and shook her backwards and forwards with all her might.

The Red Queen made no resistance whatever: only her face grew very small, and her eyes got large and green: and still, as Alice went on shaking her, she kept on growing shorter—and fatter—and softer—and rounder—and——

Chapter XI

WAKING

—it really *was* a kitten, after all.

Chapter XII

"Your Red Majesty shouldn't purr so loud," Alice said, rubbing her eyes, and addressing the kitten, respectfully, yet with some severity. "You woke me out of oh! such a nice dream! And you've been along with me, Kitty—all through the Looking-Glass world. Did you know it, dear?"

It is a very inconvenient habit of kittens (Alice had once made the remark) that, whatever you say to them, they *always* purr. "If they would only purr for 'yes,' and mew for 'no,' or any rule of that sort," she had said, "so that one could keep up a conversation! But how *can* you talk with a person if they *always* say the same thing?"

On this occasion the kitten only purred: and it was impossible to guess whether it meant "yes" or "no."

So Alice hunted among the chessmen on the table till she had found the Red Queen: then she went down on her knees on the hearth-rug, and put the kitten and the Queen to look at each other. "Now, Kitty!" she cried, clapping her hands triumphantly. "Confess that was what you turned into!"

("But it wouldn't look at it," she said, when she was explaining the thing afterwards to her sister: "it turned away its head, and pretended not to see it: but it looked a *little* ashamed of itself, so I think it *must* have been the Red Queen.")

"Sit up a little more stiffly, dear!" Alice cried with a merry laugh. "And curtsey while you're thinking what to—what to purr. It saves time, remember!" And she caught it up and gave it one little kiss, "just in honour of its having been a Red Queen."

"Snowdrop, my pet!" she went on, looking over her shoulder at the White Kitten, which was still patiently undergoing its toilet, "when *will* Dinah have finished with your White Majesty, I wonder? That must be the reason you were so untidy in my dream.—— Dinah! Do you know that you're scrubbing a White Queen? Really, it's most disrespectful of you!

"And what did *Dinah* turn to, I wonder?" she prattled on, as she settled comfortably down, with one elbow on the rug, and her chin in her hand, to watch the kittens. "Tell me, Dinah, did you turn to Humpty Dumpty? I *think* you did—however, you'd better not mention it to your friends just yet, for I'm not sure.

"By the way, Kitty, if only you'd been really with me in my dream, there was one thing you *would* have enjoyed——I had such a quantity of poetry said to me, all about fishes! To-morrow morning you shall have a real treat. All the time you're eating your breakfast, I'll

repeat 'The Walrus and the Carpenter' to you; and then you can
make believe it's oysters, dear!

"Now, Kitty, let's consider who it was that dreamed it all. This is
a serious question, my dear, and you should *not* go on licking your
paw like that—as if Dinah hadn't washed you this morning! You
see, Kitty, it *must* have been either me or the Red King. He was part
of my dream, of course—but then I was part of his dream, too! *Was*
it the Red King, Kitty? You were his wife, my dear, so you ought to
know——Oh, Kitty, *do* help to settle it! I'm sure your paw can wait!"
But the provoking kitten only began on the other paw, and pretended it hadn't heard the question.

Which do *you* think it was?

A boat, beneath a sunny sky[1]
Lingering onward dreamily
In an evening of July—

Children three that nestle near,
Eager eye and willing ear,
Pleased a simple tale to hear—

Long has paled that sunny sky:
Echoes fade and memories die:
Autumn frosts have slain July.

Still she haunts me, phantomwise.
Alice moving under skies
Never seen by waking eyes.

Children yet, the tale to hear,
Eager eye and willing ear,
Lovingly shall nestle near.

In a Wonderland they lie,
Dreaming as the days go by,
Dreaming as the summers die:

Ever drifting down the stream—
Lingering in the golden gleam—
Life, what is it but a dream?[2]

---

1. The initial letters of each line in this poem, when read downward, spell Alice Pleasance Liddell.
2. Dodgson here imagines his book as a dream he gives to children to hold against the
condition in which summers, and even memories, die. But he also hangs onto the com-
plicated and playful question with which he ends the story: do we dream (and awaken)
in real life, or in real life do we act only as the instruments of someone else's dream?
Late in his life Dodgson offered a succinct statement of this teasing speculation that
our ideas and actions are radically conditioned by something not ourselves—by, for
example, the constraints and possibilities given to us in our language and culture. "In
fact, now I come to think of it," he wrote in 1886 to Marion Richards, a young woman
whom he first met in 1875 when she was four years old, "*do* we decide questions, at all?
We decide *answers*, no doubt: but surely the questions decide *us*? It is the dog, you
know, that wags the tail—not the tail that wags the dog." *Letters* (see full citation on
p. 251): Feb. 8, 1886 II:620.

The Wasp in a Wig

The episode of the wasp in a wig was intended to occur between the White Knight's departure from Alice and her entrance into the eighth square at the end of chapter 8. In his biography of his uncle, Stuart Dodgson Collingwood quotes John Tenniel as objecting that "a *wasp* in a *wig* is altogether beyond the appliances of art." Collingwood reproduces another letter in which Tenniel judged the episode to be uninteresting and suggested, "If you want to shorten the book, I can't help thinking—with all submission—that *there* is your opportunity" (p. 146). Even though Alice's kindness to the rude and threatening Wasp furnishes a satisfying transition between the gentle interlude with the White Knight and the nightmare of the coronation dinner, Dodgson apparently did want to shorten his book. He therefore simply brought Alice to the boundary of the brook and had her jump across immediately, rather than turn back to hear the Wasp's story.

It has been known since the publication of Collingwood's biography in 1898 that the episode had been eliminated from the final version of *Through the Looking-Glass.* However, the content of the episode was not known until the galley sheets were offered at auction in 1974. The episode was published in 1977 by the Lewis Carroll Society of North America and Macmillan in *The Wasp in a Wig* (New York and London: Macmillan, 1977). The text used here is that of the 1977 publication.

The Wasp in a Wig[†]

. . . and she was just going to spring over, when she heard a deep sigh, which seemed to come from the wood behind her.

"There's somebody *very* unhappy there," she thought, looking anxiously back to see what was the matter. Something like a very old man (only that his face was more like a wasp) was sitting on the ground, leaning against a tree, all huddled up together, and shivering as if he were very cold.

"I don't *think* I can be of any use to him," was Alice's first thought, as she turned to spring over the brook:——"but I'll just ask him what's the matter," she added, checking herself on the very edge. "If I once jump over, everything will change, and then I can't help him."

So she went back to the Wasp——rather unwillingly, for she was *very* anxious to be a Queen.

"Oh, my old bones, my old bones!" he was grumbling on as Alice came up to him.

"It's rheumatism, I should think," Alice said to herself, and she stooped over him, and said very kindly, "I hope you're not in much pain?"

The Wasp only shook his shoulders, and turned his head away. "Ah, deary me!" he said to himself.

"Can I do anything for you?" Alice went on. "Aren't you rather cold here?"

"How you go on!" the Wasp said in a peevish tone. "Worrity, worrity![1] There never was such a child!"

Alice felt rather offended at this answer, and was very nearly walking on and leaving him, but she thought to herself "Perhaps it's only pain that makes him so cross." So she tried once more.

"Won't you let me help you round to the other side? You'll be out of the cold wind there."

The Wasp took her arm, and let her help him round the tree, but when he got settled down again he only said, as before, "Worrity, worrity! Can't you leave a body alone?"

"Would you like me to read you a bit of this?" Alice went on, as she picked up a newspaper which had been lying at his feet.

"You may read it if you've a mind to," the Wasp said, rather sulkily. "Nobody's hindering you, that *I* know of."

---

† Reprinted with the permission of A P Watt Limited on behalf of the Lewis Carroll Society of North America and the Executors of the C. L. Dodgson Estate, and of Macmillan, London and Basingstoke.

1. Worrity: worry. Here and in several other words and phrases, the Wasp uses words common in lower-class dialect.

So Alice sat down by him, and spread out the paper on her knees, and began. *"Latest News. The Exploring Party have made another tour in the Pantry, and have found five new lumps of white sugar, large and in fine condition. In coming back——"*

"Any brown sugar?" the Wasp interrupted.

Alice hastily ran her eye down the paper and said "No. It says nothing about brown."

"No brown sugar!" grumbled the Wasp. "A nice exploring party!"

"In coming back," Alice went on reading, *"they found a lake of treacle. The banks of the lake were blue and white, and looked like china. While tasting the treacle, they had a sad accident: two of their party were engulphed——"*[2]

"Were *what*?" the Wasp asked in a very cross voice.

"En-gulph-ed," Alice repeated, dividing the word into syllables.

"There's no such word in the language!" said the Wasp.

"It's in this newspaper, though," Alice said a little timidly.

"Let it stop there!" said the Wasp, fretfully turning away his head.

Alice put down the newspaper. "I'm afraid you're not well," she said in a soothing tone. "Can't I do anything for you?"

"It's all along of[3] the wig," the Wasp said in a much gentler voice.

"Along of the wig?" Alice repeated, quite pleased to find that he was recovering his temper.

"You'd be cross too, if you'd a wig like mine," the Wasp went on. "They jokes at one. And they worrits one. And then I gets cross. And I gets cold. And I gets under a tree. And I gets a yellow handkerchief. And I ties up my face——as at the present."

Alice looked pityingly at him. "Tying up the face is very good for the toothache," she said.

"And it's good for the conceit," added the Wasp.

Alice didn't catch the word exactly. "Is that a kind of toothache?" she asked.

The Wasp considered a little. "Well, no," he said: "it's when you hold up your head——so——without bending your neck."

"Oh, you mean stiff-neck," said Alice.

The Wasp said "That's a new-fangled name. They called it conceit in my time."

"Conceit isn't a disease at all," Alice remarked.

"It is, though," said the Wasp: "wait till you have it, and then you'll know. And when you catches it, just try tying a yellow handkerchief round your face. It'll cure you in no time!"

---

2. An archaic spelling of "engulfed." The Wasp of course does not see the spelling; he only hears Alice's pronunciation of the word
3. All along of: because of, another phrase from lower-class dialect.

He untied the handkerchief as he spoke, and Alice looked at his wig in great surprise. It was bright yellow like the handkerchief, and all tangled and tumbled about like a heap of sea-weed. "You would make your wig much neater," she said, "if only you had a comb."

"What, you're a Bee, are you?" the Wasp said, looking at her with more interest. "And you've got a comb. Much honey?"

"It isn't that kind," Alice hastily explained. "It's to comb hair with—your wig's so *very* rough, you know."

"I'll tell you how I came to wear it," the Wasp said. "When I was young, you know, my ringlets used to wave——"

A curious idea came into Alice's head. Almost every one she had met had repeated poetry to her, and she thought she would try if the Wasp couldn't do it too. "Would you mind saying it in rhyme?" she asked very politely.

"It ain't what I'm used to," said the Wasp: "however I'll try; wait a bit." He was silent for a few moments, and then began again—

> "When I was young, my ringlets waved
>   And curled and crinkled on my head:
> And then they said 'You should be shaved,
>   And wear a yellow wig instead.'
>
> But when I followed their advice,
>   And they had noticed the effect,
> They said I did not look so nice
>   As they had ventured to expect.
>
> They said it did not fit, and so
>   It made me look extremely plain:
> But what was I to do, you know?
>   My ringlets would not grow again.
>
> So now that I am old and gray,
>   And all my hair is nearly gone,
> They take my wig from me and say
>   'How can you put such rubbish on?'
>
> And still, whenever I appear,
>   They hoot at me and call me 'Pig!'
> And that is why they do it, dear,
>   Because I wear a yellow wig."[4]

"I'm very sorry for you," Alice said heartily: "and I think if your wig fitted a little better, they wouldn't tease you quite so much."

---

4. The Wasp's poem does not seem to be a parody.

"*Your* wig fits very well," the Wasp murmured, looking at her with an expression of admiration: "it's the shape of your head as does it. Your jaws ain't well shaped, though——I should think you couldn't bite well?"

Alice began with a little scream of laughter, which she turned into a cough as well as she could. At last she managed to say gravely, "I can bite anything I want."

"Not with a mouth as small as that," the Wasp persisted. "If you was a-fighting, now——could you get hold of the other one by the back of the neck?"

"I'm afraid not," said Alice.

"Well, that's because your jaws are too short," the Wasp went on: "but the top of your head is nice and round." He took off his own wig as he spoke, and stretched out one claw towards Alice, as if he wished to do the same for her, but she kept out of reach, and would not take the hint. So he went on with his criticisms.

"Then your eyes——they're too much in front, no doubt. One would have done as well as two, if you *must* have them so close——"

Alice did not like having so many personal remarks made on her, and as the Wasp had quite recovered his spirits, and was getting very talkative, she thought she might safely leave him. "I think I must be going on now," she said. "Good-bye."

"Good-bye, and thank-ye," said the Wasp, and Alice tripped down the hill again, quite pleased that she had gone back and given a few minutes to making the poor old creature comfortable.

The Text of
THE HUNTING OF THE SNARK
An Agony, in Eight Fits

An Easter Greeting

My dear child,

Please to fancy, if you can, that you are reading a real letter, from a real friend whom you have seen, and whose voice you can seem to yourself to hear, wishing you, as I do now with all my heart, a happy Easter.

Do you know that delicious dreamy feeling, when one first wakes on a summer morning, with the twitter of birds in the air, and the fresh breeze coming in at the open window——when, lying lazily with eyes half shut, one sees as in a dream green boughs waving, or waters rippling in a golden light? It is a pleasure very near to sadness, bringing tears to one's eyes like a beautiful picture or poem. And is not that a Mother's gentle hand that undraws your curtains, and a Mother's sweet voice that summons you to rise? To rise and forget, in the bright sunlight, the ugly dreams that frightened you so when all was dark——to rise and enjoy another happy day, first kneeling to thank that unseen Friend who sends you the beautiful sun?

Are these strange words from a writer of such tales as "Alice"? And is this a strange letter to find in a book of nonsense? It may be so. Some perhaps may blame me for thus mixing together things grave and gay; others may smile and think it odd that any one should speak of solemn things at all, except in Church and on a Sunday: but I think——nay, I am sure——that some children will read this gently and lovingly, and in the spirit in which I have written it.

For I do not believe God means us thus to divide life into two halves—to wear a grave face on Sunday, and to think it out-of-place to even so much as mention Him on a week-day. Do you think He cares to see only kneeling figures and to hear only tones of prayer——and that He does not also love to see the lambs leaping in the sunlight, and to hear the merry voices of the children, as they roll among the hay? Surely their innocent laughter is as sweet in His ears as the grandest anthem that ever rolled up from the "dim religious light" of some solemn cathedral?

And if I have written anything to add to those stores of innocent and healthy amusement that are laid up in books for the children I love so well, it is surely something I may hope to look

---

† Dodgson wrote this greeting in the spring of 1876, intending that it be inserted in copies of *The Hunting of the Snark*, which was published in March of that year. The greeting was also sold separately in 1876, and in 1880 Dodgson authorized another separate printing. The version printed above is a final version, slightly revised in its punctuation and a few other minor points, which was published around 1885.

back upon without shame and sorrow (as how much of life must then be recalled!) when *my* turn comes to walk through the valley of shadows.

This Easter sun will rise on you, dear child, "feeling your life in every limb," and eager to rush out into the fresh morning air—— and many an Easter-day will come and go, before it finds you feeble and grey-headed, creeping wearily out to bask once more in the sunlight—but it is good, even now, to think sometimes of that great morning when "the Sun of righteousness" shall "arise with healing in his wings."[1]

Surely your gladness need not be the less for the thought that you will one day see a brighter dawn than this——when lovelier sights will meet your eyes than any waving trees or rippling waters——when angel-hands shall undraw your curtains, and sweeter tones than ever loving Mother breathed shall wake you to a new and glorious day—and when all the sadness, and the sin, that darkened life on this little earth, shall be forgotten like the dreams of a night that is past!

Your affectionate Friend,
LEWIS CARROLL.

Inscribed to a Dear Child:[2]

IN MEMORY OF GOLDEN SUMMER HOURS

AND WHISPERS OF A SUMMER SEA

Girt with a boyish garb for boyish task,
    Eager she wields her spade: yet loves as well
Rest on a friendly knee, intent to ask
    The tale he loves to tell.

Rude spirits of the seething outer strife,
    Unmeet to read her pure and simple spright,
Deem, if you list, such hours a waste of life,
    Empty of all delight!

1. "Feeling your life in every link" is a slightly altered phrase from William Wordsworth's poem "We Are Seven" (1798); the sentence about "the Sun of righteousness" is from a hymn of the same name by Cecil Frances Alexander (1818–1895).
2. The first letters of each line spell, and the first syllables of each stanza sound, the name of Gertrude Chataway, a young girl Dodgson had met during a vacation by the sea in September 1875. He had already begun to write *The Hunting of the Snark* by this date. The last line of the poem, he wrote in his diary (November 6, 1875:6:432), came into his head July 18, 1874 (see also his statement in *"Alice* on the Stage," on pp. 276-78 of this Norton Critical Edition); he wrote the first stanza of the poem on July 22, 1874, and he wrote a good deal of the poem in the fall and winter of 1875–76, completing it in the spring of 1876. The poem was published in March 1876.

Chat on, sweet Maid, and rescue from annoy
   Hearts that by wiser talk are unbeguiled,
Ah, happy he who owns that tenderest joy,
   The heart-love of a child!

Away, fond thoughts, and vex my soul no more!
   Work claims my wakeful nights, my busy days—
Albeit bright memories of that sunlit shore
   Yet haunt my dreaming gaze!

Preface

If—and the thing is wildly possible—the charge of writing non-sense were ever brought against the author of this brief but instructive poem, it would be based, I feel convinced, on the line

"Then the bowsprit[3] got mixed with the rudder sometimes."

In view of this painful possibility, I will not (as I might) appeal indignantly to my other writings as a proof that I am incapable of such a deed: I will not (as I might) point to the strong moral purpose of this poem itself, to the arithmetical principles so cautiously inculcated in it, or to its noble teachings in Natural History—I will take the more prosaic course of simply explaining how it happened.

The Bellman, who was almost morbidly sensitive about appearances, used to have the bowsprit unshipped once or twice a week to be revarnished, and it more than once happened, when the time came for replacing it, that no one on board could remember which end of the ship it belonged to. They knew it was not of the slightest use to appeal to the Bellman about it—he would only refer to his Naval Code, and read out in pathetic tones Admiralty Instructions which none of them had ever been able to understand—so it generally ended in its being fastened on, anyhow, across the rudder. The helmsman[4] used to stand by with tears in his eyes: *he* knew it was all wrong, but alas! Rule 42 of the Code, *"No one shall speak to the Man at the Helm,"* had been completed by the Bellman himself with the words *"and the Man at the Helm shall speak to no one."* So remonstrance was impossible, and no steering could be done till the next varnishing day. During these bewildering intervals the ship usually sailed backwards.

As this poem is to some extent connected with the lay of the Jabberwock, let me take this opportunity of answering a question that has often been asked me, how to pronounce "slithy toves." The "i" in "slithy" is long, as in "writhe"; and "toves" is pronounced so as to rhyme with "groves." Again, the first "o" in "borogoves" is pronounced like the "o" in "borrow." I have heard people try to give it the sound of the "o" in "worry." Such is Human Perversity.

This also seems a fitting occasion to notice the other hard words in that poem. Humpty-Dumpty's theory, of two meanings packed into one word like a portmanteau, seems to me the right explanation for all.

---

3. A boom or spar projecting forward from the bow of a ship.
4. This office was usually undertaken by the Boots, who found in it a refuge from the Baker's constant complaints about the insufficient blacking of his three pairs of boots. [*Dodgson's note.*]

For instance, take the two words "fuming" and "furious." Make up your mind that you will say both words, but leave it unsettled which you will say first. Now open your mouth and speak. If your thoughts incline ever so little towards "fuming," you will say "fuming-furious;" if they turn, by even a hair's breadth, towards "furious," you will say "furious-fuming;" but if you have the rarest of gifts, a perfectly balanced mind, you will say "frumious."

Supposing that, when Pistol uttered the well-known words—

> "Under which King, Bezonian? Speak or die!"

Justice Shallow[5] had felt certain that it was either William or Richard, but had not been able to settle which, so that he could not possibly say either name before the other, can it be doubted that, rather than die, he would have gasped out "Rilchiam!"

Fit the First.[6]

THE LANDING.

"Just the place for a Snark!" the Bellman[7] cried,
  As he landed his crew with care;
Supporting each man on the top of the tide
  By a finger entwined in his hair.

"Just the place for a Snark! I have said it twice:
  That alone should encourage the crew.
Just the place for a Snark! I have said it thrice:
  What I tell you three times is true."

The crew was complete: it included a Boots—
  A maker of Bonnets and Hoods—
A Barrister, brought to arrange their disputes—
  And a Broker, to value their goods.

A Billiard-marker, whose skill was immense,
  Might perhaps have won more than his share—

---

5. Pistol and Shallow conduct this conversation in Shakespeare's 2 *Henry IV* (V.3).
6. *Fit* is a name for a division of a song or poem; Dodgson here also plays with its association with delirium or insanity.
7. A bellman is a town crier. Anne Clark [Amor] in her biography of Dodgson (see Selected Bibliography) quotes from the University statutes, current at least in the beginning of Dodgson's time in Oxford, a description of the duties of a functionary who is commissioned "at the death of doctors, masters, scholars, and other privileged persons, to put on the clothes of the deceased and give notice of their burial by ringing a bell which he carries in his hand" (p. 64). Among the other occupations named in this Fit, a boots (although Dodgson's note makes him a helmsman) is a servant in a hotel who, among other menial tasks, cleans and shines boots; a barrister is a lawyer who is admitted to plead before a court; a billiard-marker is the scorekeeper of a billiard game; and a broker appraises the value of goods.

But a Banker, engaged at enormous expense,
    Had the whole of their cash in his care.

There was also a Beaver, that paced on the deck,
    Or would sit making lace in the bow:
And had often (the Bellman said) saved them from wreck,
    Though none of the sailors knew how.

There was one who was famed for the number of things
    He forgot when he entered the ship:
His umbrella, his watch, all his jewels and rings,
    And the clothes he had bought for the trip.

He had forty-two boxes, all carefully packed,
    With his name painted clearly on each:
But, since he omitted to mention the fact,
    They were all left behind on the beach.

The loss of his clothes hardly mattered, because
    He had seven coats on when he came,
With three pair of boots—but the worst of it was,
    He had wholly forgotten his name.

He would answer to "Hi!" or to any loud cry,
    Such as "Fry me!" or "Fritter my wig!"
To "What-you-may-call-um!" or "What-was-his name!"
    But especially "Thing-um-a-jig!"

While, for those who preferred a more forcible word,
    He had different names from these:
His intimate friends called him "Candle-ends,"
    And his enemies "Toasted-cheese."

"His form is ungainly—his intellect small—"
    (So the Bellman would often remark)
"But his courage is perfect! And that, after all,
    Is the thing that one needs with a Snark."

He would joke with hyænas, returning their stare
    With an impudent wag of the head:
And he once went a walk, paw-in-paw, with a bear,
    "Just to keep up its spirits," he said.

He came as a Baker: but owned, when too late—
    And it drove the poor Bellman half-mad—

He could only bake Bride-cake[8]—for which, I may state,
　　No materials were to be had.

The last of the crew needs especial remark,
　　Though he looked an incredible dunce:
He had just one idea—but, that one being "Snark,"
　　The good Bellman engaged him at once.

He came as a Butcher: but gravely declared,
　　When the ship had been sailing a week,
He could only kill Beavers. The Bellman looked scared,
　　And was almost too frightened to speak:

But at length he explained, in a tremulous tone,
　　There was only one Beaver on board;
And that was a tame one he had of his own,
　　Whose death would be deeply deplored.

The Beaver, who happened to hear the remark,
　　Protested, with tears in its eyes,
That not even the rapture of hunting the Snark
　　Could atone for that dismal surprise!

It strongly advised that the Butcher should be
　　Conveyed in a separate ship:
But the Bellman declared that would never agree
　　With the plans he had made for the trip:

Navigation was always a difficult art,
　　Though with only one ship and one bell:
And he feared he must really decline, for his part,
　　Undertaking another as well.

The Beaver's best course was, no doubt, to procure
　　A second-hand dagger-proof coat—
So the Baker advised it—and next, to insure
　　Its life in some Office of note:

This the Banker suggested, and offered for hire[9]
　　(On moderate terms), or for sale,
Two excellent Policies, one Against Fire
　　And one Against Damage From Hail.

8. Wedding cake.
9. Office of note: reputable insurance agency. Hire: rent.

Yet still, ever after that sorrowful day,
   Whenever the Butcher was by,
The Beaver kept looking the opposite way,
   And appeared unaccountably shy.

Fit the Second.

THE BELLMAN'S SPEECH.

The Bellman himself they all praised to the skies—
   Such a carriage, such ease and such grace!
Such solemnity, too! One could see he was wise,
   The moment one looked in his face!

He had bought a large map representing the sea,[1]
   Without the least vestige of land:
And the crew were much pleased when they found it to be
   A map they could all understand.

"What's the good of Mercator's[2] North Poles and Equators,
   Tropics, Zones, and Meridian Lines?"
So the Bellman would cry: and the crew would reply
   "They are merely conventional signs!

"Other maps are such shapes, with their islands and capes!
   But we've got our brave Captain to thank"
(So the crew would protest) "that he's bought *us* the best—
   A perfect and absolute blank!"

This was charming, no doubt: but they shortly found out
   That the Captain they trusted so well
Had only one notion for crossing the ocean,
   And that was to tingle his bell.

He was thoughtful and grave—but the orders he gave
   Were enough to bewilder a crew.
When he cried "Steer to starboard, but keep her head
     larboard!"[3]
   What on earth was the helmsman to do?

---

1. In Henry Holiday's illustration, the map is an entirely blank rectangle marked on its margins by the directions of the compass and such phrases as "Torrid Zone," "Equator," and "South Pole."
2. Gerhardus Mercator was the sixteenth-century cartographer who devised a means of depicting the round earth on a flat map.
3. Larboard: port. The helmsman cannot obey this contradictory order.

Then the bowsprit got mixed with the rudder sometimes:
    A thing, as the Bellman remarked,
That frequently happens in tropical climes,
    When a vessel is, so to speak, "snarked."

But the principal failing occured in the sailing,
    And the Bellman, perplexed and distressed,
Said he *had* hoped, at least, when the wind blew due East,
    That the ship would *not* travel due West!

But the danger was past—they had landed at last,
    With their boxes, portmanteaus, and bags:
Yet at first sight the crew were not pleased with the view,
    Which consisted of chasms and crags.

The Bellman perceived that their spirits were low,
    And repeated in musical tone
Some jokes he had kept for a season of woe—
    But the crew would do nothing but groan.

He served out some grog with a liberal hand,
    And bade them sit down on the beach:
And they could not but own that their Captain looked grand,
    As he stood and delivered his speech.

"Friends, Romans, and countrymen, lend me your ears!"[4]
    (They were all of them fond of quotations:
So they drank to his health, and they gave him three cheers,
    While he served out additional rations).

"We have sailed many months, we have sailed many weeks,
    (Four weeks to the month you may mark),
But never as yet ('tis your Captain who speaks)
    Have we caught the least glimpse of a Snark!

"We have sailed many weeks, we have sailed many days,
    (Seven days to the week I allow),
But a Snark, on the which we might lovingly gaze,
    We have never beheld till now!

"Come, listen, my men, while I tell you again
    The five unmistakable marks

---

4. The Bellman slightly misquotes the first line of Mark Antony's oration in Shakespeare's *Julius Caesar*: the speech begins, "Friends, Romans, countrymen."

By which you may know, wheresoever you go,
   The warranted genuine Snarks.

"Let us take them in order. The first is the taste,
   Which is meagre and hollow, but crisp:
Like a coat that is rather too tight in the waist,
   With a flavour of Will-o-the-Wisp.

"Its habit of getting up late you'll agree
   That it carries too far, when I say
That it frequently breakfasts at five-o'clock tea,
   And dines on the following day.

"The third is its slowness in taking a jest.
   Should you happen to venture on one,
It will sigh like a thing that is deeply distressed:
   And it always looks grave at a pun.

"The fourth is its fondness for bathing-machines,[5]
   Which it constantly carries about,
And believes that they add to the beauty of scenes—
   A sentiment open to doubt.

"The fifth is ambition. It next will be right
   To describe each particular batch:
Distinguishing those that have feathers, and bite,
   From those that have whiskers, and scratch.

"For, although common Snarks do no manner of harm,
   Yet, I feel it my duty to say,
Some are Boojums—" The Bellman broke off in alarm,
   For the Baker had fainted away.

Fit the Third.

THE BAKER'S TALE.

They roused him with muffins—they roused him with ice—
   They roused him with mustard and cress—
They roused him with jam and judicious advice—
   They set him conundrums to guess.

When at length he sat up and was able to speak,
   His sad story he offered to tell;

5. Bathing-machines: see note 9, p. 17.

And the Bellman cried "Silence! Not even a shriek!"
    And excitedly tingled his bell.

There was silence supreme! Not a shriek, not a scream,
    Scarcely even a howl or a groan,
As the man they called "Ho!" told his story of woe
    In an antediluvian tone.[6]

"My father and mother were honest, though poor—"
    "Skip all that!" cried the Bellman in haste.
"If it once becomes dark, there's no chance of a Snark—
    We have hardly a minute to waste!"

"I skip forty years," said the Baker, in tears,
    "And proceed without further remark
To the day when you took me aboard of your ship
    To help you in hunting the Snark.

"A dear uncle of mine (after whom I was named)
    Remarked, when I bade him farewell—"
"Oh, skip your dear uncle!" the Bellman exclaimed,
    And he angrily tingled his bell.

"He remarked to me then," said the mildest of men,
    "'If your Snark be a Snark, that is right:
Fetch it home by all means—you may serve it with greens,
    And it's handy for striking a light.

"'You may seek it with thimbles—and seek it with care;
    You may hunt it with forks and hope;
You may threaten its life with a railway-share:
    You may charm it with smiles and soap—'"

("That's exactly the method," the Bellman bold
    In a hasty parenthesis cried,
"That's exactly the way I have always been told
    That the capture of Snarks should be tried!")

"'But oh, beamish[7] nephew, beware of the day,
    If your Snark be a Boojum! For then

---

6. Dodgson's willfully inaccurate use of "antediluvian"—which means "before the Deluge"—predicts the Baker's catastrophic fate.
7. Like *uffish, galumphing, Jubjub, outgrabe*, and some other words and names in the poem, this word is borrowed from "Jabberwocky."

You will softly and suddenly vanish away,
   And never be met with again!'

"It is this, it is this that oppresses my soul,
   When I think of my uncle's last words:
And my heart is like nothing so much as a bowl
   Brimming over with quivering curds!

"It is this, it is this—" "We have had that before!"
   The Bellman indignantly said.
And the Baker replied "Let me say it once more.
   It is this, it is this that I dread!

"I engage with the Snark—every night after dark—
   In a dreamy delirious fight:
I serve it with greens in those shadowy scenes,
   And I use it for striking a light:

"But if ever I meet with a Boojum, that day,
   In a moment (of this I am sure),
I shall softly and suddenly vanish away—
   And the notion I cannot endure!"

Fit the Fourth.

THE HUNTING.

The Bellman looked uffish, and wrinkled his brow.
   "If only you'd spoken before!
It's excessively awkward to mention it now,
   With the Snark, so to speak, at the door!

"We should all of us grieve, as you well may believe,
   If you never were met with again—
But surely, my man, when the voyage began,
   You might have suggested it then?

"It's excessively awkward to mention it now—
   As I think I've already remarked."
And the man they called "Hi!" replied, with a sigh,
   "I informed you the day we embarked.

"You may charge me with murder—or want of sense—
   (We are all of us weak at times):
But the slightest approach to a false pretence
   Was never among my crimes!

"I said it in Hebrew—I said it in Dutch—
    I said it in German and Greek:
But I wholly forgot (and it vexes me much)
    That English is what you speak!"

"'Tis a pitiful tale," said the Bellman, whose face
    Had grown longer at every word:
"But, now that you've stated the whole of your case,
    More debate would be simply absurd.

"The rest of my speech" (he exclaimed to his men)
    "You shall hear when I've leisure to speak it.
But the Snark is at hand, let me tell you again!
    'Tis your glorious duty to seek it!

"To seek it with thimbles, to seek it with care;
    To pursue it with forks and hope;
To threaten its life with a railway-share;
    To charm it with smiles and soap!

"For the Snark's a peculiar creature, that won't
    Be caught in a commonplace way.
Do all that you know, and try all that you don't:
    Not a chance must be wasted to-day!

"For England expects[8]—I forbear to proceed:
    'Tis a maxim tremendous, but trite:
And you'd best be unpacking the things that you need
    To rig yourselves out for the fight."

Then the Banker endorsed a blank cheque
        (which he crossed),
    And changed his loose silver for notes.[9]
The Baker with care combed his whiskers and hair,
    And shook the dust out of his coats.

The Boots and the Broker were sharpening a spade—
    Each working the grindstone in turn:
But the Beaver went on making lace, and displayed
    No interest in the concern:

8. The trite maxim is Lord Nelson's admonition to the men of his fleet before the battle of Trafalgar in 1805: "England expects every man to do his duty."
9. To cross a check is to draw lines across it, indicating that it is not negotiable but must be deposited in the account of the person to whom it is made out. "Notes" are banknotes.

Though the Barrister tried to appeal to its pride,
   And vainly proceeded to cite
A number of cases, in which making laces
   Had been proved an infringement of right.

The maker of Bonnets ferociously planned
   A novel arrangement of bows:
While the Billiard-marker with quivering hand
   Was chalking the tip of his nose.

But the Butcher turned nervous, and dressed himself fine,
   With yellow kid gloves and a ruff—
Said he felt it exactly like going to dine,
   Which the Bellman declared was all "stuff."[1]

"Introduce me, now there's a good fellow," he said,
   "If we happen to meet it together!"
And the Bellman, sagaciously nodding his head,
   Said "That must depend on the weather."

The Beaver went simply galumphing about,
   At seeing the Butcher so shy:
And even the Baker, though stupid and stout,
   Made an effort to wink with one eye.

"Be a man!" cried the Bellman in wrath, as he heard
   The Butcher beginning to sob.
"Should we meet with a Jubjub, that desperate bird,
   We shall need all our strength for the job!"

Fit the Fifth.

THE BEAVER'S LESSON.

They sought it with thimbles, they sought it with care;
   They pursued it with forks and hope;
They threatened its life with a railway-share;
   They charmed it with smiles and soap.

Then the Butcher contrived an ingenious plan
   For making a separate sally;
And had fixed on a spot unfrequented by man,
   A dismal and desolate valley.

1. "Stuff" was a slang expression used to describe meaningless or pointless words and gestures.

But the very same plan to the Beaver occurred:
   It had chosen the very same place:
Yet neither betrayed, by a sign or a word,
   The disgust that appeared in his face.

Each thought he was thinking of nothing but "Snark"
   And the glorious work of the day;
And each tried to pretend that he did not remark
   That the other was going that way.

But the valley grew narrow and narrower still,
   And the evening got darker and colder,
Till (merely from nervousness, not from good will)
   They marched along shoulder to shoulder.

Then a scream, shrill and high, rent the shuddering sky,
   And they knew that some danger was near:
The Beaver turned pale to the tip of its tail,
   And even the Butcher felt queer.

He thought of his childhood, left far behind—
   That blissful and innocent state—
The sound so exactly recalled to his mind
   A pencil that squeaks on a slate!

"'Tis the voice of the Jubjub!" he suddenly cried.
   (This man, that they used to call "Dunce.")
"As the Bellman would tell you," he added with pride,
   "I have uttered that sentiment once.

"'Tis the note of the Jubjub! Keep count, I entreat;
   You will find I have told it you twice.
'Tis the song of the Jubjub! The proof is complete.
   If only I've stated it thrice."

The Beaver had counted with scrupulous care,
   Attending to every word:
But it fairly lost heart, and outgrabe in despair,
   When the third repetition occurred.

It felt that, in spite of all possible pains,
   It had somehow contrived to lose count,
And the only thing now was to rack its poor brains
   By reckoning up the amount.

"Two added to one—if that could but be done,"
It said, "with one's fingers and thumbs!"
Recollecting with tears how, in earlier years,
    It had taken no pains with its sums.

"The thing can be done," said the Butcher, "I think.
    The thing must be done, I am sure.
The thing shall be done! Bring me paper and ink,
    The best there is time to procure."

The Beaver brought paper, portfolio, pens,
    And ink in unfailing supplies:
While strange creepy creatures came out of their dens,
    And watched them with wondering eyes.

So engrossed was the Butcher, he heeded them not,
    As he wrote with a pen in each hand,
And explained all the while in a popular style
    Which the Beaver could well understand.

"Taking Three as the subject to reason about—
    A convenient number to state—
We add Seven, and Ten, and then multiply out
    By One Thousand diminished by Eight.

"The result we proceed to divide, as you see,
    By Nine Hundred and Ninety and Two:
Then subtract Seventeen, and the answer must be
    Exactly and perfectly true.[2]

"The method employed I would gladly explain,
    While I have it so clear in my head,
If I had but the time and you had but the brain—
    But much yet remains to be said.

"In one moment I've seen what has hitherto been
    Enveloped in absolute mystery,
And without extra charge I will give you at large
    A Lesson in Natural History."

In his genial way he proceeded to say
    (Forgetting all laws of propriety,
And that giving instruction, without introduction,
    Would have caused quite a thrill in Society),

---

2. The Butcher's calculation returns to the number Three as the answer.

"As to temper the Jubjub's a desperate bird,
    Since it lives in perpetual passion:
Its taste in costume is entirely absurd—
    It is ages ahead of the fashion:

"But it knows any friend it has met once before:
    It never will look at a bribe:
And in charity-meetings it stands at the door,
    And collects—though it does not subscribe.[3]

"Its flavour when cooked is more exquisite far
    Than mutton, or oysters, or eggs:
(Some think it keeps best in an ivory jar,
    And some, in mahogany kegs:)

"You boil it in sawdust: you salt it in glue:
    You condense it with locusts and tape:
Still keeping one principal object in view—
    To preserve its symmetrical shape."

The Butcher would gladly have talked till next day,
    But he felt that the Lesson must end,
And he wept with delight in attempting to say
    He considered the Beaver his friend.

While the Beaver confessed, with affectionate looks
    More eloquent even than tears,
It had learned in ten minutes far more than all books
    Would have taught it in seventy years.

They returned hand-in-hand, and the Bellman, unmanned
    (For a moment) with noble emotion,
Said "This amply repays all the wearisome days
    We have spent on the billowy ocean!"

Such friends, as the Beaver and Butcher became,
    Have seldom if ever been known;
In winter or summer, 'twas always the same—
    You could never meet either alone.

And when quarrels arose—as one frequently finds
    Quarrels will, spite of every endeavour—
The song of the Jubjub recurred to their minds,
    And cemented their friendship for ever!

---

3. To subscribe to a charity is to contribute money.

Fit the Sixth.

THE BARRISTER'S DREAM.

They sought it with thimbles, they sought it with care;
　　They pursued it with forks and hope;
They threatened its life with a railway-share;
　　They charmed it with smiles and soap.

But the Barrister, weary of proving in vain
　　That the Beaver's lace-making was wrong,
Fell asleep, and in dreams saw the creature quite plain
　　That his fancy had dwelt on so long.

He dreamed that he stood in a shadowy Court,
　　Where the Snark, with a glass in its eye,
Dressed in gown, bands, and wig,[4] was defending a pig
　　On the charge of deserting its sty.

The Witnesses proved, without error or flaw,
　　That the sty was deserted when found:
And the Judge kept explaining the state of the law
　　In a soft under-current of sound.

The indictment had never been clearly expressed,
　　And it seemed that the Snark had begun,
And had spoken three hours, before any one guessed
　　What the pig was supposed to have done.

The Jury had each formed a different view
　　(Long before the indictment was read),
And they all spoke at once, so that none of them knew
　　One word that the others had said.

"You must know—" said the Judge: but the Snark exclaimed
　　　"Fudge!
　　That statute is obsolete quite!
Let me tell you, my friends, the whole question depends
　　On an ancient manorial right.

"In the matter of Treason the pig would appear
　　To have aided, but scarcely abetted:

---

4. Wig, gown, and bands (a pair of cloth strips hanging from the neck of the gown) are
worn by barristers when they plead before a judge.

While the charge of Insolvency fails, it is clear,
    If you grant the plea 'never indebted.'[5]

"The fact of Desertion I will not dispute:
    But its guilt, as I trust, is removed
(So far as relates to the costs of this suit)
    By the Alibi which has been proved.

"My poor client's fate now depends on your votes."
    Here the speaker sat down in his place,
And directed the Judge to refer to his notes
    And briefly to sum up the case.

But the Judge said he never had summed up before;
    So the Snark undertook it instead,
And summed it so well that it came to far more
    Than the Witnesses ever had said!

When the verdict was called for, the Jury declined,
    As the word was so puzzling to spell;
But they ventured to hope that the Snark wouldn't mind
    Undertaking that duty as well.

So the Snark found the verdict, although, as it owned,
    It was spent with the toils of the day:
When it said the word "GUILTY!" the Jury all groaned,
    And some of them fainted away.

Then the Snark pronounced sentence, the Judge being quite
    Too nervous to utter a word:
When it rose to its feet, there was silence like night,
    And the fall of a pin might be heard.

"Transportation for life"[6] was the sentence it gave,
    "And *then* to be fined forty pound."
The Jury all cheered, though the Judge said he feared
    That the phrase was not legally sound.

5. "Never indebted" is a proper plea in an action for debt: it is not a proper plea in an
   insolvency or bankruptcy action.
6. During the eighteenth century and part of the nineteenth, persons convicted of crimes in
   England were frequently transported, that is, sent to one of the British colonies to work
   out their sentences as convict laborers. Commonly, sentences of transportation in the
   nineteenth century sent convicts to Australia or New Zealand. This is one of several references in the poem (another is the Baker's inability to recall his name) that persuaded
   some contemporary reviewers that it was a satire on the trial in the early 1870s of an
   Australian butcher who claimed to be Sir Roger Tichborne, a wealthy Englishman who
   had been presumed lost at sea. The Tichborne impostor was found guilty of perjury.

But their wild exultation was suddenly checked
　　When the jailer informed them, with tears,
Such a sentence would have not the slightest effect,
　　As the pig had been dead for some years.

The Judge left the Court, looking deeply disgusted:
　　But the Snark, though a little aghast,
As the lawyer to whom the defence was intrusted,
　　Went bellowing on to the last.

Thus the Barrister dreamed, while the bellowing seemed
　　To grow every moment more clear:
Till he woke to the knell of a furious bell,
　　Which the Bellman rang close at his ear.

Fit the Seventh.

THE BANKER'S FATE.

They sought it with thimbles, they sought it with care;
　　They pursued it with forks and hope;
They threatened its life with a railway-share;
　　They charmed it with smiles and soap.

And the Banker, inspired with a courage so new
　　It was matter for general remark,
Rushed madly ahead and was lost to their view
　　In his zeal to discover the Snark.

But while he was seeking with thimbles and care,
　　A Bandersnatch swiftly drew nigh
And grabbed at the Banker, who shrieked in despair,
　　For he knew it was useless to fly.

He offered large discount—he offered a cheque
　　(Drawn "to bearer") for seven-pounds-ten:
But the Bandersnatch merely extended its neck
　　And grabbed at the Banker again.

Without rest or pause—while those frumious jaws
　　Went savagely snapping around—
He skipped and he hopped, and he floundered and flopped
　　Till fainting he fell to the ground.

The Bandersnatch fled as the others appeared
　　Led on by that fear-stricken yell:

And the Bellman remarked "It is just as I feared!"
   And solemnly tolled on his bell.

He was black in the face, and they scarcely could trace
   The least likeness to what he had been:
While so great was his fright that his waistcoat
      turned white—
   A wonderful thing to be seen!

To the horror of all who were present that day,
   He uprose in full evening dress,
And with senseless grimaces endeavoured to say
   What his tongue could no longer express.

Down he sank in a chair—ran his hands through his hair—
   And chanted in mimsiest tones
Words whose utter inanity proved his insanity,
   While he rattled a couple of bones.[7]

"Leave him here to his fate—it is getting so late!"
   The Bellman exclaimed in a fright.
"We have lost half the day. Any further delay,
   And we sha'n't catch a Snark before night!"

Fit the Eighth.

THE VANISHING.

They sought it with thimbles, they sought it with care;
   They pursued it with forks and hope;
They threatened its life with a railway-share;
   They charmed it with smiles and soap.

They shuddered to think that the chase might fail,
   And the Beaver, excited at last,
Went bounding along on the tip of its tail,
   For the daylight was nearly past.

"There is Thingumbob shouting!" the Bellman said.
   "He is shouting like mad, only hark!

---

7. One of the performers in a conventional minstrel show—Mr. Bones—rattled a pair of bones to punctuate nonsensical exchanges with other performers. Minstrel shows were enormously popular in England from the 1840s until near the end of the century. In Henry Holiday's illustration of this scene, the Banker is in blackface and holds a pair of his instrumental bones in his left hand.

He is waving his hands, he is wagging his head,
　　He has certainly found a Snark!"

They gazed in delight, while the Butcher exclaimed
　　"He was always a desperate wag!"
They beheld him—their Baker—their hero unnamed—
　　On the top of a neighbouring crag,

Erect and sublime, for one moment of time.
　　In the next, that wild figure they saw
(As if stung by a spasm) plunge into a chasm,
　　While they waited and listened in awe.

"It's a Snark!" was the sound that first came to their ears,
　　And seemed almost too good to be true.
Then followed a torrent of laughter and cheers:
　　Then the ominous words "It's a Boo—"

Then, silence. Some fancied they heard in the air
　　A weary and wandering sigh
That sounded like "—jum!" but the others declare
　　It was only a breeze that went by.

They hunted till darkness came on, but they found
　　Not a button, or feather, or mark,
By which they could tell that they stood on the ground
　　Where the Baker had met with the Snark.

In the midst of the word he was trying to say,
　　In the midst of his laughter and glee,
He had softly and suddenly vanished away—
　　For the Snark *was* a Boojum, you see.[8]

THE END.

---

8. In *The Annotated Hunting of the Snark* (see Selected Bibliography), Martin Gardner reports that Boojum is now a name that has been given to "a singularity that can form in superfluid helium-3, and that works its way to the surface where it can make a super-current softly and suddenly vanish" (p. 34).

BACKGROUNDS

Family and Education

MORTON N. COHEN

Beginnings[†]

The Dodgsons descended from north country people going back beyond the eighteenth century. In 1827 Charles Dodgson, Lewis Carroll's father, married his first cousin Frances Jane Lutwidge. The newborn son was the third of what eventually became a family of eleven children, and if these bloodlines deserve credit for the creative genius we know to be Lewis Carroll's, so perhaps must they bear the blame for the stammer endemic in Charles's speech and in the speech of most of his brothers and sisters.

The older north country Dodgsons were county families, gentry and nobility. But immediate antecedents were mostly men of the cloth, an army captain, a lawyer. While privileged, they were neither exceptionally gifted nor depraved: no geniuses, no knaves.

The Dodgsons we meet here typify the slice of Victorian society often described as upper middle class, falling between those who worked with their hands and those who did not work at all. Lacking aristocratic bearings, inherited wealth, land, or other property, they could aspire to rise in the world only by developing their minds—which they did. Money was generally a constant concern, but it never crowded out their religious fervor, devotion to social good, pursuit of learning, and dedication to improving the human condition.

* * * The Reverend Mr. Charles Dodgson received the curacy from his college, Christ Church, Oxford, in 1827, six years after taking a double first in classics and mathematics. Daresbury, seven miles from Warrington and twenty-one from Liverpool, a hamlet of 599 acres and 143 people, pleasantly situated and commanding fine prospects of the surrounding country, was virtually lost in the farming landscape. The parsonage, situated on a glebe farm a mile and

† From *Lewis Carroll: A Biography* (New York: A. A. Knopf, 1995), 4–8, 12–14. Copyright © 1995 by Morton N. Cohen. Used by permission of Alfred A. Knopf, a division of Random House, Inc.

a half from the small village, stood in rustic isolation, where "even the passing of a cart was a matter of great interest."[1]

* * *

S. D. Collingwood, Charles's nephew-biographer, who heard about life in the Daresbury parsonage at first hand, recorded that "in this quiet home the boy invented the strangest diversions for himself; he . . . numbered certain snails and toads among his intimate friends. He tried also to encourage civilised warfare among earthworms. . . ." He "seemed at this time to have . . . lived in that charming 'Wonderland' which he afterwards described so vividly; but for all that he was a thorough boy, and loved to climb the trees and to scramble about in the, marl-pits."[2] In *Alice's Adventures in Wonderland* and *Through the Looking-Glass*, the White Rabbit, the animals in the Caucus-Race, the Caterpillar, the garden of flowers, and much more owe their origin to the barnyard, the fields, and the gardens of Daresbury.

* * *

At Daresbury the father tended his flock, giving special attention to the poor; he initiated Sunday school and held service in a barge chapel of his own devising for those who worked on the canal running through the parish. He was reputed to exhibit wit and humor "in moments of relaxation," but in the main, he "was a man of deep piety and of a somewhat reserved and grave disposition."[3] To augment his meager income, he took in paying pupils. In addition to all his other work, he somehow managed to produce a monograph on religion at least once a year.

Life in the Dodgson household was busy and followed a strict regimen. Hours were allocated for games, but lighter activities did not encroach upon the severe Christian responsibilities or on time needed for lessons, reading, memorizing. Religious rituals dominated the Daresbury parsonage. The family assembled for prayers morning and evening; Bible reading was a staple; on Sunday they attended two church services and the children went to Sunday school. Both work and play were forbidden on Sunday, replaced by reading religious tomes, and the family ate cold meals to insure that the ser-

1. Collingwood, *The Life and Letters of Lewis Carroll* (see full citation on p. 299), 11.

   In the Church of England clerical appointments were often in the gift of institutions and individuals. The fact that Dodgson's father received his curacy from his college is a mark of his exceptional accomplishment as an undergraduate. So was his "double first," the award of first-class honors in his examinations in two fields of study with which he completed his undergraduate degree. The glebe farm was a parcel of land attached to the parish to provide food and income for the incumbent clergyman. [*Editor's note*]

2. Collingwood, 11–12.
3. Collingwood, 8.

vants did not have to work on the Lord's day. Even though Mr. Dodgson augmented his income by tutoring, he was pinched financially and sent reports back to Christ Church of "anxieties incidental to my situation."[4]

For her part, the cleric's lady kept busy helping her husband with parish work and bearing, rearing, and shaping her ever-increasing family: ten of her children were born in Daresbury. Complying with custom, she educated her daughters at home. Mrs. Dodgson was in her own way as remarkable as her husband, remaining cheerful and loving, taking on all her duties and burdens without complaint. One observer remembered her as "one of the sweetest and gentlest women that ever lived, whom to know was to love. The earnestness of her simple faith and love shone forth in all she did and said. . . . It has been said by her children that they never in all their lives remember to have heard an impatient or harsh word from her lips."[5]

*   *   *

Charles was her special pet; the few surviving letters she wrote to her sister Lucy show her sensitive to Charles's uncommon nature. She kept a three-part record of Charles's early reading: "Religious Reading: Private," "Religious Reading with Mama," and "Daily Reading: Useful—Private." Among the tomes he tackled at age seven was *The Pilgrim's Progress*. For his part, he sensed her angelic qualities and worshiped her above all others. Many years later, when his sister Mary gave birth to her first child, Charles wrote her: "May you be to him what your own dear mother was to *her* eldest son. I can hardly utter for your boy a better wish than that!"[6]

"Charlie," as well as the other sons, received their earliest lessons from their father. Charles progressed rapidly in his studies. When he was eight or so, Charles's mother, writing to him from Hull, where she was visiting her parents, congratulated him on "getting on so well with your Latin, and . . . [making] so few mistakes in your Exercises."[7] All children are curious, but not many so precocious as Charles: "One day, when . . . [he] was a very small boy," Collingwood wrote, "he . . . showed . . . [his father] a book of logarithms, with the request, 'Please explain.' Mr. Dodgson told him that he was much too young to understand . . . such a difficult subject. The child listened . . . and appeared to think it irrelevant, for he still insisted, '*But*, please, explain!'"[8] The father was evidently

---

4. The sentence is quoted from Christ Church Treasury Papers, MS. Estate 19, 160, January 23, 1832.
5. Collingwood, 8.
6. *Letters* I:146. (See full citation on p. 251).
7. Collingwood, 14.
8. Collingwood, 12–13.

successful in tutoring Charles and Charles diligent in his application, taking easily to his study of Latin, mathematics, the classics, and English literature. The father imbued the son with his own religious principles, and the son, in these early days, accepted the parental teachings, especially in matters of Christian doctrine, and sought to mirror his accomplished sire.

* * *

For sixteen years, Mr. Dodgson struggled in obscurity at Daresbury. But then, in 1843, when Charles was eleven, on the urging of Mr. Dodgson's old friend Charles Longley, Bishop of Ripon, and other notables, the Prime Minister, Robert Peel, awarded the elder Dodgson the living of Croft-on-Tees in the North Riding of Yorkshire, four miles south of Darlington, twenty-five miles north of the cathedral town of Ripon. * * *

In Croft Rectory, the boy grew into a youth, and his native talents emerged. Even before he was thrust in with others of his age and station at school, he proved supple in matters mechanical, creative in art, and a responsible leader and instructor of the other Dodgson children. With a carpenter's help, he built a marionette theater, composed plays, and learned to manipulate the marionettes for the presentations. Wearing a brown wig and a long white robe, he became an Aladdin, a nimble magician performing tricks to amaze and delight an admiring throng. He created charades and acted them out. He built for his elder sister Elizabeth a miniature toolbox and inscribed it "E.L.D. from C.L.D."

Drawings, verses, and short stories sprang forth, and while none is stamped with Mozartian genius, all are more than ordinary. Charles's early compositions in prose and poetry and his artwork show that his handwriting was already remarkably adult, strong, confident; his vocabulary and allusions prove him well ahead of his years; and if his drawings are crude, they do not lack force or humor. So mature does he appear so early that one wonders whether he moved from childhood directly into adulthood, somehow skipping boyhood. * * *

True, the metrics, the rhymes, even the grammar leave something to be desired, and if Charles's drawings are incondite, they at least show early signs of his interest in art. The self-confidence throughout suggests an exceptional young man in the making. Perhaps most remarkable is the tone, how he treats cherished subjects without offending. The verses bear serious titles ("Punctuality," "Charity," "Rules and Regulations"), but what he does with these virtuous subjects often surprises. In one after another, he dispatches conventional and ponderous Victorian concerns with a fresh and light stroke, with banter, irreverently but endearingly spoofing solemn rubrics. The neatest composition is the first poem, "My Fairy":

I have a fairy by my side
  Which says I must not sleep,
When once in pain I loudly cried
  It said "You must not weep."

If, full of mirth, I smile and grin
  It says "You must not laugh";
When once I wished to drink some gin
  It said "You must not quaff."

When once a meal I wished to taste
  It said "You must not bite";
When to the wars I went in haste
  It said "You must not fight."

"What *may* I do?" at length I cried,
  Tired of the painful task.
The fairy quietly replied,
  And said "You must not ask."

Moral: "You mustn't."

Here, then, Charles's brand of humor, his singular vein of genius, emerges: at thirteen, he already knows how to use it to excellent effect. These juvenile outpourings contain more than meets the eye. Behind the parodies of life at Croft lurk both a keen observer and a critic, a commentator on domestic and social conventions, a judge of family relationships, and, above all, an independent spirit. And beneath the banter run a dark strain of complaint, a smarting resentment, even gratuitous violence, all of which appear more forcefully later.

DONALD THOMAS

Facing the World†

In common with most boys of his class, the younger Charles Dodgson was educated at home until he was twelve years old. It was then necessary to find a school where he could board and learn something of the wider society for which he must prepare. He would see comparatively little of family life for the next six years. In August 1844, he was sent as a boarder to Richmond School, ten miles from Croft. It was a sensitive choice for the boy's introduction to the school

† From *Lewis Carroll: A Portrait with Background* (London: John Murray, 1996), 48–53. Reprinted by permission.

system. Richmond School was small but distinguished, dating back
to the fourteenth century. Its main building was a schoolroom of
1677 in the churchyard, where the boys sat on benches at sloping
desks with the headmaster at a rostrum at the far end, assisted in
teaching and keeping order by an usher.

The school had 120 boys, divided among the houses where they
lived. Charles Dodgson was one of sixteen boys in Swale House, the
headmaster's residence which the boarders shared with the family.
It was a small enough group to be free of the bullying rabble or
personal spite which blemished most public schools of the day.
James Tate, the son of a classical scholar who had preceded him in
the post, was known as a kind and gentle headmaster, far removed
from the sadistic pedagogues of legend. The teaching was principally of Latin and Greek, though such subjects as mathematics
could be added for an extra fee. * * *

When the young Charles Dodgson wrote to his two eldest sisters
on 5 August 1844, four days after his arrival, the ragging which he
had undergone seems hardly more than a child's game.

> They first proposed to play at "King of the Cobblers" and asked
> if I would be king, to which I agreed. Then they made me sit
> down and sat (on the ground) in a circle round me, and told me
> to say 'Go to work,' which I said, and they immediately began
> kicking me and knocking me on all sides. The next game they
> proposed was "Peter, the red lion," and they made a mark on a
> tombstone (for we were playing in the churchyard) and one of
> the boys walked with his eyes shut, holding out his finger, try-
> ing to touch the mark; then a little boy came forward to lead
> the rest and led a good many very near the mark; at last it was
> my turn; they told me to shut my eyes well, and the next min-
> ute I had my finger in the mouth of one of the boys, who had
> stood (I believe) before the tombstone with his mouth open.
> For 2 nights I slept alone and for the rest of the time with Ned
> Swire. The boys play me no tricks now.[1]

It seems that Mr Dodgson, keeping moral surveillance from ten
miles away, had demanded from his son an account of any faults
committed and a list of all the texts upon which he heard sermons
preached. The rector need not have worried. The boy's only fault to
date had been coming to dinner on one occasion after grace was said.
He could only remember the text of one of the Sunday sermons
because the other—like the sermon itself—was scarcely audible. * * *

Mr Tate's first report on his new pupil, made to the rector of Croft,
was filled with praise, except in the matter of scansion or translation

---

1. *Letters* 5 August [1844], I:5. (See full citation p. 251.)

from Latin verse, where the boy was inclined to fit the text into the metre and meaning he had already devised. 'I do not hesitate to state my opinion,' wrote James Tate, 'that he possesses, along with other and excellent natural endowments, a very uncommon share of genius.'

> Gentle and cheerful in his intercourse with others, playful and ready in conversation, he is capable of acquirements and knowledge far beyond his years, while his reason is so clear and so jealous of error, that he will not rest satisfied without a most exact solution of whatever appears to him obscure. He has passed an excellent examination just now in mathematics, exhibiting at times an illustration of that love of precise argument which seems to him natural.

In the matter of precision, the child was proving father to the man. But Tate was wise enough to add a final piece of advice to Mr Dodgson. 'You must not entrust your son with a full knowledge of his superiority over other boys.'[2] Had there been some hint in the conduct of the twelve year old that suggested priggishness or self-satisfaction?

Any such failing was to be roughly dealt with a few months after Charles Dodgson left Richmond in November 1845 to begin his public-school education in earnest. Though his father had been educated at Westminster, the school now chosen was Rugby. * * *

Charles Dodgson arrived at Rugby on his fourteenth birthday, 27 January 1846. He was speedily detected as a muff[3] and the taunt was scrawled on his possessions. To this point in his life he had known little but affection and security. He had been educated by his parents rather than consigned to a tutor or governess. The world of his family was ruled by the certainty that God is Love. Like some of the family's other members, he suffered from a stammer which was sometimes no more than a hesitation and on occasion a complete inability to articulate a word. In his new environment it was a matter for ridicule rather than sympathy. He was, in every way, an admirable target for those already in residence. * * *

Charles Dodgson disliked Rugby, though he kept his feelings from his family until after he left the school. To have done otherwise might seem like ingratitude to his father. Mr Dodgson, as his letters to his second son Skeffington showed, was not averse to giving his children a precise account of how much their education cost him. It was not until 1855, six years after he left Rugby, that the young Charles Dodgson made his feelings plain and only then in his private diary.

---

2. Collingwood, 25.
3. Muff: an awkward, unathletic person. [*Editor's note*]

During my stay I made I suppose some progress in learning of various kinds, but none of it was done *con amore*, and I spent an incalculable time in writing out impositions—this last I consider one of the chief faults of Rugby School. I made some friends there, the most intimate being Henry Leigh Bennett (as college acquaintances we find fewer common sympathies, and are consequently less intimate)—but I cannot say that I look back upon my life at a Public School with any sensations of pleasure, or that any earthly considerations would induce me to go through my three years again.[4]

* * *

Dodgson's particular reason for disliking Rugby was never stated. * * * While at Rugby, he clearly suffered and resented the imposition of "lines" for minor breaches of regulations, having to copy out the same line fifty, a hundred, or several hundred times. In 1857, he also confided to his diary the most tiresome ordeal of his schooldays. "I can say that if I had been thus secure from annoyance at night, the hardships of the daily life would have been comparative trifles to bear."[5]

Night was the time when the boys were unsupervised and when the victims of institutional bullying or casual ragging were most at the mercy of their tormentors. Bullying might take as casual a form as snatching the bedclothes from a victim and leaving him to shiver the rest of a winter night so that the stronger boy might sleep more warmly. It might be the more elaborate ritual of tossing him in a blanket to the ceiling of the high communal dormitory. * * * However, as one perpetrator later insisted, "Bold little fellows liked it." There is no indication that Charles Dodgson was such a bold little fellow.

MORTON N. COHEN

Cap and Gown[†]

When Charles entered Christ Church, it wore two faces, not exactly tragic and comedic, but dissimilar enough to reflect a split in the student body. On the one hand, the House, as insiders call Christ Church (because it embodies the Cathedral House of Christ), was (and is) known as a rich man's college, with royal and aristocratic

---

4. Collingwood, 30.
5. *Diaries*, 3:40. (See full citation on p. 254.)
† From *Lewis Carroll: A Biography*, 34–36, 41–43, 45. Copyright © 1995 by Morton N. Cohen. Used by permission of Alfred A. Knopf, a division of Random House, Inc.

connections, a surfeit of money, and a minimum of intellectual aspiration. * * *

The other face of Christ Church was one of intellectual distinction. Not only had Charles's father and his friend E. B. Pusey emerged from Christ Church, but many more men of achievement graced the roster. In the first half of the century, the crumbling walls embraced some of the most eminent churchmen in the land, some of the world's great classical scholars, and, for a time, the Professor of Poetry.[1] "In those days," recalls one chronicler, "Christ Church nearly monopolised the class list, and was the focus and centre of the intellectual life of the University."[2] * * *

On June 24, 1852, [Charles] wrote a long letter to his sister Elizabeth, while staying with his favorite uncle, Skeffington Lutwidge, a barrister and Commissioner in Lunacy. Lutwidge provided Charles with London hospitality, shared with his nephew his interest in microscopes, telescopes, and gadgets generally. Before long Skeffington introduced Charles to photography. In the letter, Charles reports that his uncle "has as usual got a great number of new oddities, including a lathe, telescope stand, crest stamp, a beautiful little pocket instrument for measuring distances on a map, refrigerator, etc., etc. We had an observation of the moon and Jupiter last night, and afterwards live animalcula in his large microscope. . . ." He continues: "Before I left Oxford, I had a conversation with Mr. Gordon and one with Mr. [Robert] Faussett [Mathematical Lecturer at Christ Church] on the work of the Long Vacation: I believe 25 hours' *hard* work a day *may* get through all I have to do, but I am not certain."[3] In the meantime, however, he enjoyed London.

His twenty-five-hour day of hard work reaped rewards. On December 9 he reports the good news to Elizabeth:

> You shall have the announcement of the last piece of good fortune this wonderful term has had in store for me, that is, *a 1st class in Mathematics*. Whether I shall add to this any honours at collections I cannot at present say, but I should think it very unlikely, as I have only today to get up the work in The Acts of the Apostles, 2 Greek Plays, and the Satires of Horace and I feel myself almost totally unable to read at all: I am beginning

1. Edward Bouverie Pusey (1800–1882) was a clergyman, professor of Hebrew at Oxford, and one of the leaders of the Oxford Movement, whose members wanted to make the liturgy and doctrines of the early Christian church prominent in contemporary Anglicanism. The Professor of Poetry at Oxford is elected for a term (ten years in the nineteenth century) and offers some public lectures during each academic year. Matthew Arnold held the post from 1857 to 1867. [*Editor's note.*]
2. [C. W. Collins], "Oxford in Fact and Fiction," *Blackwood's Magazine* 158 (1895): 890–904.
3. *Letters*, 24 June [1852], I:19–20.

to suffer from the reaction of reading for Moderations[4] . . . I am getting quite tired of being congratulated on various subjects: there seems to be no end of it. If I had shot the Dean, I could hardly have had more said about it.[5]

In spite of his apprehension, when he sits for Moderations he adds second-class honors in classics to his achievements.

Impressed by Charles's performance, Dr. Pusey wrote on December 2, 1852, to Charles's father. "I have great pleasure in telling you that I have been enabled to recommend your son for a Studentship. . . . One of the Censors brought me to-day five names; but in their minds it was plain that they thought your son on the whole the most eligible. . . . It has been very satisfactory to hear of your son's uniform steady and good conduct."[6]

It was not wholly exceptional for the best undergraduates to be appointed to studentships at Christ Church even before they earned their B.A. degrees, but the honor was conferred on few. The appointment crowned Charles's achievements with glory and security. He might, if he chose, now remain a Student the rest of his life, with lodgings, an honored place in the academic community of the finest college in the oldest university in the land, and a secure income. Although his emoluments came to thirty pounds a year, he soon augmented that by lecture fees; and * * * he earned as Senior Student two hundred pounds per annum. The appointment came with restrictions. He must proceed to holy orders and must not marry, for if he did, he would automatically lose the studentship, as his father had done. But he was not required to teach if he chose not to, nor was he expected necessarily to publish or to achieve any other distinction. If he wished, he might recline in his easy chair, his feet up by the fire, drink his claret, and smoke a pipe for the rest of his life. Indolence was not, however, the style that Charles yearned for. He took quite the opposite course.

Congratulations on his appointment poured in, but perhaps he valued his father's letter most. "My dearest Charles," it begins.

> The feelings and thankfulness with which I have read your letter just received . . . are, I assure you, beyond *my expression;* and your affectionate heart will derive no small addition of joy from thinking of the joy which you have occasioned to me, and to all the circle of your home. I say *"you* have occasioned," because, grateful as I am to my old friend Dr. Pusey for what he has done, I cannot desire stronger evidence than his own

---

4. Moderations: Like collections, a set of examinations. [*Editor's note.*]
5. *Letters,* 9 December [1852], I:22.
6. Dodgson family papers.

words of the fact that you have *won*, and well won, this honour for *yourself*, and that it is bestowed as a matter of *justice* to *you*, and not of *kindness* to *me*.[7] . . .

* * *

Back at Oxford in the autumn, he was preparing for "Greats," the final examinations for the bachelor's degree. "For the last three weeks before the examination," Collingwood wrote, "he worked thirteen hours a day, spending the whole night before the *viva voce* over his books."[8] The result was gratifying. He made first-class honors in the Final Mathematical School. On December 13 he wrote to Mary:[9]

> Enclosed you will find a list, which I expect you to rejoice over considerably: it will take me more than a day to believe it, I expect—I feel at present very like a child with a new toy, but I daresay I shall be tired of it soon, and wish to be Pope of Rome next. . . . I have just given my Scout[1] a bottle of wine to drink to my First. We shall be made Bachelors on Monday. . . . I hope that Papa did not conclude it was a 2nd by not hearing on Wednesday morning. * * *

Five days later Charles received his Bachelor of Arts.

From The Letters of Lewis Carroll, 1840–1857[†]

From his father

Ripon
January 6, 1840
[I:4]

My dearest Charles,
   I am very sorry that I had not time to answer your nice little note before. You cannot think how pleased I was to receive something in your handwriting, and you may depend upon it I will not forget your commission. As soon as I get to Leeds I shall scream out in

---

7. Collingwood, 53–55.
8. Collingwood, 57. ("Greats" is a course of study of classical Latin and Greek language and literature. [*Editor's note.*])
9. *Letters*, 13 December [1854], I:29–30.
1. Scout: servant [*Editor's note*]
† All selections from Dodgson's letters are extracted from *The Letters of Lewis Carroll*, ed. Morton N. Cohen, with the assistance of Roger Lancelyn Green. 2 vols. (New York: Oxford UP, 1979). Volume and page numbers are noted after the date of each letter. Reprinted by permission of AP Watt Ltd on behalf of Trustees of the CL Dodgson Estate and Scirand Lancelyn Green. Except where noted, annotations are by the editor of this Norton Critical Edition.

the middle of the street, *Ironmongers, Ironmongers.* Six hundred men will rush out of their shops in a moment—fly, fly, in all directions—ring the bells, call the constables, set the Town on fire. I WILL have a file and a screw driver, and a ring, and if they are not brought directly, in forty seconds, I will leave nothing but one small cat alive in the whole Town of Leeds, and I shall only leave that, because I am afraid I shall not have time to kill it. Then what a bawling and a tearing of hair there will be! Pigs and babies, camels and butterflies, rolling in the gutter together—old women rushing up the chimneys and cows after them—ducks hiding themselves in coffee-cups, and fat geese trying to squeeze themselves into pencil cases. At last the Mayor of Leeds will be found in a soup plate covered up with custard, and stuck full of almonds to make him look like a sponge cake that he may escape the dreadful destruction of the Town. Oh! where is his wife? She is safe in her own pincushion with a bit of sticking plaster on the top to hide the hump in her back, and all her dear little children, seventy-eight poor little helpless infants crammed into her mouth, and hiding themselves behind her double teeth. Then comes a man hid in a teapot crying and roaring, "Oh, I have dropped my donkey. I put it up my nostril, and it has fallen out of the spout of the teapot into an old woman's thimble and she will squeeze it to death when she puts her thimble on."

At last they bring the things which I ordered, and then I spare the Town, and send off in fifty waggons, and under the protection of ten thousand soldiers, a file and a screw driver and a ring as a present to Charles Lutwidge Dodgson, from

his affectionate Papa

To his sister Mary

Christ Church, Oxford
December 13, 1854
[I:30]

* * * I have just been to Mr. Price to see how I did in the papers, and the result will I hope be gratifying to you. The following were the sums total of the marks for each in the 1st class, as nearly as I can remember:

Dodgson 279
Bosanquet 261
Cooksoft 254
Fowler 225
Ranken 213

He also said he never remembered so good a set of men in. All this is very satisfactory. I must also add (this is a very boastful letter) that I ought to get the Senior Scholarship next term. Bosanquet will not try, as he is leaving Oxford, and the only man, besides the present First, to try, is one who got a 2nd last time. One thing more I will add, to crown all, and that is—I find I am the next 1st class Math, student to Faussett (with the exception of Kitchin, who has given up Mathematics) so that I stand next (as Bosanquet is going to leave) for the Lectureship. And now I think that is enough news for one post.

Your very affectionate Brother,
Charles L. Dodgson

To his sister Henrietta and brother Edwin

[Christ Church, Oxford]
January 31 [?1855]
[I:31]

My dear Henrietta,
My dear Edwin,
  I am very much obliged by your nice little birthday gift—it was much better than a cane would have been—I have got it on my watch chain, but the Dean has not yet remarked it.

My one pupil has begun his work with me, and I will give you a description how the lecture is conducted. It is the most important point, you know, that the tutor should be *dignified*, and at a distance from the pupil, and that the pupil should be as much as possible *degraded*–otherwise you know, they are not humble enough. So I sit at the further end of the room; outside the door (*which is shut*) sits the scout; outside the outer door (*also shut*) sits the sub-scout; halfway down stairs sits the sub-sub-scout; and down in the yard sits the *pupil*.

The questions are shouted from one to the other, and the answers come back in the same way—it is rather confusing till you are well used to it. The lecture goes on, something like this.

> *Tutor.* "What is twice three?"
> *Scout.* "What's a rice tree?"
> *Sub-Scout.* "When is ice free?"
> *Sub-sub-Scout.* "What's a nice fee?"
> *Pupil* (timidly). "Half a guinea!"
> *Sub-sub-Scout.* "Can't forge any!"
> *Sub-Scout.* "Ho for Jinny!"
> *Scout.* "Don't be a ninny!"
> *Tutor* (looks offended, but tries another question). "Divide a hundred by twelve!"
> *Scout.* "Provide wonderful bells!"

Sub-Scout. "Go ride under it yourself."
Sub-sub-Scout. "Deride the dunder-headed elf!"
Pupil (surprised). "Who do you mean?"
Sub-sub-Scout. "Doings between!"
Sub-Scout. "Blue is the screen!"
Scout. "Soup-tureen!"

And so the lecture proceeds.
   Such is Life—from

Your most affectionate brother,
Charles L. Dodgson

To his sister Mary

Ambleside
Wednesday [September 29, 1857]
[I:34]

My dear Mary,
   I am writing with the idea that this may reach you on Thursday morning. If it does not, I shall be home first, as I go on to Penrith this evening, and so home by Barnard Castle. Yesterday I took a portrait of Alfred Tennyson, which I think successful: also another of Hallam; and a group of the Marshalls, Mr. Tennyson and Hallam; and others.[1] I have got AT to write his name in my album, to go under his picture.

Your affectionate Brother,
Charles L. Dodgson

From Lewis Carroll's Diaries, 1855–1864[†]

Mar. 13. (Tu). [1855] [1:72–74]   I have been trying to form some practicable scheme for reading history, and have decided on beginning with Smythe's *Lectures*, of which I read the first this evening. When these scholarships are over, I shall be more at leisure for general reading. I hope to carry out some such scheme as this:

---

1. Alfred Tennyson (1809–1892) was the preeminent British poet of his generation; he had been named Poet Laureate by Queen Victoria in 1850. Hallam was his son; the Marshalls were the family of a successful industrialist. (See Dodgson's photograph on p. 369 of this Norton Critical Edition.)

† All diary selections are extracted from *Lewis Carroll's Diaries: The Private Journals of Charles Lutwidge Dodgson (Lewis Carroll)*, ed. Edward Wakeling, 10 vols. (Luton, UK: Lewis Carroll Society, 1993–2007). Volume and page numbers are noted after the date of each entry. Reprinted by permission of AP Watt Ltd on behalf of Trustees of the CL Dodgson Estate and Scirard Lancelyn Green. Except where noted, all annotations are by the editor of this Norton Critical Edition.

Classics: review methodically all the books I have read, and perhaps add a new one—(Æschylus?)

Divinity: keep up Gospels and Acts in Greek, and go on to Epistles.

History: as guided by Smythe.

Languages: read something French, begin Italian. (I think German had better be postponed).

Poetry: read whole poets, or at least whole poems. I think in this order—Shakespeare, Milton, Byron, Coleridge, Wordsworth(?).

Mathematics: go regularly on from the points I have fairly reached, this needs a scheme to itself.

Novels: Scott's over again to begin with(?).

Miscellaneous Studies: I should like to go on with *Etymology*, and read White, and all Trench's books, and Horne Tooke. Second *Logic*, finish Mill and dip into Dugald Stewart.

Divinity reading for Ordination: this should take precedence of all other, I must consult my Father on the subject.

Other subjects: Scripture History, Church Architecture, Anglo-Saxon, Gothic.[1]

☼   ☼   ☼

Mar. 24. (Sat). [1855] [1:78]   Senior Mathematical Scholarship adjudged to Bosanquet, it is some consolation to me to think that at least Ch. Ch. has got it. He tells me he did not do more than six questions in any one of the papers. Almond, and Norton, and myself, all gave up on the second day, so that Bosanquet and Cookson had the last paper all to themselves. It is tantalising to think how easily (?) I might have got it, if only I had worked properly during this term, which I fear I must consider as wasted. However, I have now got a year before me, and with this past term as a lesson, αὔριον ἄδιον ᾄσω²—I mean to have read by next time, Integral Calculus, Optics (and theory of light), Astronomy, and higher Dynamics. I record this resolution to shame myself with, in case March /56 finds me still unprepared, knowing how many similar failures there have been in my life already. ☼ ☼ ☼

Mar. 28. (W). [1855] [1:79]   End of examination for the Johnson: adjudged also to Bosanquet—only he, Cookson, and myself were in at the end. This completes the lesson read me by this wasted term—

---

1. William Smythe, *Lectures on Modern History* (1840); Richard Chenevix Trench's books include *On the Study of Words* (1851) and *English Past and Present* (1855): John Horne Tooke, *The Diversions of Purley* (1786, 1798); John Stuart Mill, *System of Logic* (1843); Dugald Stewart's books include *Elements of the Philosophy of the Human Mind* (1792), *Outlines of Moral Philosophy* (1794), and *The Philosophy of the Active and Moral Powers* (1828). The book by White has not been identified.
2. Theocritus: "Tomorrow I shall sing a sweeter song."

Eheu fugaces! video meliora proboque, deteriora sequor[3]—I do not
think the work of this term worth recording.

*   *   *

May 14. (M). [1855] [1:97–98]   * * *   The Dean and Canons have
been pleased to give me one of the "Bostock" Scholarships—said to
be worth £20 per year. This very nearly raises my income this year
to independence—Courage!

*   *   *

July 5. (Th). [1855] [1:108]   I went to the Boy's School[4] in the
morning to hear my Father teach, as I want to begin trying myself
soon. Some of the boys were much more intelligent than I expected.

July 8. (Sun). [1855] [1:108]   I took the first and second class of the
Boy's School in the morning—we did part of the life of St. John,
one of the "lessons" on Scripture lives. I liked my first attempt in
teaching very much.

July 10. (Tu). [1855] [1:110]   * * *   I have an idea for a new Drama
for the Marionette theatre, *Alfred the Great*, but have not yet begun
to write it. His adventures in disguise in the neatherd's hut, and in
the Danish Camp, will furnish two very effective scenes. Yesterday
I heard from Menella Smedley, returning "The Three Voices,"
which she borrowed to show to Frank Smedley: she says that he
wishes to be instrumental in publishing it and others. I do not think
I have yet written anything worthy of real publication (in which I
do not include the *Whitby Gazette* or the *Oxonian Advertiser*[5]) but I
do not despair of doing so some day.

Dec. 31. (M). [1855] [1:136]   I am sitting alone in my bedroom this
last night of the old year, waiting for midnight. It has been the most
eventful year of my life: I began it a poor bachelor student, with no
definite plans or expectations; I end it a master and tutor in Ch.
Ch., with an income of more than £300 a year, and the course of
mathematical tuition marked out by God's providence for at least
some years to come. Great mercies, great failings, time lost, talents
misapplied—such has been the past year.

---

3. A composite of quotes from Horace and Ovid, the latter from *Metamorphoses*, book 7;
   "Alas time is fleeting! I see and I commend the better way, but follow the worst."
   [Wakeling's note.]
4. The school at Croft-on-Tees, built with the help of the Dodgson family, whose members did some of the teaching.
5. Frank Smedley was a novelist; his cousin Menella was related to Dodgson's mother.
   The Whitby Gazette and the *Oxonian Advertiser* were local newspapers.

Jan. 7. (M). [1856] [2:10–11]   * * * Finished *Alton Locke*[6] * * *

If the book were but a little more definite, it might stir up many fellow-workers in the same good field of social improvement. Oh that God, in his good providence, may make me hereafter such a worker! But alas what are the means! Each has his *nostrum* to propound, and in the Babel of voices nothing is done. I would thankfully spend and be spent so long as I were sure of really effecting something by the sacrifice, and not merely lying down under the wheels of some irresistible Juggernaut. * * *

* * *

Jan. 22. (Tu). [1856] [2:26]   Wrote to Uncle Skeffington to get me a photographic apparatus, as I want some other occupation here, than mere reading and writing. * * *

Jan. 29. (Tu). [1856] [2:30]   Breakfasted with Swabey[7] to arrange about teaching in his school. We settled that I am to come at 10 on Sunday, and at 2 on Tuesdays and Fridays to teach sums. I gave the first lesson there today, to a class of eight boys, and found it much more pleasant than I expected. The contrast is very striking between town and country boys: here they are sharp, boisterous, and in the highest spirits the difficulty of teaching being, not to get an answer, but to prevent all answering at once. They seem tractable and in good order. * * *

Feb. 10. (Sun). [1856] [2:38]   Heard again from Mr. Yates,[8] he wants me to choose another name, as Dares is too much like a newspaper signature. * * *

Feb. 11. (M). [1856] [2:39]   Wrote to Mr. Yates, sending him a choice of names, 1. *Edgar Cuthwellis* (made by transposition out of "Charles Lutwidge"), 2. *Edgar U. C. Westhill* (ditto), 3. *Louis Carroll* (derived from Lutwidge = Ludovic = Louis, and Charles), 4. *Lewis Carroll* (ditto).

[Mar. 1. *Lewis Carroll* was chosen.]

Feb. 26. (Tu). [1856] [2:44]   Class again noisy and inattentive, it is very disheartening, and I almost think I had better give up teaching there for the present. * * *

---

6. Charles Kingsley's novel *Alton Locke* (1850) described the privations of clothing and agricultural workers.
7. Maurice C. Swabey was rector of St. Aldate's in Oxford.
8. Edmund Yates (1831–1894) was the editor of *Comic Times* and *The Train*, comic periodicals to which Dodgson contributed poems and fiction, including "She's All My Fancy Painted Him" and "Upon the Lonely Moor," parodies which were polished into the White Rabbit's evidence and the White Knight's song in the *Alice* books.

Feb. 29. (F). [1856] [2:44]   Left word at the school that I shall not be able to come again for the present. I doubt if I shall try again next term: the good done does not seem worth the time and trouble. * * *

Mar. 6. (Th). [1856] [2:48]   Finished lectures for the term, and took a holiday. Made friends with little Harry Liddell (whom I first spoke to down at the boats last week): he is certainly the handsomest boy I ever saw. * * *

June 26. (F). [1857] [3:73]   Spent the day (from 10½ till 5) at the Deanery, photographing with very slender success. Though I was disappointed in missing this last opportunity of getting good pictures of the party, it was notwithstanding one of the pleasantest days I have ever spent there. I had Alice and Edith with me till 12; then Harry and Ina till the early dinner at 2, which I joined; and all 4 children for the afternoon. The photographing was accordingly plentifully interspersed with swinging, back-gammon, etc.

* * *

Oct. 30. (F). [1863] [4:258–59]   May the next page, and the new month, begin a newer and better life for me! Grant it, oh God, for thy dear Son's sake! Oh may I be enabled to leave behind my sins and weaknesses, and to dedicate myself wholly to do God's will!

Wrote to Kitchin to say I was willing to be nominated as Examiner, for next year.[9] This afternoon I have to prepare a sermon to preach at Wendlebury next Sunday. May the merciful God assist me in my future life, that any preaching may not be a hollow mockery, my words leading others to repentance and good works, myself a castaway. Help me, oh God, for Christ's sake.

Nov. 18. (W). [1863] [4:261]   A memorable day. Kitchin called about half-past 11 to say he would bring the Prince to be photographed at half-past 12 (he had consented some time ago to sit). Went over to Badcock's and had everything ready when they arrived.[1] They staid {sic} about half an hour, and I took two negatives of him, a 6 × 5 half-length, and a 10 × 8 full-length. In the intervals he looked over my photographs that are mounted on cards, and he also signed his name in my album, saying as he did so that it was the *first* time he had used his new title. (He is now Crown-

9. G. W. Kitchin held the post of Mathematical Examiner. Dodgson became a friend of his family and photographed and wrote to his children. See *Lewis Carroll and the Kitchins*, ed. Morton N. Cohen (see Selected Bibliography).
1. Frederick, Crown Prince of Denmark, one of many well-known people Dodgson photographed. Badcock's was a building in Oxford that Dodgson used as a photography studio and for storage.

Prince, the news of the death of the old king having come on *Monday*). He conversed pleasantly and sensibly.

*   *   *

Oct. 21. (Tu). [1862] [4:137]   Called on the Dean to ask him if I was in any way obliged to take Priests' Orders. (I consider mine as a Lay Studentship). His opinion was that by being ordained Deacon I became a Clerical Student, and so subject to the same conditions as if I had taken a Clerical Studentship, viz. that I must take Priests' Orders within four years from my time for being M.A. and that as this was clearly impossible in my case, I have probably already lost the Studentship, and am at least bound to take Priests' Orders as soon as possible. I differed from this view, and he talked of laying the matter before the electors.

Oct. 22. (W). [1862] [4:138]   The Dean has decided on not consulting the electors, and says he shall do nothing more about it, so that I consider myself free as to being ordained Priest.

*   *   *

Dec. 31. (Th). [1864] [4:267]   Here, at the close of another year, how much of neglect carelessness, and sin have I to remember! I had hoped, during this year, to have made a beginning in parochial work, to have thrown off habits of evil, to have advanced in my work at Ch. Ch.—how little, next to nothing, has been done of all this! Now I have a fresh year before me: once more let me set myself to do some thing worthy of life "before I go hence, and be no more seen."

Oh God, grant me grace to consecrate to Thee, during this new year, my life and powers, my days and nights, myself. Take me, vile and worthless as I am: use me as Thou seest fit: help me to be Thy servant; for Christ's sake. Amen.

MICHAEL BAKEWELL

[Ordination]†

On December 22nd, 1861, 'Charles Lutwidge Dodgson, Master of Arts, Student of Christ Church in the University of Oxford (of whose courteous and pious life, conversation and competent learning and knowledge in the Holy Scriptures we were well assured)'; was admitted by Bishop Wilberforce into the Holy Order of Deacons of

---

† From *Lewis Carroll: A Biography* (London: Heinemann, 1996), 99–102. Reprinted by permission.

the Church of England. Taking Deacon's Orders was a compromise between being in the Church and being out of it, the outcome of a struggle that had been going on within Dodgson ever since he had come up to Oxford.

In his 1838 Ordination sermon, Dodgson's father had stressed that the Church required those who sought admission to sacred orders to examine and 'prove their own selves':

> She carries her enquiries into the sanctuary of the conscience, and calls upon the still small voice to respond to the awful question, 'Do you trust that you are inwardly moved by the Holy Ghost to take upon you this office and ministration to serve God for the promoting of His glory and the edifying of His people?'[1]

The still, small voice within Dodgson could only question his worthiness and suitability for taking priest's Orders at all. One of his New Year's resolutions for 1858 had been to begin reading for Ordination by the end of the year and to settle 'the subject finally and definitely in my mind'.[2] Others had no difficulty. His brother Skeffington was still intent on entering the priesthood; his friend Henry Liddon, ordained in 1853, had worked as a priest in the parish of Wantage. Another close friend, Robert Faussett, became Vicar of Cassington, a village a few miles outside Oxford. But Dodgson simply could not see himself working as a parish priest. He gave himself various reasons for this, but none of them is entirely convincing. There was his stammer, which he feared would be an impediment to carrying out his clerical duties. It was an obstacle certainly, but he had never let it stand in his way when delivering a recitation or performing in charades; however, there is no denying the terror which the prospect of delivering a sermon or reading the lesson aroused in him. He had a very deep and very real fear of being seized with a fit of stammering before a large congregation, and was afraid he might make Holy Things laughable. A second reason was that it would involve giving up the study and teaching of mathematics. As his diary shows, contemplation of algebraic and geometric problems was part of his daily pattern of thought. * * * His chief obstacle was his own conviction of his unworthiness to work as a parish priest. He was particularly concerned about being able to answer and combat the religious problems of his parishioners. He was not prepared to fob them off with easy or specious answers. During the time when the question of his ordination was weighing heavily on his mind [1857], he had a long and rather fruitless argument with his brother Wilfred on the subject of the need to respect college discipline.

1. Dodgson Family Collection, 1/4.
2. *Diaries* 3:142.

This also suggests to me grave doubts as to the work of the ministry which I am looking forward to. If I can find it so hard to prove a plain duty to one individual and that one unpractised in argument, how can I ever be ready to face the countless sophisms and ingenious arguments against religion which a clergyman must meet with?[3]

* * *

His other problem was that he was ill at ease among working class people. He knew that he could not work as a pastor to artisans and share their life. It was not in his nature.

Dodgson was also reluctant to give up the life he was living. If he proceeded to full Holy Orders one of the first things he would have to sacrifice would be the theatre. Bishop Wilberforce had declared that the resolution to attend theatres or operas was an absolute disqualification for Holy Orders. * * * The objection, however, extended only to those working as parish priests. If Dodgson could find some way of not proceeding to full Holy Orders he could continue to go to the theatre as often as he wished. There would be other sacrifices, too. Teaching may have bored and dispirited him at times, he may have become irritable with the college servants and weary of the conversation and company of his fellow dons, but his existence at Oxford was life as he wished to lead it. The atmosphere of Christ Church itself, the afternoons on the river, his photography, his little girl friends, his mathematical problems, his puzzles and conundrums, his visits to London's galleries and exhibitions—what could the life of a parish priest have to offer in compensation for the loss of these?

* * *

So Dodgson's lifestyle continued exactly as it had been before, but the mere fact of his ordination undoubtedly had a profound effect upon his inner self. He became more aware than ever of living out his life in the continual presence of God, which involved him in agonised bursts of soul-searching, though fortunately it did nothing to make him change his ways.

His trips to the theatre became more frequent than ever, as did his visits to art galleries and popular exhibitions. He devoted more and more time to his child-friends and to devising puzzles, tricks and stories for their entertainment. Every year he would lament time wasted, every year he would resolve to devote more time to the church and to works of religion, every year seemed to confirm him in his simple evangelical piety and yet every year would be lived out in the same old worldly pattern.

3. *Diaries* 3:18.

The *Alice* Books

From Lewis Carroll's Diaries, 1862–1865

July 3. (Th). [1862] [4:92–93]   Called on Mr. Henry Taylor,[1] to try and get him to come and sit for a photograph, but he was too busy: I liked his manner very much. Took a photo of Sir Michael Beach. Atkinson and I went to lunch at the Deanery, after which we were to have gone down the river with the children, but as it rained, we remained to hear some music and singing instead. The three sang "Sally come up" with great spirit.[2]

* * *

July 4. (F). [1862] [4:94–95]   Atkinson brought over to my rooms some friends of his, a Mrs. and Miss Peters, of whom I took photographs, and who afterwards looked over my albums and staid {*sic*} to lunch. They then went off to the Museum, and Duckworth[3] and I made an expedition *up* the river to Godstow with the three Liddells: we had tea on the bank there, and did not reach Ch. Ch. again till quarter past eight, when we took them on to my rooms to see my collection of micro-photographs, and restored them to the Deanery just before nine.

[On which occasion I told them the fairy-tale of "Alice's Adventures Under Ground," which I undertook to write out for Alice, and which is now finished (as to the text) though the pictures are not yet nearly done. Feb. 10, 1863]

[nor yet. Mar. 12, 1864]

["Alice's Hour in Elfland"? June 9, 1864]

---

1. Henry Taylor (1800–1886) was a dramatist, poet, and essayist who also worked as an official in the Colonial Office. Dodgson later did photograph him and his family. Michael Edward Hicks-Beach (1837–1916, later the Viscount St Aldwyn), also served in important political and government posts. Francis Home Atkinson was an Oxford acquaintance; he once served as tutor to the children of Alfred Tennyson.
2. See note 2 on p. 78 of this Norton Critical Edition.
3. Robinson Duckworth [1834–1911] was a fellow of Trinity College; he had been one of the tutors of the Prince of Wales when the prince was an undergraduate at Oxford.

["Alice's Adventures in Wonderland"? June 28.]

Nov. 13. (Th). [1862] [4:141–42]   Walked with Liddon.[4] *** On returning to Ch. Ch.I found Ina, Alice and Edith in the quadrangle, and had a little talk with them—a rare event of late. [Began writing the fairy-tale for Alice, which I told them July 4, going to Godstow—I hope to finish it by Christmas.]

May 9. (Sa). [1863] [4:197].   Heard from Mrs. MacDonald[5] about "Alice's Adventures Underground," which I had lent them to read, and which they wish me to publish.

Jan. 25. (M). [1864] [4:271–72]   Called at the "Board of Health" and saw Mr. Tom Taylor.[6] *** He also gave me a note of introduction to Mr. Tenniel (to whom he had before applied, for me, about pictures for *Alice's Adventures*). *** I called at Mr. Tenniel's, whom I found at home; he was very friendly, and seemed to think favourably of undertaking the pictures, but must see the book before deciding.

April 5. (Tu). [1864] [4:284]   Heard from Tenniell [*sic*] that he consents to draw the pictures for "Alice's Adventures Underground."

May 11. (Th). [1865] [5:74]   Met Alice and Miss Prickett in the quadrangle. Alice seems changed a good deal, and hardly for the better, probably going through the usual awkward stage of transition.[7]

---

4. Henry Parry Liddon attended Christ Church as an undergraduate with Dodgson, and accompanied him on a trip to Russia in 1867.
5. Mrs. MacDonald was the wife of George MacDonald, who had served as a minister of the Congregational Church but was at this time earning his living in London by lecturing, preaching, and writing poems and novels. He had already published one of his best-known fantastic romances, *Phantases* (1858); he was later to publish collections of fairy-stories and his most famous children's books, *At the Back of the North Wind* and *The Princess and the Goblin* (both 1871). His children, Mary and Greville, were among Dodgson's first child-friends.
6. In addition to serving as secretary to the Board of Health, Tom Taylor (1817–1880) was a prolific and successful playwright, and a frequent contributor to *Punch*, whose editor he became in 1874.
    John (later Sir John) Tenniel (1820–1914) had been drawing for *Punch* since 1850. In 1864 he was drawing its principal weekly political cartoon and was soon to become its principal cartoonist. Tenniel had made an early success in the 1840s with his illustrations to an edition of *Aesop's Fables*, but he did not often illustrate books.
7. Alice Liddell, who was ten years old in the summer of the expedition to Godstow (1862), had turned thirteen in May of 1865. Miss Prickett was governess to the Liddell children.

ALICE AND CARYL HARGREAVES

Alice's Recollections of Carrollian Days[†]

[M]y great joy was to go out riding with my father. As soon as we had a pony, he used to take one of us out with him every morning. The first pony we ever had was one given to my eldest brother Harry, called Tommy. Harry was away at school most of the time, and in any case did not care much about riding, so we always kept his pony exercised for him. * * * When Tommy got too old, my father bought a bigger pony for us. One Boxing Day this pony crossed its legs, and came down with me on the Abingdon road. My father had to leave me by the side of the road while he went off to get help. While he was gone, some strangers, out for an excursion, passed, and were kind enough to send me back to Oxford in their wagonette, lying on a feather bed, borrowed from a nearby farm. The bottom of the wagonette was not quite long enough when the door was shut, and this caused me great pain, so perhaps I was not as grateful as I should have been, for, when I got home and Bultitude[1] was carrying me indoors, I said to him, "*You* won't let them hurt me any more, will you?" at which, as he told my mother afterwards, he "nearly let Miss Alice drop." As it was, I was on my back for six weeks with a broken thigh. During all these weeks Mr. Dodgson never came to see me. If he had, perhaps the world might have known some more of Alice's Adventures. As it is, I think many of my earlier adventures must be irretrievably lost to posterity, because Mr. Dodgson told us many, many stories before the famous trip up the river to Godstow. No doubt he added some of the earlier adventures to make up the difference between *Alice in Wonderland* and *Alice's Adventures Underground*, which latter was nearly all told on that one afternoon. Much of *Through the Looking-Glass* is made up of them too, particularly the ones to do with chessmen, which are dated by the period when we were excitedly learning chess. But even then, I am afraid that many must have perished forever in his waste-paper basket, for he used to illustrate the meaning of his stories on any piece of paper that he had handy.

* * * When the time of year made picnics impossible, we used to go to his rooms in the Old Library, leaving the Deanery by the back door, escorted by our nurse. When we got there, we used to

---

† From "Alice's Recollections of Carrollian Days, As Told To Her Son, Caryl Hargreaves," *Cornhill* n. s. 73 (1932): 1–12.
1. The Liddells' coachmen. [*Editor's note.*]

sit on the big sofa on each side of him, while he told us stories, illlustrating them by pencil or ink drawings as he went along. When we were thoroughly happy and amused at his stories, he used to pose us, and expose the plates before the right mood had passed. He seemed to have an endless store of these fantastical tales, which he made up as he told them, drawing busily on a large sheet of paper all the time. They were not always entirely new. Sometimes they were new versions of old stories: sometimes they started on the old basis, but grew into new tales owing to the frequent interruptions which opened up fresh and undreamed-of possibilities. In this way the stories, slowly enunciated in his quiet voice with its curious stutter, were perfected. Occasionally he pretended to fall asleep, to our great dismay. Sometimes he said "That is all till next time," only to resume on being told that it was already next time. Being photographed was therefore a joy to us and not a penance as it is to most children. We looked forward to the happy hours in the mathematical tutor's rooms.

But much more exciting than being photographed was being allowed to go into the dark room, and watch him develop the large glass plates. What could be more thrilling than to see the negative gradually take shape, as he gently rocked it to and fro in the acid bath? Besides, the dark room was so mysterious, and we felt that any adventure might happen there! There were all the joys of preparation, anticipation, and realisation, besides the feeling that we were assisting at some secret rite usually reserved for grown-ups! Then there was the additional excitement, after the plates were developed, of seeing what we looked like in a photograph. Looking at the photographs now, it is evident that Mr. Dodgson was far in advance of his time in the art of photography and of posing his subjects.

*   *   *

Nearly all of *Alice's Adventures Underground* was told on that blazing summer afternoon with the heat haze shimmering over the meadows where the party landed to shelter for awhile in the shadow cast by the haycocks near Godstow. I think the stories he told us that afternoon must have been better than usual, because I have such a distinct recollection of the expedition, and also, on the next day I started to pester him to write down the story for me, which I had never done before. It was due to my "going on" and importunity that, after saying he would think about it, he eventually gave the hesitating promise which started him writing it down at all. This he referred to in a letter written in 1883 in which he writes of me as the "one without whose infant patronage I might possibly never have written at all." What a nuisance I must have made of myself! Still, I am glad I did it now; and so was Mr. Dodgson afterwards. It does not do to think what pleasure would have been missed if his little bright-eyed favourite had not bothered him to put pen to paper. The result was that for several years, when he went away on vacation, he took the little black book about with him, writing the manuscript in his own peculiar script, and drawing the illustrations. Finally the book was finished and given to me. But in the meantime, friends who had seen and heard bits of it while he was at work on it, were so thrilled that they persuaded him to publish it. I have been told, though I doubt its being true, that at first he thought that it should be published at the publisher's expense, but that the London publishers were reluctant to do so, and he therefore decided to publish it at his own expense. In any case, after Macmillans had agreed to publish it, there arose the question of the illustrations. At first he tried to do them himself, on the lines of those in the manuscript book, but he came to the conclusion that he could not do them well enough, as they had to be drawn on wood, and he did not know how. He eventually approached Mr. (later Sir John) Tenniel. Fortunately, as I think most people will agree, the latter accepted. As a rule Tenniel used Mr. Dodgson's drawings as the basis for his own illustrations and they held frequent consultations about them. One point, which was not settled for a long time and until after many trials and consultations, was whether Alice in Wonderland should have her hair cut straight across her forehead as Alice Liddell had always worn it, or not. Finally it was decided that Alice in Wonderland should have no facial resemblance to her prototype.

Unfortunately my mother tore up all the letters that Mr. Dodgson wrote to me when I was a small girl. I cannot remember what any of them were like, but it is an awful thought to contemplate what may have perished in the Deanery waste-paper basket. Mr. Dodgson always wore black clergyman's clothes in Oxford, but, when he took us out on the river, he used to wear white flannel trousers. He also replaced his black top-hat by a hard white straw hat on these occasions, but of course retained his black boots, because in those days white tennis shoes had never been heard of. He always carried himself upright, almost more than upright, as if he had swallowed a poker. * * *

Little did we dream then that this shy but almost brilliant logic tutor, with a bent for telling fairy stories to little girls, and for taking photographs of elderly dons, would before so many years be known all over the civilised world, and that his fairy stories would be translated into almost every European language, into Chinese and

Japanese, and some of them even into Arabic! But perhaps only a brilliant logician could have written *Alice in Wonderland!*

From The Letters of Lewis Carroll, 1864–1885

To Tom Taylor[1]

Christ Church, Oxford
June 10, 1864
[I:64–65]

My dear Sir,

You were kind enough to wish me to let you know some while before I came to town on my photographic visit, that you might see whether you could entrap any victims for me. My plans are not definitely settled yet, but, so far as I can see, I shall be in town on or before the 20th (though I could come sooner if there were reason to do so). After that I shall be photographing at various friends' houses for 2 or 3 weeks. I am obliged to speak vaguely, as my plans will be liable to change from day to day.

I have many children sitters engaged, among others, Mr. Millais',[1] who will make most picturesque subjects. Believe me

Ever yours truly,
C. L. Dodgson

P.S. I should be very glad if you could help me in fixing on a name for my fairy-tale, which Mr. Tenniel (in consequence of your kind introduction) is now illustrating for me, and which I hope to get published before Xmas. The heroine spends an hour underground, and meets various birds, beasts, etc. (*no* fairies), endowed with speech. The whole thing is a dream, but *that* I don't want revealed till the end. I first thought of "Alice's Adventures Under Ground," but that was pronounced too like a lesson-book, in which instruction about mines would be administered in the form of a grill; then I took "Alice's Golden Hour," but that I gave up, having a dark suspicion that there is already a book called "Lily's Golden Hours." Here are the other names I have thought of:

$$\text{Alice among the} \begin{cases} \text{elves} \\ \text{goblins} \end{cases} \quad \text{Alice's} \begin{cases} \text{hour} \\ \text{doings} \\ \text{adventures} \end{cases} \quad \text{in} \begin{cases} \text{elf-land} \\ \text{wonderland.} \end{cases}$$

---

1. Tom Taylor: see note 6 on p. 264. John Everett Millais (1829–1896) was a well-known painter and prominent member of a group known as the Pre-Raphaelite Brotherhood. Dodgson photographed him and his family in 1865.

Of all these I at present prefer "Alice's Adventures in Wonderland." In spite of your "morality," I want something sensational. Perhaps you can suggest a better name than any of these.

To Mrs. J. Barry[2]

Christ Church, Oxford
February 15, 1871
[I:162–63]

Dear Mrs. Barry,

I am sending you, with this, a print of the proposed frontispiece for *Through the Looking-Glass.* It has been suggested to me that it is too terrible a monster, and likely to alarm nervous and imaginative children; and that at any rate we had better begin the book with a pleasanter subject.

So I am submitting the question to a number of friends, for which purpose I have had copies of the frontispiece printed off.

We have three courses open to us:

(1) To retain it as the frontispiece.

(2) To transfer it to its proper place in the book (where the ballad occurs which it is intended to illustrate), and substitute a new frontispiece.

(3) To omit it altogether.

The last-named course would be a great sacrifice of the time and trouble which the picture has cost, and it would be a pity to adopt it unless it be *really* necessary.

I should be grateful to have your opinion (tested by exhibiting the picture to any children you think fit), as to which of these three courses is the best.

To the Lowrie Children[3]

Care of Messrs. Macmillan
29 Bedford Street, Covent Garden, London
August 18, 1884
[I:547–49]

My dear Children,

*   *   *

Some rather droll things happened about those hospitals: I sent round a printed letter, to offer the books, with a list of the

---

2. Letitia Barry was the wife of a clergyman in Yorkshire. Dodgson first photographed her children in 1863. The proposed frontispiece was Tenniel's rendering of the Jabberwock.
3. This letter was printed in *The Critic*, 29 (5 March 1898): 166–67. There is no other record of the Lowrie children, who were American, in Dodgson's diaries and letters. Their letter and Dodgson's answer were probably transmitted through his publisher. Dodgson here gives a lot of attention to what essentially is a fan letter.

Hospitals, and asking people to add to the list any I had left out. And one manager wrote that he knew of a place where there were a number of sick children, but he was afraid I wouldn't like to give them any books—and why, do you think? "Because they are Jews!" I wrote to say, of course I would give them some: why in the world shouldn't little Israelites read *Alice's Adventures* as well as other children!

Another—a "Lady Superior"—wrote to ask to see a copy of *Alice* before accepting it: for she had to be very careful, all the children being Roman Catholics, as to what "religious reading" they got! I wrote to say, 'You shall certainly see it first, if you like: but I can guarantee that the books have no religious teaching whatever in them—in fact, they do not teach anything at all." She said she was quite satisfied, and would accept the books.

But, while I am running on in this way, I'm leaving your letter unanswered. As to the meaning of the Snark? I'm very much afraid I didn't mean anything but nonsense! Still, you know, words mean more than we mean to express when we use them: so a whole book ought to mean a great deal more than the writer meant. So, whatever good meanings are in the book, I'm very glad to accept as the meaning of the book. The best that I've seen is by a lady (she published it in a letter to a newspaper)—that the whole book is an allegory on the search after happiness. I think this fits beautifully in many ways—particularly, about the bathing-machines: when the people get weary of life, and can't find happiness in town or in books, then they rush off to the seaside, to see what bathing-machines will do for them. * * *

To Alice (Liddell) Hargreaves

Christ Church, Oxford
March 1, 1885
[I:560–61]

My dear Mrs. Hargreaves,

I fancy this will come to you almost like a voice from the dead, after so many years of silence—and yet those years have made no difference, that I can perceive, in *my* clearness of memory of the days when we *did* correspond. I am getting to feel what an old man's failing memory is, as to recent events and new friends (for instance, I made friends, only a few weeks ago, with a very nice little maid of about 12, and had a walk with her—and now I can't recall either of her names!) but my mental picture is as vivid as ever, of one who was, through so many years, my ideal child-friend. I have had scores of child-friends since your time: but they have been quite a different thing.

However, I did not begin this letter to say all *that*. What I want to ask is—would you have any objection to the original MS book of

Alice's Adventures (which I suppose you still possess) being published in facsimile? The idea of doing so occurred to me only the other day. If, on consideration, you come to the conclusion that you would rather *not* have it done, there is an end of the matter. If, however, you give a favorable reply, I would be much obliged if you would lend it me (registered post I should think would be safest) that I may consider the possibilities. I have not seen it for about 20 years: so am by no means sure that the illustrations may not prove to be so awfully bad, that to reproduce them would be absurd.

There can be no doubt that I should incur the charge of gross egoism in publishing it. But I don't care for that in the least: knowing that I have no such motive: only I think, considering the extraordinary popularity the books have had (we have sold more than 120,000 of the two) there must be many who would like to see the original form.[4]

Always your friend,
C. L. Dodgson

From Lewis Carroll and the House of Macmillan

Letters, 1869–1895

To Alexander Macmillan

Christ Church, Oxford
February 15, 1869
[p. 77]

Dear Mr. Macmillan,

In view of the coming Easter season, I want you to consider once more the idea I once suggested to you—of bringing out a "cheap edition" of *Alice*. My reasons for wishing for it are *not* commercial, strictly speaking—as a commercial speculation, it may very likely not be profitable, or may even be a loss—but *that* I do not much care about. My feeling is that the present price puts the book entirely out of the reach of many thousands of children of the middle classes, who might, I think, enjoy it (below that I

---

4. With Mrs. Hargreaves's consent, the facsimile of the original version of the story was published as *Alice's Adventures Under Ground* in 1886.

† From *Lewis Carroll and the House of Macmillan*, ed. Morton N. Cohen and Anita Gandolfo (New York: Cambridge UP, 1987). Reprinted with permission of Cambridge University Press. The publishing house of Macmillan, founded in 1843 by Daniel and Alexander Macmillan, was a well-established firm that published most of Dodgson's writings, including some of his mathematical and logical works. Macmillan published Dodgson/Carroll on commission, a common arrangement in nineteenth-century Britain, in which the publisher managed the printing, advertising, and distribution of books, the author paid these costs, and the publisher took a percentage of the money from sales. See the entry in Dodgson's diary (August 2, 1865) on p. 274 of this edition.

don't think it would be appreciated). Now the only point I really care for in the whole matter (and *it* is a source of very real pleasure to me) is that the book should be enjoyed by children—and the more in number, the better. So I should be much obliged if you would make a rough calculation whether you could (by printing on cheaper paper (but keeping to *toned* unless white is decidedly cheaper), by putting more into a page, limiting the pictures to 10 or 12 of the best, and printing these separately (which I suppose would be cheaper than working them with the text: and in this case we might print *them* at any rate, on toned paper), having the edges sprinkled red instead of gilt, and the cover plain red, with no gilding on it except the title) sell the book for (say) half-a-crown, and yet make a profit if there were a good demand for it. I am not Quixotic enough to wish to sell at a loss, but I don't mind its damaging the sale of the other a little, provided we thus put the book within the reach of a new sphere of readers. If the scheme be at all a feasible one, I should much like to try it as an Easter book—and if you wished, something might be said in advertising it to secure people from thinking that it is done because the dearer edition won't sell.

*   *   *

To Alexander Macmillan

Christ Church, Oxford
February 4, 1877
[p. 134]

Dear Mr. Macmillan,

Can it be true, what a friend reports to me, that the *Looking-Glass* is out of print? And if so, how can it possibly have happened? Surely there must have been some strange carelessness, on the part of whoever is responsible for the reprinting, in letting the stock run too low before putting a fresh 3000 in hand? And I suppose that to be "out of print" just now, in the Xmas Season, means to lose the opportunity of a good many possible sales.

How has the *Snark* sold during the Xmas Season? *That*, I should think, would be a much better test of its success or failure than any amount of sale at its first coming out. I am entirely puzzled as to whether to consider it a success or failure. I hear in some quarters of children being fond of it—but certainly the Reviews condemned it in no measured terms.* * *

To George Macmillan

Christ Church, Oxford
November 25, 1880
[p. 160]

Dear Mr. George Macmillan,
   Please give Miss Graham (of "Warwick House, Salisbury Square") the leave she asks for, to reproduce the "Mad Tea Party" on a tablecloth.

* * *

To Alexander Macmillan

Christ Church, Oxford
October 14, 1888
[p. 246]

Dear Mr. Macmillan,
   Will you kindly inform Mr. A. Silver, of 84 Brook Green, that Mr. Lewis Carroll has no objection to his using Tenniel's pictures for the wall-paper which he proposes to design. Please add the suggestion that the *longer* the paper can be made, before the pattern repeats itself, the better: the thing has been already tried once, but the pattern repeated itself in about 2 yards of length, so that, even in a small room, the same picture would recur many times, with a very tedious effect. Twenty yards of length, before the pattern recurs, would be none too long.

* * *

To Frederick Macmillan

Christ Church, Oxford
December 22, 1895
[p. 326]

Dear Mr. Macmillan,
   I want to consult you about the Advertisement, of books to be given away. * * *
   My wish is to offer, to all Incumbents or Curates, copies of *Looking-Glass* (60th Thousand) for use in Village Reading Rooms, or to lend to invalids: also copies of *Nursery "Alice"* (toned) to show to children, or lend to sick children: also of *Sylvie and Bruno* (both volumes, to be bound in *plain* covers, merely with name, and with sprinkled edges) for Village Reading Rooms, or to lend to invalids.

It will be *many* years before we can hope to *sell* the great number of *Sylvie* on hand, and I would gladly give away (say) 1000,
that they may give pleasure *somewhere*.

* * *

From Lewis Carroll's Diaries, 1865–1886

Aug. 2. (W). [1865] [5: 100–101]   Finally decided on the re-print
of *Alice*,[1] and that the first 2000 shall be sold as waste paper.
Wrote about it to Macmillan, Combe and Tenniel. The total cost
will be

drawing pictures	138
cutting pictures	142
printing (by Clay)	240
binding & advertising (say)	80
	600

i.e. 6/–a copy on the 2000. If I make £500 by sale, this will be a loss
of £100, and the loss on the first 2000 will probably be £100 leaving me £200 out of pocket.

But if a second 2000 could be sold it would cost £300, and bring
in £500, thus squaring accounts: and any further sale would be a
gain: but that I can hardly hope for.

Sept. 13. (M). [1865] [5:173]   Macmillan is now printing 3000
more *Alices*. By the end of 1867 I hope to be about clear, if not
actually in pocket by it.

Jan. 27. (Sat). [1872] [6:200]   My birthday was signalised by hearing from Mr. Craik [of Macmillan] that they have now sold 15,000
Looking-Glasses, and have orders for 500 more!

Feb. 26. (M). [1872] [6:200–201]   Wrote out the Definitions etc. of
Euclid Book I on plan of improving by modern lights, but keeping
as much of the original as possible. * * * (I want the University to
bring out a revised Euclid). * * *

Nov. 23. (M) [1874] [6:368]   Ruskin came, by my request, for a talk
about the pictures Holiday is doing for the "Boojum," one (the scene

---

1. John Tenniel was dissatisfied with the appearance of the illustrations in the first printing, and Dodgson insisted on reprinting. The unbound sheets of the rejected edition
were sold to an American publisher, who brought out the book in 1866.

on board) has been cut on wood. He much disheartened me by holding out no hopes that Holiday would be able to illustrate a book satisfactorily.[2]

Nov. 2. (Tu). [1875] [6:430]   * * * Sent Macmillan 14 stanzas of the *Snark*, which I think we shall now publish this Christmas, with frontispiece only.

Ap: 18. (Tu). [1876] [6:457]   Went to the Polytechnic with Caroline and Henrietta to see Mr. G. Buckland's[3] Entertainment *Alice's Adventures*. It lasted about 1¼ hours. A good deal of it was done by dissolving views, extracts from, the story being read, or sung to Mr. [William] Boyd's music; but the latter part had a real scene and five performers (Alice, Queen, Knave, Hatter, Rabbit) who acted in dumb show, the speeches being read by Mr. Buckland. The "Alice" was a rather pretty child of about 10 (Martha Wooldridge) who acted simply and gracefully. An interpolated song for the Cat, about a footman and housemaid, was so out of place, that I wrote afterwards to ask Mr. Buckland to omit it.

Sept. 2. (Th). [1886] [8:291]   * * * On the 28th I got an application from Mr. H. Savile Clarke,[4] for leave to make a two Act Operetta out of *Alice* and *Looking-Glass*. I have written my consent, on condition of "no *suggestion* ever of coarseness in libretto or in stage business."

Dec. 22. (W). [1886] [8:309]   Today begins the sale of *Alice's Adventures Under Ground*. Tomorrow is the first performance of *Alice in Wonderland*, at the Prince of Wales' Theatre. A tolerably eventful week for me!

2. John Ruskin (1819–1900) was the best-known writer on art in the Victorian period. Henry Holiday (1839–1927), who did illustrate *The Hunting of the Snark*, worked as a painter and watercolorist, and in stained glass, as well as in black-and-white illustration.

3. George Buckland was a writer and performer of comic songs. The Polytechnic in London featured visual entertainments such as panoramas and "dissolving views," effects like those of the "Wool and Water" chapter of *Through the Looking-Glass* and the endings of both Alice books. William Boyd (1845–1928) was an Oxford graduate and clergyman whose *The Songs from Alice's Adventures in Wonderland* had been published in 1870.

4. Henry Savile Clarke (1841–1893) wrote and produced plays; he also worked as a newspaper editor and drama critic. He engaged a young composer, Walter Slaughter (1860–1903), to write the music for his version of the two *Alice* books. (Dodgson tried, without success, to persuade Clarke to include an episode from *The Hunting of the Snark*.) The play opened just before Christmas and ran in London for fifty performances.

LEWIS CARROLL

From Alice on the Stage[†]

* * *

Many a day we rowed together on that quiet stream—the three lit-tle maidens and I—and many a fairy tale had been extemporised for their benefit—whether it were at times when the narrator was "i' the vein," and fancies unsought came crowding thick upon him, or at times when the jaded Muse was goaded into action, and plod-ded meekly on, more because she had to say something than that she had something to say—yet none of these many tales got written down: they lived and died, like summer midges, each in its own golden afternoon until there came a day when, as it chanced, one of my little listeners petitioned that the tale might be written out for her. That was many a year ago, but I distinctly remember, now as I write, how, in a desperate attempt to strike out some new line of fairy-lore, I had sent my heroine straight down a rabbit-hole, to begin with, without the least idea what was to happen afterwards. And so, to please a child I loved (I don't remember any other motive), I printed in manuscript, and illustrated with my own crude designs—designs that rebelled against every law of Anatomy or Art (for I had never had a lesson in drawing)—the book which I have just had published in facsimile.[1] In writing it out, I added many fresh ideas, which seemed to grow to themselves upon the original stock; and many more added themselves when, years afterwards, I wrote it all over again for publication: but (this may interest some readers of "Alice" to know) every such idea and nearly every word of the dialogue, *came of itself.* Sometimes an idea comes at night, when I have had to get up and strike a light to note it down—sometimes when out on a lonely winter walk, when I have had to stop, and with half-frozen fingers jot down a few words which should keep the new-born idea from perishing—but whenever or however it comes, *it comes of itself.* I cannot set invention going like a clock, by any vol-untary winding up: nor do I believe that any *original* writing (and what other writing is worth preserving?) was ever so produced.

* * *

I have wandered from my subject, I know: yet grant me another minute to relate a little incident of my own experience. I was walk-

---

[†] First printed in *The Theatre* in 1887; reprinted in *The Lewis Carroll Picture Book,* ed. Stuart Dodgson Collingwood (London: T. Fisher Unwin, 1899), 163–70.
1. *Alice's Adventures Under Ground,* published by Macmillan in 1886. [*Editor's note.*]

ing on a hill-side, alone, one bright summer day, when suddenly
there came into my head one line of verse—one solitary line—"For
the *Snark* was a Boojum, you see." I knew not what it meant, then:
I know not what it means, now; but I wrote it down: and some times
afterwards, the rest of the stanza occurred to me, that being its last
line: and so by degrees, at odd moments during the next year or
two, the rest of the poem pieced itself together, that being its last
stanza. And since then, periodically I have received courteous letters from strangers, begging to know whether "The Hunting of the
Snark" is an allegory, or contains some hidden moral, or is a political satire: and for all such questions I have but one answer, "*I don't
know!*" And now I return to my text, and will wander no more.

Stand forth, then, from the shadowy past, "Alice," the child of my
dreams. Full many a year has slipped away, since that "golden afternoon" that gave thee birth, but I can call it up almost as clearly as if
it were yesterday—the cloudless blue above, the watery mirror
below, the boat drifting idly on its way, the tinkle of the drops that
fell from the oars, as they waved so sleepily to and fro, and (the one
bright gleam of life in all the slumberous scene) the three eager
faces, hungry for news of fairyland, and who would not be said "nay"
to: from whose lips "Tell us a story, please," had all the stern immu-
tability of Fate!

What wert thou, dream-Alice, in thy foster-father's eyes? How
shall he picture thee? Loving, first, loving and gentle: loving as a dog
(forgive the prosaic simile, but I know no earthly love so pure and
perfect), and gentle as a fawn: then courteous—courteous to all,
high or low, grand or grotesque, King or Caterpillar, even as though
she were herself a King's daughter, and her clothing wrought gold:
then trustful, ready to accept the wildest impossibilities with all that
utter trust that only dreamers know; and lastly, curious—wildly
curious, and with the eager enjoyment of Life that comes only in the
happy hours of childhood, when all is new and fair, and when Sin
and Sorrow are but names—empty words signifying nothing!

And the White Rabbit, what of *him*? Was *he* framed on the "Alice"
lines, or meant as a contrast? As a contrast, distinctly. For *her*
"youth," "audacity," "vigour," and "swift directness of purpose," read
"elderly," "timid," "feeble," and "nervously shilly-shallying," and you
will get *something* of what I meant him to be. I *think* the White Rabbit should wear spectacles. I am sure his voice should quaver, and
his knees quiver, and his whole air suggest a total inability to say
"Bo" to a goose!

But I cannot hope to be allowed, even by the courteous Editor of
The Theatre, half the space I should need (even if my *reader's*
patience would hold out) to discuss each of my puppets one by one.
Let me cull from the two books a Royal Trio—the Queen of Hearts,

the Red Queen, and the White Queen. It was certainly hard on my Muse, to expect her to sing of *three* Queens, within such brief compass, and yet to give to each her own individuality. Each, of course, had to preserve, through all her eccentricities, a certain queenly *dignity*. *That* was essential. And for distinguishing traits, I pictured to myself the Queen of Hearts as a sort of embodiment of ungovernable passion—a blind and aimless Fury. The Red Queen I pictured as a Fury, but of another type; *her* passion must be cold and calm; she must be formal and strict, yet not unkindly; pedantic to the tenth degree, the concentrated essence of all governesses! Lastly, the White Queen seemed, to my dreaming fancy, gentle, stupid, fat and pale; helpless as an infant; and her just *suggesting* imbecility, but never quite passing into it; that would be, I think, fatal to any comic effect she might otherwise produce.

Later Life

DEREK HUDSON

[Rooms at Christ Church]†

At the same time that his sisters went into "The Chestnuts",[1] Dodgson took possession of new rooms at Christ Church which were to be his for the rest of his life. He first occupied this spacious apartment, which had formerly belonged to Lord Bute, at the end of October, 1868. The rooms, in the north-west corner of Tom Quad, are unusually imposing among the quarters of Oxford dons and have an interior staircase communicating to an upper floor. The entrance is into a dark passage, with doors leading to a diningroom, a pantry and a small bedroom (bleakly equipped in Dodgson's day with a "japanned[2] sponge bath"). The passage leads on into a large high sitting-room—cold in winter—with windows looking out over St Aldate's and the Archdeacon's garden. The sitting-room has a further amenity in the shape of two small turret-rooms on the St Aldate's front—more curious, perhaps, than valuable, but useful for amusing young visitors.

Upstairs (these are the arrangements of 1953) we find another bedroom, a box-room, a bath-room, and a cubby-hole which Dodgson turned into a photographic dark-room. Even here was not his furthest; for he eventually obtained permission to build a studio on the roof—an erection that can hardly have been sightly and has long been removed; he first used it in October, 1871.

Although he became increasingly abstemious and eventually almost gave up eating lunch altogether, it would be a mistake to suppose that Dodgson possessed no interest in food. It will be remembered that the contents of the bottle which Alice drank had "a sort of mixed flavour of cherry-tart, custard, pineapple, roast

---

† From *Lewis Carroll: An Illustrated Biography* (New York: Clarkson Potter; London: Constable, 1977), 145–47. Copyright © 1977 by Derek Hudson. Used by permission of Random House Value Publishing, a division of Random House, Inc. All annotations are by the editor.
1. Chestnuts: The house in Guilford that Dodgson bought for his sisters in 1868, after the death of their father.
2. Japanned: treated with a hard, glossy varnish or lacquer.

turkey, toffy, and hot buttered toast", and that the taste of a Snark was "meagre and hollow, but crisp: Like a coat that is rather too tight in the waist, with a flavour of Will-o-the-wisp"—all evidence, surely, of a discriminating palate? His little dining-room at Christ Church holds memories of many dinner-parties, some of them quite elaborate, though the dishes were always placed on squares of cardboard, as he considered mats an unnecessary extravagance. In his diary, luncheons and dinners were recorded by a small diagram, showing the names of the guests and the places they occupied; he also kept a *menu* book, so that the same people should not be given the same dishes too often. After a dinner-party of eight in May, 1871, he wrote promptly to his publisher, Macmillan, to report "an invention of mine" (which does not seem to have been proceeded with).[3] This was a plan of the table with the names of the guests in the order in which they were to sit, and brackets to show who was to take in whom; one to be given to each guest.

*　*　*

Dodgson's study was simply but comfortably furnished with a large Turkey carpet, one or two arm-chairs, a crimson-covered couch and settee, and a dining-table and writing-table of mahogany. No visitor could fail to detect that its occupant was diligent and methodical. Manuscript boxes abounded, more than twenty of them—neatly labelled—being assembled in a special stand. The room also contained what was described after Dodgson's death as a "pine nest" of twelve drawers, as well as a pine reading stand with a cloth cover— this presumably being the "standing desk" at which he often liked to write. Letter scales and weights, quantities of stationery, shelves full of books, and a terrestrial globe filled much of the remaining space.

*　*　*

The pictures that hung in Dodgson's rooms were mostly of little girls, and usually had some personal association for him, either with the subject or the painter. There was a sprinkling of religious and fairy pictures, a plaster bust of a child, and one or two stock Victorian engravings, such as "Samuel" and "The Order of Release".[4] (If we could accept Reynolds's dictum that "the virtuous man alone has true taste", we should be quite satisfied.) Perhaps the most interesting of the *objets d'art* in the sitting-room was a set of William de

3. The entire letter, and Dodgson's sketch of his table arrangement, are reprinted in *Lewis Carroll and the House of Macmillan*, 95–96. (See full citation on p. 271.)
4. "The Order of Release" is a popular painting by John Everett Millais. "Samuel" may refer to "The Infant Samuel," an equally sentimental eighteenth-century painting by Joshua Reynolds. William de Morgan (1839–1917) designed decorative tiles that were admired by late-nineteenth-century advocates of good domestic design.

Morgan's famous tiles, which Collingwood says that Dodgson liked to explain by reference to *Alice in Wonderland* and *The Hunting of the Snark.*

The tiles, which figure largely in recollections of his later years, made their appearance only a decade before Dodgson's death. They were set around the fireplace and depicted a large ship (in three sections) and a number of more or less fabulous creatures, some of which Dodgson interpreted for the benefit of his child-friends as the Lory, the Dodo, the Fawn, the Eaglet, the Gryphon and the Beaver. In the intervals between these subjects, a tile showing a group of weird birds was repeated.

"Called on Mr. William de Morgan and chose a set of red tiles for the large fire-place", Dodgson wrote in his diary of March 4th, 1887. [8:321] This indicates that the tiles were not made to his order but were taken from de Morgan's stock, Dodgson making what he considered an appropriate selection.* * * The tiles remained in position until about twenty years ago when they were swept away, rather unnecessarily, to reveal the original fireplace; and with them went a plain green paper on canvas which covered the walls in Dodgson's time.

ISA BOWMAN

[A Visit to Christ Church]†

*   *   *

In the morning I was awakened by the deep reverberations of "Great Tom" calling Oxford to wake and begin the new day. Those times were very pleasant, and the rememberance of them lingers with me still. Lewis Carroll at the time of which I am speaking had two tiny turret rooms, one on each side of his staircase in Christ Church. He always used to tell me that when I grew up and became married he would give me the two little rooms, so that if I ever disagreed with my husband we could each of us retire to a turret till we had made up our quarrel!

And those rooms of his! I do not think there was ever such a fairy-land for children. I am sure they must have contained one of the finest collections of musical-boxes to be found anywhere in the world. There were big black ebony boxes with glass tops, through which you could see all the works. There was a big box with a handle, which

† From *The Story of Lewis Carroll* (London: J. M. Dent & Sons Ltd., 1899), 20–23, 18–19. Isa Bowman was a child actress whom Dodgson had seen in the company of the theatrical version of the Alice books. He met her in 1887.

it was quite hard exercise for a little girl to turn, and there must have been twenty or thirty little ones which could only play one tune. Sometimes one of the musical-boxes would not play properly, and then I always got tremendously excited. Uncle [Dodgson] used to go to a drawer in the table and produce a box of little screwdrivers and punches, and while I sat on his knee he would unscrew the lid and take out the wheels to see what was the matter. He must have been a clever mechanist, for the result was always the same—after a longer or shorter period the music began again. Sometimes when the musical-boxes had played all their tunes he used to put them in the box backwards, and was as pleased as I at the comic effect of the music "standing on its head," as he phrased it.

There was another and very wonderful toy which he sometimes produced for me, and this was known as "The Bat." The ceilings of the rooms in which he lived at the time were very high indeed, and admirably suited for the purposes of "The Bat." It was an ingeniously constructed toy of gauze and wire, which actually flew about the room like a bat. It was worked by a piece of twisted elastic, and it could fly for about half a minute.

I was always a little afraid of this toy because it was too lifelike, but there was a fearful joy in it. When the music-boxes began to pall he would get up from his chair and look at me with a knowing smile. I always knew what was coming even before he began to speak, and I used to dance up and down in tremulous anticipation.

"Isa, my darling," he would say, "once upon a time there was some one called Bob the Bat! and he lived in the top left-hand drawer of the writing-table. What could he do when uncle wound him up?"

And then I would speak out breathlessly, "He could really FLY!"

Bob the Bat had many adventures. There was no way of controlling the direction of its flight, and one morning, a hot summer's morning, when the window was wide open, Bob flew out into the garden and alighted in a bowl of salad which a scout was taking to some one's rooms. The poor fellow was so startled by the sudden flapping apparition that he dropped the bowl, and it was broken into a thousand pieces.

※　　※　　※

I remember that [his] shyness was the only occasion of anything approaching a quarrel between us.

I had an idle trick of drawing caricatures when I was a child, and one day when he was writing some letters I began to make a picture of him on the back of an envelope. I quite forget what the drawing was like—probably it was an abominable libel—but suddenly he turned round and saw what I was doing. He got up from his seat and turned very red, frightening me very much. Then he took my poor little drawing, and tearing it into small pieces threw it into the fire without a word. Afterwards he came suddenly to me, and saying nothing, caught me up in his arms and kissed me passionately. I was only some ten or eleven years of age at the time, but now the incident comes back to me very clearly, and I can see it as if it happened but yesterday—the sudden snatching of my picture, the hurried striding across the room, and then the tender light in his face as he caught me up to him and kissed me.

* * *

From Lewis Carroll's Diaries, 1871–1874

May 4. (Th). [1871] [6:146–47]   On this day, "Alice's" birthday, I sit down to record the events of the day, partly as a specimen of my life now, and partly because they include *one* new experience.* * * I went (by request of [John Richard] King, vicar of St. Peter's in the East) to visit Quartermain, who used to work for me as carpenter, and who is dying of consumption. I visited him more as a friend than as a clergyman, though I *did* read him, at his own wish, two psalms and his favourite hymn "Sun of my Soul." I *hope* that my visit may have been of some comfort to him, though I feel terribly unfit to comfort anyone in such a time.

June 5. (W). [1872] [6:215]   A day whose consequences may be of the greatest importance to me. I went to Nottingham * * * and heard Dr. Lewin[1] lecture on his system for the cure of stammering. * * * The lecture lasted until after midnight, having begun about 9.

Nov: 1 (Sun). [1874] [6:366–67]   Not being well, I stayed in all day, and during the day read the whole of Mivart's *Genesis of Species* [1871], a most interesting and satisfactory book, showing, as it does, the insufficiency of "Natural Selection" *alone* to account for the universe, and its perfect compatibility with the creative and guiding power of God. The theory of "Correspondence to Environment" is also brought into harmony with the Christian's belief.[2]

1. *Dr. J. H. Lewin's (of Virginia) Method of Curing Stammering and Stuttering* was published in Baltimore in 1858 and 1871.
2. St. George Jackson Mivart (1827–1900), a zoologist, accepted at the beginning of his career Darwin's ideas of evolution by natural selection, but later, in his attempt to reconcile evolution with his religious beliefs, argued the impossibility of natural selection to account for certain organic features, such as the development of the eye.

From The Letters of Lewis Carroll, 1868–1897

To Margaret Cunnynghame[3]

Christ Church
Oxford
January 30, 1868
[I:112–13]

No carte[4] has yet been done of me that does real justice to my *smile*; and so I hardly like, you see, to send you one—however, I'll consider if I will or not—meanwhile, I send a little thing to give you an idea of what I look like when I'm lecturing. The merest sketch, you will allow—yet still I think there's something grand in the expression of the brow and in the action of the hand.

* * *

Your affectionate friend,
C. L. Dodgson

---

3. Margaret Cunnynghame was the daughter of a family whom Dodgson met on a visit to his own family. She was thirteen when she received this letter.
4. Carte: a visiting card bearing a photograph.

To Bert Coote[5]

The Chestnuts, Guildford
June 9 [?1877]
[I:276–77]

My dear Bertie,

I would have been very glad to write to you as you wish, only there are several objections. I think, when you have heard them, you will see that I am right in saying "No."

The first objection is, I've got no ink. You don't believe it? Ah, you should have seen the ink there was in *my* days! (About the time of the battle of Waterloo: I was a soldier in that battle.) Why, you had only to pour a little of it on the paper, and it went on by itself! *This* ink is so stupid, if you begin a word for it, it can't even finish it by itself.

The next objection is, I've no time. You don't believe *that*, you say? Well, who cares? You should have seen the time there was in *my* days! (At the time of the battle of Waterloo, where I led a regiment.) There were always 25 hours in the day—sometimes 30 or 40.

The third and greatest objection is, my *great* dislike for children. I don't know why, I'm sure: but I *hate* them—just as one hates arm-chairs and plum-pudding! You don't believe *that*, don't you? Did I ever say you would? Ah, you should have seen the children there were in my days! (Battle of Waterloo, where I commanded the English army. I was called "the Duke of Wellington" then, but I found it a great bother having such a long name, so I changed it to "Mr. Dodgson." I chose that name because it begins with the same letter as "Duke.") So you see it would never do to write to you.

Have you any sisters? I forget. If you have, give them my love. I am much obliged to your Uncle and Aunt for letting me keep the photograph.

I hope you won't be much disappointed at not getting a letter from

Your affectionate friend,
C. L. Dodgson

---

5. Bert Coote (1867–1938), ten years old when he received this letter, was an actor whose long theatrical career extended to the making of films in the 1930s.

To Mrs. A. L. Mayhew[6]

Christ Church, Oxford
May 26, 1879
[I:337–39]

Dear Mrs. Mayhew,

*   *   *

If Saturday afternoon is fine, I shall be glad to have Janet as soon after 2 as she can be got here. If you cannot come yourself, Ruth and Ethel might bring her—or, if you have other places you wish to go to, and like to leave her for an hour or two, I shall be most happy to take charge of her: but in either of these cases I should like to know *exactly* what is the minimum of dress I may take her in, and I will strictly observe the limits. I hope that, at any rate, we may go as far as a pair of bathing-drawers, though for *my* part I should much prefer doing without them, and shall be very glad if you say she may be done "in any way she likes herself."

But I have a much more alarming request to make than *that*, and I hope you and Mr. Mayhew will kindly consider it, and not hastily refuse it. It is that the same permission may be extended to Ethel. Please consider my reasons for asking the favour. Here am I, an amateur-photographer, with a deep sense of admiration for *form*, especially the human form, and one who believes it to be the most beautiful thing God has made on this earth—and who hardly ever gets a chance of photographing it! Did I ever show you those drawings Mr. Holiday did for me, in order to supply me with some graceful and unobjectionable groupings for children without drapery? He drew them from life, from 2 children of 12 and 6—but I thought sadly, "*I* shall never get 2 children of those ages who will consent to be subjects!" and now at last I seem to have a *chance* of it. I could no doubt hire *professional* models in town: but, first, they would be ugly, and, secondly, they would *not* be pleasant to deal with: so my only hope is with *friends*. Now your Ethel is beautiful, both in face and form; and is also a perfectly simple-minded child of Nature, who would have no sort of objection to serving as model for a friend she knows as well as she does me. So my humble petition is, that you will bring the 3 girls, and that you will allow me to try some groupings of Ethel and Janet (I fear there is no use naming Ruth as well, at her age, though *I* should have no objection!) without any drapery or suggestion of it.

6. The Mayhew daughters were the children of an Oxford clergyman and his wife. In 1879 the younger daughter was six or seven years old; the older daughter, Ethel, was about eleven years old.

I need hardly say that the pictures should be such as you might if you liked frame and hang up in your drawing-room. On no account would I do a picture which I should be unwilling to show to all the world—or at least all the artistic world.

If I did not believe I could take such pictures without any lower motive than a pure love of Art, I would not ask it: and if I thought there was any fear of its lessening *their* beautiful simplicity of character, I would not ask it.

I print all such pictures *myself*, and of course would not let any one see them without your permission.

I fear you will reply that the one *insuperable* objection is "Mrs. Grundy"—that people will be sure to hear that such pictures have been done, and that they will *talk*. As to their *hearing* of it, I say "of course. All the world are welcome to hear of it, and I would not on any account suggest to the children not to mention it—which would at once introduce an objectionable element"—but as to people *talking* about it, I will only quote the grand old monkish(?) legend:

> They say:
> Quhat do they say?
> *Lat them say!*[7]

* * *

I write all this, as a better course than coming to say it. *I* can be more sure of saying exactly what I mean—and you will have more leisure to think it over.

Sincerely yours,
C. L. Dodgson

To Mrs. A. L. Mayhew

Christ Church, Oxford
May 28, 1879
[I:341]

Dear Mrs. Mayhew,

Thanks for your letter. After my last had gone, I wished to recall it, and take out the sentence in which I had quite gratuitously suggested the possibility that you *might* be unwilling to trust me to photograph the children by themselves in undress. And now I am more than ever sorry I wrote it, as it has accidentally led to your telling me what I would gladly have remained ignorant of. For I hope you won't think me *very* fanciful in saying I should have no pleasure in doing any such pictures, now that I

---

7. "Thay haif said, Quhat say thay, Lat thame say" was adopted as the motto of the Earls Marischal of Scotland.

know I am not thought fit for only permitted such a privilege except on condition of being under chaperonage. I had rather do no more pictures of your children except in full dress: please forgive all the trouble I have given you about it.

*   *   *

Sincerely yours,
C. L. Dodgson

To an unidentified recipient

[? Mid-1882]
[I:463]

. . . I am a member of the English Church, and have taken Deacon's Orders, but did not think fit (for reasons I need not go into) to take Priest's Orders. My dear father was what is called a "High Churchman," and I naturally adopted those views, but have always felt repelled by the yet higher development called "Ritualism."

But I doubt if I am fully a "High Churchman" now. I find that as life slips away (I am over fifty now), and the life on the other side of the great river becomes more and more the reality, of which *this* is only a shadow, that the petty distinctions of the many creeds of Christendom tend to slip away as well—leaving only the great truths which all Christians believe alike. More and more, as I read of the Christian religion, as Christ preached it, I stand amazed at the forms men have given to it, and the fictitious barriers they have built up between themselves and their brethren. I believe that when you and I come to lie down for the last time, if only we can keep firm hold of the great truths Christ taught us—our own utter worthlessness and His infinite worth; and that He has brought us back to our one Father, and made us His brethren, and so brethren to one another—we shall have all we need to guide us through the shadows.

Most assuredly I accept to the full the doctrines you refer to—that Christ died to save us, that we have no other way of salvation open to us but through His death, and that it is by faith in Him, and through no merit of ours, that we are reconciled to God; and most assuredly I can cordially say, "I owe all to Him who loved me, and died on the Cross of Calvary." . . .

To an agnostic

Christ Church, Oxford
May 31, 1897
[II:1122]

. . . In the Agnostic view of Christianity, it seems to be expected, sometimes, that Christians should be able to *prove* what they believe, by arguments which a reasonable man *must* accept as valid, whatever his *wishes* may be.

This is the case with (say) mathematics. If a proposition of Euclid were put before a man, able to understand it, but very anxious *not* to believe it, he would not be able to help himself: he *must* believe it.

This is *not* the case with Christianity. Some of its beliefs are what would be called in Science "Axioms," and are quite incapable of being *proved*, simply because *proof* must rest on something already granted: but this does not exist in the case of Axioms: if there were anything already granted, which could be used in proving them, they would not be "Axioms," but "Theorems." The existence of Free Will is an Axiom of this kind. Consequently, if, in any discussion between two persons, one accepts some Axiom needed in the discussion, and the other does not, there is no more to be said: further discussion is useless.

The other beliefs of Christianity are mostly, if not wholly, believed as a *balance of probabilities*: one who is resolved *not* to believe never finds himself *compelled* to believe: there is always room for *moral* causes to come in, such as humility, truthfulness, and, above all, the resolution to *do what is right*.

No discussion, between two persons, can be of any use, until each knows clearly *what* it is that the other asserts.

MORTON N. COHEN

The Man's Faith[†]

Thus, in mathematics, Charles sought reasoned proofs of logical propositions; in matters of religion, he recognized that although, as in Euclidean geometry, a believer had to accept certain axioms, he must move on from them to religious tenets that depend in part on intuition, the balance of probabilities, and moral causes.

---

† From *Lewis Carroll: A Biography*, 372–73. Copyright © 1995 by Morton N. Cohen. Used by permission of Alfred A. Knopf, a division of Random House, Inc. All annotations are by the editor.

Charles must have realized that his altered view of religion would not be welcome in the main Church, nor would his liberal notions be acceptable on the hearth at Croft, in the sitting room at Guildford, or with many of his stiff-collared colleagues in Common Room. T. B. Strong, who had ample opportunity to converse with Charles, refers to his disinclination to discuss religion: "It is difficult to speak of a side of his character in regard to which he was very reserved."[1] "I *hate* all theological controversy," Charles confessed to Mrs. Rix (July 7, 1885). "It is wearing to the temper, and is I believe (at all events when viva voce) worse than useless." [*Letters* II, 586] Controversy is, in any case, a breeding ground for animosity, for hate, and Charles believed that love "makes the world go round."

What have we here, then, in Charles Dodgson? * * * The sum of his beliefs, like Coleridge's and Maurice's,[2] defies labels. But like Coleridge and Maurice, he harbored a reverence for the past, a holy respect for the Bible and the teachings of Christ, an insistence on inner knowledge, a reliance on intuition and conscience—in other words, a mixture of elements that we can call both liberal and conservative. When all is said and done, he was his own man, having forged a faith intricately wrought and unique.

There emerges a man who thought carefully, deeply, and constantly about what is right and wrong, who asked all the crucial questions about life and death, good and evil, seeking answers from congenial guides, and ultimately tested and shaped his own faith and destiny. He was, in essence, a solid Christian, and he lived by Christian principles, more diligently than most of those high-minded churchmen who despised his moderation.

Charles's faith did not, then, derive entirely from domestic and schoolhouse instruction; even though he aligned himself with his father, he rejected much of his father's teaching. Looking inward, as he so often did, must have gone against the grain of accepting traditional dicta without examining them. "God has given . . . [us] conscience (that is an intuitive sense of 'I ought,' 'I ought not'), and this . . . we ought to obey," he wrote Mary Brown (December 26, 1889). [*Letters* II:772–73] When he said that we must subject our faith to conscience, he echoed not his father, but Coleridge and Maurice, particularly Coleridge's Reason. He subscribed to a belief

---

1. [Thomas Banks Strong], "Lewis Carroll"' *Cornhill* 4 (no. 4): 303–10. Strong (1861–1944) was a colleague of Dodgson's at Christ Church, later dean of the college, vice chancellor of the University, and successively bishop of Ripon and of Oxford.
2. Samuel Taylor Coleridge (1772–1834), poet and essayist, and Frederick Denison Maurice (1805–1872), clergyman, educator, and controversial writer on religious topics, became important figures in the Broad Church, an ample term used to describe mid- and late-nineteenth-century attempts to mediate among divisions of doctrine and liturgy within the Anglican Church and to accommodate Christian belief to the findings and ideas of current, especially German, biblical scholarship.

in the spark of divinity he found within himself, the spark that his two mentors helped him recognize.

*   *   *

If a human being "acts without attending to that inner voice," Charles wrote to Mary Brown (December 26, 1889), ". . . he is . . . doing wrong, *whatever* the resulting act may be. . . . Don't worry yourself with questions of *abstract* right and wrong. When you are puzzled go and tell your puzzle to your Heavenly Father . . . and pray for guidance, and then do what seems best to *you*, and it will be accepted by Him." [*Letters*, II:772–73]

From Lewis Carroll's Diaries, 1880–1891

Sep. 3. (F). [1880] [7:292–93]   Little Edith Blakemore was allowed (for the first time) to go alone to the shore in search of me. I took her about with me a little and then home. In the afternoon I fell in with the three little "jersey" girls, and made acquaintance with the parents—name Godby: the children being Nellie, Katie, and Phyllis. Mr. Godby, though he looks commercial is an Oxford man. I promised *Alice* for little Nellie, and also promised a *Snark* to a quite new little friend, Lily Alice Godfrey, from New York aged 8, but talked like a girl of 15 or 16, and declined to be kissed on wishing goodbye, on the ground that she "never kissed gentlemen." It is rather painful to see the lovely simplicity of childhood so soon rubbed off: but I fear it is true that there are no children in America.

*   *   *

May 14. (Sat). [1881] [7:335]   Took the longest walk (I believe) I have ever done—round by Dorchester, Didcot and Abingdon—27 miles—took eight hours—no blisters, I rejoice to find, and I feel very little tired.

Oct. 18. (Tu). [1881] [7:371]   6 p.m. I have just taken an important step in life, by sending to the Dean a proposal to resign the Mathematical Lectureship at the end of this year. I shall now have my whole time at my own disposal, and, if God gives me life and continued health and strength, may hope, before my powers fail, to do some worthy work in writing—partly in the cause of Mathematical education, partly in the cause of innocent recreation for children, and partly, I hope (though so utterly unworthy of being allowed to take up such work) in the cause of religious thought. May God bless the new form of life that lies before me, that I may use it according to His holy will!

Feb. 6. (F). [1891] [8:549–50]   I must have fainted just at the end of morning chapel, as I found myself, an hour afterwards, lying on the floor of the stalls; and had probably struck my nose against the hassock, as it had been bleeding considerably. It is the first time I fainted quite away. I sent for Dr. Brooks. I had some headache afterwards, but felt very little the worse. It is of course possible it may have been epilepsy and not fainting: but Dr. Brooks thinks the latter.[1]

Feb. 12. (Th). [1891] [8:551]   Nearly well again, though still not free from headache. Dr. Brooks now thinks it was an epileptic attack, passing off into sleep. The only previous attack was on morning of December 31, 1885, more than five years ago.

Sept. 12. (Sat). [1891] [8:580]   Last evening I had another experience of 'seeing fortifications'.[2] * * *

E. M. ROWELL

To Me, He Was Mr. Dodgson[†]

When I first saw Lewis Carroll I was a sixth-form girl[1] at the Oxford High School. One morning at school the word went around that 'Mr Dodgson' was coming to give some lectures to the sixth on symbolic logic. To me the name 'Mr Dodgson' meant nothing, and when someone said casually, 'Lewis Carroll, you know,' I acquiesced in the synonym but my mind was blank as before.

I had of course always known *Alice in Wonderland*, but to me Alice and the White Rabbit and the Red Queen—and the Dormouse and the Mad Hatter and the Cheshire Cat—were endowed with all the vitality and reality and being of an age-old myth; and how they had managed to get into a book was really neither here nor there. In short, at the age of fifteen I was quite oblivious of the fact that Lewis Carroll had written *Alice in Wonderland*,

---

1. Sadi Ranson-Polizzotti, Jenny Woolf, and Peter van Vugt (see Selected Bibliography) consider the probability that Dodgson suffered from epilepsy and/or migraine. According to Ranson-Polizzotti, "Almost all of the things that happen in Wonderland correlate directly to various seizure states" (40). Walter Tyrell Brooks was Dodgson's Oxford physician.
2. Dodgson's phrase for his experience of seeing dark bars, perhaps a symptom of migraine.
† From *Harpers* 186 (1943): 319–23, A somewhat shorter version is reprinted in *Lewis Carroll: Interviews and Recollections*, ed. Morton Cohen (Iowa City: U of Iowa P, 1989), 129–34. Reprinted by permission of AP Watt Ltd on behalf of Morton N. Cohen. Annotations are by the editor of this Norton Critical Edition.
1. Ethel Rowell was sixteen or seventeen years old when Dodgson met her in 1894. She became a lecturer in mathematics at the Royal Holloway College.

and neither 'Lewis Carroll nor' 'Mr Dodgson' had any associations for me.

When Mr Dodgson stood at the desk in the sixth-form room and prepared to address the class I thought he looked very tall and seemed very serious and rather formidable, beyond that I did not go and, with the ready docility of a schoolgirl of the nineties, I soon settled down to the subject in hand and forgot the lecturer in his own fascinating 'Game of Logic'.

* * *

The day after Mr. Dodgson gave us his last lecture, I received from him this letter:

Ch. Ch., Oxford
April 18. /94.
[*Letters* II:1019–20]

My dear Ethel,

(I would gladly write "Miss Rowell" if I thought you would prefer it, but, with more than forty years' interval of age, the other way seems more natural.)

You did your logic so *very* well, that it occurs to me to ask whether you would like, and could spare the time, to have some more lessons during the vacation. If so, I will come and speak to your Mother, and see if any such arrangement can be made.

I should be very glad to do it; and it would be a real help in the book I am at work on.

yours very sincerely
C. L. Dodgson.

The lessons began almost at once, and in those summer holidays I went to and fro to Mr Dodgson's rooms in Christ Church; we worked through the first proofs of the book, and as the subject opened out I found great delight in this my first real experience of the patterned intricacies of abstract thought.

In the beginning my inveterate docility got in the way; I could find nothing to comment on and my response was limited to a repetitive 'Yes, yes . . . yes, I see.' I was ready to accept everything that was put before me. One day after a long series of such feeble affirmatives Mr Dodgson put down his pen and, looking at me with his rather crooked smile, 'You do make the lion and the lamb consort together in your caravanserai, don't you?' he said. I did not understand and thought he was paying me a compliment, so I hastened to say deprecatingly 'Oh! but I'm afraid I don't get on easily with everybody.' 'He looked at me with his kindest smile and said:' 'Well, my dear, let us leave the lamb to fend for itself, and get back to our muttons, shall we?'

His words were Greek to me, but in their very strangeness they lingered in my memory, and much later I understood both his criticism of me and the patience with which he so gently withdrew it in the face of my ignorance.

I did not understand, but I realized that he found my shallow receptivity disappointing. And presently I managed to face the thing more squarely, to halt the flow of passive response, to tell myself and to tell my teacher what I found difficult or obscure in his reasoning. By his own real wish to know what I was thinking Mr Dodgson compelled me to that independence of thought I had never before tried to exercise. I had always learned very easily, and such ready assimilation of all and sundry had filled my mind with a company of somnolent ideas which, awake, must surely have been at odds with one another. Mr Dodgson's protest of the lion and the lamb was indeed justified. But gradually under his stimulating tuition I felt myself able in some measure to judge for myself, to select, and, if need be, to reject.

But while he was urging me to exercise my critical faculties Mr Dodgson at the same time bestowed on me another gift of aspect more gracious. He gave me a sense of my own personal dignity. He was so punctilious, so courteous, so considerate, so scrupulous not to embarrass or offend, that he made me feel that I counted—counted not as much as anyone else, and certainly not more than anyone else, but just in and as myself. There was nothing competitive or precarious in this counting, and thus my own keen awareness of awkwardness, ignorance, and inadequacy could not inhibit this new sense of the freedom of selfhood.

In Mr Dodgson's presence I felt proud and humble, with the pride and humility which are the grace and personality, grace conferred thus upon an ignorant schoolgirl by the magnanimity of a proud and very humble and very great and good man. And then Mr Dodgson gave me his affection—the reflection, in our own particular relation, of his great-hearted concern for all children. He was so patient of all one's limitations, so understanding, so infinitely kind.

* * *

I became a student at the Royal Holloway College in October, 1895, and after that I saw Mr Dodgson very rarely; but I was sure of his friendly interest, and I never felt out of touch with him.

When it was suggested that I should go on from Honors Moderations to work for the Final Honors School Examination in Mathematics at Oxford he was gently concerned and made an urgent protest to my mother on the grounds that the proposed course was altogether unsuitable for a girl, that the work was far too exacting and would impose a strain which might even upset my mental balance! My brother remembers vividly how his distressful apprehensions and vehement opposition reduced my mother to tears. I think he was always very conscious both of the qualities and of the disabilities of

women, and perhaps he overemphasized the differences in tempera-
ment and in capacity between men and women. But he was never for
a moment patronizing to women or to children; he 'consulted' one
about this or that and took careful and serious account of any opinion
given. He was always completely at ease with women and children,
and I fancy he was happier with them than in the company of men.

Throughout my college course he always answered my letters,
and he kept me in touch with the work he was doing.

KAROLINE LEACH

[Dodgson's Friendships with Women]†

* * *

Our fascination with Lewis Carroll and his works remains undi-
minished, but at its centre is the image of a Victorian clergyman,
shy and prim, locked in perpetual childhood; a man who, said Virginia Woolf, "had no life", who sought comfort and companionship
exclusively through friendships with "little girls", and who almost
invariably lost interest in them when they reached puberty. In his
biography Morton N. Cohen describes Carroll as a man with "dif-
fering sexual appetites", who "desired the companionship of female
children". More crudely, but perhaps also more honestly, the popular press has labelled him a "paedophile". It is certainly true that, if
Dodgson was alive to take the "Beggar Maid" and others of his
photographs today, he would probably find himself the object of
less flattering attention from the authorities.

* * *

An exception is Hugues Lebailly, a Professor of English Cultural
Studies at the Sorbonne, who has shown in papers such as "Charles
Lutwidge Dodgson, Eminent Ruskinian" (1996) and "C. L. D. and
Females" (2001) that Dodgson's MS diaries contain several entries
expressing his admiration for the adult female form in works of art,
and his enthusiasm for the "pretty" actresses, such as Gwynne Herbert and Milly Palmer, he saw at the theatre. "[Rossetti] showed us
many beautiful pictures", reads one such entry (April 18, 1865:
Diaries 5: 70–72), "two quite new: the bride going to meet the bride-
groom (from Solomon's Song) and Venus with a background of roses."
The latter picture is the notorious "Venus Verticordia", which

---

† From "The Real Scandal: Lewis Carroll's Friendships with Adult Women," *Times Literary
  Supplement* (February 8, 2002), 13–15. © Karoline Leach, News International Trading
  Ltd, 2002.

shocked and disgusted much of the art establishment when it was publicly displayed.

*   *   *

Lebailly's work on the lost realities of Victorian "child-worship" (in "C. L. Dodgson and the Victorian Cult of the Child", 1998) makes clear the extent to which Carroll's artistic and emotional "obsession" with little girls was and remains a misunderstood expression of this strange phenomenon. In the course of my own researches for a screenplay, I discovered that the man revealed in the MS diaries manifestly was not "exclusively focused on children". On the contrary, he recorded numerous relationships with grown women. And analysis of his published correspondence showed that out of nearly 500 letters to so-called child-friends, only 117 were actually to pre-teen children, while 152 were to girls aged between fourteen and seventeen, and 225 were to women aged over eighteen (the oldest being forty-two).

What the figures unambiguously make clear is that he did not, as the biographies maintain, lose interest in his "child-friends" once they reached the age of puberty; in fact large numbers of his "child-friends" were already teenagers or grown women when his friendships with them began. For reasons which will become clear, Dodgson preferred to refer to them as "children", but manifestly they were not. Similarly, there is no sign that his contemporaries considered him to be sexually "strange" about small girls. In fact, it was not his supposed predilection for little girls that raised eyebrows, but his numerous "unconventional" relationships with women, both married and single. The modern misapprehension is a bizarre construct, a mixture of deliberate deception on the part of Dodgson and his family, pure accidental muddle and misunderstanding.

A powerful mythology already surrounded the name "Lewis Carroll" before he died. It was saturated in the mores and symbols of the Victorian cult that equated a love of children with moral perfection and innocence. Carroll quickly grew to embody this cult and, by the early 1890s, he was being presented in the press as a latter-day saint, a "genuine lover of children" (*Harper's Monthly Magazine*, July 1890), living in "an El Dorado of innocent delights" (*Illustrated London News*, April 1891). Even people who knew him well, such as Gertrude Thomson, writing in the *Gentlewoman* of January 1898 (the year of his death), could create impossibly idealized images of Carroll as "some delicate ethereal spirit enveloped for the moment in a semblance of common humanity".

This was an image that Dodgson was happy to foster from time to time for his own reasons—but it was never in any sense a reality.

As his diaries and letters make plain, he liked to take women friends such as Constance Burch, Beatrice Hatch, Gertrude Chataway and Winifred Stevens (to mention just four) on holiday with him. At Oxford, he enjoyed tête-à-tête dinners with them that might last well into the night, and he was known to escort married women up to London for the weekend; they occasionally stayed overnight with him in his sisters' Guildford home. Not surprisingly, this generated gossip, which sometimes amused but often enraged him. He joked frequently about "Mrs Grundy", the fictional guardian of middle-class morality, claiming she dogged his footsteps incessantly. "Just now she—Mrs G.—is no doubt busy talking about me and another young friend of mine—a mere child only four or five and twenty—whom I have brought down from town to visit my sisters", he wrote to Maud Standen on April 14, 1884 [*Letters*, II:536–37]. (The "young friend" on that occasion was the artist Theodosia Heaphy.)

It was in order to evade some of this disapproval that he began to manipulate the developing Carroll myth by occasionally implying, or at least allowing others to assume, that his many girlfriends were somewhat younger than they really were. For, according to Victorian mores, a girl under the age of fourteen was a "safe" companion for a bachelor, since she was assumed to be below the age of sexual availability. There was nothing wrong in a man taking a child for a holiday by the sea. When writing to his more straitlaced friends, therefore, Dodgson used language cleverly to infantilize his female companions, describing them as "children" even when they were twenty-five years old. This pretence met with ready acceptance from his many admirers and from the Victorian public.

* * *

From Lewis Carroll's Diaries, 1885–1892

Mar. 29. (Sun). [1885] [8:179–82] Never before have I had so many literary projects on hand at once. For curiosity I will here make a list of them:

(1) *Supplement to Euclid and His Modern Rivals*, now being set up in pages. * * * I think of printing 250. [published Ap. 1885]

(2) Second edition of *Euclid and His Modern Rivals*, this I am correcting for press, and shall embody above in it. [published Nov. 1885][1]

---

1. The *Supplement to Euclid and His Modern Rivals*, and the second edition of that book (first published in 1879), were published by Macmillan in 1885.

(3) A book of Mathematical curiosities, which I think of calling *Pillow Problems, and other Mathematical Trifles.*[2] This will contain Problems worked out in the dark, Logarithms without Tables, Sines and Angles ditto, a paper I am now writing, on "Infinities and Infinitesimals," condensed Long Multiplication, and perhaps others.

(4) *Euclid V*, treating Incommensurables by a method of Limits, which I have nearly completed.[3]

(5) *Plain Facts for Circle-Squarers* which is nearly complete, and gives actual proof of limits 3.14158, 3.14160.

(6) A symbolical Logic, treated by my algebraic method (see 23/12/84).[4]

(7) *A Tangled Tale*, with answers, and perhaps illustrated by Mr. Frost [published December 1885][5]

(8) A collection of Games and Puzzles of my devising, with fairy-pictures by Miss E. G. Thomson. This might also contain my "Memoria Technica" for dates etc., my "Cipher-writing," scheme for Letter-registration, etc. etc.[6]

(9) *Nursery "Alice,"* for which 20 pictures are now being coloured by Mr. Tenniel.[7] [published]

(10) Serious poems in *Phantasmagoria*. I think of calling it "Reason and Rhyme," and hope to get Mr. Furniss to draw for it.[8]

(11) *Alice's Adventures Under Ground*, a facsimile of the MS. book, lent me by "Alice" (Mrs. Hargreaves). I am now in correspondence with Dalziel about it.[9] [published]

(12) *Girls' Own Shakespeare*. I have begun on *Tempest*.

2. "Pillow-Problems Thought Out During Sleepless Nights" was incorporated in *Curiosa Mathematica Part II*, published by Macmillan in 1893.
3. Dodgson incorporated his revisions to *Euclid V* (1868), and *Plain Facts for Circle-Squarers*, in *Curiosa Mathematica, Part I: A New Theory of Parallels* (1888).
4. *Symbolic Logic Part 1, Elementary*, Dodgson's demonstration of how to do logic by using rules like those of mathematics, was published by Macmillan in 1896. *Part 2*, for more advanced students, was not published, but it has been reassembled from proofs and notes by William Warren Bartley III (see Selected Bibliography).
5. Arthur B. Frost (1851–1928) was an American book illustrator and painter who studied and worked in London.
6. This collection was never published. E. Gertrude Thomson (1850–1929) illustrated books and worked in stained glass. Dodgson sketched in her studio and became a close friend.
7. *The Nursery Alice* was published in 1889.
8. The sentimental poems in *Phantasmagoria* (1869) were collected in *Three Sunsets and Other Poems*, published by Macmillan in 1898 and illustrated by Ms. Thomson. Harry Furniss (1854–1915) was the illustrator of the *Sylvie and Bruno* books (1889, 1893).
9. The facsimile of the manuscript that Dodgson prepared for Alice Liddell was published by Macmillan in 1886. The Dalziels were a firm of engravers.

(13) New edition of *Parliamentary Representation*, embodying supplement etc.[1]

(14) New edition of *Euclid I, II*, for which I am now correcting edition 4.[2]

(15) The new child's book, which Mr. Furniss is to illustrate. * * * I have settled on no name as yet, but it will perhaps be *Sylvie and Bruno*. [published]

I have other shadowy ideas, e.g. a Geometry for Boys, a volume of Essays on theological points freely and plainly treated, and a drama on *Alice*: * * * but the above is a fair example of "too many irons in the fire"!

Aug. 13. (W). [1890] [8:524]   Went to the "Phonograph" again, at end of lecture, to hear the "private audience" part. Listening through tubes, with the nozzle to one's ear, is *far* better and more articulate than with the funnel: also the music is much sweeter. It is a pity. * * * that we are not 50 years further on in the world's history, so as to get this wonderful invention in its perfect form. It is now in its infancy; the new wonder of the day, just as I remember Photography was about 1850.

Ap. 3. (Sun). [1892] [8:612]   Once more I have to thank my Heavenly Father for the great blessing and privilege of being allowed to speak for Him! May he bless my words to help some soul on its heavenward way. I preached at the College Servants' Service on the last words of Rev. 3.1.[3]

STUART DODGSON COLLINGWOOD

[An Old Bachelor][†]

*   *   *

An old bachelor is generally very precise and exact in his habits. He has no one but himself to look after, nothing to distract his attention

1. The expurgated version of Shakespeare's plays was not completed. A revised edition of Dodgson's *Principles of Parliamentary Representation* (1884), his use of mathematics to assure proportional representation in elected bodies, was not published.
2. A fifth edition of *Euclid Books I, II* was published in 1886.
3. "Blessed is he that readeth, and they that hear the words of this prophecy, and keep those things which are written therein: for the time is at hand."
† From *The Life and Letters of Lewis Carroll (Rev. C. L. Dodgson)* (London: T. Fisher Unwin, 1898), 265–67, 389–91, and 329–31. Reprinted by permission of AP Watt Ltd on behalf of Trustees of the CL Dodgson Estate and Scirard Lancelyn Green. Annotations are by the editor of this Norton Critical Edition.

from his own affairs; and Mr. Dodgson was the most precise and exact of old bachelors. He made a précis of every letter he wrote or received from the 1st of January, 1861, to the 8th of the same month, 1898. These précis were all numbered and entered in reference-books, and by an ingenious system of cross-numbering he was able to trace a whole correspondence, which might extend through several volumes. The last number entered in his book is 98, 721.

He had scores of green cardboard boxes, all neatly labelled in which he kept his various papers. These boxes formed quite a feature of his study at Oxford, a large number of them being arranged upon a revolving bookstand. The lists, of various sorts, which he kept were innumerable; one of them, that of unanswered correspondents, generally held seventy or eighty names at a time, exclusive of autograph-hunters whom he did not answer on principle. He seemed to delight in being arithmetically accurate about every detail of life.

He always rose at the same hour, and, if he was in residence at Christ Church, attended College Service. He spent the day according to a prescribed routine, which usually included a long walk into the country, very often alone, but sometimes with another Don, or perhaps, if the walk was not to be as long as usual, with some little girl-friend at his side. When he had a companion with him, he would talk the whole time, telling delightful stories or explaining some new logical problem; if he was alone, he used to think out his books, as probably many another author has done and will do, in the course of a lonely walk. The only irregularity noticeable in his mode of life was the hour of retiring, which varied from 11 p.m. to four o'clock in the morning, according to the amount of work which he felt himself in the mood for.

He had a wonderfully good memory, except for faces and dates. The former were always a stumbling-block to him, and people used to say (most unjustly) that he was intentionally short-sighted. One night he went up to London to dine with a friend, whom he had only recently met. The next morning a gentleman greeted him as he was walking. "I beg your pardon," said Mr. Dodgson, "but you have the advantage of me. I have no remembrance of having ever seen you before this moment." "That is very strange," the other replied, "for I was your host last night!" Such little incidents as this happened more than once.

* * *

It was only to those who had but few personal dealings with him that he seemed stiff and "donnish"; to his more intimate acquaintances, who really understood him, each little eccentricity of manner or of habits was a delightful addition to his charming and interesting personality. That he was, in some respects, eccentric cannot be denied; for instance he hardly ever wore an overcoat, and always wore a tall hat, whatever might be the climatic conditions. At dinner in his rooms small pieces of cardboard took the place of table-mats; they answered the purpose perfectly well, he said, and to buy anything else would be a mere waste of money. On the other hand, when purchasing books for himself, or giving treats to the children he loved, he never seemed to consider expense at all.

He very seldom sat down to write, preferring to stand while thus engaged. When making tea for his friends, he used, in order, I suppose, to expedite the process, to walk up and down the room waving the teapot about, and telling meanwhile those delightful ancedotes of which he had an inexhaustible supply.

* * *

He had a strong objection to staring colours in dress, his favourite combination being pink and grey. One little girl who came to stay with him was absolutely forbidden to wear a red frock, of a somewhat pronounced hue, while out in his company.

At meals he was very abstemious always, while he took nothing in the middle of the day except a glass of wine and a biscuit. Under these circumstances it is not very surprising that the healthy appetites of his little friends filled him with wonder, and even with alarm. When he took a certain one of them out with him to a friend's house to dinner, he used to give the host or hostess a gentle warning, to the mixed amazement and indignation of the child, "Please be careful, because she eats a good deal too much."

Another peculiarity, which I have already referred to, was his objection to being invited to dinners or any other social gatherings; he made a rule of never accepting invitations. "Because you have invited me, therefore I cannot come," was the usual form of his refusal. I suppose the reason of this was his hatred of the interference with work which engagements of this sort occasion.

He had an extreme horror of infection, as will appear from the following illustration. Miss Isa Bowman and her sister, Nellie, were at one time staying with him at Eastbourne, when news came from home that their youngest sister had caught the scarlet fever. From that day every letter which came from Mrs. Bowman to the children was held up by Mr. Dodgson, while the two little girls, standing at the opposite end of the room, had to read it as best they could. Mr. Dodgson, who was the soul of honour, used always to turn his head to one side during these readings, lest he might inadvertently see some words that were not meant for his eyes.

* * *

The following is an extract from a letter written in 1896 [*Letters* Sept. 28, 1896: II: 1099–1100] to one of his sisters, in allusion to a death which had recently occurred in the family:—

> It is getting increasingly difficult now to remember *which* of one's friends remain alive, and *which* have gone "into the land of the great departed into the silent land."[1] Also, such news comes less and less as a shock, and more and more one realises that it is an experience each of *us* has to face before long. That fact is getting *less* dreamlike to me now, and I sometimes think what a grand thing it will be to be able to say to oneself, "Death is *over* now; there is not *that* experience to be faced again."
>
> I am beginning to think that, if the *books* I am still hoping to write are to be done at *all*, they must be done *now*, and that I am *meant* thus to utilise the splendid health I have had, unbroken, for the last year and a half, and the working powers that are fully as great as, if not greater, than I have ever had. I brought with me here the MS., such as it is (very fragmentary and unarranged) for the book about religious difficulties,[2] and I meant, when I came here, to devote myself to that, but I have changed my plan. It seems to me that *that* subject is one that hundreds of living men could do, if they would only try, *much* better than I could, whereas there is no living man who could (or at any rate who would take the trouble to) arrange and finish and publish the second part of the "Logic." Also, I *have* the Logic book in my head; it will only need three or four months to write out, and I have *not* got the other book in my head, and it might take years to think it out. So I have decided to get Part ii. finished *first*, and I am working at it day and night. I have taken to early rising, and sometimes sit down to my work before seven, and have one and a half hours at it before breakfast. The book will be a great novelty, and will help, I fully believe, to make the study of Logic far *easier* than it now is. And it will, I also believe, be a help to religious thought by giving *clearness* of conception and of expression, which may enable many people to face, and conquer, many religious difficulties for themselves. So I do really regard it as work for *God*.

Another letter, written a few months later to Miss Dora Abdy [*Letters* II:1112], deals with the subject of "Reverence," which Mr. Dodgson considered a virtue not held in sufficient esteem nowadays:—

---

1. A translation by Henry Wadsworth Longfellow of a line in a German poem by Johann Gaudenz von Salis-Seewis.
2. This book was to be a series of essays on difficult questions of religious belief. Dodgson wrote at least one essay (on eternal punishment). He wrote to a nephew to whom he sent a draft of this essay that he would discuss only those religious difficulties that affected conduct, and that did not conflict with certain principles he called axioms: for example, that human beings possess free will, that they are responsible for choosing wrong, that they are responsible to a person, and that "This person is perfectly good."

My dear Dora,—In correcting the proofs of "Through the Looking-Glass"[3] (which is to have "An Easter Greeting" inserted at the end), I am reminded that in that letter (I enclose a copy), I had tried to express my thoughts on the very subject we talked about last night—the relation of *laughter* to religious thought. One of the hardest things in the world is to convey a meaning accurately from one mind to another, but the *sort* of meaning I want to convey to other minds is that while the laughter of *joy* is in full harmony with our deeper life, the laughter of amusement should be kept apart from it. The danger is too great of thus learning to look at solemn things, in a spirit of *mockery*, and to seek in them opportunities for exercising *wit*. That is the spirit which has spoiled, for me, the beauty of some of the Bible. Surely there is a deep meaning in our prayer, "Give us an heart to love and *dread* Thee." We do not mean *terror*: but a dread that will harmonise with love; "respect" we should call it as towards a human being, "reverence" as towards God and all religious things.

Yours affectionately,
C. L. Dodgson

DONALD THOMAS

[Death][†]

When his own death came, he would be packed and ready for the journey but there was also the matter of what would be left behind. There were, for example, the nude photographs from the 1870s. He had kept them all, though their subjects were now grown women. He wrote to Beatrice Hatch during his illness of 1895 asking her what she would like done with five studies of her [*Letters* II:1052]. It was plain that on his death there must be a bonfire of many papers, sketches, photographs and other items. When the time came, part of his diary was found to be torn out, covering the troubled Oxford summer weeks of 1879 and the gossip circulated by Mrs Owens.[1] Perhaps it was done by his executors but more likely Dodgson himself had removed it.

---

3. The proofs to which Dodgson refers are presumably those of the 1897 edition, for which Dodgson wrote a preface (see p. 101 of this Norton Critical Edition).
† From *Lewis Carroll: A Portrait with Background* (London: John Murray, 1996), 352–53. Copyright © Donald Thomas, 1996. Reprinted by permission of A. M. Heath & Co. Ltd.
1. Mrs. Sydney Owens was the wife of a Christ Church colleague of Dodgson's and the mother of a seventeen-year-old woman whom Dodgson kissed at parting, thinking that she was younger. His somewhat playful letter of apology did not appease Mrs. Owens, and she began circulating gossip about his custom of entertaining and photographing young girls. [*Editor's note*]

In the autumn of 1897, he was preoccupied by working out rules for a new system of long division. After his meeting with Gertrude Thomson on 20 November he returned to Oxford. Ten days before Christmas, the weather was so warm that he was working in his sitting room without a fire and with the window open. The temperature was still fifty-four degrees. On 19 December he sat up until 4 a.m., trying to solve a problem that had been sent him from New York and which involved finding three equal rational-sided right-angle triangles. He found two and then went to bed.

Two days before Christmas, he caught the afternoon train for Guildford and spent much of the time over Christmas working on the second part of *Symbolic Logic* and correcting the proofs of *The Three Sunsets*. On 5 January 1898, a telegram arrived announcing the death of the Reverend Charles Collingwood of Southwick near Sunderland, the husband of Dodgson's sister Mary. Dodgson wrote back, enclosing £50 to cover immediate expenses. To his nephew Stuart Dodgson Collingwood he wrote a business letter [*Letters* II:1155–56] warning him to get a signed agreement from the undertakers on the cost of the funeral and reminding the young man that he and his mother 'have no money to throw away.'

In his letter of 5 January to his sister Mary, he added that he would not be able to travel north for the funeral, though she had asked him to come at once. He had a bronchial cold and Dr Gabb had forbidden him to undertake the journey. In a few days, the bronchial symptoms were worse and Dr Gabb ordered him to bed. A nurse was brought in. Dodgson lay propped on the pillows and his breathing 'rapidly became hard and laborious.' He asked one of his sisters to read him a hymn whose verses ended with the refrain, 'Thy Will be done.' He described the illness as 'a great trial of his patience.' On 13 January, he said to the sister who was with him. 'Take away those pillows, I shall need them no more.' On the following day, at about half past two in the afternoon, as Stuart Dodgson Collingwood described it, 'One of his sisters was in the room at the time, and she only noticed that the hard breathing suddenly ceased.' She called the nurse who came at once and 'hoped that this was a sign that he had taken a turn for the better.' When she saw him, it was evident that he was dead. They summoned Dr Gabb. The doctor looked at the smooth and unlined face, then went down to the sitting-room where Dodgson's sisters were waiting and said, 'How wonderfully young your brother looks!'[2]

He was buried in the graveyard on the hill at Guildford, after a service at St Mary's, taken by the rector and Francis Paget, now Dean of Christ Church. The ceremony was simple and inexpensive,

2. Collingwood, 347–48.

as he had stipulated, remembering the difficulties caused at pro-
bate by extravagance in his father's funeral. There were relatively
few mourners. * * *

Gertrude Thomson accompanied her 'Beloved Friend' and at his
death showed publicly a degree of attachment which had been con-
cealed during twenty years of his life.

> A grey January day, calm, and without a sound, full of the
> peace of God which passeth all understanding. A steep, stony,
> country road, with hedges close on either side, fast quickening
> with the breath of the premature spring. Between the withered
> leaves of the dead summer a pure white daisy here and there
> shone out like a little star. A few mourners slowly climbed the
> hill in silence, while borne before them on a simple hand-bier
> was the coffin, half hid in flowers. Under an old yew, round
> whose gnarled trunk the green ivy twined, in the pure white
> chalk earth his body was laid to rest, while the slow bell tolled
> the passing—
>
> > Of the sweetest soul
> > That ever look'd with human eyes.[3]

---

3. Tennyson, *In Memoriam* VII, ll. 11–12. [*Editor's note*]

CRITICISM

CHARLES DICKENS

From Frauds Upon the Fairies[†]

We must assume that we are not singular in entertaining a very great tenderness for the fairy literature of our childhood. What enchanted us then, and is captivating a million of young fancies now, has, at the same blessed time of life, enchanted vast hosts of men and women who have done their long day's work and laid their grey heads down to rest. It would be hard to estimate the amount of gentleness and mercy that has made its way among us through these slight channels. Forbearance, courtesy, consideration for poor and aged, kind treatment of animals, love of nature, abhorrence of tyranny and brute force—many such good things have been first nourished in the child's heart by this powerful aid. It has greatly helped to keep us, in some sense, ever young, by preserving through our worldly ways one slender track not overgrown with weeds, where we may walk with children, sharing their delights.

In an utilitarian age, of all other times, it is a matter of grave importance that Fairy tales should be respected. Our English red tape is too magnificently red ever to be employed in the tying up of such trifles, but every one who has considered the subject knows full well that a nation without fancy, without some romance, never did, never can, never will, hold a great place under the sun. The theatre, having done its worst to destroy these admirable fictions—having in a most exemplary manner destroyed itself, its artists, and its audiences, in that perversion of its duty—it becomes doubly important that the little books themselves, nurseries of fancy as they are, should be preserved.[1] To preserve them in their usefulness, they must be as much preserved in their simplicity, and purity, and innocent extravagance, as if they were actual fact. Whosoever alters them to suit his own opinions, whatever they are, is guilty, to our thinking, of an act of presumption, and appropriates to himself what does not belong to him.

We have lately observed, with pain, intrusion of a Whole Hog of unwieldy dimensions into the fairy flower garden. The rooting of the animal among the roses would in itself have awakened in us nothing but indignation; our pain arises from his being violently

† From *Household Words* 8, 184 (October 1, 1853): 97, 101. Reprinted in *The Dent Uniform Edition of Dickens' Journalism*, Vol. 3: *"Gone Astray" and Other Papers from Household Words, 1851–59*, ed. Michael Slater, (Columbus, OH: Ohio State UP, 1998), 166–74. Annotations are by the editor of this Norton Critical Edition.
1. Theatrical burlesques and pantomimes, popular all through the Victorian period, regularly used fairy-tale plots and characters as platforms for punning dialogue, comical comment on people and events in the news, and farcical stage business.

driven in by a man of genius, our own beloved friend, MR. GEORGE
CRUIKSHANK.[2] That incomparable artist is, of all men, the last who
should lay his exquisite hand on fairy text. In his own art he understands it so perfectly, and illustrates it so beautifully, so humorously, so wisely, that he should never lay down his etching needle to
"edit" the Ogre, to whom with that little instrument he can render
such extraordinary justice. But, to "editing" Ogres, and Hop o'-my-
thumbs, and their families, our dear moralist has in a rash moment
taken, as a means of propagating the doctrines of Total Abstinence,
Prohibition of the sale of spirituous liquors, Free Trade, and Popular
Education. For the introduction of these topics he has altered the
text of a fairy story; and against his right to do any such thing we
protest with all our might and main. * * *

Now, it makes not the least difference to our objection whether
we agree or disagree with our worthy friend, Mr. Cruikshank, in
the opinions he interpolates upon an old fairy story. Whether good
or bad in themselves, they are, in that relation, like the famous definition of a weed; a thing growing up in a wrong place. He has no
greater moral justification in altering the harmless little books than
we should have in altering his best etchings. If such a precedent
were followed we must soon become disgusted with the old stories
into which modern personages so obtruded themselves, and the
stories themselves must soon be lost. With seven Blue Beards in the
field, each coming at a gallop from his own platform mounted on a
foaming hobby a generation or two hence would not know which
was which, and the great original Blue Beard would be confounded
with the counterfeits. Imagine a Total abstinence edition of Robinson Crusoe, with the rum left out. Imagine a Peace edition, with
the gunpowder left out, and the rum left in. Imagine a Vegetarian
edition, with the goat's flesh left out. * * * Robinson Crusoe would
be "edited" out of his island in a hundred years, and the island
would be swallowed up in the editorial ocean.

* * *

Frauds on the Fairies once permitted, we see little reason why they
may not come to this, and great reason why they may. The Vicar of
Wakefield[3] was wisest when he was tired of being always wise. The
world is too much with us, early and late. Leave this precious old
escape from it, alone.

2. George Cruikshank (1792–1878) was one of the most accomplished and best-known of
   early- and mid-nineteenth-century caricaturists and book illustrators. He illustrated a
   translation of fairy tales by the brothers Grimm (1823) and some of Dickens's novels.
   Dickens greatly admired Cruikshank's work, but he protested when Cruikshank, a
   reformed alcoholic, turned fairy tales into tracts against the use of alcohol.
3. The principal character in Oliver Goldsmith's novel of the same name (1766).

CHRISTINA ROSSETTI

From Goblin Market [1862]†

A young woman, Laura, is tempted by a pack of goblins to buy and taste their exotic fruit: "Currants and gooseberries, / Bright-fire barberries, / Figs to fill your mouth, / Citrons from the South, / Sweet to tongue and sound to eye; / Come buy, come buy." Laura succumbs, but on the next day she can no longer see or hear the goblins, and she withers with unsatisfied desire. Her sister Lizzie tries to save her by going to the goblins and allowing herself to be covered with the juices of their fruit: "Eat me, drink me," she says to her sister when she returns, "love me." But the juices are bitter when Laura tries to taste them on Lizzie's body. Rossetti resolves her brilliant fantasy by making it a parable of sisterly and perhaps Christlike sacrifice and redemption. [*Editor's note*]

* * *

Her lips began to scorch,
That juice was wormwood to her tongue,
She loath'd the feast:
Writhing as one possessed she leap'd and sung,
Rent all her robe, and wrung
Her hands in lamentable haste,
And beat her breast.
Her locks streamed like the torch
Borne by a racer at full speed,
Or like the mane of horses in their flight,
Or like an eagle when she stems the light
Straight toward the sun,
Or like a caged thing freed,
Or like a flying flag when armies run.

Swift fire spread through her veins, knocked at her heart,
Met the fire smouldering there
And overbore its lesser flame;
She gorged on bitterness without a name:
Ah! fool, to choose such part
Of soul-consuming care!
Sense failed in the mortal strife:
Like the watch-tower of a town
Which an earthquake shatters down,
Like a lightning-stricken mast,

---

† From *The Complete Poems of Christina Rossetti*, Vol. 1, ed. R. W. Crump (Baton Rouge: Louisiana UP, 1979), 24–26.

Like a wind-uprooted tree
Spun about,
Like a foam-topped waterspout
Cast down headlong in the sea,
She fell at last;
Pleasure past and anguish past,
Is it death or is it life?

          Life out of death.
That night long Lizzie watched by her,
Counted her pulse's flagging stir,
Felt for her breath,
Held water to her lips, and cooled her face
With tears and fanning leaves:
But when the first birds chirped about their eaves,
And early reapers plodded to the place
Of golden sheaves,
And dew-wet grass
Bowed in the morning winds so brisk to pass,
And new buds with new day
Opened of cup-like lilies on the stream,
Laura awoke as from a dream,
Laughed in the innocent old way,
Hugg'd Lizzie but not twice or thrice;
Her gleaming locks showed not one thread of gray,
Her breath was sweet as May,
And light danced in her eyes.
          Days, weeks, months, years
Afterwards, when both were wives
With children of their own;
Their mother-hearts beset with fears,
Their lives bound up in tender lives;
Laura would call the little ones
And tell them of her early prime,
Those pleasant days long gone
Of not-returning time:
Would talk about the haunted glen,
The wicked, quaint fruit-merchant men,
Their fruits like honey to the throat,
But poison in the blood;
(Men sell not such in any town):
Would tell them how her sister stood
In deadly peril to do her good,
And win the fiery antidote:
Then joining hands to little hands

Would bid them cling together,
"For there is no friend like a sister,
In calm or stormy weather;
To cheer one on the tedious way,
To fetch one if one goes astray,
To lift one if one totters down,
To strengthen whilst one stands."

GILLIAN AVERY

Fairy-Tales for Pleasure[†]

1865—*Alice's Adventures in Wonderland* comes within the decade of [Frederic Farrar's] *Eric, or Little by Little* (1858), [Charles Kingsley's] *The Water Babies* (1863), and *Jessica's First Prayer* (1867) [by "Hesba Stretton," pseudonym of Sarah Smith], but the pious, the moralistic, and the didactic are as much absent from its pages as if they had never existed at all in children's literature. For some children the charm of the Alice books may rest on the sheer fantasy— Alice's extraordinary changes of size, the Cheshire Cat's grin, the pig baby; for others on the relentless logic with which Carroll works out his ideas, so that in Looking-Glass Country, where everything works backwards, Alice has to walk in the opposite direction to the place she wants to reach in order to arrive there, is given a dry biscuit by the Red Queen to quench her thirst after running, and learns to pass a cake round first and cut it up afterwards. Another amusing ingredient is the clever use of words—the puns of the Gnat, the Mock Turtle's verbal confusions, like the four branches of Arithmetic— Ambition, Distraction, Uglification, and Derision; of the use, in comparisons by the White Knight, of adjectives in the wrong sense—wind "as strong as soup", or, of himself struck upside down in his helmet, "as fast as lightning". But possibly the most refreshing thing of all about these books is the way the nonsense is set in sparkling contrast, against a background of dull, everyday, schoolroom life.

However far Alice wanders through Wonderland or Looking-Glass Country, she is constantly reminded of things she has learned, but always in a gloriously muddled way, which makes the real subjects seem equally nonsensical. For instance there are the parodies. Schoolroom poetry still consisted of pious, moralizing verses, like 'How doth the little busy bee', and ''Tis the voice of the sluggard', by Isaac Watts, and Jane Taylor's 'Twinkle, twinkle, little star'. These are triumphantly

---

† From *Nineteenth Century Children: Heroes and Heroines in English Children's Stories, 1780–1900* (London: Hodder, 1965), 129–36. Reprinted by permission. Annotations are by the editor.

metamorphosed into 'How doth the little crocodile improve his shining tail', ''Tis the voice of the lobster', 'Twinkle, twinkle, little bat'. 'Star of the Evening', a song the Liddell children had learned, becomes the Mock Turtle's 'Soup of the Evening'. The difficult steps of the quadrille become the riotous romp of the lobster quadrille; historical facts about the Anglo-Saxons are repeated by the Mouse as the dryest things he knows, to restore Alice and the other creatures after their involuntary swim in the Pool of Tears; while morals to stories, always a bane of the nursery, are parodied by the Duchess's ridiculous habit of appending an utterly irrelevant 'moral' to every statement she makes—"Flamingoes and mustard both bite. And the moral of that is—'Birds of a feather flock together.'" The Red Queen is the concentrated essence of all governesses, giving rapid instructions on etiquette—"Look up, speak nicely, and don't twiddle your fingers all the time . . . Curtsey while you're thinking what to say. It saves time."

Through the Looking-Glass ends with the ridiculous examination of Alice by the two queens, rushing through schoolroom subjects, and turning them all upside down.

> "'Can you do Subtraction? Take nine from eight.'"
>
> "'Nine from eight I can't, you know,' Alice replied very readily; 'but—'
>
> "'She can't do Subtraction,' said the White Queen. "Can you do Division? Divide a loaf by a knife—what's the answer to *that*?"
>
> "'I suppose—' Alice was beginning, but the Red Queen answered for her. "Bread and butter, of course." . . .
>
> "'Do you know Languages? What's the French for fiddle-de-de?"
>
> "'Fiddle-de-de's not English,' Alice replied gravely.
>
> "'Whoever said it was?" said the Red Queen.
>
> "Alice thought she saw a way out of the difficulty, this time. "If you'll tell me what language fiddle-de-dee is, I'll tell you the French for it!" she exclaimed triumphantly.
>
> "But the Red Queen drew herself up rather stiffly, and said, 'Queens never make bargains.'"

By treating the world of lessons and governesses with such playfulness, Lewis Carroll reduces it from the terrifying place it must sometimes have seemed to a manageable absurdity. In this way the Alice books strike as strong a blow against didacticism and cramming as did Felix Summerly's manifesto against Peter Parleyism.[1] One of

---

1. The pseudonym "Peter Parley" was invented by Samuel Goodrich, an American writer of children's books, and adopted by several British writers who exploited the popularity of the Peter Parley books in England. In the prospectus to *The Home Library* (1841–49), Sir Henry Cole, who used the pseudonym Felix Summerly, characterized "Peter Parleyism" as being hostile to fancy and tenderness in its emphasis on conveying information and moral instruction.

the best features of the books is that although in the course of her adventures Alice may be bullied and cross questioned by the creatures she meets ("I never was so ordered about before, in all my life, never!"), she always takes final control, overcoming the hostility of the court of the Queen of Hearts with her cry—"Who cares for you? . . . You're nothing but a pack of cards!"; and shaking the stiff, dictatorial, governessy Red Queen in *Through the Looking-Glass*, back to a soft, fat, round, black kitten. It is wishfulfilment of the most appealing kind.

* * *

NINA AUERBACH

Alice and Wonderland: A Curious Child†

"What—is—this?" he said at last.
"This is a child!" Haigha replied eagerly, coming in front of Alice to introduce her . . . "We only found it today. It's as large as life, and twice as natural!"
"I always thought they were fabulous monsters!" said the Unicorn. "Is it alive?"

For many of us Lewis Carroll's two *Alice* books may have provided the first glimpse into Victorian England. With their curious blend of literal-mindedness and dream, formal etiquette and the logic of insanity, they tell the adult reader a great deal about the Victorian mind. Alice herself, prim and earnest in pinafore and pumps, confronting a world out of control by looking for the rules and murmuring her lessons, stands as one image of the Victorian middle-class child. She sits in Tenniel's first illustration to *Through the Looking-Glass and What Alice Found There* in a snug, semi-foetal position, encircled by a protective armchair and encircling a plump kitten and a ball of yarn. She seems to be a beautiful child, but the position of her head makes her look as though she had no face. She muses dreamily on the snowstorm raging outside, part of a series of circles within circles, enclosures within enclosures, suggesting the self-containment of innocence and eternity.

Behind the purity of this design lie two Victorian domestic myths: Wordsworth's "seer blessed," the child fresh from the Imperial Palace and still washed by his continuing contact with "that immortal sea," and the pure woman Alice will become, preserving an oasis for God and order in a dim and tangled world. Even Victorians

† From *Victorian Studies* 17 (1973): 31–47. Reprinted by permission of the author and *Victorian Studies*. Reprinted by permission of Indiana University Press.

who did not share Lewis Carroll's phobia about the ugliness and uncleanliness of little boys saw little girls as the purest members of a species of questionable origin, combining as they did the inherent spirituality of child and woman. Carroll's Alice seems sister to such famous figures as Dickens' Little Nell and George Eliot's Eppie,[1] who embody the poise of original innocence in a fallen, sooty world.

Long after he transported Alice Liddell to Wonderland, Carroll himself deified his dream-child's innocence in these terms:

> What wert thou, dream-Alice, in thy foster-father's eyes? How shall he picture thee? Loving, first, loving and gentle: loving as a dog (forgive the prosaic simile, but I know of no earthly love so pure and perfect), and gentle as a fawn: . . . and lastly, curious—wildly curious, and with the eager enjoyment of Life that comes only in the happy hours of childhood when all is new and fair, and when Sin and Sorrow are but names—empty words, signifying nothing![2]

From this Alice, it is only a step to Walter de la Mare's mystic icon, defined in the following almost Shelleyan image: "She wends serenely on like a quiet moon in the chequered sky. Apart, too, from an occasional Carrollian comment, the sole medium of the stories is *her* pellucid consciousness."[3]

But when Dodgson wrote in 1887 of his gentle dream-child, the real Alice had receded into the distance of memory, where she had drowned in a pool of tears along with Lewis Carroll, her interpreter and creator. The paean quoted above stands at the end of a long series of progressive falsifications of Carroll's first conception, beginning with Alice's pale, attenuated presence in *Through the Looking-Glass*. For Lewis Carroll remembered what Charles Dodgson and many later commentators did not, that while *Looking-Glass* may have been the dream of the Red King, *Wonderland* is Alice's dream. Despite critical attempts to psychoanalyze Charles Dodgson through the writings of Lewis Carroll, the author of *Alice's Adventures in Wonderland* was too precise a logician and too controlled an artist to confuse his own dream with that of his character. The question "who dreamed it?" underlies all Carroll's dream tales, part of a pervasive Victorian quest for the origins of the self that culminates in the controlled regression of Freudian analysis. There is no equivocation in Carroll's first *Alice* book: the dainty child carries the threatening kingdom of Wonderland within her. A closer look

1. Little Nell is a character in *The Old Curiosity Shop* (1840–41); Eppie is in *Silas Marner* (1861) [*Editor's note*].
2. "Alice on the Stage," *The Theatre*, 9 (April 1, 1887): 181.
3. Walter de la Mare, *Lewis Carroll* (London: 1932), 55.

at the character of Alice may reveal new complexities in the senti-mentalized and attenuated Wordsworthianism many critics had assumed she represents, and may deepen through examination of a single example our vision of that "fabulous monster," the Victorian child.

Lewis Carroll once wrote to a child that while he forgot the story of *Alice*, "I think it was about 'malice.'"[4] Some Freudian critics would have us believe it was about phallus.[5] Alice herself seems aware of the implications of her shifting name when at the beginning of her adventures she asks herself the question that will weave through her story:

> "I wonder if I've been changed in the night? Let me think: *was* I the same when I got up this morning? I almost think I can remember feeling a little different. But if I'm not the same, the next question is, 'Who in the world am I?' Ah, *that's* the great puzzle!"

Other little girls traveling through fantastic countries, such as George Macdonald's Princess Irene and L. Frank Baum's Dorothy Gale, ask repeatedly "*where* am I?" rather than "*who* am I?" Only Alice turns her eyes inward from the beginning, sensing that the mystery of her surroundings is the mystery of her identity.

Even the above-ground Alice speaks in two voices, like many Victorians other than Dodgson-Carroll:

> She generally gave herself very good advice, (though she very seldom followed it), and sometimes she scolded herself so severely as to bring tears into her eyes; and once she remem-bered trying to box her own ears for having cheated herself in a game of croquet she was playing against herself, for this curi-ous child was very fond of pretending to be two people.

The pun on "curious" defines Alice's fluctuating personality. Her eagerness to know and to be right, her compulsive reciting of her lessons ("I'm sure I can't be Mabel, for I know all sorts of things") turn inside out into the bizarre anarchy of her dream country, as the lessons themselves turn inside out into strange and savage tales of animals eating each other. In both senses of the word, Alice becomes "curiouser and curiouser" as she moves more deeply into Wonderland; she is both the croquet game without rules and its violent arbiter, the Queen of Hearts. The sea that almost drowns

---

4. Letter to Dolly [Agnes] Argles, 28 November 1867. [*Letters* I:107–108]
5. See Martin Grotjahn, "About the Symbolization of *Alice's Adventures in Wonderland*," *American Imago, 4* (1947): 34, for a discussion of Freud's "girl = phallus equation" in relation to Alice.

her is composed of her own tears, and the dream that nearly oblit-
erates her is composed of fragments of her own personality.[6]

As Alice dissolves into her component parts to become Wonderland, so, if we examine the actual genesis of Carroll's dream child,
the bold outlines of Tenniel's famous drawing dissolve into four
separate figures. First, there was the real Alice Liddell, a baby belle
dame, it seems, who bewitched Ruskin as well as Dodgson.[7] A
small photograph of her concludes Carroll's manuscript of *Alice's
Adventures under Ground*, the first draft of *Wonderland*. She is
strikingly sensuous and otherworldly; her dark hair, bangs, and
large inward-turned eyes give her face a haunting and a haunted
quality which is missing from Tenniel's famous illustrations. Carroll's own illustrations for *Alice's Adventures under Ground* reproduce her eerieness perfectly. This Alice has a pre-Raphaelite langour
and ambiguity about her which is reflected in the shifting colors of
her hair.[8] In some illustrations, she is indisputably brunette like
Alice Liddell; in others, she is decidedly blonde like Tenniel's model
Mary Hilton Badcock; and in still others, light from an unknown
source hits her hair so that she seems to be both at once.

* * *

The demure propriety of Tenniel's Alice may have led readers to see
her role in *Alice's Adventures in Wonderland* as more passive than it
is. Although her size changes seem arbitrary and terrifying, she in
fact directs them; only in the final courtroom scene does she change
size without first wishing to, and there, her sudden growth gives
her the power to break out of a dream that has become too dangerous. Most of Wonderland's savage songs come from Alice: the Caterpillar, Gryphon and Mock Turtle know that her cruel parodies of
contemporary moralistic doggerel are "wrong from beginning to
end."[9] She is almost always threatening to the animals of Wonder-

6. Edmund Wilson's penetrating essay, "C. L. Dodgson: The Poet Logician," is the only
   criticism of *Alice* to touch on the relationship between dream and dreamer in relation
   to Alice's covert brutality: "But the creatures that she meets, the whole dream, *are*
   Alice's personality and her waking life. . . . [S]he . . . has a child's primitive cruelty. . . .
   But though Alice is sometimes brutal, she is always well-bred." Wilson cites as examples of brutality her innuendos about Dinah to the mouse and birds. *The Shores of
   Light*, 2nd ed. (1952; rpt. New York: 1967), 543–44.
7. See Florence Becker Lennon, *The Life of Lewis Carroll*, rev. ed. (New York: 1962), 151,
   for Ruskin's beatific description of a secret nocturnal tea party presided over by Alice
   Liddell.
8. Lewis Carroll knew the Rossetti family and photographed them several times. Dante
   Gabriel Rossetti later claimed that Carroll's Dormouse was inspired by his own pet
   wombat. Perhaps his elongated, subtly threatening heroines had a deeper, if more indirect, impact on Carroll.
9. It is significant that the Alice of *Looking-Glass*, a truly passive figure, is sung *at* more
   than she sings; the reverse is true in *Wonderland*. Tweedledum and Tweedledee sing
   the most savage song in *Looking-Glass*, "The Walrus and the Carpenter," which seems
   to bore Alice.

land. As the mouse and birds almost drown in her pool of tears, she eyes them with a strange hunger which suggests that of the *Looking-Glass* Walrus who weeps at the Oysters while devouring them behind his handkerchief. Her persistent allusions to her predatory cat Dinah and to a "nice little dog, near our house," who "kills all the rats" finally drive the animals away, leaving Alice to wonder forlornly—and disingenuously—why nobody in Wonderland likes Dinah.

Dinah is a strange figure. She is the only above-ground character whom Alice mentions repeatedly, almost always in terms of her eating some smaller animal. She seems finally to function as a personification of Alice's own subtly cannibalistic hunger, as Fury in the Mouse's tale is personified as a dog. At one point, Alice fantasizes her own identity actually blending into Dinah's:

> "How queer it seems," Alice said to herself, "to be going messages for a rabbit! I suppose Dinah'll be sending me on messages next!" And she began fancying the sort of thing that would happen: '"Miss Alice! Come here directly, and get ready for your walk!" "Coming in a minute, nurse! But I've got to watch this mousehole till Dinah comes back, and see that the mouse doesn't get out."

While Dinah is always in a predatory attitude, most of the Wonderland animals are lugubrious victims; together, they encompass the two sides of animal nature that are in Alice as well. But as she falls down the rabbit hole, Alice senses the complicity between eater and eaten, looking-glass versions of each other:

> "Dinah, my dear! I wish you were down here with me! There are no mice in the air, I'm afraid, but you might catch a bat, and that's very like a mouse, you know. But do cats eat bats, I wonder?" And here Alice began to get rather sleepy, and went on saying to herself, in a dreamy sort of way, "Do cats eat bats? Do cats eat bats?" and sometimes, "Do bats eat cats?" for, you see, as she couldn't answer either question, it didn't matter which way she put it.

We are already half-way to the final banquet of *Looking-Glass*, in which the food comes alive and begins to eat the guests.

Even when Dinah is not mentioned, Alice's attitude toward the animals she encounters is often one of casual cruelty. It is a measure of Dodgson's ability to flatten out Carroll's material that the prefatory poem could describe Alice "in friendly chat with bird or beast," or that he would later see Alice as "loving as a dog . . . gentle as a fawn." She pities Bill the Lizard and kicks him up the chimney, a state of mind that again looks forward to that of the

Pecksniffian[1] Walrus in *Looking-Glass*. When she meets the Mock Turtle, the weeping embodiment of a good Victorian dinner, she restrains herself twice when he mentions lobsters, but then distorts Isaac Watts's *Sluggard* into a song about a *baked* lobster surrounded by hungry sharks. In its second stanza, a Panther shares a pie with an Owl who then becomes dessert, as Dodgson's good table manners pass into typical Carrollian cannibalism. The more sinister and Darwinian aspects of animal nature are introduced into Wonderland by the gentle Alice, in part through projections of her hunger onto Dinah and the "nice little dog" (she meets a "dear little puppy" after she has grown small and is afraid he will eat her up) and in part through the semi-cannibalistic appetite her songs express. With the exception of the powerful Cheshire Cat, whom I shall discuss below, most of the Wonderland animals stand in some danger of being exploited or eaten. The Dormouse is their prototype: he is fussy and cantankerous, with the nastiness of a self-aware victim, and he is stuffed into a teapot as the Mock Turtle, sobbing out his own elegy, will be stuffed into a tureen.

Alice's courteously menacing relationship to these animals is more clearly brought out in *Alice's Adventures under Ground*, in which she encounters only animals until she meets the playing cards, who are lightly sketched-in versions of their later counterparts. When expanding the manuscript for publication, Carroll added the Frog Footman, Cook, Duchess, Pig-Baby, Cheshire Cat, Mad Hatter, March Hare, and Dormouse, as well as making the Queen of Hearts a more fully developed character than she was in the manuscript.[2] In other words, all the human or quasi-human characters were added in revision, and all develop aspects of Alice that exist only under the surface of her dialogue. The Duchess' household also turns inside out the domesticated Wordsworthian ideal: with baby and pepper flung about indiscriminately, pastoral tranquillity is inverted into a whirlwind of savage sexuality. The furious Cook embodies the equation between eating and killing that underlies Alice's apparently innocent remarks about Dinah. The violent Duchess' unctuous search for "the moral" of things echoes Alice's own violence and search for "the rules."[3] At the Mad Tea Party, the Hatter extends Alice's "great interest in questions of eating and drinking" into an insane *modus vivendi*; like Alice, the Hatter and the Duchess sing savage songs about eating that embody

1. Pecksniff is a piously hypocritical character in Dickens's *Martin Chuzzlewit* (1843–44) [*Editor's note*].
2. In *Alice's Adventures under Ground*, Queen and Duchess are a single figure, the Queen of Hearts and Marchioness of Mock Turtles.
3. Donald Rackin makes the same point in "Alice's Journey to the End of Night," *PMLA* 81 (1966): 323.

the underside of Victorian literary treacle. The Queen's croquet game magnifies Alice's own desire to cheat at croquet and to punish herself violently for doing so. Its use of live animals may be a subtler extension of Alice's own desire to twist the animal kingdom to the absurd rules of civilization, which seem to revolve largely around eating and being eaten. Alice is able to appreciate the Queen's savagery so quickly because her size changes have made her increasingly aware of who she, herself, is from the point of view of a Caterpillar, a Mouse, a Pigeon, and, especially, a Cheshire Cat.

The Cheshire Cat, also a late addition to the book, is the only figure other than Alice who encompasses all the others. William Empson discusses at length the spiritual kinship between Alice and the Cat, the only creature in Wonderland whom she calls her "friend."[4] Florence Becker Lennon refers to the Cheshire Cat as "Dinah's dream-self," and we have noticed the subtle shift of identities between Alice and Dinah throughout the story. The Cat shares Alice's equivocal placidity: "The Cat only grinned when it saw Alice. It looked good-natured, she thought: still it had *very* long claws and a great many teeth, so she felt it ought to be treated with respect." The Cat is the only creature to make explicit the identification between Alice and the madness of Wonderland: "'. . . we're all mad here. I'm mad. You're mad.' 'How do you know I'm mad?' said Alice. 'You must be,' said the Cat, 'or you wouldn't have come here.' Alice didn't think that proved it at all." Although Alice cannot accept it and closes into silence, the Cat's remark may be the answer she has been groping toward in her incessant question, "who am I?"[5] As an alter ego, the Cat is wiser than Alice—and safer—because he is the only character in the book who is aware of his own madness. In his serene acceptance of the fury within and without, his total control over his appearance and disappearance, he almost suggests a post-analytic version of the puzzled Alice.

✳   ✳   ✳

Presented from the point of view of her older sister's sentimental pietism, the world to which Alice awakens seems far more dreamlike and hazy than the sharp contours of Wonderland. Alice's lesson about her own identity has never been stated explicitly, for the stammerer Dodgson was able to talk freely only in his private language of puns and nonsense, but a Wonderland pigeon points us toward it:

---

4. In *Looking-Glass*, the pathetic White Knight replaces the Cheshire Cat as Alice's only friend, another indication of the increasing softness of the later Alice. William Empson, *Some Versions of Pastoral*, 2nd ed. (London: 1950).
5. Jan B. Gordon, "The *Alice* Books and the Metaphors of Victorian Childhood," relates the *Alice* books to Michel Foucault's argument that in the nineteenth century, madness came to be regarded as allied to childhood rather than to animality, as it had been in the eighteenth century. *Aspects of Alice*, edited by Robert Phillips (New York: 1971), 101.

"You're a serpent; and there's no use denying it. I suppose you'll be telling me next that you never tasted an egg!"

"I have tasted eggs, certainly," said Alice, who was a very truthful child; "but little girls eat eggs quite as much as serpents do, you know."

"I don't believe it," said the Pigeon; "but if they do, why, then they're a kind of serpent: that's all I can say."

This was such a new idea to Alice, that she was quite silent for a minute or two[6]

Like so many of her silences throughout the book, Alice's silence here is charged with significance, reminding us again that an important technique in learning to read Carroll is our ability to interpret his private system of symbols and signals and to appreciate the many meanings of silence. In this scene, the golden child herself becomes the serpent in childhood's Eden. The eggs she eats suggest the woman she will become, the unconscious cannibalism involved in the very fact of eating and desire to eat, and finally, the charmed circle of childhood itself. Only in *Alice's Adventures in Wonderland* was Carroll able to fall all the way through the rabbit hole to the point where top and bottom become one, bats and cats melt into each other, and the vessel of innocence and purity is also the source of inescapable corruption.

* * *

We return once more to the anomaly of Carroll's Alice, who explodes out of Wonderland hungry and unregenerate. By a subtle dramatization of Alice's attitude toward animals and toward the animal in herself, by his final resting on the symbol of her mouth, Carroll probed in all its complexity the underground world within the little girl's pinafore. The ambiguity of the concluding trial finally, and wisely, waives questions of original guilt or innocence. The ultimate effect of Alice's adventures implicates her, female child though she is, in the troubled human condition; most Victorians refused to grant women and children this respect. The sympathetic delicacy and precision with which Carroll traced the chaos of a little girl's psyche seems equalled and surpassed only later in such explorations as D. H. Lawrence's of the young Ursula Brangwen in *The Rainbow*, the chaos of whose growth encompasses her hunger for violence, sexuality, liberty, and beatitude. In the imaginative literature of its century, *Alice's Adventures in Wonderland* stands alone.

6. Empson (270) refers to this passage as the Pigeon of the Annunciation denouncing the serpent of the knowledge of good and evil.

DONALD RACKIN

Blessed Rage: The *Alices* and the Modern Quest for Order[†]

> Three centuries lay between the promulgation of the Copernican theory and the publication of the *Origin of Species*, but in the sixty-odd years which have elapsed since that latter event the blows have fallen with a rapidity which left no interval for recovery. The structures which are variously known as mythology, religion, and philosophy, and which are alike in that each has as its function the interpretation of experience in terms which have human values, have collapsed under the force of successive attacks and shown themselves utterly incapable of assimilating the new stores of experience which have been dumped on the world. With increasing completeness science maps out the pattern of nature, but the latter has no relation to the pattern of human needs and feelings. . . . Standards are imaginary things, and yet it is extremely doubtful if man can live well, either spiritually or physically, without the belief that they are somehow real. Without them society lapses into anarchy and the individual becomes aware of an intolerable disharmony between himself and the universe.
>
> —Joseph Wood Krutch, *The Modern Temper*[1]

If Alice's survival and development depend on her imposition of a firm, albeit artificial, vision of order and purpose on a world with no inherent principles of such order and purpose, if the stability of her self-image and sense of freedom depend on becoming a successful player of mere games, a competent actress in a constructed play universe with rules, so to speak, of her own making, then the *Alices* constitute a telling dream representation of their author's own plight. Understanding this relationship between Dodgson's inner life, his legendary rage for standards and order, and the functions of order and disorder in his public imaginative works illuminates both the sources of his creative urge and the strange, curiously resilient power of the *Alices*.

A few examples will suffice. In a search for the "meaning" of the *Alices*, what can be made, for instance, of the fact that these creations of an extremely imaginative artist celebrated in particular for the indeterminacy of his free-flowing narratives are also the creations of a man who for 50 years kept a meticulous register of the contents of every letter he wrote or received—summaries of more than 98,000 letters, many of them little more than minor business

† From *Alice's Adventures in Wonderland and Through the Looking-Glass: Nonsense, Sense, and Meaning* (New York: Twayne Publishers, 1991), 88–103. Reprinted by permission.
1. 1929; reprinted New York: Harcourt, Brace, and World, 1956, 12–13.

notes? Or what light is shed on the *Alices* by the fact that this supremely playful comic genius who created books teeming with disorder at the same time maintained a faithful record of the many luncheons and dinners he gave throughout many years of a sociable lifetime, with diagrams showing where each guest sat and lists of just what dishes were served? Or what can we say of this trenchant satirist of obsessiveness (almost all the *Alice* creatures are chronic obsessives) who himself seriously threatened to break off relations with his publisher of 30 years' standing because he found slight printing imperfections in the eighty-four thousandth copy of one of his popular children's books, then in print for 20 years, but who denied publicly throughout his life that he had anything to do with those masterpieces of free, mad nonsense and disorder signed by Lewis Carroll?

Wherever one looks, abundant biographical evidence indicates that Dodgson was so passionately devoted to regularity in his every-day affairs that his orderliness bordered on the pathological. But he was by no means unique: most of us are acquainted with people like him, people who manifest their extraordinary need for order by obsessively regulating and standardizing their daily lives. This behavior seems to express a deep-seated anxiety about the messiness that surrounds human consciousness, an anxiety about the morally random nature of an existence that can never satisfy the human mind's need for regularity, completeness, and control. On guard against the apparently mindless chaos that threatens their beliefs, their trust, and sometimes their very sanity, people who suffer from such anxiety often fill their waking lives with artificial structure—with manufactured systems and rules their wills (like their cultures' wills) impose on the disorderly matter and events they inevitably encounter. Like the child Alice, who in the maddening anarchy of her underground dream adventures persists in citing and looking for "rules," these devotees of order continually apply artifical constructs and systems to tidy up and temporarily regularize what their unconscious minds recognize as permanent chaos—the endlessly incomplete, absurd, "dreadful confusion" (*Looking-Glass*) that underlies our rationalized, futilely constructed, so-called waking world.

Scientific studies demonstrating the strict mechanical order inherent in nature, like Darwin's revolutionary explanations of nature's puzzling randomness, variation, and waste (*The Origin of Species* was published less than three years before Dodgson told his first *Alice* story to Alice Liddell and her sisters in 1862), cannot even begin to dispel such people's desperate sense of underlying anarchy. Indeed, these vexed souls are likely to find in visions like Darwin's further evidence of ultimate moral chaos; for such amoral, unprogressive, and strictly mechanical order in nature offers little

human comfort, little or no power to resolve the anxieties modern
men and women often suffer in contemplating the morally meaningless process that is nature and their only home. Instead of finding in Darwinian and post-Darwinian science some solution to the
metaphysical vexations of apparently random natural variety, these
obsessively orderly people—and by no means are they always scientifically naive—might very well find there objective, daytime cor-
roborations of their worst nightmares: a chilling panorama of the
pointless, mindless, inescapable mechanisms in which science has
now placed them firmly and forever. And, consequently, they might
easily find themselves, in their need for a corresponding moral pattern, for individual or collective human significance, terrifyingly
alone—powerless aliens in a careless, indifferent, absurd universe.
When Alice in her subterranean Wonderland cries because she is,
as she says, "so *very* tired of being all alone here!" (*Wonderland*),
she pines not only for the human companionship she has lost, but
also for some familiar signposts of intelligible order that her fellow
humans dream or construct for themselves in their darkness above
nature's ultimate emptiness. The religious and metaphysical assumptions that once answered the basic human need for orderly, complete, and permanent explanations and reasons beyond the reach of
reason had thinned out and vanished for a great number of Victorian
intellectuals during their lifetimes, destroyed by a natural, innocent,
childlike curiosity like Darwin's—and like Alice's. The resulting
God-less void was terrifying. It still is.

✳ ✳ ✳

Evil / Live

The fault here lies of course in life itself. When Alice complains to
the Cheshire Cat that the croquet game seems to have no rules, she
couples this with "and you've no idea how confusing it is all the
things being alive" (*Wonderland*). After Darwin, life—"being
alive"—becomes almost by definition a maddening moral confusion. The lovable imp Bruno in Carroll's *Sylvie and Bruno Concluded* (1893), seeing the letters EVIL arranged by Sylvie on a board
as one of his "lessons" and asked by Sylvie what they spell, exclaims,
"Why it's LIVE, backwards!" The narrator (clearly associated with
the author) sympathetically adds in parentheses, "(I thought it was,
indeed)." Some Carroll critics cite this passage as a clue to Dodgson's psychology; but they generally miss its direct and crucial relationship to Carroll's "backwards" literary dream fantasies—to the
evil confusion in all the living things being alive, to the darkness
and old chaos inherent in living and dying nature after Darwin's
simple biological vision has settled on the world, after innocent,

childlike Darwinian curiosity and the need for extrahuman completion and stasis have enticed us "backwards" down the rabbit hole and behind our manufactured anthropomorphic looking-glasses.

Carroll's comedy, then, contributes to the final destruction of a sustaining vision of nature and human nature in orderly harmony, moving steadily and according to divine rules toward some divine end. Such a vision hopefully concludes the chief philosophical poem of the age, Tennyson's *In Memoriam* (1837–50). Tennyson's long elegy ends with a rather forced, hopeful assertion that the human race (along with all natural creation) moves inexorably along a clear path toward a higher state of being and consciousness, where nature will make complete moral sense "like an open book" and where, ultimately, the seemingly mindless, random, amoral multiplicity, and violent waste of "Nature, red in tooth and claw" (*In Memoriam*, 56, line 15) will attain the coherent singleness of an orderly cosmos lovingly designed for humankind and justly ruled by one God:

> That God, which ever lives and loves,
> One God, one law, one element,
> And one far-off divine event,
> To which the whole creation moves.
> (131, lines 141–44)

The natural moral progress, the sense of unitary, purposeful, God-given order and natural motion within an ultimate rest celebrated here by Tennyson (and by Tennyson's stunning music) were by mid-century already a kind of outdated, forced, wishful vision for many intellectuals (and probably for Tennyson himself in his less public roles). And, among other things, the *Alice* books should be understood as representing the completion of this disillusionment— a strangely comical announcement of a new age of dark human consciousness.

Indeed, in *Wonderland* the sort of wishful progressive evolutionism voiced at the end of *In Memoriam* and echoed in much conventional mid- and late-Victorian literature is ridiculed with particular ferocity: for example, a baby can *devolve* into a pig as easily as a pig can *evolve* into a baby. (Darwin's theory, as it was first advanced, made no progressive claims: evolution dealt with adaptive *changes* in species, not with their rise on the hierarchical escalator of moral, spiritual development in some great, God-devised chain of being.) In Carroll's comic vision, moreover, motion is mere motion without first cause or final goal. And despite Alice's queening and the implied checkmate at the end of her looking-glass chess game, no one really wins by progressing logically and by deliberately reaching some known and desired end—or everyone wins, as in the pointless caucus race, which in itself nonsensically destroys the very grounds of all teleology. * * * [Alice] does progress in her Wonderland quest, but only toward a recognition that she must give up that quest and revert to infantile, dependent innocence, denying her frighteningly vivid perceptions of nature's careless, amoral, and unprogressive dance.

Alice's Evidence

* * *

In order to survive, Alice—like the hyperorderly Charles Dodgson—must create a meaningfully ordered, word-dependent game world out of the morally unintelligible void, and often in opposition to clear evidence from the nature of which we humans are an inseparable part. It could be said that such order is made in spite; and the spiteful element in Dodgson's rejections of disorder (like his clearly spiteful, outspoken rejections of babies and little boys because of their natural messiness) remains never far from the surface of his *Alice* fantasies. Alice's own spitefulness ("Who cares for *you*. . . . You're nothing but a pack of cards!" [*Wonderland*], for example) is one of Carroll's means to make her characterization believably human. It also helps explain why modern readers frequently admire what they see as her heroism. Like many spiteful heroines and heroes of failed causes in stage tragedies, Alice is a not altogether attractive figure. But we still admire, even cherish her as our courageous surrogate because she unwittingly learns to act heroically when she fails to find the order she seeks in the surrounding natural chaos. She thus becomes for many modern readers what she undoubtedly was for Dodgson: a naive champion of the doomed human quest for ultimate meaning and lost Edenic order. In the *Alices*, as in twentieth-century existential thought, human meaning is made in spite of the void, and, in making her order and meaning out of, essentially, *nothing*, the brave child Alice spitefully makes—for herself and for us, her elders and her successors—what we might very well call sense out of nonsense, something out of nothing. Ironically, like the nihilistic villain Edmund who declares near the end of *King Lear*, "Some good I mean to do, / Despite of mine own nature," Alice, in resisting her instinctive fears and the moral nothingness of her adventures, somehow makes of her spitefulness an affirmation of the human spirit.

But this is not to say that the *Alice* books are little *King Lear*s. For all their tragic implications, they are of course basically, overwhelmingly comic. Accordingly, their heroine, besides persevering and fighting back, has the practical good sense of a comic, rather than a tragic, figure. At the end of each book, she has the good sense to do another necessary human thing, to run away, suppressing the

reality of her own true dream-visions and substituting for that reality
the comfortable dreams of her above-ground world's waking state.

In any case, Alice's imposed order becomes all the more admirable and precious because of its fragility (the way the *Alice* books
have become the cherished, sometimes sacrosanct, possession of
deeply troubled adults). The comic tone at the end of *Wonderland*,
for example, like the customary tone of Carroll's adult narrator, is so
sure of itself because it is ultimately so unsure of itself, because it is
forged in shaky anxiety, emerging suddenly and full-blown from the
rejection of an orderly person's nightmare of complete disorder. Like
the total rejection of any bad dream we have just broken off, Carroll's concluding pages seem to deny completely the validity of
adventures that have all the luminosity of our truest experiences,
whose creatures and insanities will continue to live indefinitely, we
sense, after we reject them and wake to our fragile daydreams of
cosmic order. Therefore, the endings of both *Alice* books, contrived
and sentimental as they might be, are paradoxically appropriate
and true to our ordinary ambiguous experience. Brazen (and frightened) Alice rejects all her evidence as nonsense and dream; chaos
and old night are ironically dispelled by mere teatime and a little
kitty cat (both fine and delicate symbols of insouciant high civilization); and the final narratives, palpably artificial constructions
though they be, seem to explain away sensibly whatever residual
conviction of the dream adventures' relevance and validity might
persist—in dreamers, readers, or writers whose waking moments
are shaped by and dedicated to humanly constructed order.

The Search for Order

* * *

Like a haughty member of the upper classes staring down an incon-
trovertible but class-threatening fact, like a colonial official maintaining an ideologically constructed order against actual rebellion
in some God-forsaken outpost of European imperialism and "civilization," the frame story of each *Alice* book stands in direct, defiant
opposition to the body of the book, the vivid adventures themselves. When Humpty Dumpty tells Alice, "the question is . . .
which is to be master—that's all" (*Looking-Glass*), his assertion—
like Alice's early declaration that the "great puzzle" is "Who in the
world am I?" (*Wonderland*)—has profound existential, linguistic,
political, social, and economic significance. He is master of his
world because he *chooses* to believe he is in spite of the actual circumstances and because in his class-ordered, hierarchical, money-
driven world, he has the power (words and money and force) and
the elevated position (class and proper diction) to pay for and com-

mand obedience—and thus a kind of existence and order. Who "in the world" we are (and who we are "in the world") is a function of how we order (master, boss about, bully, verbalize, and force into a coherent order) our essentially unorderable worlds. Never mind that the ideological grounds, the "natural" justification for our mastery over members of lower classes and conquered peoples or over the intransigent moral chaos underlying all classes and systems are, after Darwin and the disappearance of God, as fragile as Humpty Dumpty's eggshell and as precarious as his perch. At the end of her *Looking-Glass* adventures, Alice says of their "dreadful confusion," "I can't stand this any longer!" (*Looking-Glass*). Similarly, at the end of her *Wonderland* adventures she finally decides she will have no more of their even more dreadful confusion. Like Humpty Dumpty, she decides for herself what to call this dreaded and uncontrollable chaos—and she calls it a "curious dream," mere "nonsense" (sense though it most certainly appears to be). So too do the ends of both fantasies define as "wonderful" and "nonsense" what we and Alice have just experienced vividly as frightening reality, asserting through their structure as well as their content that they too will have none of it. For at this point in the adventures and the narratives there appears no sane choice for humans but to seize power, to impose the fragile, artificial, arbitrary order of above-ground human law, culture, and social convention, using their shaky words and signs as the primary means of mastery.

Of course, like the White Knight, who says of his silly upside-down box "it's my own invention," we sometimes allow ourselves to recognize that such order and such power are merely our own silly, upside-down inventions of a world made whole. But generally we keep up our guard, and such chilling recognitions come to us only indirectly and even then artfully disguised in oblique fantasies, jokes, nonsense, games, and dreams—not straight and not in that uncensored daylight we choose to call sober, unadorned everyday life. Besides, we are also well aware at some level of comprehension of the final danger: if our eggshell, invented, but coherent waking world really fell and shattered, we too, like the imperious but fragile Humpty Dumpty, could never be put together again.

✳ ✳ ✳

Alice as Artist

Moreover, because she is child, dreamer, liar, and namegiver, Alice is also, in many ways, artist—a player of very special games. And like many modern artists, she moves toward creating an ominous, rather illusory beauty and order out of dangerous, disorderly, and

essentially ugly and grotesque materials—not by denying the existence of these materials, but rather by shaping them into what she
(and we) can call patterned, plotted "adventures," through her
human, blessed rage for order.

In a sense, then, Carroll's naive child-heroine prefigures the central spirit behind the twentieth-century dependence on art as an
essential, if fragile, source for those transcendent visions of coherence that are necessary to make human existence bearable. Wallace
Stevens's unnamed singer in the heart of darkness at Key West—at
the tip, that is, of a fragile civilization, a final dot in a vast dark
sea—sings "among / The meaningless plungings of water and the
wind." She could easily be a direct descendant of Carroll's Alice.
Her attractiveness to Stevens's adult speaker standing in the darkness is like the appeal of the innocent child Alice Liddell to the
experienced, order worshiper Charles Dodgson—and the appeal of
the *Alice* books to a modern reader:

> It was her voice that made
> The sky acutest at its vanishing.
> She measured to the hour its solitude.
> She was the single artificer of the world
> In which she sang. And when she sang, the sea,
> Whatever self it had, became the self
> That was her song, for she was the maker.
>
> Then we,
> As we beheld her striding there alone,
> Knew that there never was a world for her
> Except the one she sang and, singing, made.
> ("The Idea of Order at Key West," lines 34–43)

A naive forerunner of the modern artist-hero figure, Alice resists
succumbing to the despair provoked by her perceptions of absurdity. Instead of drowning in her own tears (a primal salt sea filled
with the life of all those Darwinian natural creatures—and with a
carefully drawn ape significantly in the center of Dodgson's original *Under Ground* illustration, she leads the way to that fantastical
shore where games can still be played and tales told. Along with her
fastidious creator, Alice persists, despite many daunting setbacks,
and finally seems to win the game for us all.

✳   ✳   ✳

JAMES R. KINCAID

The Wonder Child in Neverland[†]

* * *

Everything in Wonderland either generates a game or has to go sit and sulk. Since no attention at all is paid to the sulkers, they soon see the error of their ways and offer themselves up to the game. The Mock Turtle dallies with deep sadness, the Queen with death, the Duchess with sentimentality and with morals. This last, her quick ability to locate the moral that everything has within it, is of great interest to us, since it seems so close to textual interpretation, and may offer the secret of how to make interpreting fun. For the Duchess, the comment "The game seems to be going on rather better now" can be taken to mean "Oh, 'tis love, 'tis love, that makes the world go round." Or, she says, it can mean that the world goes round by everybody minding his business (much the same thing), in turn meaning "Take care of the sense, and the sounds will take care of themselves." The Duchess, poststructurally adept, seizes on secret puns, hidden disconnections, takes them in her beak, and drops them into craters. * * * It is a proud interpretive activity and a frisky one. Even the concluding Wonderland trial offers a hilarious romp with logic, linguistic certainty, and the control we imagine we have over events and consequences.

But the most unembarrassed view of what play can do comes in the simplest of the frolicsome activities, the Caucus Race. Here Dodgson is drawn in himself, taking on the form of the Dodo, just for the fun of it. The Dodo reads out the non-rules, not to constrain but to shoo away any constraints. Instead of giving rules, he gives out invitations, not a representation of experience but the thing itself: "the best way to explain it is to do it." The course is marked out "in sort of a circle"—"'the exact shape doesn't matter,' it said"— and all who were nearby and wanted to join in (which was everybody) "began running when they liked, and left off when they liked." Though it is not clear that the race has anything like an ending, it is felt only fitting that there should be a prize; so the Dodo, after some thought, declares, "*Everybody* has won, and *all* must have prizes." Such play opens us up to wild delights.

Delights which Alice would prefer, thank you just the same, to forego. She responds to the invitations offered to her with polite

† From *Child-Loving: The Erotic Child and Victorian Culture* (New York: Routledge, 1992), 290–98. Reprinted by permission.

refusals, though she keeps going, keeps being tempted, keeps making us think that just possibly she will slide over into sloth and devilment. Despite her curiosity, however, she is generally a well-ordered adult, prudent and respectful of conventions, even when she fails to recognize the basis for or implications of these conventions. She wants above all to stay in command of her world, Wonderland included, and reaches time and again for just those devices which had seemed so natural when she had been taught them—the ordering of predatory hierarchies, for instance. She tends to understand and value levels of being in terms of who eats what or whom, a grisly view whose genteel disguises are quietly removed in Wonderland. "Do cats eat bats?," she wonders as she falls, and sometimes "'Do bats eat cats?' for, you see, as she couldn't answer either question, it didn't much matter which way she put it." Any warm-blooded noun might be inserted, we suppose—bat, cat, rat, goat, slug, or Alice—so long as the key, *eat*, remained constant. She seems unable to avoid connecting the eaters with their dinners, chatting up mice and birds about cats and turning the delightful lobster quadrille into a feast, where the merry dancers are threatened by her own practices—"I've often seen them at dinn–."

As with "Idleness and Mischief," she often turns for security to prim prudential poems of the sort adults thrust at children (then and now). Trying to recover a sense of who she *is*, Alice runs for answers to the worst part of her culture. It is very sad and irksome, what with all the Wonderland creatures singing to her and waving brightly colored (if not very tasteful) banners telling her not to worry about the sort of identity that grown-ups give you. But Alice keeps after these poems, poems with titles like "'Tis the voice of the sluggard" or "The Old Man's Comforts and How He Gained Them." This last, better known as "You are old, Father William," stands as a direct rebuke if not to Alice then certainly to the cautious, CPA assumptions she is wanting to make. The poem Alice is trying to remember features an old man braying about how he spent all his youth preparing for his nineties and now what an abundant payoff he has had. He never once forgot, he says, that "youth could not last;/I thought of the future, whatever I did, / That I never might grieve for the past." As a result of hoarding his youth in this way, he is now "cheerful," collecting divine interest and entertaining callers with reflections on his favorite topic: "You are cheerful, and love to converse upon death, / Now tell me the reason, I pray." Not even Alice can hold such a vision in Wonderland; its prudential economy has no meaning there. As a result, all Alice can get from the situation is a rollicking poem about a somersaulting, upside-down, eel-balancing, ointment-selling, punning old man who has no notion that yesterday has any connection to tomorrow, that one might or might not save, or that there is any God or Death one might be "cheerful" about. He even becomes tired with his questioner, bored with anyone who really would think to ask for advice, when he could ask for marmalade.

*   *   *

Nor does she learn the most important lessons of all, that things do not conclude in Wonderland, that they cannot be understood in terms of goals or ends, and that new modes of seeing might be not only useful but happy substitutions. Time and again, she wants to tie things up and send them off, write a report and file it. The Mock Turtle's old-boy (or -girl or -it) memories (or anticipations or lies) of a quite remarkable school it attended (or is attending or will be attending or never did attend) include an idea whose time had certainly come: lessons should lessen, else there is no reason for their name—ten hours one day, nine the next, and so on. Alice feels, first, stung by this praise of a school she did not frequent; but then she tries to understand the lessening system. What, she wonders, happened on the eleventh day, a vacation? That's it! "'And how did you manage on the twelfth?' Alice went on eagerly." Earlier, at the great tea-party, formed as a ring of eternity, Alice tries to find in the circle a stopping point, tries to reinsert linear time into a world where it's always tea-time; she wants it all to be over: as the party moves round and round, Alice cannot keep from asking "what happens when you come to the beginning again?" Where Wonderland has most to offer, Alice calls up her strongest resistance.

All the same, we never lose hope of somehow educating this child into childhood. She does not, for one thing, always have her back up, hissing. We are led into this work by the promise that the child can be cuddled. The prefatory poem, "All in the golden afternoon," is a basking verse, one that laps and strokes and suggests a recapture in memory so perfect that the past will flood the present, erasing that distinction and, with it, the one between the adult and child. Early on, as Alice goes down the rabbit hole, there is a nestling intimacy implied between the narrator and the child who allows such attentions: "She generally gave herself very good advice (though she very seldom followed it)," humor whose very feebleness signals a private understanding. Again, at the very end, the child is there, or seems to be, for snuggling. She is still "little Alice," and through her sister provides the final enticing image. But notice how it is no longer suggested that Alice participates in this, even hears the jokes. They are still private jokes, but they are now so confidential as to be solitary. Through our surrogate, Alice's sister, we can only moon over memories or paint a picture of the future that tries to soften the pain of the child's desertion. Alice has run off from the scene; the sister, the adult, is left alone to make the best of things; though the best doesn't amount to much:

> Lastly, she pictured to herself how this same little sister of hers would, in the after-time, be herself a grown woman; and how she would keep, through all her riper years, the simple and loving heart of her childhood; and how she would gather about her other little children, and make *their* eyes bright and eager with many a strange tale, perhaps even with the dream of Wonderland of long ago; and how she would feel with all their simple sorrows, and find a pleasure in all their simple joys, remembering her own child-life, and the happy summer days.

The adult tries to hold something, to keep the child from becoming so resoundingly ordinary and familiar. The adult wants not to bring the child close but to keep it at a distance, hold it at arm's length. Otherwise, we cannot move in a field of desire at all. We can always pretend, with Alice's sister, that somehow Alice will be different, that adulthood will not destroy her Otherness, that she will keep, in memory and in her heart, something simpler. But deep inside, even while spinning this story, we acknowledge that the magic did not take, that Alice has no simplicity to maintain or regain, that she will not even, in a vulgar and pathetic idea we could not keep ourselves from adding, use the story to bring other children to us, others with bright and eager eyes. She could never tell the story. She didn't get it.

*   *   *

Looking-Glass Losses

The second story almost gives up before it begins, gives up on any real recapturing effort, and sees what may be harvested from the consolations of melancholy. It is a book written not only for but by Alice's sister. But even Alice's sister is not quite resigned to going out like a candle, and, despite everything, the players behind the glass keep holding out to Alice timid entreaties, shy, red-faced, and foot-shuffling expressions of half-hope that she will yet join the fun. The erotics in Looking-Glass, in other words, are similar to those in Wonderland, depending on a fluid, shifting Other, sliding in and out of focus, offering glimpses and then taking them away, rescuing the adult from despair and then abandoning him. We are in a shaded world now, no longer in golden afternoons; but every now and then we think that—maybe, though probably not, but possibly—the clouds are parting.

The opening poem, "Child of the pure unclouded brow," provides a short form of the play of desire encouraged in the work as a whole, a desire rooted in glum loneliness and self-pity, bitterness and puzzlement, broken, though, by tantalizing suggestions that what is gone may not be gone, that what never was might be regained. The poem begins by saluting the child and then at once slipping into the lip-quivering acknowledgment that "thou and I are half a life asunder." This distance is so extreme it nearly smothers desire: "I have not seen thy sunny face, / Nor heard thy silver laughter. / No thought of me shall find a place / In thy young life's hereafter—." These are lines uttered with a sleeve brushing across eyes which are darting daggers through the tears. They look like exit lines: if what we've said were really so, if that is what we really thought, things would have to stop right here. But in looking-glass land, so much older and tireder than Wonderland, these sorts of things are always being said and then withdrawn; the child is recurrently being disowned and then given just one more chance. In this prefatory poem, we are rushed right past the sad finale into appeals to the child to keep the action going, to learn how to remember. All that is asked is that the child listen to the story, but the asking is very much in the form of threats: listen or die! Of course, we threaten in metaphors: "unwelcome beds," "melancholy maidens," and the raging, killing cold outside. "Within," on the other hand, is "the firelight's ruddy glow, / And childhood's nest of gladness." Don't leave the nest and you will not die after all! It is not too late, maybe, even now, to return. The story is written to point out the return route or, even better, to ask you to stay, since maybe you really haven't gone after all. "The magic words will hold thee fast: / Thou shalt not heed the raving blast." That is almost believable at times; it almost seems that the magic might work its spell, name and fix the child. That it does not hold the child is obvious, is the whole point: *Through the Looking-Glass* builds its longing out of the paltry materials of what might have been.

*   *   *

Partly to screen ourselves from the real terror, that the child is no longer there, we enter into play with dark things. We hope somehow that we can wish into being what is hopeless, learn along with the White Queen how to live with "impossible things," making as many as six of them come to visit before breakfast. But we acknowledge that these things must be born out of frightening forms. Humpty Dumpty romps with rootless language, a system of connecting with one another that has no connections. There may be no ties with one's past, no remembering even the horror—unless one makes a memo of it. Here, as in the shop run by the Sheep, the shelf we want to pick from always becomes empty; the beautiful rushes we think we have gathered melt away like snow. The Other is more than elusive here; it is always on the edge of disappearing. Perhaps grimmest of all are the pleas made through the Gnat, soft and persistent attempts to woo Alice to come join us and be a child again. The Gnat wants contact, wants jokes; but Alice knows none and finds the Gnat's offerings so poor that their communion, so much desired by the Gnat, finally dwindles to conversation about death. But we keep hoping that play somehow will be revived in the next county or in the next square. For instance, after calmly eradicating the Gnat, Alice is given another invitation, delivered by a beautiful Fawn. In the Wood of No Names where the Fawn leads her, they come together, even touch. But names in the form of order and power return to get them; and the vision is shattered—only to spring back before us again just round the next bend.

* * *

The child seems to appear here only in a series of goodbyes, last encounters between a forlorn adult and a barely polite, distracted child or child-that-was. The Gnat and the fawn are succeeded by the climactic farewell with the White Knight, a scene so packed with love and self-pity it is hard to see how Alice could fail to respond. But fail she does, not crying at anything like the rate the Knight had forecast and hardly concealing her impatience as he rides off, so she can trip quickly over the last brook and be a Queen, mate a King, and confirm her betrayal.

There had once been yet another farewell, with an old wasp, where Alice had acted with more Wendy-like kindness,[1] where the grumpy old (about-to-die, actually) Wasp is stirred to acknowledge her kindness—"Good-bye, and thank-ye"—, and where Alice gets a little warm glow from her charity: she was "quite pleased that she had gone back and given a few moments to make the poor old creature comfortable." This chapter on the wasp was never published, and all child-lovers know why. Alice thoughtlessly tripping over the brook, turning her back on the dear old White Knight is terrible— but it has its erotic possibilities. The scene can be replayed and made to come out differently; or, if all else fails, forced to yield the pleasures of indignation. But Alice as familiar, kindly, mothering Wendy: that is crushing. The Otherness of betrayal can be dealt with, but not the prosaic dullness of the sick-nurse. We can, after all, find a way to play with loss, with the elusive and maddening Alice and Peter Pan. We never really wanted them caged.

1. Kincaid reads Wendy in J. M. Barrie's *Peter Pan, or the Boy Who Would Not Grow Up* (1904) as a maternal figure [*Editor's note.*]

MARAH GUBAR

Reciprocal Aggression[†]

* * *

Crucially, one of the adult ideas Alice resists most vehemently during her adventures is the message that she should remain a child forever. "Now if you'd asked *my* advice," Humpty Dumpty pompously observes, "I'd have said 'Leave off at seven.'" Unmoved by this absurd proposal, Alice indignantly informs him that "I never ask advice about growing" and—when he continues to press her—she firmly changes the subject: "They had had quite enough about the subject of age, she thought." Similarly, when the officious railway guard tells her, "You're traveling the wrong way," Alice completely ignores this complaint, even when another gentleman on the train seconds it by suggesting that she take a return ticket. "Indeed I sha'n't!" Alice retorts, and a few pages later she reaffirms her commitment to moving forward: "for I certainly won't go *back*."

Rather than interpreting such moments as unproblematic evidence for Carroll's own desire to arrest the girlchild in place, we should instead recognize that they represent his willingness to grapple, quite self-consciously, with the question of how damaging this particular adult yearning is, and how young people should respond to it. In other words, Carroll acknowledges this arresting impulse as one of the impositions that pushy adults place on children. What should children do when confronted with such nudging? If we assume that Alice is intended to function as a positive role model, the foregoing incidents send the message that young people should refuse to listen to such nonsense and get away from the adult in question as fast as possible. Alice's encounter with the White Knight toward the end of *Through the Looking-Glass* likewise promotes this idea. Many critics maintain that the White Knight functions as a stand-in for Carroll, interpreting his determination to hold Alice prisoner as an admission of the author's own longing to freeze the child in place. Indeed, this scene does stage a skirmish between an adult who wants to capture and slow down a child and the child herself, who is determined to move forward and graduate to more grown-up status: "'I don't want to be anybody's prisoner,'" Alice announces, "I want be a Queen."

What critical accounts of this scene rarely acknowledge is that this conflict is *instantly* resolved in favor of Alice; in response to her

† From *Artful Dodgers: Reconceiving the Golden Age of Children's Literature* (New York: Oxford UP, 2009), 120–24. Reprinted by permission of Oxford University Press.

declaration, the Knight promptly gives up his claim on her and agrees to help her move forward: "'So you will, when you've crossed the next brook. . . . I'll see you safe to the end of the wood—and then I must go back.'" Like many other scenes in the *Alice* books, then, this one invites children to regard adult desires as something they can say no to: it is less about arrest than about *resisting* arrest, something Alice does over and over again during the course of her adventures. Constantly disengaging herself from a variety of unpleasant interactions, Alice operates as an escape artist from the very first scene—in which she flees the prosaic company of her sister—to the final moments of both adventures, when she busts out of the chaotic fantasyland created by Carroll.

Moreover, Carroll strongly implies that Alice is right to resist the pressure to remain childlike by introducing readers to a number of characters who are absurd and unattractive precisely because they are cases of arrested development. Although they are clearly identified as "men," for example, the Tweedle brothers look "like a couple of great school-boys" and behave like infants; besides their fussing and fighting over a rattle, their extreme egotism leads Alice to denounce them as "Selfish things!" They and the equally querulous Humpy Dumpty are literally arrested; when Alice first sees the Tweedles, they stand so still that she forgets they are alive and gazes at them as if they are "wax-works." Here Carroll links being frozen in place with being objectified; elsewhere he goes so far as to link this state with death. When Alice spots Humpty Dumpty, his expression is so "fixed" that she assumes "he must be a stuffed figure." Although this embryonic character tries to persuade Alice of the benefits of remaining frozen at an early age, his own dire fate demonstrates the nonviability of that kind of life. By emphasizing the self-centeredness of these childlike figures, Carroll anticipates [J. M.] Barrie's un-Romantic habit of associating eternal innocence with "heartless" egocentrism.

Despite these indications that Carroll intends to deride the adult yearning for eternal youth, the characterization of the White Knight shows how conflicted he remains in regard to this issue. A decidedly childish figure himself, the Knight seems designed to elicit amused sympathy rather than harsh ridicule. Although he clearly desires to detain Alice and delay her development, this "gentle," "mild," "kindly" figure is hardly portrayed as a villain. Indeed, the narrator informs us that in later years, Alice recalls the occasion of listening to his song very fondly. Moreover, however problematic the Knight's desire to control and arrest Alice may be, this "foolish" character is so ineffectual, so easy to resist, that such solicitations wind up seeming fairly harmless. Yet at the same time, * * * this scene rather ruthlessly exposes and mocks the tendency of narcissistic adults to assume ownership over and project their own feelings onto children. Wandering through the world "with his eyes shut, muttering to himself," the Knight ignores and misreads Alice, making this one of many scenes in the second *Alice* book that explore the "subjective distortions by which we remake others into imaginary self-reflections."[1]

Moreover, by having the White Knight spout a parody of Wordsworth, Carroll associates such self-involved fantasizing specifically with Romantic discourse. Like so many other interpolated texts in the *Alice* books, the Knight's song dwells on the perils of entering into a relationship characterized by fake or failed mutuality. In it, Carroll sends up the self-absorption of the poet-narrator of "Resolution and Independence" (1807), suggesting that his efforts to draw the old leech-gatherer into conversation do not attest to any desire for genuine communication or reciprocity. Thus, in Carroll's version, the Wordsworthian narrator ignores everything the "aged aged man" says in response to his questions. His extreme egotism is hilarious, but the parody conveys a real concern that artists, in their narcissism, can actually harm the hapless objects of their attention. Thus, Carroll's poet-narrator physically abuses the subject of his tale, shaking the old man "from side to side, / Until his face was blue" and accompanying his often-reiterated question with violence: "I cried, 'Come, tell me how you live!' / And thumped him on the head."

As Ruth Berman notes, Carroll's phrasing here recalls another Wordsworth poem in which the object under interrogation is a child; in "Anecdote for Fathers" (1798), the speaker repeatedly demands that his child explain himself ("Why? Edward, tell me why?") while physically accosting him ("I said and took him by the arm") [lines 48, 26]. Rather unfairly, Carroll suggests that the Wordsworthian narrator is himself unaware of how his desires constrain the liberty, self-expression, and well-being of his child addressee. Keen to avoid what he views as a highly unself-conscious and aggressive authorial stance, Carroll repeatedly emphasizes his own recognition that being figured as the subject of other people's imaginings can constitute a painful form of subjection for the child.[2]

Indeed, Alice so dislikes the idea of belonging to another person's dream that a few scenes after she tearfully dismisses this possibility as "nonsense," she contemplates going back to rouse the Red King

---

1. U. C. Knoepflmacher, *Ventures into Childland: Victorians, Fairy Tales, and Femininity* (Chicago: U Chicago P, 1998), 222.
2. Ruth Berman, "White Knight and Leech Gatherer: The Poet as Boor," *Mythlore* 33 (Autumn 1982): 29–31. As Berman notes, this is a very unsympathetic reading of Wordsworth, since the father himself recognizes that he has dealt with his son in a rough, insensitive way at the end of "Anecdote for Fathers." Clearly, Wordsworth was not incapable of perceiving the boorishness of his own narrators.

in order to reassure herself that her Wonderland adventure really is "*my* dream"—and this despite the fact that the Tweedles have warned her that waking him up might make her vanish like a blown-out candle. Just as Carroll's photographs often alert viewers to his own invisible presence, the many moments in the *Alice* books that raise the possibility that Alice is "fabulous" rather than "real" draw our attention to the author hovering behind the scenes. Indeed, the very last line of *Through the Looking-Glass* invites such exposure; although it asks child readers to decide whether the Red King or Alice dreamed up the preceding story, an astute audience member might well propose another answer entirely.

At the same time, by creating a child protagonist who constantly finds herself having poems, stories, and songs inflicted on her by nonsensical men, Carroll dramatizes the plight of the child bombarded by other people's discourse, which of course includes Alice Liddell and other young readers of his books. In the process, he manages to undercut the cheery notion that children's literature exists merely to entertain children—an idea the *Alice* books are often credited with popularizing. After hearing that the Tweedle brothers regaled Alice with verse, Humpty brags, "'I can repeat poetry as well as other folk, if it comes to that.'" "Hoping to keep him from beginning," Alice hastily exclaims "'Oh, it needn't come to that!'" But of course it does:

> "The piece I'm going to repeat," he went on without noticing her remark, "was written entirely for your amusement."
>
> Alice felt that in that case she really *ought* to listen to it; so she sat down, and said "Thank you" rather sadly.

Carroll here sends up the whole idea of writing "for" children. Humpty Dumpty professes to have composed children's literature: a poem created solely to entertain a particular child. Yet this claim is obviously specious, since he has just met Alice (and in any case seems far less interested in her than in himself and his own pronouncements). Worse than that, Carroll suggests, the mere act of designating the child as the intended addressee can exert a coercive, silencing effect; the child is essentially being asked to sit down and shut up, a point made explicit during Humpty's rendition of the poem, when he "severely" informs Alice that she should stop inserting her own commentary in between his lines: "'You needn't go on making remarks like that,' Humpty Dumpty said: 'they're not sensible, and they put me out.'"

Carroll's decision to represent Alice as immersed in discourse not of her own making and his habit of dwelling on his heroine's artificiality—her status as a figment of someone else's imagination—are closely related. If we acknowledge that outside influences strongly shape selfhood, we must face the possibility that even our dreams are not our own—an idea that might make anyone weep. Alice's tears attest to how painful it is to conceive of oneself as a scripted being rather than an autonomous, totally authentic agent. Yet rather than regard this problem as unique to childhood, Carroll conceives of such belatedness as another point of connection between young and old. For the White Knight scene vividly illustrates that children are not the only ones imbued with ideologies not of their own making; adults, too, must cope with their profound unoriginality. Although the Knight prides himself on his power of invention, his ideas are either absurd or—in the case of his song—derivative. Not only does the plot of his poem come from Wordsworth, "the tune *isn't* his own invention"; according to the highly acculturated Alice, "it's '*I give thee all, I can no more.*'" Adults, Carroll suggests, absorb, conform to, and improvise on various cultural influences, too, including and especially the kind of Romantic discourse about childhood that he himself frequently reiterates, reanimates, and caricatures.

Such keen recognition about the difficulty of being genuinely inventive and innovative might help explain why Carroll never allows his heroine to evolve into a full-fledged creative agent. Despite her willingness to say no, Alice ultimately remains a relatively unresistant reader: just as she wants to echo Watts when she first arrives in Wonderland, so too she promises after her final departure to "repeat 'The Walrus and the Carpenter'" to Dinah the next morning. And although Carroll flirts with the idea that children can wrest away the pen, he does not really take it seriously as a genuine possibility. It is grown-ups who control the world of children's fiction, as Alice herself recognizes. * * *

ROBERT M. POLHEMUS

Lewis Carroll and the Child in Victorian Fiction†

* * * Carroll is important as a writer who makes fun of what Jacqueline Rose calls "the whole ethos of language as always reliable or true."[1] As the child knows and shows, language is anything but a neutral, transparent medium that simply reflects an existing reality. Linguistic power creates a joyous surge of identity and also a knowledge of otherness, as Alice learns in *Looking-Glass* when she finds

† From *The Columbia History of the British Novel*, ed. John Richetti, et al. (New York: Columbia UP, 1994), 601–606. Copyright © 1994 Columbia University Press. Reprinted with permission of the publisher.
1. Jacqueline Rose, *The Case of Peter Pan, or The Impossibility of Children's Fiction* (London: Macmillan, 1984).

herself alienated from the faun once they pass out of the "wood of no names" and back into the realm of human language. Carroll stresses throughout both the delight and the farce of misunderstanding that are inherent in words and dialogue. The texts render what children feel about language as they struggle to master it: that it is slippery, confusing, hard, rule-ridden, and frustrating, but also creative, pleasurable, and full of play. Language proves our social being and determines our fate, but, as a child learns, it is also the means for defining and expressing our desires, our individuality, our confusions, our subjective freedom, and our bonds. We live by linguistic fictions. In Carroll, many of the characters act out verbal structures, for instance, Humpty Dumpty, the Tweedles, and even Alice, whose movements in *Looking-Glass* exactly conform to the predictive words of the Red Queen at the beginning.

Carroll helped to lead in making language a great subject for thought and comedy and literature, but for him it is nothing to be idealized. It can never be a precise communication system because it is inseparable from its users. From the first in *Through the Looking-Glass*, Carroll tells us that Alice moves in a dream world composed of words that exist independently of personal will. When the White King exclaims of his pencil, "It writes all manner of things that I don't intend," he is talking about the unmanageable nature of language, and he previews its role in the book, and in twentieth-century intellectual history. And when "Jabberwocky" appears to Alice, we know that we are in a fictional world of sense, absurdity, and wordplay all at once, like a child trying to fathom language.

> 'Twas brillig, and the slithy toves
> Did gyre and gimble in the wabe:
> All mimsy were the borogoves,
> And the mome raths outgrabe.

The verse foreshadows the whole book. The extreme tensions in the poem—between the unconventional use of language (invented vocabulary) and the conventional (normal syntax, grammar, rhythm, and rhyme), between referential significance and self-contained nonsense—define and energize Carroll. "Jabberwocky" puts the focus on the very *fact* of language itself, whose very existence—as children see and feel—is just as marvelous, just as fantastic, as any of the meanings it conveys.

Even as the figure of the child in the last two centuries has called forth interpretation, assertions of authority, and projection, so has Carroll's fiction. Lewis Carroll's work is particularly susceptible to the regressive tendencies of critics and writers who find in it images, words, meanings, and emotions that liberate, clarify, articulate, and give play to their own ideas, longings, and obsessions. Alice defines her readers as their dreams and childhoods do.

Read what has been written about Carroll and you find a wonderland of interpretation. It has been argued, for example, that Queen Victoria wrote the Alice books, that Alice is a phallus, that she is an imperialist, that she is an existential heroine, a killjoy, a sex-tease, or a symbol for what every human being should try to be like in the face of an outrageous universe; it has been claimed that her pool of tears represents the amniotic fluid, that the Caucus race parodies Darwin, that it sports with Victorian theories about the Caucasian race, that the Alice books may contain a secret history of the Oxford movement, that they allegorize Jewish history, that the "Pig and Pepper" chapter is a description of toilet training, that the White Queen stands for John Henry Newman and the Tweedles for Bishop Berkeley; that these tales are dangerous for children, that they are literally nonsense and do not refer to the real world; that Carroll was a latent homosexual, an atheist, a schizophrenic, a pedophile, a faithful Christian, a fine man. Some of this criticism is brilliant, some is lunatic, some is both by turns, some is hilarious, much of it is fascinating and insightful, nearly all of it is entertaining, and most of it is offered with the dogmatic surety of Humpty Dumpty, who says, "I can explain all the poems that ever were invented—and a good many that haven't been invented just yet." My purpose here is not to patronize other commentators but to show that something in the nature of the writing itself—some vacuum of indeterminacy—sucks in a wide variety of reaction and engagement. Children are subject to authority, but Carroll puts authority in doubt and questions it. The Alice fiction deals with the crisis of authority in modern life, and readers are drawn to solve it. People project their wishes and beliefs and concerns onto these fictions as they lay them upon children. Like the parables of the Bible, like dreams, like depicted fantasies, Carroll stimulates a hermeneutics of subjective ingenuity and a multiplicity of views. These malleable texts resist closure of meaning; they remain open-ended and dialogical.

Of course, I am giving my own interpretation of Carroll, and obviously it stresses his use of a problematic dream-child in an anti-authoritarian, carnivalesque literary comedy and centers on the way that child opens up the play of language, the unconscious mind, and floating, contradictory desires. The world he creates is both referential and nonreferential, both like the world we live in and a different, fantasy world of nonsense. When the Mock Turtle tells Alice that in school he learned "Reeling and Writhing" and the different branches of arithmetic, "Ambition, Distraction, Uglification, and Derision," the text offers both an example of nonsensical, creative wordplay that breaks free of "reality" and a satire on what real children actually do learn in real schools. Through the child, Carroll gets across his sense of a fantastic, alternative world of being, a sense of rebellious knowledge of actuality, a sense of humor (i.e., putting life in a play-frame), and a sense of the importance and imprecision of language.

*   *   *

In "The Emperor's New Clothes," a child exposes the ruler's nakedness by cutting through lies and illusions to give people the perspective they need for seeing their own gullibility and the ruses of power. That's how Carroll works. He makes the child his protagonist, her dreams his narrative; and he pretends that children are his only audience so that he can rid himself and others of inhibitions and repressions. Through the child, he strips away both personal and social conventions and prejudices (e.g., you must not think or talk disrespectfully of parents, royalty, or "sacred" things; life should make sense; we all speak the same language; personalities are coherent; poetry is elevated; a well-brought-up little girl does not harbor murderous thoughts; the world of childhood is simple); he holds them up to ridicule and sets loose possibilities for imagining the unthinkable (e.g., original words and fantastic physical beings, the pleasure of the obliteration of others, the animation of the inanimate, the stupidity of mothers and fathers; the joys of madness). In the reversed looking-glass of his art, Carroll uses Alice to show up the silly childishness—in its pejorative sense—and the arbitrary limits of the so-called adult world. He proves in the Alice books that even in the most outwardly conventional and time-serving of adults there may be a wild and brave child struggling to get out and mock the withering realities that govern life. Such is the hope of this comedy of regression.

Carroll's way is to begin and frame his text with mawkish, sentimental descriptions of childhood. It is as if, in his introductory poems and in the opening monologue of *Looking-Glass* featuring the girl-child, he is trying to represent the most morally unobjectionable being that he and his fellow Victorians could conceive of in order to smother his psychic censor in a well of treacle. Watch a child alone at play with its toys and dolls and after a while you may begin to hear and see these figures taking on roles that dramatize aspects of the child's life. Different tones and voices arise, words come out that reveal thoughts and visions neither you nor the child knew it possessed. Carroll's fiction is like that. In *Looking-Glass*, after Alice babbles, "I wonder if the snow *loves* the trees and fields that it kisses them so . . . and . . . says 'go to sleep, darlings'" and Dr. Dodgson appears to lull himself to sleep, Mr. Carroll suddenly bursts through the looking-glass and through the double wall of superego and sentimentality: he quotes Alice saying, "Nurse! Do let's pretend that I'm a hungry hyaena, and you're a bone!" That explodes the pious little-girl image and releases manic, unpredictable energy into the text and a typically resonant complexity into the character of Alice.

* * *

Not surprisingly, the character and function of Alice have become bones of critical contention, I have put her by and large in a favorable light, but some in the late twentieth century, focusing on problems of race, class, and gender, judge her more negatively. She has been seen as a quintessential figure of Victorian ethnocentrism for her continual attempts to bring her own standards, customs, mores, and manners to bear on the beings and circumstances she meets in her wonderlands. Carroll does sometimes betray his own upper-class biases, and he does render Alice's privileged-class assurance, especially in her occasional bouts of snobbery and patronization in the early chapters of *Wonderland*. She can also be seen as an example of essentialist gender stereotyping that makes the Victorian girl into a litany of virtues (and Alice surely displays most of humanity's good qualities). Such views have merit and interest, but they miss the dream psychology and the plurality of being Carroll imagines for her and also, I think, the main historical point: this writer moved one of history's most notoriously marginalized groups of beings, children, to the center of existence.

He could identify with the otherness of childhood, and its diversity; and in narrating the progress of Alice on her journeys he could reveal, as Freud would do in his famous essay "A Child is Being Beaten," one of the momentous secrets of childhood—and life: the imaginative processes of transposed and projected violence. Of course, Carroll is, among other things, a colonialist of childhood. He imposes upon a child and children his own dream of childhood, his sense and definition of a child. But this dream is fluid, and he is also a liberator of childhood. The Alice tales end with the question of whose dream this is and here Carroll touches upon the imperialism of desire. The question suggests a sense of fiction's mediation between author, audience, and cultural context, and, fittingly in a book about a child, it opens up the subject of custody.

* * *

ELIZABETH SEWELL

The Balance of Brillig[†]

* * *

It is important to take a fairly wide field, because the authoritarian Humpty Dumpty, backed up later by Carroll himself, has suggested an over-simple explanation. Humpty Dumpty undertakes to interpret the hard words, says that *brillig* is four o'clock in the afternoon, when you start broiling things for dinner, and then goes on to *slithy* which he maintains is a combination of lithe and slimy: 'You see—it's like a portmanteau—there are two meanings packed up into one word.' To this Carroll adds in the Snark Preface. 'Humpty Dumpty's theory, of two meanings packed into one word like a portmanteau, seems to me the right explanation of all.'

* * *

There is a more interesting remark earlier in the conversation, and it may be as well to start here rather than with the portmanteau theory. Alice and Humpty have been having a difference of opinion about the noun 'glory', to which Humpty attributes an entirely personal meaning. When Alice complains, Humpty says that he intends to be master of his own house, and continues with the remark that adjectives are pliable and verbs tough. 'They've a temper, some of them—particularly verbs: they're the proudest—adjectives you can do anything with, but not verbs.' It is certain that in Nonsense vocabulary nouns and adjectives play by far the biggest part. Mr. Partridge[1] in his classification of the vocabulary of *Jabberwocky* gives four new verbs, *gimble, outgrabe, galumphing* and *chortled*, to ten new adjectives and eight new nouns.

* * *

We can assume that the writers wanted their sentences containing Nonsense words to look like genuine sentences bearing reference, and that they found nouns and adjectives better for their purpose than verbs. If Nonsense words are to appear to be one of a class, it must be in order that they should carry conviction as words rather than gibberish. *Brillig, Cloxam, Willeby-Wat* have no more reference than *Hey nonny no* or *Hi diddle diddle*, but they seem to have,

---

† From *The Field of Nonsense* (London: Chatto and Windus Ltd., 1952), 116–29. Reprinted by permission.
1. Eric Partridge, "The Nonsense Words of Edward Lear and Lewis Carroll," in *Here, There and Everywhere* (London: 1950), 162–88 [*Editor's note*].

because they are presented to us as nouns or adjectives, and remind us of other words which have reference.

*   *   *

We can move on now to an example of Nonsense wording; a very short one will do to start with:—

> . . . and shun
> The frumious Bandersnatch.

The verb is simple and familiar; we are left with a noun and an adjective. Humpty Dumpty's commentary on the poem does not go beyond the first verse, but the similar phrase, 'the slithy toves' is dealt with as follows: 'Well "*slithy*" means "lithe and slimy" . . . "*toves*" are something like badgers—they're something like lizards— and they're something like corkscrews.' The noun is treated as if it were a technical term, a label and no more, and is invested at once with Nonsense properties. * * * The adjective is an example of Humpty Dumpty's portmanteau, and *frumious* is of the same type. Carroll says of it in the Snark Preface that it is a combination of 'fuming' and 'furious'. To take the adjectives first, *slithy* and *frumious*, it seems curious that Humpty Dumpty should have got by so easily on his portmanteau theory, for when one looks at it, it becomes very unsatisfactory. It would fit a pun well enough, in which there are precisely that—two meanings (or more than two) packed up in one word. But *frumious*, for instance, is not a word, and does not have two meanings packed up in it; it is a group of letters without any meaning at all. What Humpty Dumpty may have meant, but fails to say, is that it looks like two words, 'furious' and 'fuming', reminding us of both simultaneously. It is not a word, but it looks like other words, and almost certainly more than two. * * *

Nonsense words which do not act in this way, *Jubjub*, for instance, must have their function as technical terms made clear at once, and this in fact is what happens:

> Beware the Jubjub bird . . .

> Should we meet with a Jubjub, that desperate bird,
> We shall need all our strength for the job!

On the whole, however, the first of these two forms is the commoner, a Nonsense word reminding the mind of other words which it resembles. It is important, for if a word does not look like a word, so to speak, the mind will not play with it. Carroll coins examples of this sort, *Mhruxian* and *grurmstipths* from *Tangled Tales* or the 'occasional exclamation' of the Gryphon, *Hjckrrh* from *The Mock Turtle's Story*. Words such as these do not interest the mind; but dongs and toves look strangely familiar, and the mind can enjoy itself with them. * * * We are left with a half-conscious perception of verbal likenesses, and, in consequence, the evocation of a series of words.

It looks as if Nonsense were running on to dangerous ground here, for two of its rules are (*a*) no likenesses are to be observed, and (*b*) no trains of association are to be set up. At this point we shall have to go back to the Snark Preface for a moment, for, although we have rejected Carroll's suggestion that Humpty Dumpty's theory will cover all the Nonsense words, making the portmanteau into an umbrella, there is an interesting remark a little later on. Discussing the alternative of saying 'fuming-furious' or 'furious-fuming', Carroll says, 'but if you have that rarest of gifts, a perfectly balanced mind, you will say "frumious".' It is a hint that here as elsewhere Nonsense is maintaining some kind of balance in its language.[2] After all, Humpty Dumpty who is the chief language expert in the Alices is himself in such a state; Carroll could have made any of his characters discourse upon words, and it is interesting that the one who in fact does so was 'sitting, with his legs crossed like a Turk, on the top of a high wall—such a narrow one that Alice quite wondered how he could keep his balance.' * * *

Nonsense has a fear of nothingness quite as great as its fear of everythingness. Mr. Empson says in *Some Versions of the Pastoral*[3] that the fear of death is one of the crucial topics of the Alices, but it will be simpler for us at present to think of it as a fear of nothingness.

> . . . 'for it might end, you know,' said Alice to herself, 'in my going out altogether, like a candle. I wonder what I should be like then?'

> 'You know very well you're not real.'
> 'I *am* real!' said Alice, and began to cry.

The Snark breaks the rules here, for in Fit the Seventh someone has 'softly and suddenly vanished away', that is, has become nothingness. Nonsense does not deal in any kind of physical or metaphysical nothingness, one needs to remember. It deals in words. Where these are normal and are acting normally, there cannot be a nothingness in so far as they are concerned, for words have reference to experience. 'Word implies relation to creatures' (Aquinas, *Summa [Theological]*, Pt. I, Q. 34, Art. 4). The only way in which

---

2. Belle Moses in *Lewis Carroll in Wonderland and at Home* (New York: 1910) quotes him as saying of his Nonsense language, 'A perfectly balanced mind could understand it' (6).
3. William Empson, "The Child as Swain," *Some Versions of Pastoral* (London: Chatto and Windus; New York: New Directions, 1935)

nothingness could set in might be by some sort of separation between words and things, by things having no words attached to them or by words without reference to things. It comes down to a question of names.

* * *

It is interesting that such a case is dealt with explicitly in *Through the Looking-Glass*, in Alice's entry into the wood where things have no name. This is at the end of Chapter III, *Looking-Glass Insects*, a very significant chapter despite its rather limited title, for it is all about words and names. It starts with Alice trying to make a survey of the country and attempting to name, as one might do in geography, the mountains and rivers and towns. Then comes the scene in the railway carriage * * * with [its] remark, 'Language is worth a thousand pounds a word!' Soon after this, two remarks are made to Alice about knowing her own name and knowing the alphabet, and then begins a series of puns, made by the Gnat. It is as if, having got words and references put together at this point (as they were not at the beginning of the chapter, where Alice says, 'Principal mountains—I'm on the only one, but I don't think it's got any name') and having realized the value of it—worth a thousand pounds a word—one can start playing with it. Puns, as we have seen, are a safe enough game for Nonsense, because they are real portmanteaux, where the two meanings are distinct but are incongruously connected by an accident of language formation. After the puns, Alice and the Gnat discuss the purpose of names, and whether they have any use. Then follows another game with words: Alice's horse-fly becomes a rocking-horse-fly, the butterfly a bread-and-butter-fly. A piece of each word is allowed to develop * * * all out of proportion. Images in Nonsense are not allowed to develop, to turn into or mingle with other images as happens in dreams and poetry; but words may do so, provided they merely develop into another word, and by their development accentuate an incongruity. Here again, circumstantial details are given at once: 'Its wings are thin slices of bread-and-butter, its body is a crust, and its head is a lump of sugar.' Looking-Glass Insects, in fact, are not insects at all but compounds of words to which are added lists of properties in the best Nonsense manner.

The next stage is a further discussion on names. 'I suppose you don't want to lose your name? . . . only think how convenient it would be if you could manage to go home without it!' Alice is a little nervous about such an idea, and the Wood where things have no names, to which she proceeds immediately after this conversation, is frighteningly dark. Once in it, she cannot remember her own name or give a name to any of the objects round her. This is a terrifying situation, but Carroll preserves the readers from it by subjecting Alice alone to the experiment; the passage in the book makes no attempt to forgo the use of names. It is at this point that Alice meets the Fawn, a pretty creature 'with its large gentle eyes . . . Such a sweet soft voice it had!' It asks her name, and she makes a similar enquiry, but neither can remember, and they proceed lovingly—the word is Carroll's own—till they emerge from the wood. There each remembers its name and identity, and in a flash they are parted.

This passage is one of the most interesting in the Alices. There is a suggestion here that to lose your name is to gain freedom in some way, since the nameless one would no longer be under control: 'There wouldn't by any name for her to call, and of course you wouldn't have to go, you know.' It also suggests that the loss of language brings with it an increase in loving unity with living things. It is words that separate the fawn and the child.

* * *

Nonsense is a game with words. Its own inventions wander safely between the respective pitfalls of 0 and 1, nothingness and everythingness; but where words without things are safe enough, things without words are far more dangerous. To have no name is to be a kind of nothing:—

> 'What do you call yourself?' the Fawn said . . .
> She answered rather sadly, 'Nothing just now.'

But it is also to have unexpected opportunities for unity and that is a step towards everythingness. We are safe with *brillig* and the *Jabberwock* because that is a fight, a dialectic and an equilibrium; but * * * something has crept in here which words cannot cover, cannot split up and control. There is a nostalgia in each of these scenes:—

> Alice stood looking after it, almost ready to cry with vexation at having lost her dear little fellow-traveller so suddenly.

* * *

But Nonsense can admit of no emotion—that gate to everythingness and nothingness where ultimately words fail completely. It is a game to which emotion is alien, and it will allow none to its playthings, which are words and those wielders of words, human beings. Its humans, like its words and things and Nonsense vocabulary, have to be one, and one, and one. There is nothing more inexorable than a game.

JEAN-JACQUES LECERCLE

The Pragmatics of Nonsense[†]

* * * We might sum up the dialectics of subversion and support according to the following moments, or stages.

The first stage consists in the realisation that in Wonderland, conversationally and otherwise, all is not well—all is not as the governess says it should be. As we know, 'is' has a sad tendency to part ways with 'ought' at an early stage. Alice always remains polite and cooperative, she does as she is bid and is willing to help—the characters do not conform to this irreproachable mode of behaviour. They are gruff, argumentative, insulting and generally unjust. Like Alice, we are shocked at their sophistry and their recourse to eristics. Like her, we realise that these people take advantage of certain *perversions* of language. For this is not simply the unpleasant idiosyncrasies of a mere pack of cards, to be forgotten when we all wake up—these are perversions of *language*, which threaten us with the same pitfalls in our waking state. There is no escaping them, except perhaps by proceeding to the second stage of the dialectics.

Language is an immoral universe. Those perversions seem to bring success to whoever indulges in them. More often than not Alice remains speechless, for she who believes in the maxims of good breeding and grammar is always surprised at the actions that breach them. There is violence in such perverse deviations: characters are liable to be 'suppressed', like the Dormouse in the trial scene in *Alice's Adventures in Wonderland*, deprived of the use of their heads, or destroyed in various ways. * * * The fabric of social life, and the fabric of language, are torn, and *subversion* triumphs. There are no rules left in this social and linguistic chaos, the best emblems of which are the game of croquet and the poem 'They told me you had been to her' in *Alice's Adventures in Wonderland*. All we can do is watch Alice drift aimlessly, and drift ourselves, as all rules and regularities of language and behaviour dissolve. The characters in Wonderland are not even like the villains in Dickens, who know what they are about and will get their comeuppance— they are not evil, but characterised by an arbitrary and thoughtless general acrimony, the linguistic equivalent of the state of nature.

This, however, is only a superficial, or temporary, description of the world of nonsense, which is destined to be cancelled when we reach the third stage of our dialectics. To the interpretation of

† From *Philosophy of Nonsense: The Intuitions of Victorian Nonsense Literature* (New York: Routledge, 1994), 112–14. Copyright © 1994 Routledge. Reproduced by permission of Taylor & Francis Books UK.

Wonderland in terms of existential angst, there will always be an answer accusing Alice, that prim Victorian miss, of invading the Eden of Wonderland and spoiling it with her silly and mean rules and conventions.[1] It might be argued that when she states that it is rude to make personal remarks, she brings guilt and therefore chaos into a natural state of interpersonal freedom where the concept 'rude' does not even exist. Both versions, however, are inadequate: Wonderland is neither totally chaotic nor totally blissful and free. In fact, rather than by chaos, Wonderland is characterised by the emergence of another order, one which is less constraining and more surprising perhaps, but which is nevertheless fairly orderly. The society of Wonderland has its own order—albeit partial and apparently incoherent: one takes turns at deciding the subject of the conversation, as Humpty Dumpty points out; one changes places around the tea table, when the Mad Hatter says that the time has come. And the world of nonsense is itself fairly regular: as we have seen, language is not at all dissolved, but exploited. The rule of exploitation is provided in the preface to *Through the Looking-Glass*. It is a rule of *inversion*, not subversion. The game of nonsense, and the Wonderland it calls into being are the negative moment in the pedagogic dialectics of the acquisition by the child of good manners, in society as in conversation. Once Alice has perceived this negative inverted order she learns to conform to the new rules and to use them for her own purposes. She then becomes a formidable opponent and sometimes triumphs over characters who are, after all, merely cards and chess pieces.

This is the dialectics of the transformation of the pragmatically *infans* into the conversationally skilful speaker. As a result, inversion leads to the fourth stage, *conversion*, when Alice, who has learnt the rules the hard way, comes to accept them; not as painful impositions, but as freely accepted necessities. The linguistic social contract is signed; the importance of linguistic and polite conventions (the definition of which entails their reciprocal recognition by the agents) is firmly impressed on the child's mind. Wonderland is, as far as the rules of politeness and conversation are concerned, the equivalent of the initial situation in Rawls,[2] when the principles of justice and fairness are inevitably chosen.

The mention of Rawls's fictitious, or fictional, 'initial situation' is deliberate. If conversion were to be the climax of my dialectics, we would end up with a cooperative view of conversation and dialogue, and support would overshadow subversion. Since this is obviously not

---

1. James R. Kincaid, "Alice's Invasion of Wonderland," *Publications of the Modern Language Association* 88 (1973): 92–99.
2. John Rawls, *A Theory of Justice* (Cambridge: Harvard UP, 1971).

the case, we need a fifth stage, which I propose to call, if you will pardon the nonsensical coinage, *transversion*. The *Aufhebung*[3] of subversion into conversion, which is the global pedagogic aim pursued by nonsense texts, leaves a trace. Alice is, and is not, a conventional speaker. She will always remember, as the closing words of *Alice's Adventures in Wonderland* state, 'the happy summer days,' not because they will be banal memories of childhood, but because she has undergone an experience which has changed her for good. This ambivalent stage is the true climax of my dialectics. Alice's acceptance of the conventions of linguistic behaviour is no blind adherence, but rather a show of limited and displaced confidence—literally displaced by her journey through Wonderland, that is across the rules and their subversion. This is the moral of nonsense. Rules of language and conventions there are, but one can only conform to them if one has transformed them, if one still transgresses them, or, to borrow a famous phrase, if one supports them, but only under erasure.[4]

GILLES DELEUZE

Thirty-Third Series of Alice's Adventures[†]

* * *

Alice has three parts, which are marked by changes of location. The first part (chapters 1–3), starting with Alice's interminable fall, is completely immersed in the schizoid element of depth. Everything is food, excrement, simulacrum, partial internal object, and poisonous mixture. Alice herself is one of these objects when she is little; when large, she is identified with their receptacle. The oral, anal, and urethral character of this part has often been stressed. But the second part (chapters 4-7) seems to display a change of orientation. To be sure, there is still, and with renewed force, the theme of the house filled by Alice, her preventing the rabbit from entering and her expelling violently the lizard from it (the schizoid sequence child-penis-excrement). But we notice considerable modifications. First, it is in being too large that Alice how plays the role

---

3. *Aufhebung*: ·Georg Wilhelm Friedrich Hegel (1770–1831) and other philosophers use this word to describe the state of an idea (thesis) when it meets its antithesis and is both changed and preserved. [*Editor's note.*]

4. In the writing of the philosopher Jacques Derrida (1930–2004), a word is "under erasure" when it is not exactly appropriate to the idea being expressed but the language offers no better word. [*Editor's note.*]

† From *The Logic of Sense*, tr. Mark Lester, ed. Constantin V. Boundas (New York: Columbia UP, 1990), 234–37. Copyright © 1990 Columbia University Press. Reprinted with permission of the publisher. Copyright © 1969 by Les   Editions de Minuit. Reprinted by permission of Georges Borchardt, Inc. for Les Editions de Minuit.

of the internal object. Moreover, to grow and to shrink no longer occur only in relation to a third term in depth (the key to be reached or the door to pass through in the first part), but rather act of their own accord in a free style, one in relation to the other— that is, they act on high. Carroll has taken pains to indicate that there has been a change, since now it is drinking which brings about growth and eating which causes one to shrink (the reverse was the case in the first part). In particular, causing to grow and causing to shrink are linked to a single object, namely, the mushroom which founds the alternative on its own circularity. Obviously, this impression would be confirmed only if the ambiguous mushroom gives way to a good object, presented explicitly as an object of the heights. The caterpillar, though he sits on top of the mushroom, is insufficient in this regard. It is rather the Cheshire Cat who plays this role: he is the good object, the good penis, the idol or voice of the heights. He incarnates the disjunctions of this new position: unharmed or wounded, since he sometimes presents his entire body, sometimes only his cut off head; present or absent, since he disappears, leaving only his smile, or forms itself from the smile of the good object (provisional complacency with respect to the liberation of sexual drives). In his essence, the cat is he who withdraws and diverts himself. The new alternative or disjunction which he imposes on Alice, in conformity with this essence, appears twice: first, a question of being a baby or a pig, as in the Duchess' kitchen; and then as the sleeping Dormouse seated between the Hare and the Hatter, that is, between an animal who lives in burrows and an artisan who deals with the head, a matter of either taking the side of internal objects or of identifying with the good object of heights. In short, it is a question of choosing between depth and height.[1] In the third part (chapters 8–12), there is again a change of element. Having found again briefly the first location, Alice enters a garden which is inhabited by playing cards without thickness and by flat figures. It is as if Alice, having sufficiently identified herself with the Cheshire Cat, whom she declares to be

---

1. In both cases the cat is present, since he appears initially in the Duchess' kitchen and then counsels Alice to go to see the hare "or" the hatter. The Cheshire Cat's position in the tree or in the sky, all of his traits, including the terrifying ones, identify him with the superego as the "good" object of the heights (idol): "(The Cat) looked good-natured, (Alice) thought: still it had *very* long claws and a great many teeth, so she felt that it ought to be treated with respect." The theme of the entity of the heights, which slips away or withdraws, but which also fights and captures internal objects, is a constant in Carroll's work—it will be found in all of its cruelty in the poems and narratives in which angling occurs (see, for example, the poem "The Two Brothers," in which the younger brother serves as bait). In *Sylvie and Bruno*, the good father, withdrawn to the kingdom of fairies and hidden behind the voice of a dog, is essential; this masterpiece, which also puts into play the theme of the two surfaces—the common surface and the magic or fairy surface—would require a lengthy commentary. * * *

her friend, sees the old depth spread out in front of her, and the animals which occupied it become slaves or inoffensive instruments. It is on this surface that she distributes her images of the father—the image of the father in the course of a trial: "They told me you had been to her, / And mentioned me to him. . . ." But Alice has a foreboding of the dangers of this new element: the manner in which good intentions run the risk of producing abominable results, and the phallus, represented by the Queen, risks turning into castration (" 'Off with her head!' the Queen shouted at the top of her voice"). The surface is burst, ". . . the whole pack rose up into the air, and came flying down upon her. . . ."

One could say that *Through The Looking-Glass* takes up this same story, this same undertaking, but that things here have been displaced or shifted, the first moment being suppressed and the third greatly developed. Instead of the Cheshire Cat being the good voice for Alice, it is Alice who is the good voice for her own, real cats—a scolding voice, loving and withdrawn. Alice, from her height, apprehends the mirror as a pure surface, a continuity of the outside and the inside, of above and below, of reverse and right sides, where "Jabberwocky" spreads itself out in both directions at once. After having behaved briefly once again as the good object or the withdrawn voice vis-à-vis the chess pieces (with all the terrifying attributes of this object or this voice), Alice herself enters the game: she belongs to the surface of the chessboard, which has replaced the mirror, and takes up the task of becoming queen. The squares of the chessboard which must be crossed clearly represent erogenous zones, and becoming-queen refers to the phallus as the agency of coordination. It soon appears that the corresponding problem is no longer that of the unique and withdrawn voice, and that it has rather become the problem of multiple discourses: what must one pay, how much must one pay in order to be able to speak? This question appears in almost every chapter, with the word sometimes referring to a single series (as in the case of the proper name so contracted that it is no longer remembered); sometimes to two convergent series (as in the case of Tweedledum and Tweedledee, so much convergent and continuous as to be indistinguishable); and sometimes to divergent and ramified series (as in the case of Humpty Dumpty, the master of semantemes and paymaster of words, making them ramify and resonate to such a degree as to be incomprehensible, so that their reverse and right sides are no longer distinguishable). But in this simultaneous organization of words and surfaces, the danger already indicated in *Alice* is specified and developed. Again, Alice has distributed her parental images on the surface: the White Queen, the plaintive and wounded mother; the Red King, the withdrawn father, asleep from the fourth chapter onward. But, traversing all depth and height, it is the Red Queen who arrives—the phallus become the agent of castration. It is the final debacle again, this time finished off voluntarily by Alice herself. Something is going to happen, she declares. But what? Would it be a regression to the oral-anal depths, to the point that everything would begin anew, or rather the liberation of another glorious and neutralized surface?

The psychoanalytic diagnosis often formulated with respect to Lewis Carroll notes the following: the impossibility of confronting the Oedipal situation; flight before the father and renunciation of the mother; projection onto the little girl, identified with the phallus but also deprived of a penis; and the oral-anal regression which follows. Such diagnoses, however, have very little interest, and it is well known that the encounter between psychoanalysis and the work of art (or the literary-speculative work) cannot be achieved in this manner. It is not achieved certainly by treating authors, through their work, as possible or real patients, even if they are accorded the benefit of sublimation; it is not achieved by "psychoanalyzing" the work. For authors, if they are great, are more like doctors than patients. We mean that they are themselves astonishing diagnosticians or symptomatologists. There is always a great deal of art involved in the grouping of symptoms, in the organization of a *table* where a particular symptom is dissociated from another, juxtaposed to a third, and forms the new figure of a disorder or illness. Clinicians who are able to renew a symptomatological table produce a work of art; conversely, artists are clinicians, not with respect to their own case, nor even with respect to a case in general; rather, they are clinicians of civilization. In this regard, we cannot follow those who think that Sade has nothing essential to say on sadism, nor Masoch on masochism. It seems, moreover, that an evaluation of symptoms might be achieved only through a *novel*. It is not by chance that the neurotic creates a "familial romance,"[2] and that the Oedipus complex must be found in the meanderings of it. From the perspective of Freud's genius, it is not the complex which provides us with information about Oedipus and Hamlet, but rather Oedipus and Hamlet who provide us with information about the complex.

* * *

The neurotic can only actualize the terms and the story of his novel: the symptoms are this actualization, and the novel has no other meaning. On the contrary, to extract the non-actualizable

---

2. In a familial (or "neurotic") novel, the symptoms are "actualized" in the plot and characters. The "novel as a work of art," on the contrary, disengages "the *event* which it counteractualizes in fictive characters," which is why a work of art cannot be used as an expression of its creator's symptoms. [*Editor's note.*]

part of the pure event from symptoms, * * * to go from the physical surface on which symptoms are played out and actualizations decided to the metaphysical surface on which the pure event stands and is played out, to go from the cause of the symptoms to the quasi-cause of the *œuvre*—this is the object of the novel as a work of art, and what distinguishes it from the familial novel. In other words, the positive, highly affirmative character of desexualization consists in the *replacement of psychic regression by speculative investment*. This does not prevent the speculative investment from bearing upon a sexual object—since the investment disengages the event from it and poses the object as concomitant of the corresponding event: what is a little girl? An entire *œuvre* is needed, not in order to answer this question but in order to evoke and to compose the unique event which makes it into a question. The artist is not only the patient and doctor of civilization, but is also its pervert.

Of this process of desexualization and this leap from one surface to another, we have said almost nothing. Only its power appears in Carroll's work: it appears in the very force with which the basic series (those that esoteric words subsume) are desexualized to the benefit of the alternative to eat/to speak; but also in the force with which the sexual object, the little girl, is maintained. Indeed, the mystery lies in this leap, in this passage from one surface to another, and in what the first surface becomes, skirted over by the second. From the physical chessboard to the logical diagram, or rather from the sensitive surface to the ultra-sensitive plate—it is in this leap that Carroll, a renowned photographer, experiences a pleasure that we might assume to be perverse.

MICHAEL HOLQUIST

What Is a Boojum? Nonsense and Modernism[†]

* * *

The *Snark* is the most perfect nonsense which Carroll created in that it best exemplifies what all his career and all his books sought to do: achieve pure order. For nonsense, in the writings of Lewis Carroll, at any rate, does not mean gibberish; it is not chaos, but the opposite of chaos. It is a closed field of language in which the meaning of any single unit is dependent on its relationship to the system of the other constituents. Nonsense is "a collection of words or events which in their arrangement do not fit into some recognized

† From *Yale French Studies* 43 (1969): 145–64. Reprinted by permission of the publisher and the author.

system" [Elizabeth Sewell, *The Field of Nonsense*, 25], but which constitute a new system of their own. As has recently been said, "what we have learned from Saussure is that, taken singly, signs do not signify anything, and that each one of them does not so much express a meaning as mark a divergence of meaning between itself and other signs . . . The prior whole which Saussure is talking about cannot be the explicit and articulate whole of a complete language as it is recorded in grammars and dictionaries . . . the unity he is talking about is a unity of coexistence, like that of the sections of an arch which shoulder one another. In a unified whole of this kind, the learned parts of a language have an immediate value as a whole, and progress is made less by addition and juxtaposition than by the internal articulation of a function which in its own way is already complete."[1] My argument here is that *The Hunting of the Snark* constitutes such a whole; it is its own system of signs which gain their meaning by constantly dramatizing their differences from signs in other systems. The poem is, in a small way, its own language. This is difficult to grasp because its elements are bound up so closely with the syntax, morphology, and, fleetingly, the semantics of the English language.

Some illustrations, taken from Carroll, may help us here. In the book which most closely approximates the completeness of the system in the *Snark, Through the Looking-Glass*, Humpty Dumpty says in a famous passage: "'When *I* use a word . . . it means just what I choose it to mean—neither more nor less.' 'The question is,' said Alice, 'whether you *can* make words mean so many different things.' 'The question is,' said Humpty Dumpty, 'which is to be master—that's all.'" This last remark is a rebuke to Alice, who has not understood the problem: it is not, as she says, to "make words mean so many *different* things." It is to make a word mean just *one* thing, the thing which its user intends and nothing else. Which is to be master—the system of language which says "'glory' doesn't mean 'a nice knockdown argument'" or Humpty who says it does mean that, and in his system, only that. Nonsense is a system in which, at its purest, words mean only one thing, and they get that meaning through divergence from the system of the nonsense itself, as well as through divergence from an existing language system. This raises, of course, the question of how one understands nonsense. It is a point to which I will return later; for the moment suffice it to say that if meaning in nonsense is dependent on the

1. Maurice Merleau-Ponty, "Indirect Language and the Voices of Silence," *Signs*, tr. Richard C. McCleary (Evanston: Northwestern UP, 1964), 39–40. [Ferdinand de Saussure (1857–1913) was a linguist whose best-known work was translated into English as *A Course in General Linguistics* (*Editor's note*).]

field it constructs, then the difference between nonsense and gibberish is that nonsense is a system which can be learned, as languages are learned. Thus the elements of the system can be
perceived relationally, and therefore meaningfully, within it. Gibberish, on the other hand, is unsystematic.

What this suggests is that nonsense, among other things, is
highly abstract. It is very much like the pure relations which obtain
in mathematics, where ten remains ten, whether ten apples, ten
horses, ten men or ten Bandersnarks. This is an important point,
and helps to define one relationship of nonsense to modernism. For
it suggests a crucial difference between nonsense and the absurd.
The absurd points to a discrepancy between purely human values
and purely logical values. When a computer announces that the
best cure for brain cancer is to amputate the patient's head, it is,
according its system, being logical.[2] But such a conclusion is unset-
tling to the patient and absurd to less involved observers. The
absurd is a contrast between systems of human belief which may
lack all logic, and the extremes of a logic unfettered by human disorder. Thus the absurd is basically play with order and disorder.
Nonsense is play with order only. It achieves its effects not from
contrasting order and confusion, but rather by contrasting one system of order against another system of order, each of which is logical in itself, but which cannot find a place in the other.

*   *   *

The best argument against the *Snark's* allegorization remains, of
course, the poem itself. The interpretation which follows is based
not only on the poem itself, but on the various ways in which it *is*
itself. That is, the poem is best understood as a structure of resistances to other structures of meaning which might be brought to it.
The meaning of the poem consists in the several strategies which
hedge it off as itself, which insure its hermetic nature against the
hermeneutic impulse. Below are six of the many ways by which the
poem gains coherence through inherence.

1. The dedication poem to Gertrude Chataway appears at first
   glance to be simply another of those treacly Victorian set
   pieces Dodgson would compose when he abandoned nonsense for what he sometimes thought was serious literature. But a second reading reveals that the poem contains
   an acrostic: the first letter of each line spells out Gertrude

2. For raising the problems of the relationship between nonsense and the absurd, and for
   the computer example, I am grateful to my friend Jan Kott.

Chataway; a third reading will show that the initial word in the first line of each of the four quatrains constitute another acrostic, Girt, Rude, Chat, Away. This is the first indication in the poem that the words in it exist less for what they denote in the system of English then they do for the system Carroll will erect. That is, the initial four words of each stanza are there less to indicate the four meanings present in them before they were deployed by Carroll they at first convey (clothed, wild, speak, begone) than they are to articulate a purely idiosyncratic pattern of Carroll's own devising.

2. Another index of the systematic arbitrariness of the poem is found in the second quatrain of the first Fit: "Just the place for a Snark! I have said it twice: / That alone should encourage the crew. / Just the place for a Snark! I have said it thrice: / What I tell you three times is true." The rule of three operates in two ways. First of all it is a system for determining a truth that is absolutely unique to this poem. When in Fit 5 the Butcher wishes to prove that the scream he had heard belongs to a Jubjub bird, he succeeds in doing so by repeating three times, "Tis the voice of the Jubbub!" Now, there will be those who say that there is no such thing as a Jubjub bird. But in fact, in the system of the Snark poem, there is—and his existence is definitively confirmed through the proof which that system *itself* provides in the rule of 3. In the game of nonsense that rule, and only that rule, works. The system itself provides the assurance that only it can give meaning to itself.

*　*　*

3. The same effect of an arbitrariness whose sense can be gleaned only from the poem itself is to be found in the various names of the crew members: Bellman, Boots, Bonnet-maker, Barrister, Broker, Billiard-marker, Banker, Beaver, Baker, and Butcher. They all begin with a B. And much ink has been spilled in trying to explain (from the point of view of the allegory a given critic has tried to read into the *Snark*) why this should be so. The obvious answer, if one resists the impulse to substitute something else for the text, is that they all begin with B *because they all begin with B*. The fact that they all have the same initial sound is a parallel that draws attention to itself because it is a parallel. But it is only a parallel at the level where all the crew members on this voyage will be referred to by nouns which have an initial voiced bilabial plosive. In other words, it is a parallel that is

rigidly observed, which dramatizes itself, but only as a dynamic *process* of parellelism, and nothing else.

4. Another way in which the poem sets up resistances which frustrate allegory is to be found in the fifth Fit. The butcher sets out to prove that two can be added to one. "Taking three as the subject to reason about— / A convenient number to state— / We add seven and ten, and then multiply out / By one thousand dimished by eight.

The result we proceed to divide, as you see, / By nine hundred and ninety and two: / Then subtract seventeen, and the answer must be / Exactly and perfectly true."

And in fact the answer is perfectly true—but it is also what you begin with. The equation begins with 3—the number the Butcher is trying to establish—and it ends with 3. The math of the equation looks like this:

$$\frac{(X + 7 + 10)(1000 - 8)}{992} - 17 = X;$$ which simplifies to x, or a pure integer.

The equation is a process which begins with no content and ends with no content. It is a pure process which has no end other than itself. It is thus perhaps the best paradigm of the process of the whole poem: it does what it is about. It is pure surface, but as Oscar Wilde once observed, "there is nothing more profound than surface."

5. A fifth way in which the poem maintains its structural integrity is found in the many coinages it contains, words which Humpty Dumpty defines as portmanteau words, two meanings packed into one word like a portmanteau; words which Gilles Deleuze, in the most comprehensive study of Carroll's significance for language, *Logique du Sens*, has so charmingly translated as "les mots-valies" [Paris: 1969, 59, 268–78]. Carroll, in the introduction to the *Snark* writes, ". . . take the two words 'fuming' and 'furious.' Make up your mind that you will say both words, but have it unsettled which you will say first. Now open your mouth and speak. If your thoughts incline ever so little towards 'fuming' you will say 'fuming-furious;' if they turn by even a hair's breadth towards 'furious,' you will say 'furious-fuming;' but if you have that rarest of gifts, a perfectly balanced mind, you will say 'frumious.'"

"If you have that rarest of gifts, a balanced mind . . . ," in other words, you will find just the right word, and not some approximation. In the seventh Fit, when the Banker is attracked by the Bandersnatch, the bird is described as having "frumious jaws." And the Banker, utterly shaken, chants "in the mimsiest tones," a combination of miserable and flimsy. For a bird which exists only in the system of nonsense, adjectives used to describe objects in other systems will not do; they are not precise enough, and so the system itself provides its own adjective for its own substantive. Since only the Banker has ever been attacked by a Bandersnatch, it is necessary to find a unique adjective adequate to this unique experience: thus "mimsiest." This attempt to find just the right word, and no other, resulting finally in coinages, is another way in which Carroll's search for precision, order, relates him to language as an innovative process in modern literature.

* * *

But the portmanteau word is also the third element of a three part progression, from one, furious, to two, fuming, to three, frumious. Like the rule of three it results in a new "truth," and like the rule of three it is a unique kind of syllogism. In order to get a logical conclusion to the syllogism, it must grow out of a divergence between two prior parallel statements.

This is an important point if one is to see the logic which determines that Carroll's system is a *language* and not gibberish. * * * Carroll's portmanteaux are *words* and not gibberish because they operate according to the rule which says that all coinages in the poem will grow out of the collapse of two known words into a new one. Carroll can deploy words he invents and still communicate because he does so according to rules. Whereas an expression of gibberish would be a sound pattern whose meaning could not be gleaned from its *use* according to rules: an expression of gibberish would be a sound pattern whose meaning could not be gleaned either from the syntactic or morphological principles provided by its use, or which would be deducible according to such principles in a known language system. Nonsense, like gibberish, is a violence practiced on semantics. But since it is systematic, the sense of nonsense can be learned. And that is the value of it: it calls attention to language. Carroll's nonsense keeps us honest; through the process of disorientation and learning which reading him entails, we are made aware again that language is not something we know, but something alive, in process—something to be discovered.

6. The final structure of resistance I'd like to mention is contained in perhaps the most obvious feature of the poem, its

rhyme. William K. Wimsatt, in a well-known essay, makes the point that in a poem the rhyme imposes "upon the logical pattern of expressed argument a kind of fixative counter-pattern of alogical implication."[3] He goes on to say that "rhyme is commonly recognized as a binder in verse structure. But where there is need for binding there must be some difference or separation between the things to be bound. If they are already close together, it is supererogatory to emphasize this by the maneuver of rhyme. So we may say that the greater the difference in meaning between rhyme words the more marked and the more appropriate will be the binding effect."

*   *   *

Professor Wimsatt suggests that "the words of a rhyme, with their curious harmony of sound and distinction of sense, are an amalgam of the sensory and the logical, or an arrest and precipitation of the logical in sensory form; they are the icon in which the idea is caught" (165). I read this to mean that two words which are disparate in meaning result, when bound by rhyme, in a new meaning which was not contained in either of them alone. In other words, you get a kind of rule of three at work. Like the syllogism, two disparate but related elements originate a third. Thus understood, the rhyme of traditional verse has the effect of meaningful surprise; two rhymes will constitute a syllogism resulting in a new association.[4]

But this is not true of nonsense verse. "They sought it with thimbles, they sought it with care; / They pursued it with forks and hope; / They threatened its life with a railway-share; / They charmed it with smiles and soap." This stanza begins each of the last four Fits, and may stand as an example for what rhyme does throughout the poem. The rhyme words, "care, railway-share," and "hope, soap" would be very different from each other in traditional verse, and binding effects of the sort Professor Wimsatt has demonstrated in Pope or Byron would be possible. Because the language of most verse is simply a more efficiently organized means of making sense of the sort that language *outside* verse provides. Thus, while very different, some kind of meaningful association could be made of them capable of catching an idea.

But "care," "railway-share," "hope" and "soap" in this quatrain have as their ambiance *not* the semantic field of the English language, but the field of Carroll's nonsense. In traditional verse "rhyme

3. *The Verbal Icon*, 3rd edition (New York: 1963), 153.
4. For a detailed study of sound/sense patterns in verse see: A. Kibedi Varga, *Les Constantes du poème* (The Hague, 1963), 39–42, 91–121.

words . . . can scarcely appear in a context without showing some difference of meaning" [Wimsatt 156]. But if the whole context of a poem is *without* meaning, its separate parts will also lack it. There can be no differences in meaning between words because they are all equally meaningless in this context. So the reader who attempts to relate rhyme to meaning in Carroll's poem will be frustrated. The syllogism of rhyme, which in other verse has a new meaning as its conclusion, ends, in Carroll's verse, where it began. Instead of aiding meaning, it is another strategy to defeat it. Language in nonsense is thus a seamless garment, a pure cover, absolute surface.

٭   ٭   ٭

For the moral of the *Snark* is that it has no moral. It is a fiction, a thing which does not seek to be "real" or "true." The nineteenth century was a great age of system building and myth makers. We are the heirs of Marx and Freud, and many other prophets as well, all of whom seek to explain *everything*, to make sense out of *everything* in terms of one system or another. In the homogenized world which resulted, it could be seen that art was nothing more than another—and not necessarily privileged—way for economic or psychological forces to express themselves. As Robbe-Grillet says, "Cultural fringes (bits of psychology, ethics, metaphysics, etc.) are all the time being attached to things and making them seem less strange, more comprehensible, more reassuring."[5]

Aware of this danger, authors have fought back, experimenting with new ways to insure the inviolability of their own systems, to invite abrasion, insist on strangeness, create fictions. Lewis Carroll is in some small degree a forerunner of this saving effort. To see his nonsense as a logic is thus far from being an exercise in bloodless formalism. That logic insures the fictionality of his art, and as human beings we need fictions. As is so often the case, Nietzsche said it best: "we have art in order not to die of the truth."[6]

After having stressed at such length that everything in the *Snark* means what it means according to its own system, it is no doubt unnecessary, but in conclusion I would like to answer the question with which we began. What is a Boojum? A Boojum is a Boojum.

5. "A Path for the Future of the Novel," in Maurice Nadeau, *The French Novel Since the War*, tr. A. M. Sheridan Smith (London, 1967), 185. [Alain Robbe-Grillet (1922–2008) was important in formulating and promoting new developments in fiction and film in the 1950s and after. (*Editor's note.*)]
6. *The Will to Power* (1909–10), Book III, Section 822.

ROGER TAYLOR

"All in the Golden Afternoon": The Photographs of Charles Lutwidge Dodgson[†]

When Dodgson decided to take up photography in 1856, it was regarded as the very latest thing—a fashionable pastime that allowed gentlemen to demonstrate their interest in technology, chemistry, and optics as well as to reveal their artistic tendencies. Perhaps it was this symbiosis between science and art that initially attracted Dodgson, but more likely it was the conceptual framework of photography that appealed to his fertile imagination. Through the ground glass of his camera, the view of his world would have been turned upside down and laterally inverted. People hung upside down; the foreground took the place of sky; what lay to the right now appeared on the left. Change the focal length of the lens and large things became small. Shift the focus of the lens and solid objects dissolved until they disappeared from view.

In the deep yellow light of the darkroom, other magic was at work. The alchemy of developing solutions made images appear out of thin air, with the invisible becoming visible, the third dimension reduced to two. Watching the glass plate develop offered a conundrum of reversed tones where white became black and black, white. In the world of photography, the positive became negative and the negative, positive. The transient became permanent and the established, fugitive. Nothing was ever quite what it seemed. To the imagination of the man who was later to write *Alice's Adventures in Wonderland* and *Through the Looking-Glass and What Alice Found There*, all of this must have seemed infinitely appealing.

Although photography may have been attractive to Dodgson for these reasons, there was an even more profound reason he wished to become a photographer. It is clear that he enjoyed a highly developed visual sensibility. Throughout his life he was concerned with the appearance of things and in his diaries noted his response to particular scenes at the theater or works of art at the Royal Academy. When writing, especially for children, he filled his texts with a rich tapestry of images that have endured through countless generations. Given this sensibility, it is hardly surprising that Dodgson wanted to be recognized as an artist. From a very early age he sketched and drew. The family magazines he wrote as a boy at

† From Roger Taylor and Edward Wakeling, *Lewis Carroll, Photographer: The Princeton University Library Albums* (Princeton: Princeton UP, 2002), 11–13, 28–29, 50–51, 66, and 111. Reprinted by permission of the author.

Croft are full of his thumbnail illustrations, which owe more to the comic works of Thomas Hood than to fine art.[1] These childish efforts reveal an early interest in combining narrative structure and pictorial expression, something to which he would return with photography. Later, he drew the illustrations for the manuscript version of *Alice's Adventures Under Ground* that he gave to Alice Liddell as a Christmas present in 1864.

Despite the charm and appeal of these drawings, Dodgson realized his own shortcomings as an artist and looked for other ways to express himself visually. It was the eminent artist and amateur photographer Sir William Newton who suggested "the Camera is by no means calculated to teach the principles of art; but to those who are already well-informed in this respect, and have had practical experience, it may be the means of considerable advancement."[2] Photography offered the perfect way forward and met a number of criteria important to Dodgson. It was not solely a medium of artistic expression, but also a scientifically complex business that required total mastery of each delicate stage of manipulation if it were to succeed. The discipline and order demanded by the process suited Dodgson's love of self-control and sense of purpose. Being the most fashionable hobby that a young man of his social class and education could pursue, it also gave him privileged access to individuals and situations that might otherwise have been denied him. For all these reasons, photography became critically important to the fulfillment of Dodgson's emotional needs and personal development.

*   *   *

Dodgson seldom wrote expansively about photography in his diary. We get brief glimpses of his successes and failures with remarks about "photographing with very slender success." [*Diary* June 26, 1857, 3:73] We learn about whom he photographed and whether he thought them beautiful or striking. We read about his problems with the developing bath and about the faulty safe-light that fogged his plates. He concentrated upon technical matters with never a word about photographic aesthetics or what kind of results he strove to achieve. As so often with Dodgson, we have to look elsewhere to get a bearing on his attitudes and values. In "Hiawatha's Photographing,"[3] his use of irony to describe a portrait session

---

1. Thomas Hood (1799–1845) was a comic poet and illustrator, the editor of a series of *Comic Annuals* and a contributor to *Punch* and other comic journals in the 1830s and 1840s. [*Editor's note.*]
2. In Cuthbert Bede [pseud. Rev. E. Bradley], *Photographic Pleasures* (London: T. McLean, 1855), 33.
3. In *The Complete Works of Lewis Carroll* [see Selected Bibliography], 768–72.

reveals by inversion (a very Carrollian trait) what he valued most about his own photography:

> First the Governor, the Father:
> He suggested velvet curtains
> Looped about a massy pillar;
> And the corner of a table,
> Of a rosewood dining-table.
> He would hold a scroll of something,
> Hold it firmly in his left-hand;
> He would keep his right-hand buried
> (Like Napoleon) in his waistcoat;
> He would contemplate the distance
> With a look of pensive meaning,
> As of ducks that die in tempests.

The pretentious wife fares little better, overadorned in jewels and satin, "Far too gorgeous for an empress. / Gracefully she sat down sideways, / With a simper scarcely human, / Holding in her hand a bouquet / Rather larger than a cabbage." The plain daughter wanted to be taken with a look of "passive beauty," which consisted of squinting and drooping eyes and a "smile that went up sideways / To the corner of the nostrils." Here, in order to make his point, Dodgson comically embellished the pretensions of those aspiring members of the middle classes who sat for studio portraits. But through this satire he positioned himself at the opposite end of the photographic spectrum, where self-assurance, simplicity, beauty, and a lack of ostentation were hallmarks of his class; Dodgson was nothing if not a snob. These values carry through into his photographs, where neither velvet drapes, Napoleonic poses, bouquets, or unpleasant features intrude upon his compositions. Instead, Dodgson's sitters are distinguished, noble, handsome, or beautiful, with never an anxious face to upset the countenance of his idealized world. They are his heroes, heroines, child friends, relatives, and colleagues, all of whom belonged to his social circle, or the one to which he aspired.

* * *

Of all the photographs Dodgson made during his visits to Monk Coniston Park,[4] his portrait of Tennyson and [his son] Hallam in the company of the Marshall family is the most remarkable. Tennyson sits upon a daybed set beneath a tall window, with little Hallam snuggled into his protective lap. To one side sit the Marshalls,

---

4. Monk Coniston Park, in the Lake District in the north of England, was the vacation home of the Marshall family. The Tennysons were on holiday in a house nearby. [*Editor's note.*]

their daughter Julia seated on the floor between the legs of her parents, her face turned in perfect profile. Dodgson's use of light and the structure of his composition break the established photographic conventions of the day. The photograph is dominated by a series of verticals created by the window frame, shutter, and drapes. These alternating bands of light and dark establish a rhythmic flow across the upper part of the image that begins and ends with bands of darkness to contain the composition. At the center of the picture the dark frame of the window coincides with the back of the daybed, effectively dividing the picture into two distinct parts; that of the Tennysons and that of the Marshalls.

This division is reinforced by differences in pose. Tennyson sits hunched on the daybed, with his arms protectively wrapped around Hallam and his knees drawn up as if to shield the boy from the camera. From the dark shadow of his face Tennyson's eye glints warily at the camera, watchful and mistrusting. This is a cameo portrait of a father protecting his son from a world he knows to be wicked and threatening. The Marshalls adopted an altogether different set of poses. True to the image of a Victorian industrialist, James Marshall sits bolt upright, his face set with an unyielding expression. His wife, her head slightly bowed as if in thought, leans upon her husband, his arm around her. Seated at their feet, their daughter Julia is sheltered from the world on both sides by the impressive barrier of her father and the skirts of her mother. Here we have two expressions of parental affection: the one loving but hermetic, the other cool and unresponsive. * * * Dodgson moved past the immediate subject matter of Tennyson and Marshall to direct attention to relationships between children and their parents.

* * *

Not all Dodgson's photographs were elaborately staged and formally posed. In one notable example the very opposite is the case. He promised Kathleen Tidy, the daughter of friends in Yorkshire, that he would photograph her for her seventh birthday. When his first attempt "failed" he tried again two days later on her birthday but "with little success." [*Diaries* April 1, 1858, 3:169, 170] When Dodgson chose to photograph Kathleen perched on the branch of a tree, he cast aside all previous conceptions of photographic portraiture in favor of the unconventional. As a rule, photographers did not take portraits with the subject's face partially obscured by branches. Why did Dodgson deliberately choose this unorthodox setting and how did he expect the photograph to succeed? Was it that he subconsciously wanted to liberate the child and give her a degree of freedom that her attire and social position made impossible? Although we can never know Dodgson's true intent, we

Plate 35
Tennysons and Marshalls
29 September 1857
Monk Coniston Park, Ambleside
5¼ × 5⅝ in. (13.1 × 14.3 cm)
A(I): 34

recognize the achievement of his portrait because of its modernity. It has all the spontaneity of a snapshot made in an instant with a Kodak. The portrait has little formal compositional structure. The intervening branches become confused with the tartan pattern of the skirt to create a web of detail that veils the figure. Kathleen's face, the usual focus of attention in a portrait, is crisscrossed with twigs, one of which appears to press into her cheek. The differential focus of the branches heightens the sense of intrusion, as if the photographer had glanced upward to discover Kathleen hiding in the tree. Everything about this photograph suggests it was made spontaneously, whereas the reverse was the case, with Dodgson struggling to create a successful image. But to Dodgson, the mathematician with a profound love of logic, the most logical thing for him to do was to be illogical.

※   ※   ※

During the course of Dodgson's twenty-five years as a photographer, it is hardly surprising that his involvement with photography ebbed and flowed in response to his circumstances and other commitments. But there was never a real crisis about how he was to move forward to the next season and the next body of work. His concentration on portraiture ensured that he would never be short of material so long as he could get out and about to meet new and interesting families and their children. Concentrating largely, though not exclusively, on children as sitters enabled him to regenerate his enthusiasm with each new discovery. To him, children were magical, a gift from God that gave meaning and purpose to his life as a bachelor, reverend gentleman, and children's author. Their enjoyment of his company reaffirmed his sense of humanity and kept the vital spark of his creativity very much alive as part of his daily life. Only weeks before his death on 14 January 1898 he was still meeting children, sketching with Gertrude Thomson, and sitting up until 4 A.M. trying to solve a mathematical problem that had been sent him. Charles Lutwidge Dodgson was no ordinary man. He was a polymath of remarkable talent whose legacy still enriches our lives through his literature and this extraordinary body of photographs.

CAROL MAVOR

Utopographs, or The Myth of Everlasting Flowers[†]

*   *   *

Part of the appeal of understanding little girls as without sex is that it is avoidance of death. For sex is always connected with death. Little girls eventually leave their childhood beds * * * only to fly to their wedding bed, which brings them to their birthing bed, which brings them that much closer to their deathbed. (As Carroll wrote in the prefatory poem to *Through the Looking-Glass:* "We are but older children, dear, / Who fret to find our bedtime near.") In order to stop this flight, Carroll ensured that his little girls would always be beautiful and everlasting by capturing them on the photographic plate (an everlasting flower bed), before their eventual bloom of womanly breasts and hips, and their unstoppable wilt. Carroll's little girls, pasted into his albums, were flattened flower buds—some from last spring, others from many springtimes ago—all pressed, pasted, preserved, and arranged into Victorian albums. All about

† From *Pleasures Taken: Performances of Sexuality and Loss in Victorian Photographs* (Durham, NC: Duke UP, 1995), 25–27, 42. Reprinted by permission of the author.

the same age, despite different birthdates. Carroll wanted his child-friends to be forever little, to remain as Persephone was *before* she plucked the tender, sweet-smelling narcissus that metaphorically stood for her own breakage, loss, and marked change. Carroll wanted to avoid the disappointment and anxiety that Alice experiences when she futilely attempts to hold onto her plucked "dream-rushes" in *Through the Looking-Glass*. The "darling scented rushes" are symbols of Carroll's girl-child friends.

*   *   *

The photograph became, for Carroll, the contradictory medium to hold the little girl forever young in the looking glass. We can see the photograph as temporal in the sense that it records a specific moment, a split second in the young sitter's life, yet also as "eternal" in that it is everlasting and not subject to change (neither a moment, nor eternity). The little girls are strange Marinesque flowers, sexual but without the sexual organs to generate themselves;[1] their only reproduction is photographic reproduction, infinitely repeated as sameness.* * *

But the split between temporality and eternity is not the only contradiction within the photograph. There is also a play between "real" and "unreal"—much as the little girl is "sexual" and "not sexual" or "woman" and "not woman." Barthes addresses the paradox of the photographic medium in "The Photographic Message," where he argues that the photograph is paradoxical due to the coexistence of two messages,

> the one without a code (the photographic analogue), the other with a code (the "art" or the treatment, or the "writing," or the rhetoric, of the photograph); structurally, the paradox is clearly not the collusion of a denoted message and a connoted message (which is the—probably inevitable—status of all the forms of mass communication), it is that here the connoted (or coded) message develops on the basis of a message *without a code.*[2]

In the case of Carroll's photography, we can see that the photograph is a portmanteau of the art object and reality. Like the large leather suitcase that opens up into two compartments, two bags in one (or even like the invented portmanteau double-words of Carroll's *Looking-Glass* world), the photograph is the baggage that encases the two: the photographic "analogue" / the denoted message and the connoted message / the treatment of the photograph—its "art."

---

1. John Marin (1870–1953) was an American painter and watercolorist whose seascapes and landscapes especially are marked by delicate forms and diffused light. [*Editor's note.*]
2. In *Image/Music/Text*, tr. Stephen Heath (New York: Hill and Wang, 1977), 19.

That the photograph presents itself as both real and not real allows
Carroll to believe in the myth of everlasting flowers, the myth that
girls like Alice Liddell will remain "forever little."

*   *   *

This undecidability is poignantly demonstrated in a scene, which is
neither fictitious nor true, from Gavin Millar's film, *Dreamchild*
(1985). The scene features Alice, her mother, one of Alice's sisters,
"Mr. Dodgson," and Mr. Duckworth seated in a row boat that is
floating down a beautiful river lined with wild flowers and (perhaps) "real scented rushes." Alice stories have been told. It has been
a perfect summer day . . . until now. Mr. Dodgson has begun to
stare at Alice. His eyes are filled with an overwhelming, uncomfortable sort of love. His gaze, painful for all involved, does not go
unnoticed by Alice. It is clear that she has *experienced* it before and
that her sister has seen it before (but neither girl blushes). Without
warning, Alice puts a stop to the look by giving Mr. Dodgson a big
cold splash of river water right in the eyes. Humiliation washes over
his face. The water streams down his cheeks, as if he were crying
the incredulous tears of the Mock Turtle—as if he were shedding
not drops but gallons of tears (as Alice once did in Wonderland). If
Mr. Dodgson were not entirely speechless, he would be stuttering.
Mrs. Liddell sternly insists that Alice apologize to him. Then, with
unnerving "knowledge" and defiance, Alice not only apologizes but
also uses her white lace handkerchief to soak up the water from
Mr. Dodgson's pathetic face—sensually drawing the moment out as
if the water were tears, tears shared between lovers, until we and
Alice's mother cannot take it anymore. His gaze, a white lace handkerchief, a performative little girl, a sexuality without parameters:
these are the contradictions at play, in those photographs of Carroll's that feature a "complex fantasm" we call "the girl."

JEAN GATTÉGNO

Mathematics†

*   *   *

As long as he was lecturing—in other words, until 1881—Carroll
used his mathematical talents in the service of pedagogy, producing manuals, glossaries, books of problems and exercises, etc., for
students. His many works on Euclid were also, in a more general

† From *Lewis Carroll: Fragments of a Looking Glass*, tr. Rosemary Sheed (New York:
  Crowell, 1974), 143–48. Reprinted by permission.

way, written with this kind of concern to popularize. He certainly sought, in addition, to defend a geometry that was under attack from all sides, though he never examined the non-Euclidian geometries. Equally certainly, in his linking of algebra and geometry, he was endeavoring to follow the mathematical developments of the day. But the thing above all that he was aiming to do was to translate into a language accessible to everybody (or almost everybody) ideas and problems traditionally the preserve of specialists. His method of popularizing was intelligent and sometimes humorous, especially in his masterpiece in that field, *Euclid and His Modern Rivals*. As the title indicates, the author wanted to ensure Euclid's triumph over his rivals—in respect to his fundamental postulate concerning parallels. But the form he chose is somewhat unusual: a trial in Hell, with Minos and Rhadamanthus sitting in judgment on the "Euclid-wreckers." In this dramatic style, twelve of the latter (with their manuals) are dispatched by Carroll to Mathematical Hell. Aware that his readers might find this approach surprising, especially coming from the pen of "Charles L. Dodgson, M.A., Senior Student and Mathematical Lecturer of Christ Church, Oxford," the author provides an apologia in a prologue, headed with a quotation from Horace:

> *Ridentem dicere verum*
> *Quid vetat?*[1]

> It is presented in a dramatic form partly because it seemed a better way of exhibiting in alternation the arguments on the two sides of the question; partly that I might feel myself at liberty to treat it in a rather lighter style than would have suited an essay, and thus to make it a little less tedious and a little more acceptable to my unscientific readers.
>
> In one respect this book is an experiment and may chance to prove a failure: I mean that I have not thought it necessary to maintain throughout the gravity of style which scientific writers usually affect, and which has somehow come to be regarded as an 'inseparable accident' of scientific teaching. I never could quite see the reasonableness of this immemorial law: subjects there are, no doubt, which are in their essence too serious to admit of any lightness of treatment—but I cannot recognize Geometry as one of them. * * *

Aside from the originality of this approach to Euclid, the style is noteworthy, for it prefigures an event then in gestation, which was to occur the following year: the entry into mathematics of "Lewis

---

1. "What is to prevent a laughing man from saying what is true?" (*Euclid* . . . London, 1882, pp. ix–x).

Carroll." Though, in fact, all the works I have so far mentioned were attributed to C. L. Dodgson, it was in 1880 that there began to appear—in a women's magazine, *The Monthly Packet*—what was to be published in full in 1885 as *A Tangled Tale*.[2] The terms in which Carroll introduces it are strongly reminiscent of the Euclid prologue:

> The writer's intention was to embody in each Knot [problem] (like the medicine so dexterously, but ineffectually, concealed in the jam of our early childhood) one or more mathematical questions—in Arithmetic, Algebra, or Geometry, as the case might be—for the amusement, and possible edification, of the fair readers of that Magazine.

It is not only in its title, plainly avowing itself a "tale," and its structure, divided into ten short stories, independent yet inter-linked, that Carroll takes over from Dodgson, the Mathematical Tutor. Above all, it is in the reference to *Alice*, explicit in the word "knot," which sends us directly back to one of Alice's unintentional puns in the chapter, "A Caucus-Race and a Long Tale." And lest any doubts remain, Carroll returns to the theme in his conclusion, explaining why he cannot continue the tale *ad infinitum*:

> My puppets were neither distinctly *in* my life (like those I now address), nor yet (like Alice and the Mock Turtle) distinctly *out* of it. [p. 152]

A Tangled Tale, then, with its mixture of fiction-cum-nonsense and mathematics (Carroll always gave the answers to the problems he had set after his readers had sent in their own) represents a marked change. Mathematics, which the literary writer had up to then excluded from his domain, was now invading it, but being altered in the process. *Having been a science, they were becoming a game.*[3] And it was his vocation as a teacher, his desire to communi-cate, that led to the change. Indeed, the thing was all of a piece: remember that it was in 1881 that Carroll resigned the Lectureship, and in 1877 that he had written the first *Memoria Technica*, a mne-monic game in which his taste for figures and his love of words are perfectly combined. And, though the first part of *Curiosa Mathemat-ica* (published in 1888) was still very Euclidian, the second (1893) had developed into something quite different—a series of "Pillow

2. London, 1885. Reproduced in *Pillow Problems and a Tangled Tale* (New York, Dover, 1958).
3. Note, though, that the idea of trying to turn mathematics into a game dated back to 1856 at least. During his brief experience at teaching schoolchildren, he wrote in his diary: "Varied the lesson at the school with a story, introducing a number of sums to be worked out" [Feb. 5, 1856: *Diaries* 2:34]

Problems," as the subtitle called them. Both were, in fact, signed "Charles L. Dodgson," but the changeover from the demonstration of the first to the problems (with solutions appended) of the second represented precisely that changeover from theory to games that we have been witnessing.

The introduction to *Pillow Problems* leaves us in no doubt, since Carroll makes a point of stressing that it is not with any aim of advancing science, but simply to satisfy the need to occupy the empty hours of the day, or the night, that he presents these games:

> My motive, for publishing these Problems, with their mentally-worked solutions, is most certainly *not* any desire to display powers of mental calculation. Mine, I feel sure, are nothing out-of-the-way; and I have no doubt there are many mathematicians who could produce, mentally, much shorter and better solutions. It is not for such persons that I intend my little book; but rather for the much larger class of *ordinary* mathematicians, who perhaps have never tried this resource, when mental occupation was needed, and who will, I hope, feel encouraged—by seeing what can be done, after a little practice, by one of *average* mathematical powers—to try the experiment for themselves, and find in it as much advantage and comfort as I have done. [xiii–xiv]

The word *comfort* is perhaps a little surprising, as Carroll himself remarks, and it leads him on to a passage which is often quoted in support of hypotheses regarding his "religious doubts" and "sexual obsessions":

> Perhaps I may venture, for a moment, to use a more serious tone, and to point out that there are mental troubles, much worse than mere worry, for which an absorbing subject of thought may serve as a remedy. There are sceptical thoughts, which seem for the moment to uproot the firmest faith; there are blasphemous thoughts, which dart unbidden into the most reverent souls; there are unholy thoughts, which torture, with their hateful presence, the fancy that would fain be pure.

A far cry, it seems, from the "games" we were speaking of earlier. But only partly so. For, though it is true that these lines express a gravity we do not associate with entertainment, they also introduce a new factor into mathematics, and use it for a purpose very different from its traditional role. The aim here is not mathematical, or scientific—not even as in applied science—but something quite different: to turn mathematics into a pure *pastime* is a really fundamental change.

It was as a pastime, furthermore, that Carroll returned to mathematics and made it part of his everyday life. To judge from his diaries, the last years of his life were absolutely shot through with his "discoveries"—always worked out mentally, and always following the same pattern: sleeplessness or interrupted sleep, and then a sudden illumination. This note, dated November 12, 1897 [*Diaries* 9:351] is a typical example:

> An inventive morning! After waking, and before I had finished dressing, I had devised a new, and much neater, form in which to work my Rules for Long Division, and also decided to bring out my *Games and Puzzles* and Part III of *Curiosa Mathematica*, in *Numbers*, in paper covers, paged consecutively, to be ultimately issued in boards.

Mathematics, from the science it had been when he was an undergraduate, from the discipline it had represented when he was a Lecturer, had become both a "curiosity" and, literally, an essential pastime.

That it was essential to him is not sufficiently recognized. Several of his biographers, referring to one of the very few mathematicians who have troubled to compare Carroll's work with the mathematics of his day,[4] have assented to his conclusion: "In all of Dodgson's mathematical writings, it is evident that he was not an important mathematician." And even though Bourbaki[5] is of a somewhat different opinion, I would not go to the stake in defense of Carroll's contribution to the science of mathematics. On the other hand, I think it important to stress the major part played not only by his mathematical training, but, more importantly, by his profound immersion in mathematics, in both his work[6] and his life. For it is that immersion that accounts for the mass of pamphlets, letters, and lampoons which filled so much of his leisure during the second half of his life—pieces which, whether arguing the finer points of a system of proportional representation or proposing a new method for the rotation of proctors[7] (and in one year he published no fewer than five texts on each of these subjects), were all quite definitely mathematically inspired. * * *

---

4. Warren Weaver, "Lewis Carroll, Mathematician," *Scientific American*, April 1956.
5. N. Bourbaki speaks of the "theorems on linear systems with real or complex coefficients thus elucidated, in an obscure textbook, with characteristic attention to detail, by the famous author of *Alice in Wonderland*" (*Eléments d'histoire des mathématiques*, Paris, 1969, p. 87).
6. I would refer readers to Elizabeth Sewell's excellent book, *The Field of Nonsense*, London, 1952.
7. "Proctors" were members of the teaching staff appointed in rotation to ensure the maintenance of discipline among the students within the area of the university.

HELENA M. PYCIOR

[Mathematics and Humor]†

Augustus de Morgan introduced chapter II of his *Trigonometry and Double Algebra* of 1849 with a précis of symbolical algebra: "*With one exception*, no word nor sign of arithmetic or algebra has one atom of meaning throughout this chapter, the object of which is *symbols, and their laws of combination*, giving a *symbolic algebra*."[1] Slightly over fifteen years later, Lewis Carroll's Alice interrupted the trial of the Knave to state her opinion of the nonsense verse read by the White Rabbit. "*I* don't believe," Alice declared, "there's an atom of meaning in it."

The concidence of language in De Morgan's algebraic textbook and Carroll's *Alice's Adventures in Wonderland* is not accidental. Charles Lutwidge Dodgson's mathematical training and interests influenced the literary works he published under the pseudonym of Lewis Carroll. The *Alices* embodied the mathematician Dodgson's misgivings about symbolical algebra, the major British contribution to mathematics of the first half of the nineteenth century. The theme of meaninglessness, emphasized in earlier interpretations of the *Alices*,[2] can be traced back to Dodgson's encounter with the symbolical approach; the roots of his nonsense verse may also be in symbolical algebra, which stressed in mathematics structure over meaning.

* * *

Dodgson's mature introduction to advanced mathematics, including symbolical algebra, seems to have taken place a decade before publication of *Alice in Wonderland*—during the summer of 1854 when, nearing completion of his undergraduate program at Christ's Church, Oxford (which was sorely deficient in mathematics and science), he studied mathematics under Bartholomew Price, then a fellow and tutor of Pembroke College. From Price, Dodgson learned calculus "swimmingly." [*Letters* Aug 23, 1854, I.29]. In addition, he discussed algebra with Price. * * * Thus, also from Price, Dodgson

† From "At the Intersection of Mathematics and Humor: Lewis Carroll's *"Alices"* and Symbolical Algebra," *Victorian Studies* 28.1 (1984): 149, 161–63, 165–66, 168–70. Reprinted by permission of Indiana University Press.

1. Augustus De Morgan, *Trigonometry and Double Algebra* (London: Taylor, Walton, and Maberly, 1849), 101. I wish to thank Roland Stromberg, who encouraged me to write a paper on humor and Victorian mathematics.
2. See, for example, Donald Rackin, "Alice's Journey to the End of Night," *PMLA* 81 (1966): 313–326, and "Blessed Rage: Lewis Carroll and the Modern Quest for Order," in *Lewis Carroll: A Celebration*, ed. Edward Guiliano (New York: Clarkson Potter, 1982), 15–25.

probably acquired a familiarity with and ambivalence towards symbolical algebra. As indicated by one of Dodgson's letters written during this summer to Mary Dodgson [*Letters* I.26–29], Price encouraged him to question the legitimacy of extending algebraic terms to cover situations beyond their original definitions. Dodgson now asked what multiplication of lines could mean. Multiplication of a real number by a counting number is easy to conceptualize and define. Thus, four times five involves taking five four times, or adding five to five to five to five. [But] nineteenth-century mathematics had moved far beyond multiplication by counting numbers. Negatives were routinely multiplied by negatives, imaginaries by imaginaries, and even lines by lines. Taking his characteristically literal approach, Dodgson questioned the appropriateness of using a single term "multiplication" to cover operations on such different objects as numbers and lines. As he explained, "my question was solely one of *words*. 'What likeness is there in the two *operations* to justify our calling them by the same *name*?' I am not nearly satisfied yet on the subject." [*Letters* I.28]

* * *

Dodgson ignored symbolical algebra because it was inimical to the traditional view of mathematics which he held to the end of his life: algebraic meaninglessness and arbitrariness went directly counter to his deep-seated belief in the absolute certainty or truth of mathematics. It was, indeed, according to Dodgson, its certainty which made mathematics superior to other sciences and therefore attractive to the human mind. Thus in *Curiosa Mathematica*, Dodgson explained that other sciences led to provisional knowledge, but:

> The charm [of mathematics] lies chiefly, I think, in the absolute *certainty* of its results: for that is what, beyond almost all mental treasures, the human intellect craves for. Let us only be sure of *something*! More light, more light! . . . "And, if our fate be death, give light and let us die!"[3] This is the cry that, through all the ages, is going up from perplexed Humanity, and Science has little else to offer, that will really meet the demands of its votaries, than the conclusions of Pure Mathematics. (xv)

Dodgson's reference to "absolute *certainty*" made it clear that, for him, mathematics guaranteed more than logical certainty (or assurance of the logical affiliation of certain ideas). It guaranteed

---

3. "More light": the last words of Goethe on his deathbed. "And if our fate be death" is a line from a poem by John Keble (1792–1866) in *The Christian Year* (1866), "Sixth Sunday after Epiphany." [*Editor's note*]

truth—in Dodgson's words, "certain universally-true Theorems," some of which were "provable from genuine Axioms (i.e. from Axioms whose self-evident character is indisputable)." Attending Dodgson's belief in self-evident axioms leading to true theorems was, of course, commitment to the meaningfulness of mathematics. According to him, mathematics began first of all with human penetration of the meaning of the axioms, and then assent to them. "Now," he wrote, "there is one preliminary step, that is absolutely indispensable before the human intellect can accept any Axiom whatever: and that is, it must attach some *meaning* to it. We cannot, rationally, either assent to, or deny, any Proposition the words of which convey to us no idea" (*Curiosa Mathematica*, xv, 62, 67–68). Thus the certainty—and hence the beauty and intellectual significance—of mathematics depended ultimately on meaningful, self-evident axioms, the opposite of the meaningless, arbitrary signs, symbols, and rules of symbolical algebra. It is, then, no wonder that Dodgson, mathematical teacher and author, steered clear of the new algebra.

While symbolical algebra found no place in Dodgson's mathematics and teaching, there is evidence to suggest that it worried him and played upon his imagination in such a way that he was led to express his concern in the *Alices*. Dodgson's struggle with the question of algebraic meaning, hinted at in his letter to Mary Dodgson in the summer of 1854, and his composition of the germs of *Alice in Wonderland* coincided in time. As a fellow student in Price's reading party of the summer of 1854 later recounted:

> Dodgson and I were both pupils of Professor Bartholomew Price . . . in a mathematical Reading Party at Whitby in the summer of 1854. It was there that *Alice* was incubated. Dodgson used to sit on a rock on the beach, telling stories to a circle of eager young listeners of both sexes. These stories were afterwards developed and consolidated into their present form.[4]

Thus, it was with visions of lines multiplied by lines, quantities less than nothing, and symbolical algebra dancing in his head that Dodgson first set about constructing an other-world (the underground) in which meaninglessness and arbitrariness prevailed.

*   *   *

[The *Alices* refer] directly and indirectly to the breakdown of mathematics as a science of absolute truths following development of the symbolical approach to algebra. Alice's recognition of the

---

4. Footnote in *Letters* 1:26. Quotation from [Thomas Fowler], "Our Lewis Carroll Memorial," *St. James Gazette* 36 (March 11, 1898): 7.

potential meaninglessness and arbitrariness of mathematics, in fact, comes early in *Alice in Wonderland*. Subjected to the vagaries of her underground experience, such as changes in her size, Alice comes to question even her identity. She wonders if she is Ada or Mabel, two of her above-ground friends. In this epistemological crisis, reminiscent of Descartes' in the *Discourse on Method*, Alice imitates the French philosopher by trying to establish what she knows with certainty. It is not surprising that Alice turns first to mathematics, given its privileged position in Victorian culture. If there is any truth or certainty in the natural world, her Victorian contemporaries would have agreed, it is evidenced by mathematics. But at this point mathematics fails to prove a bedrock of knowledge. Alice multiplies in a nondecimal base and finds that the multiplication leads nowhere in particular. For review, Alice says:

> "I'll try if I know all the things I used to know. Let me see: four times five is twelve, and four times six is thirteen, and four times seven is—oh dear! I shall never get to twenty at that rate! However, the Multiplication Table doesn't signify: let's try Geography."

Carroll's choice of a varying nondecimal base is designed, I believe, to indicate the arbitrariness of mathematics.[5] Mathematicians are free to calculate in any base they choose; there is nothing sacred about the base ten. But in addition to the arbitrariness of mathematics, the passage alludes to its meaninglessness. Alice clearly states that "the Multiplication Table doesn't signify." Besides punning on the meaninglessness of mathematics, the verb "signify" for Carroll may also have been associated with mathematical writings of the symbolical algebraists, where it was frequently used.[6] Their main point—and Alice's as expressed here—was that algebra (in Alice's case, arithmetic) is basically meaningless, that its symbols (here, numbers) stand for nothing in particular. Alice finds that mathematics is no mainstay of truth and certainty, and cannot save her from the madness of the underground world. Viewed from this perspective, the meaninglessness and arbitrariness of symbolical algebra provide a key to the meaninglessness and arbitrariness of Carroll's underground world.

* * *

---

5. For a brief discussion of different interpretations of Alice's calculations, see Gardner, *The Annotated Alice*, 23. [See Selected Bibliography.]
6. In *Trigonometry and Double Algebra*, De Morgan used the term "significant algebras" for those in which all symbols and combinations of symbols were meaningful (101).

The argument that Lewis Carroll had symbolical algebra in mind fits well with the meaninglessness which Donald Rackin[7] finds in the *Alices*. * * * According to Rackin, Alice's "quest serves, vicariously, as the reader's metaphorical search for meaning in the lawless, haphazard universe of his deepest consciousness":

> Merely to list the reverses Alice encounters in Wonderland is to survey at a glance an almost total destruction of the fabric of our so-called logical, orderly, and coherent approach to the world. Practically all pattern, save the consistency of chaos, is annihilated. First, there are the usual modes of thought— ordinary mathematics and logic: in Wonderland they possess absolutely no meaning. Next are the even more basic social and linguistic conventions: these too lose all validity. . . . [T]he essence of Alice's adventures beneath commonly accepted ground is the grimmest comedy conceivable, the comedy of man's absurd condition in an apparently meaningless world. [313–14]

Alice, of course, finally rebels against the meaninglessness of Wonderland. According to Rackin, the rebellion sets in when she meets the King and Queen of Hearts. As the rulers of Wonderland, they "should hold the secret of their realm's meaning and be the ultimate source of its order." But the King, Queen, and their attendants are, as Rackin says, "mere abstract, manufactured, and arbitrary symbols—just a pack of cards, pictures of kings and queens, men and women" [322].

Here Dodgson's acquaintance with symbolical algebra can illuminate Rackin's analysis. The *Alices* deal with the search for meaning in a meaningless world—a world in which even mathematics no longer signifies. The loss of meaningful mathematics is tantamount to the loss of human certainty, since as Dodgson indicated in his mathematical works, mathematics alone guaranteed absolute truth.

* * *

This response of Carroll to symbolical algebra in the *Alices*, then, suggests that the crises of faith which the Victorians experienced were not always the result of the breakdown of religion under the impact of science. Carroll was concerned instead, albeit humorously, with the breakdown of older mathematical certainty under the impact of the new algebra.

Elizabeth Sewell's view of nonsense as a game similarly accords well with the claim for symbolical algebra as an antecedent of Carroll's literary works. "If neither prose nor poetry," she asks, "can

7. "Alice's Journey to the End of Night" [see Selected Bibliography]. [*Editor's note.*]

provide the necessary structure for Nonsense, is there some other system by which language could be organized into an independent and consistent, if nonsensical, structure?" She finds such structure in game rules, or "an enclosed whole, with its own rigid laws which cannot be questioned within the game itself."[8] This description fits symbolical algebra, or any other modern mathematical system. But more importantly from an historical perspective, in appealing to the analogy of the game, Sewell hit on the exact analogy used by De Morgan when trying to explain symbolical algebra to his contemporaries. As early as 1835, for example, De Morgan compared mathematics to dominoes; later, he compared symbolical algebra to putting together a dissected map whose pieces had been turned upside down.

In short, the theses of the tradition of combining mathematics and humor as a background to Dodgson's stories and of an integral relationship between his algebraic views and the *Alices* are well supported. The latter thesis also fits well with earlier interpretations of the *Alices*. The facts that the *Alices* deal with a search for meaning in a meaningless world, that Dodgson's nonsense emphasizes structure over meaning, that the analogy of a game is appropriate to his literature, and that Dodgson was acquainted with and yet uneasy about the symbolical approach all point to symbolical algebra as a major influence on the *Alices*. The *Alices* were, at least partly, expressions of Dodgson's anxiety over the loss of certainty implicit in mathematicians' acceptance of the symbolical approach. Alice's bewilderment in Wonderland paralleled Dodgson's bewilderment in the mathematical world of the symbolical algebraists. Alice's response to the chaos of the underground—retreat—paralleled Dodgson's response to symbolical algebra—the ignoring of it in his serious mathematical writings and teachings. But while Alice could flee Wonderland and leave the chaos behind, Dodgson could never completely escape the symbolical approach. Denied a place in his mathematics, the themes and techniques of symbolical algebra found an outlet in his fantasy writings.

8. *The Field of Nonsense* [see pp. 346–50 of this Norton Critical Edition], 24–25.

Selected Bibliography

Works excerpted for this edition are not listed here.

DODGSON'S WRITINGS, LETTERS, AND DIARIES

Alice's Adventures Under Ground: A Facsimile of the Original Lewis Carroll Manuscript. Microfilm. Ann Arbor: University Microfilms, 1964; New York: Panda, 1953; London: Pavilion, 1985.

Bartley, William Warren, III, ed. *Lewis Carroll's Symbolic Logic.* New and updated ed. New York: C. N. Potter, 1986. The excellent introduction makes a good case for Dodgson's innovative thinking as a mathematical logician.

Brown, Sally. *The Original Alice: From Manuscript to Wonderland.* London: British Library, 1997.

Cohen, Morton N., ed. *Lewis Carroll and the Kitchins: Containing Twenty-five Letters Not Previously Published and Nineteen of His Photographs.* New York: Lewis Carroll Society of North America, 1980.

———. *The Selected Letters of Lewis Carroll.* 2nd ed. Basingstoke: Macmillan, 1989.

———, and Edward Wakeling, eds. *Lewis Carroll and His Illustrators: Collaborations and Correspondence, 1865–1898.* Ithaca, NY: Cornell UP, 2003.

Fisher, John, ed. *The Magic of Lewis Carroll.* New York: Simon and Schuster, 1973.

Gardner, Martin. *The Universe in a Handkerchief: Lewis Carroll's Mathematical Recreations, Games, Puzzles, and Word Play.* New York: Copernicus, 1996.

———, ed. *The Annotated Alice: Alice's Adventures in Wonderland & Through the Looking-Glass—The Definitive Edition.* New York: Norton, 2000.

———, ed. *The Annotated Hunting of the Snark: The Full Text of Lewis Carroll's Great Nonsense Epic—The Definitive Edition.* With illustrations by Henry Holiday. New York: Norton, 2006.

Goodacre, Selwyn H., ed. *Lewis Carroll's Alice's Adventures in Wonderland* (Pennyroyal Press edition). With notes by James R. Kincaid and illustrations by Barry Moser. West Hatfield, MA: Pennyroyal Press, 1982.

———. *Lewis Carroll's Through the Looking-Glass, and What Alice Found There* (Pennyroyal Press edition). With notes by James R. Kincaid and illustrations by Barry Moser. West Hatfield, MA: Pennyroyal Press, 1982.

Green, Roger Lancelyn, ed. *The Diaries of Lewis Carroll.* Two vols. New York: Oxford UP, 1954. Superseded by Edward Wakeling's edition of *Lewis Carroll's Diaries* (see citation on p. 254), but useful for notes and commentary.

Guiliano, Edward, ed. *The Complete Illustrated Works of Lewis Carroll.* Illustrated by John Tenniel, et al. New York: Avenel Books, 1982. Includes the *Alice* books (and *Alice's Adventures Under Ground*), *The Hunting of the Snark*, the two volumes of *Sylvie and Bruno*, *A Tangled Tale*, and volumes of Dodgson's comic and sentimental poetry.

Hudson, Derek, ed. *Useful and Instructive Poetry.* London: G. Bles, 1954. Carroll's earliest poems.

Kelly, Richard, ed. *Alice's Adventures in Wonderland.* 2nd ed. Buffalo, NY: Broadview, 2011. Includes *Alice's Adventures Under Ground*, *The Nursery Alice*, contemporary reviews of *Wonderland*, and a list of films and TV productions.

Kincaid, James R., ed. *Lewis Carroll's The Hunting of the Snark: An Agony, in Eight Fits.* Illustrations by Barry Moser. Berkeley: U of California P, 1983.

Mathematical Recreations of Lewis Carroll. Two volumes. New York: Dover Publications, 1958. Includes the first volume of *Symbolic Logic, The Game of Logic, Pillow-Problems,* and *A Tangled Tale.*

McDermott, John Francis, ed. *The Russian Journal, and Other Selections from the Works of Lewis Carroll.* 1935; rpt. New York: Dover Publications, 1977.

Milner, Florence, ed. *The Rectory Umbrella and Mischmasch.* London: Cassell and Co., 1932. Two of Carroll's comic domestic magazines.

The Pamphlets of Lewis Carroll (four-volume series). Charlottesville, VA: UP of Virginia, 1993, 1994, 2001, 2010.

Tanis, James, and John Dooley, eds. *Lewis Carroll's The Hunting of the Snark.* With illustrations by Henry Holiday. Los Altos, CA: Bryn Mawr College Library, 1981.

BIBLIOGRAPHIES

Fordyce, Rachel. *Lewis Carroll: A Reference Guide.* Boston: G. K. Hall, 1988.

Gattégno, Jean, ed. "Bibliographie selective: Lewis Carroll's *Alice Adventures in Wonderland.*" *Cahiers Victoriens et Édouardians* 40 (1994): 153–62.

Guiliano, Edward. "Lewis Carroll: A Sesquicentennial Guide to Research." *Dickens Studies Annual* 10 (1982): 263–310.

———, ed. *Lewis Carroll: An Annotated International Bibliography, 1960–77.* Charlottesville: UP of Virginia, 1980.

Lovett, Charles C., ed. *Lewis Carroll and the Press: An Annotated Bibliography of Charles Dodgson's Contributions to Periodicals.* New Castle, DE: Oak Knoll P, 1999.

Preston, Michael J. *A Concordance to the Verse of Lewis Carroll.* New York: Garland, 1985.

———. *A KWIC Concordance to Lewis Carroll's* Alice's Adventures in Wonderland *and* Through the Looking-Glass. New York: Garland, 1986.

Sigler, Carolyn. "Lewis Carroll Studies, 1983–2003." *Dickens Studies Annual* 34 (2004): 375–413.

Williams, Sidney Herbert. *A Bibliography of the Writings of Lewis Carroll (Charles Lutwidge Dodgson, M.A.).* London: "Bookman's Journal," 1924.

———. *The Lewis Carroll Handbook: Being a New Version of a Handbook of the Literature of the Rev. C. L. Dodgson* [1931]. Rev. and augmented by Roger Lancelyn Green [1962], and further rev. by Denis Crutch. Folkestone, UK: Dawson, 1979.

Weaver, Warren. *Alice in Many Tongues: The Translations of* Alice in Wonderland. Madison: U of Wisconsin P, 1964.

BIOGRAPHIES

Amor, Anne Clark. *Lewis Carroll: A Biography.* London: Dent, 1979.

———. *The Real Alice: Lewis Carroll's Dream Child.* London: M. Joseph, 1981.

Cohen, Morton N., ed. *Lewis Carroll: Interviews and Recollections.* Iowa City: U of Iowa P, 1989.

Foulkes, Richard. *Lewis Carroll and the Victorian Stage: Theatricals in a Quiet Life.* Burlington, VT: Ashgate, 2005.

Furniss, Harry. "Recollections of 'Lewis Carroll.'" *Strand* 35 (1908): 48–52. Furniss illustrated both volumes of *Sylvie and Bruno.*

Green, Roger Lancelyn. *Lewis Carroll.* New York: H. Z. Walck, 1962.

Imholtz, August A., Jr., and Charlie Lovett, eds. *In Memoriam Charles Lutwidge Dodgson 1832–1898: Obituaries of Lewis Carroll and Related Pieces.* New York: Lewis Carroll Society of North America, 1998.

Kelly, Richard Michael. *Lewis Carroll.* Rev. ed. Boston: Twayne, 1990.

Leach, Karoline. *In the Shadow of the Dreamchild: A New Understanding of Lewis Carroll.* Chester Springs, PA: Dufour Editions, 1999.

Lebailly, Hugues. "Charles Lutwidge Dodgson's Diaries: The Journal of a Victorian Playgoer (1855–1897)." *The Carrollian* 7 (2001): 16–39.

Lennon, Florence Becker. *The Life of Lewis Carroll (Victoria Through the Looking Glass)*. 3rd ed. New York: Dover, 1972.

Lovett, Charles C. *Lewis Carroll among His Books: A Descriptive Catalogue of the Private Library of Charles L. Dodgson*. Jefferson, NC: McFarland, 2005.

Moses, Belle. *Lewis Carroll in Wonderland and At Home: The Story of His Life*. New York and London: D. Appleton and Company, 1910.

Pudney, John. *Lewis Carroll and His World*. New York: Thames & Hudson, 1976.

Ranson-Polizzotti, Sadi. "What About Lewis Carroll?: Going Underground." *Biography and Source Studies* 8 (2009): 37–58.

Sigler, Carolyn, "Was the Snark a Boojum? One Hundred Years of Lewis Carroll Biographies." *Children's Literature* 29 (2001): 229–43.

Taylor, Alexander. *The White Knight: A Study of C. L. Dodgson (Lewis Carroll)*. 1952; rpt. Philadelphia: Dufour Editions, 1963.

Vugt, Peter van. "C. L. Dodgson's Migraine and Lewis Carroll's Literary Inspiration: A Neurolinguistic Perspective." *Linguistica Antverpiensia* 28 (1994): 151–61.

Winchester, Simon. *The Alice Behind Wonderland*. New York: Oxford, 2011.

Woolf, Jenny. *The Mystery of Lewis Carroll: Discovering the Whimsical, Thoughtful and Sometimes Lonely Man Who Created Alice in Wonderland*. New York: St. Martin's, 2010.

COLLECTIONS OF ESSAYS

Bloom, Harold, ed. *Lewis Carroll* (Modern Critical Views series). New York: Chelsea House, 1987.

Burstein, Mark, ed. *A Bouquet for the Gardener: Martin Gardner Remembered*. Beltsville, MD: Lewis Carroll Society of North America, 2011.

Crutch, Denis, ed. *Mr. Dodgson: Nine Carroll Studies, with a Companion-Guide to the Alice at Longleat Exhibition*. London: Lewis Carroll Society, 1973.

Jones, Jo Elwyn, and J. Francis Gladstone. *The Alice Companion: A Guide to Lewis Carroll's Alice Books*. Basingstoke: Macmillan, 1998.

Guiliano, Edward, ed. *Lewis Carroll—A Celebration: Essays on the Occasion of the 150th Anniversary of the Birth of Charles Lutwidge Dodgson*. New York: C. N. Potter, 1982.

———. *Lewis Carroll Observed: A Collection of Unpublished Photographs, Drawings, Poetry, and New Essays*. New York: C. N. Potter, 1976.

———, and James R. Kincaid, eds. *Soaring with the Dodo: Essays on Lewis Carroll's Life and Art*. New York: Lewis Carroll Society of North America, 1982.

Hollingsworth, Cristopher, ed. *Alice beyond Wonderland: Essays for the Twenty-First Century*. Iowa City: U of Iowa P, 2009. Includes essays by Hollingsworth, Stephen Monteiro, and Franz Meier on photography, and Elizabeth Throesch on the new mathematics and the Alice books.

Moore, Alice, and Richard Landon. *All in the Golden Afternoon—The Inventions of Lewis Carroll: An Exhibition Selected from the Joseph Brabant Collection*. Toronto: Thomas Fisher Rare Book Library, 1999. Includes essays on photography, letters, and illustrations.

Phillips, Robert S., ed. *Aspects of Alice: Lewis Carroll's Dreamchild as Seen through the Critics' Looking-Glasses, 1865–1971*. New York: Vanguard, 1971.

Rackin, Donald, ed. *Alice's Adventures in Wonderland: A Critical Handbook* (Wadsworth Guide to Literary Study). Belmont, CA: Wadsworth, 1969.

LITERARY STUDIES

Ayres, Harry Morgan. *Carroll's Alice*. New York: Columbia UP, 1936.

Blake, Kathleen. *Play, Games, and Sport: The Literary Works of Lewis Carroll*. Ithaca, NY: Cornell UP, 1974.

———. "Alice's Adventures in Wonderland." In *The Hero's Journey*. Ed. Harold Bloom, 11–24. New York: Bloom's Literary Criticism, 2009.

———. "Lewis Carroll (Charles Lutwidge Dodgson)." In *Victorian Novelists After 1885* (Dictionary of Literary Biography). Vol. 18. Ed. William E. Fredeman and Ira Bruce Nadel. Detroit: Gale Research Co., 1983, 43–61.

Carpenter, Humphrey. "Alice and the Mockery of God." In *Secret Gardens: A Study in the Golden Age of Children's Literature*. Boston: G. Allen & Unwin, 1985, 44–69.

Carr, Annabel. "The Art of the Child: Turning the Lens on Lewis Carroll." *Literature & Aesthetics* 19.2 (2009): 123–37.

Cixous, Hélène. "Introduction to *Through the Looking-Glass* and *The Hunting of the Snark*." *New Literary History* 13.2 (1982): 231–51.

Eagleton, Terry. "Alice and Anarchy." *New Blackfriars* 53.629 (Oct. 1972): 447–55.

Ede, Lisa. "An Introduction to the Nonsense Literature of Edward Lear and Lewis Carroll," In *Explorations in the Field of Nonsense*. Ed. Wim Tigges. Amsterdam: Rodopi, 1987, 47–60.

Elwyn Jones, Jo, and J. Francis Gladstone. *The Red King's Dream; or, Lewis Carroll in Wonderland*. London: Jonathan Cape, 1995.

Empson, William. "The Child as Swain." In *Some Versions of Pastoral*. London: Chatto & Windus, 1935, 246–77.

Henkle, Roger B. "Comedy from Inside." In *Comedy and Culture: England 1820–1900*. Princeton: Princeton UP, 1980, 201–11.

———. "The Mad Hatter's World." *Virginia Quarterly Review* 49 (1973): 99–117.

Irwin, Michael. "Alice: Reflections and Relativities." In *Rereading Victorian Fiction*. Ed. Alice Jenkins and Juliet John. New York: St. Martin's, 2000, 115–28.

Kenner, Hugh. "Art in a Closed Field." *Virginia Quarterly Review* 38.4 (1962): 597–613.

Kérchy, Anna. "Ambiguous Alice: Making Sense of Lewis Carroll's Nonsense Fantasies." In *Does It Really Mean That? Interpreting the Literary Ambiguous*. Ed. Kathleen Dubs and Janka Kaščáková. Newcastle: Cambridge Scholars, 2010, 104–20.

Kincaid, James R. "Alice's Invasion of Wonderland." *Publications of the Modern Language Association* 88.1 (1973): 92–99.

Knoepflmacher, U. C. "Avenging Alice: Christina Rossetti and Lewis Carroll." *Nineteenth-Century Literature* 41.3 (1986): 299–328.

Madden, William A. "Framing the Alices." *Publications of the Modern Language Association* 101.3 (1986): 362–73.

Massey, Irving. *The Gaping Pig: Literature and Metamorphosis*. Berkeley: U of California P, 1976, 76–97.

Polhemus, Robert M. "Carroll's *Through the Looking-Glass* (1871): The Comedy of Regression." In *Comic Faith: The Great Tradition from Austen to Joyce*. Chicago: U of Chicago P, 1980, 245–93.

Rackin, Donald. "Alice's Journey to the End of Night." *Publications of the Modern Language Association of America* 81.5 (Oct. 1966): 313–26.

Robson, Catherine. "Reciting Alice: What Is the Use of a Book without Poems?" In *The Feeling of Reading: Affective Experience in Victorian Literature*. Ed. Rachel Ablow. Ann Arbor: U of Michigan P, 2010, 93–113.

Sewell, Elizabeth. *Lewis Carroll: Voices from France*. Ed. Clare Imholtz. New York: Lewis Carroll Society of North America, 2009.

Stoffel, Stephanie Lovett. *The Art of Alice in Wonderland*. New York: Smithmark Publishers, 1998.

Wheat, Andrew R. "Dodgson's Dark Conceit: Evoking the Allegorical Lineage of Alice." *Renascence: Essays on Values in Literature* 61 (2009): 103–23.

White, Donna. "The Game Plan of *The Hunting of the Snark*." *Proceedings of the Second International Lewis Carroll Conference*. Ed. Charlie Lovett. Silver Spring, MD: Lewis Carroll Society of North America, 1994, 112–18.

Wilson, Edmund. "C. L. Dodgson: The Poet-Logician." In *The Shores of Light: A Literary Chronicle of the Twenties and Thirties*. New York: Farrar, Straus, and Young, 1952, 540–50.

HISTORICAL STUDIES

Batchelor, John. "Dodgson, Carroll, and the Emancipation of Alice." In *Children and Their Books: A Celebration of the Work of Iona and Peter Opie*.

Ed. Gillian Avery and Julia Briggs. New York: Clarendon Press, 1989, 187–99.

Clark, Beverly Lyon. "Lewis Carroll's Alice Books: The Wonder of Wonderland." In *Touchstones: Reflections on the Best in Children's Literature*. Vol. 1. Ed. Perry Nodelman. West Lafayette, IN: Children's Literature Association, 1985, 44–52.

Coveney, Peter. *The Image of Childhood: The Individual and Society—A Study of the Theme in English Literature*. Rev. ed. Harmondsworth: Penguin, 1967.

Cripps, Elizabeth A. "Alice and the Reviewers." *Children's Literature* 11 (1983): 32–48.

Darton, F. J. Harvey. *Children's Books in England: Five Centuries of Social Life*. 3rd ed. Rev. Brian Alderson. New Castle, DE: Oak Knoll Press, 1982.

Dusinberre, Juliet. *Alice to the Lighthouse: Children's Books and Radical Experiments in Art*. Basingstoke: Macmillan, 1987, 69–80.

Geer, Jennifer. "'All Sorts of Pitfalls and Surprises': Competing Views of Idealized Girlhood in Carroll's *Alice* Books." *Children's Literature* 31 (2003): 1–24.

Gray, Donald J. "The Uses of Victorian Laughter." *Victorian Studies* 10.2 (Dec. 1966): 145–76.

———. "Victorian Comic Verse; or, Snakes in Greenland." *Victorian Poetry* 26.3 (1988): 211–30.

Helson, Ravenna. "The Psychological Origins of Fantasy for Children in Mid-Victorian England." *Children's Literature* 3 (1974): 66–76.

Henkle, Roger B. "Spitting Blood and Writing Comic: Mid-Century British Humor." *Mosaic* 9.4 (1976): 77–90.

Higbie, Robert. "Lewis Carroll and the Victorian Reaction Against Doubt." *Thalia: Studies in Literary Humor* 3.1 (1980): 21–28.

Hunt, Peter. "The Fundamentals of Children's Literature Criticism: *Alice's Adventures in Wonderland* and *Through the Looking-Glass*." In *The Oxford Handbook of Children's Literature*. Ed. Judith L. Mickenberg and Lynne Vallone. New York: Oxford UP, 2011, 23, 35–51.

Jenkins, Ruth. "Imagining the Abject in Kingsley, MacDonald, and Carroll: Disrupting Dominant Values and Cultural Identity in Children's Literature." *The Lion and the Unicorn* 35.1 (Jan. 2011): 67–87.

Knoepflmacher, U. C. "Little Girls Without Their Curls: Female Aggression in Victorian Children's Literature." *Children's Literature* 11 (1983): 14–31.

Lebailly, Hugues. "C. L. Dodgson and the Victorian Cult of the Child." *The Carrollian* 4 (1999): 3–31.

Leslie, Shane. "Lewis Carroll and the Oxford Movement." *London Mercury* 28 (1933): 233–39.

Lovell-Smith, Rose. "Eggs and Serpents: Natural History Reference in Lewis Carroll's Scene of Alice and the Pigeon." *Children's Literature* 35 (2007): 27–53.

Mayer, Jed. "The Vivisection of the Snark." *Victorian Poetry* 47.2 (2009): 429–48.

Moss, Anita. "Lewis Carroll." *Writers for Children: Critical Studies of Major Authors since the Seventeenth Century*. Ed. Jane M. Bingham. New York: Scribner's, 1988, 117–27.

Ostry, Elaine, "Magical Growth and Moral Lessons; or, How the Conduct Book Informed Victorian and Edwardian Children's Fantasy." *The Lion and the the Unicorn* 27.1 (2003): 27–56.

Pattison, Robert. "Children in Children's Literature." In *The Child Figure in English Literature*. Athens: U of Georgia P, 1978, 135–59.

Prickett, Stephen. "Consensus or Nonsense?" In *Victorian Fantasy*. Rev. ed. Waco, TX: Baylor UP, 2005, 109–37.

Rackin, Donald. "Corrective Laughter: Carroll's Alice and Popular Children's Literature of the Nineteenth Century." *The Journal of Popular Culture* 1.3 (1967): 243–55.

Reinstein, Phyllis Gila. *Alice in Context*. New York: Garland, 1988.

Reichertz, Ronald. *The Making of the Alice Books: Lewis Carroll's Use of Earlier Children's Literature*. Buffalo, NY: McGill-Queen's UP, 1997.

Sale, Roger. *Fairy Tales and After: From Snow White to E. B. White*. Cambridge: Harvard UP, 1978, 101–26.

Susina, Jan. *The Place of Lewis Carroll in Children's Literature*. New York: Routledge, 2010.

LANGUAGE AND LINGUISTICS

Adam, Rose. "Lewis Carroll's 'Jabberwocky': Non-Sense not Nonsense." *Language and Literature* 4.1 (1995): 1–15.
Baum, Alwin L. "Carroll's Alices: The Semiotics of Paradox." *American Imago* 34 (1977): 86–108.
Flescher, Jacqueline. "The Language of Nonsense in Alice." *Yale French Studies* 43 (1969): 128–44.
Fordyce, Rachel, and Carla Marello, eds. *Semiotics and Linguistics in Alice's World*. New York: de Gruyter, 1994. Includes essays by Isabelle Nières on Tenniel's interpretation of the *Alice* books, Antal Bókay on "Alice in Analysis," and Maurizio De Ninno's "Naked, Raw Alice" on semiotics and Claude Lévi-Strauss.
Kirk, Daniel F. *Charles Dodgson, Semiotician*. Gainesville: U of Florida P, 1962.
Lakoff, Robin Tolmach. "Lewis Carroll: Subversive Pragmatist," *Pragmatics* 3 (1993): 367–85.
Marret, Sophie. "Metalanguage in Lewis Carroll." *SubStance* 22, no. 2/3, issue 71/72 (1993): 217–27.
May, Leila Silvana. "Language-Games and Nonsense: Wittgenstein's Reflection in Lewis Carroll's Looking-Glass." *Philosophy and Literature* 31.1 (2007): 79–94.
Muskat-Tabakowska, E. "General Semantics Behind the Looking-Glass." *ETC.: A Review of General Semantics* 27.4 (1970): 483–92.
Nilsen, Don L. F. "The Linguistic Humor of Lewis Carroll," *Thalia: Studies in Literary Humor* 10 (1988): 35–41.
Pitcher, George. "Wittgenstein, Nonsense, and Lewis Carroll." *Massachusetts Review* 6.3 (1965): 591–611. Rpt. in *English Literature and British Philosophy*. Ed. S. P. Rosenbaum. Chicago: U of Chicago P, 1971, 229–50.
Schwab, Gabriele. "Nonsense and Metacommunication: Reflections on Lewis Carroll." In *The Play of the Self*. Eds. Ronald Bogue and Mihai I. Spariosu. Albany: State U of New York, 1994, 157–79.
Shibles, Warren A. "A Philosophical Commentary on *Alice's Adventures in Wonderland*." In *Wittgenstein: Language & Philosophy*. Dubuque, IA: W. C. Brown Book Co., 1969, 14–45.
Sorensen, Roy A. "A Plenum of Palindromes for Lewis Carroll." *Mind* 109 (2000): 17–20.
Sutherland, Robert D. *Language and Lewis Carroll*. The Hague: Mouton, 1970.
Turner, Beatrice. "'Which Is To Be Master?': Language as Power in *Alice in Wonderland* and *Through the Looking-Glass*." *Children's Literature Association Quarterly* 35.3 (2010): 243–54.

MATHEMATICS AND PHILOSOPHY

Abeles, Francine F. "Algorithms and Mechanical Processes in the Work of Charles L. Dodgson." *Proceedings of the Second International Lewis Carroll Conference*. Ed. Charlie Lovett. Silver Spring, MD: Lewis Carroll Society of North America, 1994, 97–106.
Bartley, William Warren III, "Lewis Carroll as a Logician." *Times Literary Supplement*, June 15, 1973, 655–66.
———. "Lewis Carroll's Lost Book on Logic." *Scientific American* 227.1 (1972): 38–46.
Beale, Tony. "C. L. Dodgson: Mathematician." In *Mr. Dodgson* (see Denis Crutch, Collections of Essays), 26–33.
Black, Duncan. *A Mathematical Approach to Proportional Representation: Duncan Black on Lewis Carroll*. Boston: Springer, 1996.
———. "Lewis Carroll and the Theory of Games." *American Economic Review* 59.2 (1969): 206–10.

Heath, Peter Lauchlan. *The Philosopher's Alice.* New York: St. Martin's P, 1974.
Holbrook, David. *Nonsense Against Sorrow: A Phenomenological Study of Lewis Carroll's Alice Books.* London: Open Gate, 2001.
Johnson, Charles W. *Philosophy in Literature.* Vol. 1. San Francisco: EMText, 1992.
Laporte, Henri. *Alice au pays des Merveilles: Structures Logiques et Représentations du Désir.* Paris: Mame, 1973.
Sacksteder, William. "Looking Glass: A Treatise on Logic." *Philosophy and Phenomenological Research* 27.3 (1967): 338–55.
Sherer, Susan. "Secrecy and Autonomy in Lewis Carroll." *Philosophy and Literature* 20.1 (1996): 1–19.
Weaver, Warren. "Lewis Carroll, Mathematician." *Scientific American* 194.4 (Apr. 1956): 116–28.
Wilson, Robin J. *Lewis Carroll in Numberland: His Fantastical Mathematical Logical Life—An Agony in Eight Fits.* New York: Allen Lane, 2008.

GENDER

Armstrong, Nancy. "The Occidental Alice." *Differences* 2.2 (1990): 3–40.
Ciolkowski, Laura E. "Visions of Life on the Border: Wonderland Women, Imperial Travelers, and Bourgeois Womanhood in the Nineteenth Century." *Genders* 27 (1998).
Cohen, Morton N. "Lewis Carroll and the Education of Victorian Women." In *Nineteenth-Century Women Writers of the English-Speaking World.* Ed. Rhoda B. Nathan. New York: Greenwood P, 1986, 27–35.
Golden, Catherine J. "The Book as Portal." In *Images of the Woman Reader in Victorian British and American Fiction.* Gainesville: UP of Florida, 2003, 187–201.
Lebailly, Hugues. "Charles Lutwidge Dodgson's Infatuation with the Weaker and More Aesthetic Sex Reexamined." *Dickens Studies Annual* 32 (2003): 339–62.
Little, Judith. "Liberated Alice: Dodgson's Female Hero as Domestic Rebel." *Women's Studies* 3.2 (1971): 195–205.
Pierce, Joanna Tapp. "From Garden to Gardener: The Cultivation of Little Girls in Carroll's *Alice* Books and Ruskin's 'Of Queens' Gardens.'" *Women's Studies* 29.6 (2000): 741–61.
Polhemus, Robert M. "The Maiden Tribute: Lot's Daughters through the Victorian Looking-Glass." In *Lot's Daughters: Sex, Redemption, and Women's Quest for Authority.* Stanford: Stanford UP, 2005, 197–216.
Robson, Catherine. "Lewis Carroll and the Little Girl: The Art of Self-Effacement." In *Men in Wonderland: The Lost Girlhood of the Victorian Gentleman.* Princeton: Princeton UP, 2001, 129–53.
Talairach-Vielmas, Laurence. "Drawing 'Muchnesses' in Lewis Carroll's *Alice's Adventures in Wonderland.*" In *Moulding the Female Body in Victorian Fairy Tales and Sensation Novels.* Burlington, VT: Ashgate, 2007, 49–65.
White, Laura Mooneyham. "Domestic Queen, Queenly Domestic: Queenly Contradictions in Carroll's *Through the Looking-Glass.*" *Children's Literature Association Quarterly* 32.2 (2007): 110–28.

PSYCHOANALYTIC STUDIES

Burke, Kenneth. "The Thinking of the Body." In *Language as Symbolic Action: Essays on Life, Literature, and Method.* Berkeley: U of California P, 1966, 308–43. Reprinted from *Psychoanalytic Review* 50 (1963): 375–413.
Dimock, George. "Childhood's End: Lewis Carroll and the Image of the Rat." *Word & Image* 8.3 (1992): 183–205.
Faimberg, Haydée. "The Snark Was a Boojum." *International Review of Psycho-Analysis* 4 (1977): 243–49.
Feldstein, Richard. "The Phallic Gaze of Wonderland." In *Reading Seminar XI: Lacan's Four Fundamental Concepts of Psychoanalysis.* Ed. Richard Feldstein, Bruce Fink, and Maire Jaanus. Albany: State U of New York, 1995, 149–74.
Gattégno, Jean, and Alain Schifres. "Alice in Analysis," *Réalités* 201 (Aug. 1967): 58–61.

Greenacre, Phyllis. *Swift and Carroll: A Psychoanalytic Study of Two Lives.* New York: International Universities P, 1955.

——. "'It's My Own Invention': A Special Screen Memory of Mr. Lewis Carroll, Its Force and Its History," and "On Nonsense." In *Emotional Growth: Psychoanalytic Studies of the Gifted and a Great Variety of Other Individuals.* Vol. 2. New York: International Universities P, 1971, 438–578, 592–615.

Grotjahn, Martin. "About the Symbolization of Alice's Adventures in Wonderland." *American Imago* 4.4 (1947): 32–41.

Lopez, Alan. "Deleuze with Carroll: Schizophrenia and Simulacrum in the Philosophy of Lewis Carroll's Nonsense." *Angelaki* 9.3 (2004): 101–20.

Schilder, Paul. "Psychoanalytic Remarks on *Alice in Wonderland* and Lewis Carroll." *Journal of Nervous and Mental Diseases* 87.2 (Feb. 1938): 159–68.

ILLUSTRATIONS

Hancher, Michael. *The Tenniel Illustrations to the "Alice" Books.* Columbus: Ohio State UP, 1985.

Lovell-Smith, Rose. "The Animals of Wonderland: Tenniel as Carroll's Reader." *Criticism* 45.4 (2003): 383–415.

Mespoulet, Marguerite. *Creators of Wonderland.* New York: Arrow, 1934.

Mitchell, Charles. *The Designs for the Snark.* Rpt. in *The Annotated Hunting of the Snark* (see Dodgson's Writings, Letters, and Diaries), 83–115.

Ovenden, Graham, ed. *The Illustrators of* Alice in Wonderland *and* Through the Looking Glass. Intro. John Davis. Rev. ed. New York: St. Martin's, 1979.

PHOTOGRAPHY

Alexander, James R. "Sentiment and Aesthetics in Victorian Photography: The Child Portraits of C. L. Dodgson." *The Carrollian* 17.2 (2006): 2–67.

Cohen, Morton N. *Reflections in a Looking Glass: A Centennial Celebration of Lewis Carroll, Photographer.* Includes essays by Mark Haworth-Booth and Roy Flukinger, as well as plates. New York: Aperture, 1998.

——, ed. *Lewis Carroll, Photographer of Children: Four Nude Studies.* New York: The Rosenbach Foundation, 1978.

Gernsheim, Helmut. *Lewis Carroll, Photographer.* Rev. ed. New York: Dover, 1969.

——, ed. *Lewis Carroll: Victorian Photographer.* London: Thames & Hudson, 1980.

Mallardi, Rosella. "The Photographic Eye and the Vision of Childhood in Lewis Carroll." *Studies in Philology* 107.4 (2010): 548–72.

Nickel, Douglas R. *Dreaming in Pictures: The Photography of Lewis Carroll.* New Haven, CT: Yale UP, 2002. Includes plates.

Ovenden, Graham. *Pre-Raphaelite Photography.* New York: St. Martin's, 1984.

Roegiers, Patrick. *Le visage regardé, ou, Lewis Carroll, dessinateur et photographie: essai.* Paris: Créatis, 1982.

Vallone, Lynne. "Reading Girlhood in Victorian Photography." *The Lion and the Unicorn* 29.2 (2005): 190–210.

THE AFTERLIFE OF ALICE

Brooker, Will. *Alice's Adventures: Lewis Carroll and Alice in Popular Culture.* New York: Continuum, 2004.

Brown, Jennifer Stafford. "Surrealists in Wonderland: Aspects of the Appropriation of Lewis Carroll." *Canadian Review of Comparative Literature* 27 (2000): 128–43.

Burton, Tim, dir. *Alice in Wonderland.* 2010. Los Angeles: Walt Disney Pictures, et al. Movie / DVD.

Del Tredici, David. *Final Alice: A Cantata for One Voice.* Chicago Symphony Orchestra, conducted by Sir George Solti. Eloquence Australia B0015U0OO6, 1976, CD.

Fritz, Sonya Sawyer. "Alice Still Lives Here: The Implied Victorian Reader and Film Adaptations of Lewis Carroll's Alice Books." In *Crossing Textual Boundaries in International Children's Literature*. Ed. Lance Weldy. Newcastle upon Tyne: Cambridge Scholars Publishing, 2011, 109–22.

Geronimi, Clyde, dir. *Alice in Wonderland*. 1951. Los Angeles: Walt Disney Pictures. Movie / DVD.

Israel, Kali. "Asking Alice: Victorian and Other Alices in Contemporary Culture." In *Victorian Afterlife: Postmodern Culture Rewrites the Nineteenth Century*. Eds. John Kucich and Dianne F. Sadoff. Minneapolis: U of Minnesota P, 2000, 252–87.

Kérchy, Anna. "Wonderland Lost and Found? Nonsensical Enchantment and Imaginative Reluctance in Revisionings of Lewis Carroll's Alice Tales." In *Anti-Tales: The Uses of Disenchantment*. Eds. Catriona McAra and David Calvin. Newcastle upon Tyne: Cambridge Scholars Publishing, 2011, 62–74.

Langridge, Roger. *Snarked!: Book One, Forks and Hope; Book Two: Ships and Sealing Wax*. Los Angeles: KaBoom, 2012. Comic book / graphic novel: Story of the further adventures of the Walrus and the Carpenter, and other characters from the *Alice* books and *The Hunting of the Snark*. Book Three, the final installment, is forthcoming.

Leitch, Thomas. "The Ethics of Infidelity." In *Adaptation Studies: New Approaches*. Eds. Christa Albrecht-Crane and Dennis Cutchins. Madison, NJ: Farleigh Dickinson UP, 2010, 61–77.

Long, Carol Y. "Alice's Adventures in Wonderland: From Book to Big Screen." In *The Antic Art: Enhancing Children's Literary Experience through Film and Video*. Eds. Lucy Rollin and Jill P. May. Fort Atkinson, WI: Highsmith, 1993, 131–40.

Lovett, Charles C. *Alice on Stage: A History of the Early Theatrical Productions of Alice in Wonderland, Together with a Checklist of Dramatic Adaptations of Charles Dodgson's Works*. Westport, CT: Meckler, 1990. See also August A. Imholtz, "Alice on Stage II: An Initial Supplement to the Lovett Checklist," *The Carrollian* 14 (2004): 62; Edward Wakeling, "Alice on Stage III: Another Supplement to the Lovett Checklist," *The Carrollian* 16 (2005): 62–63; and Clare Imholtz, "Alice on Stage IV: The Lord Chamberlain's Plays," *The Carrollian* 20 (2007): 18–37.

McLeod, Norman, dir. *Alice in Wonderland*. 1933. Los Angeles: Paramount Studios. Cast includes W. C. Fields, Cary Grant, and Gary Cooper. Movie / DVD.

McWilliam, Rohan. "Jonathan Miller's Alice in Wonderland (1966): A Suitable Case for Treatment." *Historical Journal of Film, Radio and Television* 31.2 (2011): 229–46.

Millar, Gavin, dir. *Dreamchild*. 1985. London: Thorn EMI, et al. Movie / DVD.

Miller, Jonathan, dir. "Alice in Wonderland" (episode of *The Wednesday Play*). 1966. London: BBC. Television / DVD.

Newman, Kim. "Go Ask Alice: A Review of Tim Burton's *Alice in Wonderland*." *Sight and Sound* 20 (2010): 32–34.

Noon, Jeff. *Automated Alice*. Illustrated by Harry Trumbore. New York: Doubleday, 1996. Futuristic sequel to the *Alice* books.

Roiphe, Katie. *Still She Haunts Me*. New York: Dial Press, 2001. Fictionalized account of Dodgson's relationship with Alice Liddell.

Sewell, Byron W. *Lewis Carroll in the Popular Culture: A Continuing List*. New York: Lewis Carroll Society of North America, 1976.

Sigler, Carolyn, ed. *Alternative Alices: Visions and Revisions of Lewis Carroll's Alice Books*. Lexington: UP of Kentucky, 1997.

Sinker, Mark. "Alice through the Lens." *Sight and Sound* 228 (2010): 35–38.

Slavitt, David R. *Alice at 80: A Novel*. Garden City, NY: Doubleday, 1984.

Swados, Elizabeth. *Alice at the Palace*. Directed by Emile Ardolino. 1982. New York: New York Shakespeare Festival. Television / DVD.

Willing, Nick, director. *Alice in Wonderland*. 1999. Potsdam: Bablesberg International Film Produktion; New York: NBC. Cast includes Whoopi Goldberg, Robbie Coltrane, and Ben Kingsley. Television movie / DVD.